"Joseph D'Lacey is one of our best new horror writers, delivering surprises, intensity, and scares aplenty with each new book. And with every book, he's upping his game."

Tim Lebbon, author of The Heretic Land

"Dreadfully visionary. Appallingly inspired. One could wear out a thesaurus trying to articulate the singular fusion of qualities that has come to define Joseph D'Lacey's work. Alternately (and sometimes simultaneously) horrifying, mesmerizing, shocking, unsettling, and beautiful, and always deeply intelligent, it's utterly unlike anything else I'm aware of. It's also utterly wonderful."

Matt Cardin, author of To Rouse Leviathan

"An exceptional piece of apocalyptic/horror/fantasy fiction."

Tor.com

"D'Lacey's passages are rife with urgency... its message on environmental issues, meticulous setting of scene, and successful intertwining of the characters' narratives makes for an engaging read."

Publishers Weekly

"If you're a horror fan and you're not already reading Joseph D'Lacey you had better have a bloody good excuse."

The Eloquent Page

BY THE SAME AUTHOR

JOSEPH D'LACEY

The Book of the Crowman

THE BLACK DAWN
VOL II

ANGRY
ROBOT

ANGRY ROBOT
A member of the Osprey Group

Lace Market House,
54-56 High Pavement,
Nottingham
NG1 1HW
UK

Angry Robot/Osprey Publishing,
PO Box 3985,
New York,
NY 10185-3985,
USA

www.angryrobotbooks.com
The crow rode

An Angry Robot paperback original 2014

ISBN: 978 0 85766 348 1
Ebook ISBN: 978 0 85766 349 8

Printed in the United States of America

9 8 7 6 5 4 3 2 1

For Ishbel, without whose selflessness and support the work could not have been done.

PART I

TO WAR

"…comes the Crowman, people. He walks where there is pestilence. He walks where there is war. He weaves a cloak of blackness for he is the black sunrise of the black dawn. For he is the son of the broken land and the wrathful sky. For where he walks there is destruction and decay, the old world cast down in dust and ashes. For he is judgement made flesh. And you shall perish or be raised up at the touch of his black feathers. And you shall vanish into darkness behind his cloak or be set free by it into the light. The black poppy of Death sprouts in the Crowman's bootprints. He shall plant a black seed of silence in the earth and none can know what will spring from that seed…"

Prophecy, partial, Black Dawn era scrapbook, Coventry,
author unknown

"…the voice of the Great Spirit is heard in the twittering of birds, the rippling of mighty waters, and the sweet breathing of flowers. If this is Paganism, then at present, at least, I am a Pagan."

Zitkala-Sa – Lakota Sioux, 1876-1938

"the ravens rise to heaven
a sky of black scimitars to war!
at the beck of morrigan, they come
to drip a bead of death from every beak

by the thousand they scrape the air
screamin caw! caw!
lie down in the earth you men
the time of men is over!

'til only a scarecrow stands
arms stretched out to east and west
stone grey eyes surveyin the fallen
straw lips and fingers twitchin in the wind
and whisprin tis good, tis good…"

Untitled verse, pre-Black Dawn era scrapbook, Ward archive, London, author unrecorded

PROLOGUE

The war is over but the land remains hushed.

Great tracts of England are as grey and dead as leprous flesh but, here and there, the green of Mother Earth persists; lush pockets of riotous overgrowth murmur with birdsong and the scurrying of small creatures, awakening once more. In some places the fields, ungrazed for years by sheep or cattle, have returned to grassland, occasionally swaying to the touch of the still slumbering wind.

And where the calcified arteries of road and motorway once ran, choked with the noise and fumes of trucks and cars, now those sclerotic highways have been broken by quakes or have vanished into fathomless rifts. Those that remain are entombed by an arch of luxuriant foliage; the pressing in from both sides of the verges and embankments, clutching the tarmac until it ruptures allowing even more growth to sprout though.

The cities are dead. Many have sunk back into the land, absorbed by tremors that turned the earth beneath them to liquid. London is a barely populated ruin. Manchester is a vast lake of shaken soil. All that remains of Birmingham are the tops of its highest buildings. The Ward are falling, the Green Men reclaiming the land day by day.

A Bright Day is coming.

But Mother Earth, she sleeps yet, still feverish after cleansing herself of the sickness that humankind became, not yet trusting that we have remembered her as the giver of all nourishment and substance and the receiver of our remains in death. Nor is there any certainty that such a trust will ever return.

As for the Crowman, I never doubted him. After all, I knew him more intimately than most. One could say I was his progeny, perhaps, for he made me everything that I am. He is here still; his spirit stronger than ever in the land and in the hearts of its people. I prophesied his coming, I told the Green Men he was among them and would lead them into battle. He did all that and more, blessing every soul who loved the land with the chill caress of his black feathers. He walks with all of us.

And what of Gordon Black, the boy whose task it was to seek out the Crowman and reveal him to the world? Did he succeed? Did he fulfil his destiny?

Even though I have glimpsed the future, I cannot say for certain. The prophecies have come to me and I have recorded them, but my spirit will have returned to the wind for many generations before his story truly has its end.

Though Gordon may have overcome every obstacle and though he may have been equal to every task and though, in the finish, he might even have found the Crowman and shown him to the world, what was all that worth without another to keep his story alive? Yes, the people told his tale, but even those who witnessed aspects of it never saw the whole. And you know how people can be when they have a story to tell; their embellishments cloud the truth. Gordon Black needed someone to tell his story plain and true, to keep it alive in the hearts of us all. Only then would his deeds have any meaning. Only in the passing on from one soul to another, in the most accurate telling, could they have a purpose.

It fell to me to be the first chronicler of Gordon Black's life and mission, to tell it right for the good of all. The Crowman chose me; he made me. To keep him alive in story. Even now, I find it hard to believe that he would choose a man with a black heart, whose ways were those of theft and rape. Me, whose eyes are pitted and white with blindness, whose skin is scarred, whose body is broken, whose fingers are bent and almost useless. I am the first Keeper. Many better souls will follow me but I am proud of my place in all this and I would not change a word of it simply to show myself in a better light.

For all of this, though, for all I've been witness to as a whole man and as a blind man with a new way of seeing, I still cannot say whether any of it matters, or if a single word of it has made a difference. For, though the Crowman's story is already becoming distant in time and his wonders grow all around us, I see there is a child yet to be born who holds all of this in her hands. Somewhere, even now, she walks the Black Feathered Path in the hope of becoming a Keeper. If she is equal to this task, and no simple matter is it, there will be something special about her, something powerful.

The strict codes of the Black Feathered Path will not keep untruths and substitutions from creeping into the Crowman's history over the passing generations. This young woman might be the one to bring Gordon's journey of discovery back to the world through the most exact recounting of all, the final telling. Only a woman has the power to do it. If she can complete the path, hers will be the history that ensures our future: The Book of the Crowman.

All this I have seen and yet it has not been my place to know the outcome. I am the first Keeper and I have done everything I can. For good or ill, I have played my part. This much you already know, whether you believe me or not: without the teller there is no tale.

1

Dirty rain fell on the woman's paling cheeks and neck, leaving gritty streaks. The heavy droplets pattered into her staring eyes but she barely blinked. A small hole in the front of her throat pulsed with dark upwellings. The blood, diluted by the filthy downpour, pooled behind her head, and her long greying hair became indistinguishable from the bare soil. Her right hand still clutched a longbow, her knuckles yellow with tension as though its curved shaft was keeping her alive.

She'd been on the ground for almost a minute already but the sound of hot lead penetrating flesh and cracking bone remained the loudest sound in Gordon's head, far louder than the report of the gun it came from. The other four who now crouched around her, all Green Men and Women, were young and inexperienced, not really fighters at all. They'd been breaking up an old wardrobe for firewood in a backstreet of Fulham when the Ward attacked.

The nearest cover was a long-abandoned playground where they'd cowered, only returning fire from behind a concrete play tunnel when the advancing Wardsmen were within range of their bows. The woman's first arrow had flown true, hitting a Wardsmen in the chest but in almost that same instant, a Ward rifleman had also found his mark.

Gordon knew the Ward would regroup and advance first; they were trained. The survivors he'd had fallen in with were not. And though they may have hated the Ward, they feared them more.

Nearest the wounded woman, whose name Gordon still didn't know, knelt Kieran, looking pale and confused. His hands shook as he reached towards her face. Kieran was the one who'd told Gordon how he'd seen the Crowman flitting through the streets of Fulham late at night, leaving a blessing of black feathers wherever the Green Men sheltered. Kieran was seventeen, the same age as Gordon, and seemed sincere. In other times they might have become friends but Gordon had learned to share as little information with people as he could get away with while he gathered as much intelligence about his objective as possible. Out of habit Gordon hadn't told Kieran and his crew his real name. Right now he was David Cook.

A bullet hit their cover, blasting chips of concrete into the air and raising a puff of dust. Kieran started back, pulling his hands away. Another bullet slapped into the wet dirt near the wounded woman's head, spraying Kieran with a mist of earth and blood. They all moved closer to the tunnel, dragging the woman with them. Kieran began to cry.

"Mum? Mum! What do we do now?" The rain in the woman's eyes had begun to pool and spill like tears. Kieran looked at Gordon. "Why isn't she waking up, Dave? It's just a little hole."

The others pressed their backs to the concrete pipe and tried to shrink as more rifle fire came down on their position. Gordon closed his eyes and pressed a fist to his forehead.

They'll be coming around the sides any minute. We'll be slaughtered.

As he had the thought, the firing stopped. A voice called across the open ground between the two parties.

"We know you have Gordon Black with you. Send him out, unarmed, and we'll let the rest of you go. You all know the alternative."

Kieran frowned.

"Gordon Black? I've heard that name. Isn't he some kind of psychopath?"

Gordon shrugged, lips downturned.

"I have no idea." He pulled Kieran closer. "Listen, we've got an opportunity here. Who's the best shot?"

"Me, I guess. But we can't shoot now. They're negotiating. It's not right."

"They're not negotiating," said Gordon. "The Ward never negotiate. Take one of them out, right now, and I'll make all this go away. Doesn't matter if you miss. It'll give me enough time to find cover."

Kieran shook his head.

"What are you going to do?" He asked. "What *can* you do?"

A bullet thumped into the dirt near Gordon's boot. He drew his knees to his chest.

"Your mum's dying, Kieran. The Ward are the ones who did it. Just give me a chance."

Kieran put his face close to Gordon's.

"If you run away, I'll find you. And I'll cut your fucking throat."

Gordon smiled.

"A second. That's all I need, Kieran. Please."

The voice came once more across no-man's land.

"We know he's there. Send him out unarmed and you can save yourselves."

Kieran nocked and an arrow and hauled on the string, drawing the bow into a tight D. The moment he stood from cover, Gordon darted into the open and ran. He heard the awful silence in which he imagined Kieran scanning for a target and sighting it. He never heard the arrow fly, only the several reports of Ward rifles. He glanced back as he exited the playground and saw Kieran crouched once more, a grin on his face. It was then that the scream came, that of a man on the wrong end of a nightshade-dipped arrowhead. With a grim smile, Gordon sprinted freely now, safe in the cover of a high brick wall.

Gordon moved among the Wardsmen like a ripple on dark water. Their focus was the playground, the concrete pipe and the people crouched behind it, so Gordon's presence, casual and assured but utterly silent, was something they only sensed when the blade of his lock knife parted the skin below their jawbones and severed their windpipes.

Two were already propped against a chunk of fallen masonry, dying from their arrow wounds. They saw him but their comrades-in-arms, immune to their agonies and intent on their prey, ignored their crying and gesturing. Two more fell to their knees clutching their throats in shock and disbelief before the three remaining realised they were under attack. Only one of them carried a rifle and he turned it now on Gordon Black.

With only ten feet between them, the rifleman's shot from the hip went wide. Frowning, he raised his weapon to the correct position, aimed and fired again. The boy stepped clear even as the Wardsman's finger closed on the trigger. Then Gordon was upon him, turning his world briefly red then black. One of the two remaining was the unit's commander, his belt pulled tight on his grey overcoat, hinting at the hungry, wasted flesh beneath. The brimmed hat once worn by Ward agents had been replaced by grey riot helmets. But neither the commander nor his final man carried a firearm – ammunition was a finite resource now. The commander raised instead a long heavy stick made of hickory and his subordinate pulled free a well-oiled and honed machete.

"You agreed to let them go." Said Gordon.

The unit commander blinked.

"There were... conditions."

Gordon stood with his legs slightly apart and his arms hanging relaxed at his sides. His right hand was slick and red, his knife dripping. He shrugged.

"They've been met."

"I don't understand."

Gordon made a show of impatience.

"Do I have to spell it out? You wanted Gordon Black and you've got him."

He watched the look that passed between the two men. It used to amuse him, this moment, but he couldn't smile about killing any more. It was too much like a task now, something wrong and unpleasant; something that had to be done nevertheless. They were young, these two. A little older than him, perhaps, but not as experienced. Not by a long way. They'd been sent out to find him. To bring him back. How many like this had there been over the last three years? Gordon couldn't recall. They wanted to do their duty, to make good on their orders.

You stupid, stupid boys.

The whistle and snick of slim projectiles finding their warm fleshy home caused Gordon to jump back. For a few seconds longer the stunned Wardsmen stood there, taking in the truth as the nightshade crept into their systems, slowly making good on what the arrowheads had begun. Gordon looked into the commander's eyes for a long time before loping back to the playground.

Gordon found Kieran kneeling at his mother's side, head hanging, tears dripping from his nose.

"She couldn't hold on, Dave."

The others stood back, fidgeting and red-faced. When Gordon looked at them they couldn't meet his eyes.

He crouched beside Kieran, placing a hand on the boy's shoulder.

"Let me look," he whispered.

When Kieran didn't respond, Gordon put his knees on the sodden ground and placed his ear to her chest. There was no movement and the rain had already chilled her body. Gordon closed his eyes and heard the distant cawing of a thousand crows. The sounds merged into a roaring hiss and he felt the first globules of Black Light pulsing behind his fingertips.

Kieran's voice cut through the static in his head. Holding the Black Light back made Gordon's guts turn over but he managed to stem its flow for a moment.

"What did you do to them?"

Gordon didn't understand at first. Was Kieran asking about the healings? Did he already know about the Black Light?

"Who?"

"The patrol."

"Oh…" Gordon put a fist to his mouth, fighting to keep his gorge from rising. "I… uh… shut them down."

"How many men?"

"Three. You took the last two."

"We thought you were going to distract them. Get them to turn their backs so we could get away. How did you kill three armed Wardsmen?"

Black Light swirled and expanded in Gordon's palms. He swallowed back his nausea. Willed the dark energy away.

"I was lucky." He began to cough, to choke. "They were new recruits. Didn't really know what they were about. Does it matter?"

Kieran stood up.

"Yes, mate. It matters. It matters a lot. I don't think your name's David Cook." He jabbed a dirty, blood-caked finger towards Gordon's face. "I think you're the one they were looking for. We've heard about you – the boy who's looking for the Crowman. The boy who cuts up Wardsmen wherever he goes. But you got it wrong this time, mate. You lied to us and you got my mother killed."

Gordon thrust his palms against his forehead, squeezing his eyes shut.

How can I be the enemy to the people I'm trying to help?

He let his hands drop to his sides and raised his head to meet Kieran's eyes. Even with the fury of his mother's death still hot in his blood, the boy could not hold his gaze. Gordon allowed the Black Light to come, feeling it bead and swell at his fingertips, letting it drip like venom to the wet ground. Where the spent, dead earth had been the colour of charcoal, the droplets of Black Light brought colour: deep fertile brown and the first stirrings of green growth. Kieran and his crew backed away.

Gordon looked at them, weeping. He sank to his knees.

"Just do one thing for me," he said. "If you truly are Green Men, if you value this land and believe in her future, never... *ever*... speak of this."

Gordon let his hands be drawn towards the woman. Anything he could do to lessen the impact of what he was about to do was a bonus. His hands went to her throat, as though he intended to throttle her. The Black Light, gravitating to sickness and death, found its lodestone.

He felt the bullet dislodge from the woman's cervical vertebrae and travel forwards and out towards his hands. With deft fingers, he removed the mangled lead slug and dropped it to the ground. He returned his hand to her neck and sensed the wound shrinking closed within, the flesh reconnecting, the entry hole sealing.

The woman blinked. She coughed. Her eyes focussed on Gordon, with his hands still clasped at her throat, and she screamed. The scream of the living with no wish to die.

Gordon leapt up and ran, no idea which direction to take and half expecting the whistle of arrows to follow him. He sprinted from the playground and from the ruined park, taking left turns and right turns as haphazardly as he could. It was the healings that brought both Green Men and Ward out looking for him, the rumours of a boy with power. The gift was a threat to his mission. Faces peered from broken windows and shelters in rubble. He knew that everyone who saw him would remember his passing. Anyone who ran among the streets of London now, had something to run from.

"Never again," he whispered as he fled. "Never again."

Archibald Skelton regarded the dead Wardsmen in silence for a long time. Three years of pursuing the boy had done little to reduce his cask-like paunch or the amphibious blubber of his face. However, his surviving eye was keener than ever.

Blood had turned the churned brick and masonry of their

position black, as though the three men whose throats had been cut had leaked oil. Their faces were stiff and ashen in the permanent gloom that choked the streets of the capital; each expression of horrified acceptance more like studies in stone than true death. The four men with arrow wounds lay collapsed and staring, but all of the fallen reminded Skelton of toy soldiers. Perhaps it was their youth that gave them that aspect, perhaps the casual ease with which they appeared to have been dispatched.

"They were just youngsters," said Skelton. "We should have sent men with more history. More guile."

When there was no response, Skelton glanced over at his long-serving partner. The hulk that was Mordaunt Pike might also have been dead for all the colour in his sunken cheeks, for all the movement in his limbs. Even Pike's eyes were dim and unfocused, waiting for a true threat to rouse the power in his massive hands or a command to fire the resolute circuitry of his mind.

"It was the boy, of course," continued Skelton in the wheezed tones of a schoolmistress.

At that, there was a stiffening of muscle in Pike's huge frame, an almost mechanical creak from deep within him. Skelton smirked.

"I wonder how many he's taken now, Pike," he said. "How many of our boys have gone down under that dirty little blade of his, do you think?"

Pike straightened, eliciting further groans from the cabling of his joints. Something ignited in his eyes and he seemed to see the final position of the Ward unit, the dead men and the playground beyond, for the first time.

"Sometimes, I think he's too smart for us," said Skelton. "Too… strong."

The machinery of Pike's body strained beneath his grey trench coat and he turned to face Skelton. Cold rage glowed in his eyes. He was alive once more. He took a step towards his partner, towering over him. Skelton swallowed the wonderful dread in his throat but there was nothing he could do to prevent the hot stiffening at his groin. Pike's eyes, the headlamps of some killer automaton, blazed with hate.

"Gordon Black's life will be a short one," he said in a monotone. "We're getting closer all the time. And he'll pay, Skelton. We'll make him pay. For all of this."

Skelton's pulse beat thick and heavy at his neck. He took a white handkerchief from his pocket and patted his forehead. As much as he adored the lethal energy that rolled off Pike when they discussed the boy, the fact was that they were running out of time.

In three years of searching, coming tantalisingly close to capturing the boy so many times, they still didn't have him. Sometimes, in the small hours, when Pike's engine was a faint rumble of snores from across the room, Skelton wondered if they were doomed. So many of the cataclysmic prophecies had already come true: the earthquakes and epidemics, the floods and landslides. In those anxious and debilitating insomniac watches, Skelton could almost believe that if they didn't stop Gordon Black soon, the Crowman's work would be complete and the Ward would be as extinct as everyone else. By morning, though, such thoughts would always have disappeared to the realms of paranoid fantasy, where they belonged.

One thing Skelton was certain of: once they had Gordon Black, the world would be the Ward's. Forever.

Taking a deep breath, Skelton reached for Pike's shoulder, ended up with his waxy, swollen fingers on the bigger man's biceps. Pike's eyes watched the contact, the coals of fury still smouldering in his gaze.

Skelton swallowed and spoke.

"Listen, Mordaunt..." For a moment words escaped him. He swallowed again. "You know I feel the same way as you about the boy, about everything. But look around, man. There's not much world left to save from the Crowman. Look at these youths, their lifeblood joining the torrent of such that Gordon Black has already spilled. Three years, Mordaunt. Three years and we haven't seen him, haven't so much as grabbed at his coattails."

Pike's slab of a hand, cold and vicelike, removed Skelton's from his arm. Death crouched in his eyes.

"What are you saying?"

It took all he had but Skelton held his partner's gaze. He thanked God for love and the strength it gave him. He became formal once again, his partner's superior – just as he'd always been when they were in uniform.

"We're going to change our approach, Pike." And, as Skelton's heartbeat clattered on, bearing feelings he had no words to express, it came to him what they must do. He took Pike's arm again, only for a moment. "Walk with me," he said. "I have an idea."

2

As the sun sets behind the hovels and squats on the far side
of the river in Shep Afon, Mr Keeper and Carrick Rowntree
sit on the soft silt and smoke their pipes beside a small fire. A
little farther up the riverbank, wrapped in a blanket, Megan
sleeps, exhausted by the effects of the sacrament and the
journey it took her on. Sometimes she murmurs or cries out,
kicking weakly at the sandy earth and causing Mr Keeper to
cast her a concerned glance.

"We could take a room at one of the inns," he says. "She's
been through a lot."

Carrick looks unconcerned.

"What could be more renewing than being cradled in the
arms of the Earth Amu?" he says.

Mr Keeper shakes his head.

"I know. It's stupid of me. But she's been through such a
lot. And she's still so young. I want to… make it up to her.
She deserves a reward."

"A night spent on one of Shep Afon's splintery pallets is no
reward for one who seeks the Crowman. Look at her, Aaron.
She's at home right where she is. Besides," says Carrick,
patting something hidden inside his tunic. "You know as well
as I do that Megan has already taken her reward."

For a while there is no sound but the plunge and slop of the market town's creaking waterwheels and the distant murmur of trader's voices raised in cheer as they throng the taverns around the hub.

"It took me years to see our work as anything other than a curse," Mr Keeper says eventually. "Even now there are days when I think things might have been simpler if I'd stayed in my apa's smithy. He was a bastard to me and never taught me a damn thing worth repeating but I'd have known, of a morning, what was in store for me between sunrise and nightfall. Hell, Carrick, I'd be happily shoeing horses now. Making pokers and mending gates, instead of worrying about the future. And her."

"You'd have your own children, Aaron. You'd be just as worried about them and just as worried about the future. We Keepers are folk, plain as anyone else. The only difference is the knowledge we hold and the burden it bestows upon us."

Mr Keeper taps the ash from the bowl of his pipe and refills it. He lights it with a stick from their fire. As the light fades from the day, the glow of the flames picks out the deepening creases in his forehead, around his eyes and mouth. He looks at his old master.

"Carrick…" He hesitates for long moments. "The story has been eroded over the generations. The people tell it wrong around their hearths when evening comes. They don't understand the Crowman like they used to. If we lose the thread of his life, we're finished. You know that. All of this rests on her shoulders now." Mr Keeper takes a long pull on his pipe stem. "It sometimes strikes me as unreasonable that an innocent must carry such a load."

"There are no mistakes in this world. She's where she's meant to be."

Mr Keeper's eyes flash.

"Don't try to placate me, Carrick. Those are worn out words. They have no meaning now. Nothing is certain. Nothing is 'meant to be'."

The old man sighs but when Mr Keeper glances over it's a smile he sees on Carrick Rowntree's face.

"Listen, Aaron, if it makes you feel any better, I was just as concerned about you."

"Really?"

"Of course. I lost a great deal of sleep over it. But you should understand that it's absolutely right and proper to fret about your life's work. Our work is the Black Feathered Path and we can't help but care for those who travel it. If we didn't, well, all this would be nothing more than a joke. A bad one." Carrick Rowntree glances at Megan's huddled form. "The girl is strong. She is equal to the task. Guide her right and you're giving everyone a chance at the future." The old man shakes his head, again good-naturedly. "You're no different than when you came to me, Aaron, all those years ago. A boy who held a vision. What did I always tell you?"

"Don't be distracted by what others are doing. Concentrate on what you're doing."

"Exactly. You need to do the same now. Get your part in all this right and Megan will get hers right. It has to be that way around or nothing will work."

Mr Keeper clamps his pipe between his teeth and scoots closer to his old master so that he can whisper.

"She's a young woman, Carrick. The first there's ever been. It's not as simple as working with a lad. Everything I do or say, it has to be correct. And I can't just give her a beating when she gets it wrong like you used to do with me."

The old man chuckles.

"It's not funny," says Mr Keeper. "I have to think carefully before I speak and act. On every single occasion. And I have to maintain a certain… distance. It would be so much more comfortable if it was a boy."

"No it wouldn't. Lads are troublesome. They don't concentrate and they think they know better than you do. They'll earn themselves a beating every day given half the chance. Just like you did." Carrick takes Mr Keeper's arm in his old fingers. "Listen to me, Aaron. As a friend. What you have with Megan is unprecedented. It's as much a challenge for you as it is for her and that is absolutely as it should be. Guiding her, teaching her our ways as you do, you are forced to maintain a sacred mindset throughout. You are required to respect the girl as you respect… who?"

Mr Keeper blinks.

"Are you testing me?"

"Indeed I am. Answer the question, Aaron."

Mr Keeper's anger rises.

"Listen Carrick, there's too much water under the bridge for this. How dare you sit there and think you can treat me like a…" The answer comes to him and Mr Keeper's annoyance vanishes. "Great Spirit," he whispers. "Oh dear sweet heaven above."

"Do you see?" asks the old man.

Very slowly, Mr Keeper nods.

"I don't know why I never saw it before."

"Because it was right in front of you, Aaron. That's how it always is. The Earth Amu has sent a girl child. Even in the Black Dawn the time of men was waning. It was men whose ideas forced the Crowman from blackness into existence. And though we've changed, made amends and redressed the balance to some degree, men alone cannot heal the wounds they inflicted. Only a woman can do that. I've seen things in the weave, Aaron. Women already wearing the mantle of Keeper in many lands across the water. But this girl," Carrick nods in Megan's direction. "Well, she is different – special. And that is why, if she can complete the path, Megan will be the one who changes our world forever, bringing harmony where even the Keepers have failed to find it. Even now, Aaron, there are factions out there in our land, all men, who search for the lost knowledge, who thirst for its resurrection. And they are dedicated. They will not stop and we must find a way to deal with them."

"But what in heaven's name can one young woman do against all that, Carrick?"

"The fact that neither of us knows the answer should be reason enough to realise that it is time for a daughter of the land to take her turn. This is what the Earth Amu wants. It's what the Crowman wants. And it's the reason you and I exist, Aaron. Everything we've ever done and the wrongs of every generation before us will be met here and now by this girl. And it is up to you to train her right and well or all is lost." Carrick Rowntree's fingers clasp harder over Mr Keeper's arm. "Hold your commitment, Aaron. Continue to lead her as you have thus far. Give her the best chance you can, and she in turn will give us a chance. One last chance for us all."

Megan stands on the silty river bank watching Mr Keeper and Carrick Rowntree and listening to their hushed conversation. She sees her own blanket-wrapped form, curled in exhaustion close by, and senses the ache in her belly even though for now she is disembodied, her spirit abroad within the weave.

The seepage between her legs is strong and steady and it will soon be time to change the cloth she surreptitiously placed there before collapsing into sleep. One thing is immediately clear: neither Mr Keeper nor his teacher can see her in the weave, even though that very afternoon they both travelled with her, quietly keeping watch over her in the guise of two wrens as she searched for the Crowspar. It was soon after she returned that her bleed began, and she is in no doubt that the Keepers' blindness is due to her moon. Her womanhood increases her abilities in the weave: Silence. Invisibility. Who knows what more?

I'm free!

Her delight, however, is brief. What has passed between the two elders is enough to clip these newfound secret wings. Now that the men have fallen into silence, Megan decides she has heard enough. The only power she holds right now is the power to flee, to be away from the weight of destiny, if only for a while.

She turns from her guardians and takes a few tentative steps up the bank toward the rocks that lead up to Shep Afon's hub and the now deserted market place. Glancing back she sees neither Mr Keeper nor Carrick Rowntree look up from their spiral of worries. Climbing the rocks is easy. Though her body is heavy with fatigue and the lingering effects of the sacrament, her spirit is light and fleet of foot. In seconds she stands on the wall separating the market from the river, finding herself between two worlds. One is the world she knows, the world where Mr Keeper is her guide and protector. The other is the new world, the weave, the byways of which she has never trodden entirely alone.

She hops down into the deserted hub where not a scrap of waste from the day's trading remains. Even the beggars and stray dogs have moved on and the only noise now comes from the inns and taverns that line the hub.

Megan hesitates.

All this freedom and no idea where to begin. She closes her eyes for a moment and waits for a draw or ripple in the weave. It is barely a blink before she senses a glow among the inns and the pull that accompanies it. She takes a step into the marketplace but stops to look back over the low boundary wall. The Keepers seem very small and far away even though if she spoke quietly they would be able to hear.

She turns her back on them.

The boards and trestles that the traders leased for their day of commerce are now stacked in stone archways out of the weather. The hub of Shep Afon is a broad, perfect ring of compacted grit nestling in a semi-circle of the river's meander, the inns, taverns and other premises forming the opposite half of the circle. At the centre of the market place, Megan stops, opening herself to prompts from the weave. When a distracted wind skitters across the deserted expanse, Megan hears the voices of a thousand stallholders, their songs and cries now whispered in the body of the breeze.

One voice, that of a woman, is clearer than all the rest.

Save us all. The girl's got the Scarecrow in her.

The pull from the weave intensifies and Megan begins to walk again, her pace quickening. She makes for a slim property, sandwiched between two inns. The building is timber-framed, its front wall formed in bulging sections of dun coloured daub, as though the inns on each side are crushing it. There is no sign to say what manner of business it houses, but to be in the commercial centre of the village, Megan assumes some sort of trade must occur on the premises.

She approaches the warped, splintering door and is about to knock when it opens and two men stumble out. Trying to support each other and failing, the pair blunder right through Megan and collapse to the ground, laughing. She shivers, nauseated by the sensation, but the men have no awareness of her whatsoever.

"I've had better donkeys," slurs one.

"I've had better... weasels," says the other.

"Weasels?"

"Er, yeah. Big, fat stripy weasels."

"You mean badgers?"

"Badgers. Yeah."

The two men roll around, laughing so hard they can't get up.

"You can say what you like 'bout Shep Afon's dubious... snatch rental... 'stablishments," says the larger of the two men, with difficulty. He gains his feet and hauls his thinner friend upright. "But the beer's bloody excellent. Let's have another pint."

The drunks stagger away leaving a yeasty, sweaty reek in their wake. The door has closed behind them but the pull from behind it is even stronger now. Megan closes her eyes and passes through the weathered wood like a breath through gauze.

Beyond it, oil lamps illuminate a tiny reception area where a heavyset matriarch keeps watch like a bloated bird of prey. Her sour disdain, worn like scarring, lifts into a smile of lascivious and ingratiating welcome the moment a knock sounds at the front door. Megan steps clear of the brothel's mistress, not wanting to repeat the sensation of flesh passing through the pure glow of her weave body. As a group of three traders stumble in, Megan lets the draw pull her through a curtain of red ribbons, along a slim corridor with closed doors to her right and up a flight of uneven steps that she knows would creak loudly had she a more substantial form.

On the next level, the rooms run to her left but the pull still comes from above. Noises emanate from most of the rooms; giggles, squeals, and grunts mostly but sometimes sounds of choking and sobbing. Megan concentrates on the draw from overhead but she can't shut out the animalistic voices, nor can she imagine what they signify: something more complex than the rutting of beasts.

Only in Gordon's world has she seen stairs rising more than two levels but here they take her to a third and still the steps in the sandwich house lead up. The fourth flight ends at a door with a red rose painted on it and this is where the pull emanates from. Megan ascends and listens. She hears nothing but she can sense life on the other side. She passes through the door.

Within, the roof of the sandwich house forms the tightly cocked ceiling of the room, the joists and rafters in plain view. A small wind-eye gives onto the market place, quite the vantage point for an observer. The bed, large by Megan's reckoning, looks as though a fight has taken place in it. The room smells thick with the mingled scents of men and women. Well, one woman. The one who now sits remaking her face at a tiny dressing table in a mirror little bigger than her own face. It is in this mirror that her eyes glance at some movement in her periphery and then lock with Megan's. Her free hand flies to her mouth but the cry it was intended to stifle is already out. The woman turns on her stool.

Darkness falls. Mr Keeper and Carrick Rowntree move closer to their fire while Megan slumbers nearby. Mr Keeper is lost in a reverie, his eyes drawn by ghosts of flame and starlight on the surface of the river. Carrick Rowntree adds wood to the fire, stirring up a plume of sparks to attract his old pupil's attention.

"I have to leave in the morning, Aaron."

Mr Keeper doesn't look at him.

"I know."

"I won't be coming back this time."

Mr Keeper sighs and looks over the flames at the man who guided him on the Black Feathered Path; so long ago it might be someone else's life, someone else's memories. The emotions of that time, though, are as fresh as spring buds. He has no remedy for the pain it causes to think of the old man leaving. Carrick became the father he'd never dared believe existed. Stern but fair, always encouraging yet willing to let a boy make mistakes and, more importantly, learn from them. He watches Carrick through the fire and smoke and fancies he sees the history of a thousand souls alive in the old man's eyes.

Carrick slips a hand between the fold of his layers of warm clothing.

"If I forget to give you this, however, I will be obliged to return and find you, making tomorrow's departure a far less dramatic affair and costing me a good deal of unnecessary effort."

He holds out his hand, away from the flames, and Mr Keeper reaches across. The touch of the crystal is like frozen midnight in his palm. He shivers and spends long moments turning it over in his hands, watching the way it absorbs the flickering firelight.

"When Megan is ready, you must give her the Crowspar. If, as you believe, she is the girl in the prophecy, then she is the last of our kind. The one who cleaves us to the land forever."

After a while, Mr Keeper flips the Crowspar up into the air, catches it deftly and secretes in one of his many pockets in a manner that appears to be final. Within a few moments, though, the crudely carved artefact is somehow back in his hands, its facets traced and its contours explored by Mr Keeper's agitated fingers.

He leans closer to the fire and lowers his voice to a whisper.

"I don't like to admit it, Carrick – especially not to you – but I've no idea what I'm going to tell Megan about this. The crystal is the one aspect of his life I've never truly understood."

The old man might be smiling or frowning. The flames make it impossible to tell. Mr Keeper thinks he is angry at first but eventually Carrick does respond, his voice equally hushed.

"That's because its role in the Crowman's story extends into our time, into this moment. The telling will not be complete until a woman walks the path. Only then will any of us really know what the Crowspar may be or what its purpose is. Megan is the first to have found and retrieved the black crystal. I would like to believe she will know what to do with it when the time comes. I can only assume that she will find her instructions somewhere within the Crowman's story. One thing I do know, Aaron: if you're right – if she is who you think she is – hers will be the finest, most accurate telling of all."

At that moment, Megan whimpers in her sleep. By the firelight, Mr Keeper can make out the fear and anxiety on her face. He almost gets up to comfort her but checks himself, knowing there's nothing more he can do except allow her to rest. Tomorrow they must begin the journey home and she'll need her strength.

"She'll be alright, Aaron."

Embarrassed that his concerns must show on his face, Mr Keeper sighs and turns back to the fire.

"I hope you're right, Carrick."

"She has you to guide her. She can do no better than that."

Mr Keeper doesn't know how to respond to the compliment. It's not the sort of thing Carrick Rowntree usually comes out with. In the end he settles for familiar territory.

"One more pipe?"

His old teacher nods.

"One more. And then we must sleep. Tomorrow will find us on the long road once more."

They fill their pipes and smoke in silence as the fire dies down.

3

"You," says the woman. "I prayed I'd not see your kind ever again." Whatever fright she felt is fast replaced by suspicion and anger. "Yet here you are on the very same day." The woman, tense but hard of the eye, spends long moments studying Megan. "What brings you to my room?"

Megan wants to put the woman at her ease, to answer simply but she struggles.

"The... shape of the weave."

"Listen, Scarecrow girl, I know cocks and I know futures. I don't know no weave."

Megan blushes and looks away. The woman rises and approaches. She stands in front of Megan, one shoulder bare, her arms folded.

"How did you get past the mistress?"

"She didn't..." Megan clears her throat. "...see me." Fearing the woman might call for the mistress or simply kick her back down the stairs, Megan starts to talk without really thinking. "I had to find you. You said you'd tell my fortune. I wanted you to but Mr Keeper wouldn't allow it. Please, I have to know."

The woman snorts in disgust.

"That's it?" She almost smiles. "Listen, girl–"

"I'm Megan."

"Megan then. You're a bright spark. Pretty too. This is your future: you'll be happy. A good husband, enough to eat, a healthy brood. Go on back to your Keeper."

"No. You don't understand. I already know that's not my fate. I'm walking the Black Feathered Path. I need to see where it leads."

"Don't Keepers have the power to see both behind *and* ahead?"

"Yes. But we're forbidden to serve ourselves with our own knowledge. It's meant only for the good of the land and the people."

The woman's hostility begins to drop away.

"And you hold to that?"

"Of course. If the path is not defined, the way is not clear. Besides, I want to complete my training. For myself and for everyone."

The woman considers Megan for a few silent moments and then holds out her hand.

"Come. Sit with me for a spell."

Megan smiles and reaches towards her. Her fingers to pass right through the woman's hand and they both flinch as though stung.

"Fuck. What are you, girl?"

A sickening shiver overwhelms Megan and she staggers back towards the door. The woman stares.

"Please don't be afraid," Megan says. "Help me. I know you can do it. Help me to see."

The woman isn't shocked for long. Her edge returns almost immediately and she folds her arms across her chest.

"If you want the future you must pay for it. How will you do that, ghost girl? With ghost money?"

Megan's mind whirls. She is so close. She hears heavy footfalls on the stairs and drunken laughter. The woman shakes her head.

"Time you were away."

"No. Wait. We can make it... a trade."

"Believe me, little one, all you've got that I want is your looks and your youth and I don't think you'll be wanting to part with those."

The footsteps reach the door and a strong hand hammers against it.

"Please," Megan whispers. "I have something to give you. This can't be a mistake. You need me and I need you. I'm sure of it."

The woman considers. The hammering comes again.

"Fuck off!" she yells.

After a pause a slurred male voice says:

"The mistress said top room."

"The mistress is drunk. I've got my moon."

"I'm not fussed."

"Well, I am so fuck off like I told you."

After some indistinct muttering the footsteps clomp back down the creaking stairs and the hammering assails a different door. The woman's gaze fixes once more on Megan.

"So. What can a girl like you possibly do for me?"

Megan closes her eyes and stretches into the weave around the woman knowing she has one chance to get this right and very little time in which to do it. Immediately she senses pain in the woman's womb and bladder. She sees black spots there: years of untreated disease, the scarring from two abortions and several rapes.

But this long-term physical damage is nothing next to the shadows that crowd the woman's aura: dark spirits feeding on the degradation of leased flesh, drinking the woman's shame and pain despite her efforts to maintain some sort of prostitute's nobility. Megan is not frightened by the spirits. Far from it. She is incensed at their leechlike cling and the barefaced simplicity of their intentions. But she knows if the woman could see what attends her at every moment of the day she would be insane with terror.

Megan can also tell that the woman's true ability is that of a seer. But her profession and the shadows it has plunged her into are clouding her skills almost beyond use. The woman barely believes in her own gift, using it as a way to bring in an extra meal or two on the days when Shep Afon's market is busy. There is only one thing to do, and Megan has never done it before.

Using her hands in the weave, she reaches into the woman's belly and strokes the scars with her fingertips, fingertips that begin to spark with white light. As the light grows she lets it blast away the decade or more of infection that has caused so much inflammation and discomfort. Guided only by instinct, Megan works fast inside the woman's body and as she works she prays, calling in the only spirit being she knows she can trust to answer.

The oil lamps in the room flicker and dim. The woman doesn't notice. Her eyes stare ahead and her body is rigid, as though time has stopped. Megan prays harder, putting all her fury into her invocations.

"Here's a place for your darkness," she whispers. "Here's a place for your light."

From somewhere distant in the weave, Megan hears a familiar sound and nods to herself with a grim smile. The whine of huge black wings scything the air gains volume fast. The light from the two oil lamps becomes little more than an ochre stain as flitting shadows crowd the attic room. Their blackness is deep, sleek and midnight pure, astonishingly beautiful in comparison with the tainted darkness of the psychic parasites clinging to the whore like ivy.

Time in the physical world stops. The woman is frozen, unblinking. Megan's fingers work at speed, seeking out sickness and obliterating it with light, loosening gnarls of scarred vulval and uterine flesh, returning rosy health to abused tissues. The gurning, lasciviously fascinated beings that wait in the woman's energy field draw back from Megan's brightness and purity, scowling at the intrusion of anything that doesn't feed their salacious appetites. Yet her light is enough to distract them from the pristine dark that now occupies every corner of the woman's room, a dark that advances with a feathery whisper until it surrounds them. Obsidian beaks and claws extend from every direction and only then do the spirits notice the force that stalks them. They try to shrink away but the Crowman's influence is everywhere. The beaks and claws close over the spirits, matching their frequency with ease; puncturing and cutting into them as though they were flesh. The spirits howl.

"Take them," whispers Megan. "Take them away from her forever."

A wind rises in the tiny room, sudden as a squall, and vast wings beat at the air. With a sound like tearing hessian the dark spirits are ripped from the woman's aura and for a moment her unblinking eyes widen in pain. The wind increases, causing Megan to narrow her eyes against its force.

In an instant the room returns to silence. The wind is gone, the darkness has dissolved. The oil lamps brighten and Megan senses a purity as though the energy in the attic has been somehow scrubbed white. Even the smell of the soiled sheets has been neutralised. The room is fresh, as is the face of the woman. Megan withdraws her hands from the weave of the prostitute's body and the woman's eyes gradually refocus.

She looks around the room as though not recognising it. Her eyes meet Megan's and she collapses forward, into her open arms. Megan wills substance back into her own form and holds the prostitute tight. She glances once more around the exposed beams and rafters, making certain the room is clear. She strokes the woman's back.

"It's alright," she says. "Everything will be different now. Everything will be better."

But whether the woman hears or not, Megan can't tell; the sound of her weeping is too loud. To the departed darkness, and the echoing whisper of black silken wings, Megan whispers:

"Thank you."

4

Dear Gordon,

There's so much I want to say to you. But now that I've finally
managed to get some paper and a pencil, I don't know where to start.
The most important thing is I'm alive. I wish I could tell you about
Mum, Dad and Angela but I don't know what happened to them or
where they are. We were separated the day the Ward came for us and I
haven't seen them since. Oh, Gordon, I miss them so much it makes my
chest hurt. Like there's a raw wound inside that will never heal. But I
miss you the most. Sometimes I cry really hard, the way I imagine insane
people do, and I want to smash my head against the wall so hard that
I'll – well, you know. I probably shouldn't say things like that but if
you're still out there, I know you'll understand. Wardsman Boscombe
– he lets me call him Bossy when no one's around – says you're alive.
He never says it to me but I'm sure he has connections among the Green
Men. He says he hears stories about you sometimes. Probably nothing
more than rumours, I know, but it gives me hope and I need that in here.
Bossy's not like the others. He never beats me. He's the one who got me
this stuff so I can write to you. He says he has "friends". He says he can
get these letters to you. All he asks is a small price every now and again.
Is it true you fought with Skelton and Pike? That you cut them both with
Dad's knife? I'm so proud of you Gordon. If I had a knife here I'd

••••

Gordon squatted against a brick wall and looked up into the sky.

It was saturated with smoke, dust and low cloud. Charcoal-dark flakes floated down and settled on his already grimy clothes; a snow of ash from the thousands of tiny fires which now kept the people of London warm or cooked their food – those fortunate enough to find it. The permanent smog smelled of sulphur, spent coal and burnt wood. The sun rarely broke through, even in the open country, and four seasons had become two: a warm, wet monsoon and a frozen winter.

From the pack beside him – a sturdy but modest rucksack containing his parents' last letters, his diary and the scrapbook of Crowman prophecies, extra layers, a flysheet and small blanket, whatever food he could salvage and a few other necessities – he withdrew a tin of salmon, spiked it with his dad's old lock-knife and worked it open. The blade was thinner and curved almost to a crescent by three years of honing. The once angular wooden handle had worn smooth to abide in Gordon's right palm. With the tin's lid prised back, the stink of the city was banished for a moment by the oily reek of fish. Saliva flooded his mouth making the glands in his throat sting and ache. His stomach worked against itself, groaning. He spiked a lump of pink flesh, inspected it briefly and popped it into his mouth.

He chewed for a long time before swallowing.

There was no opportunity for a second bite; a noise in the distance brought him to his feet. Nearby, there was an impact hole in the wall, almost perfectly round but for the jagged edges of bricks. There was damage like this all over London, across every city he'd passed through, blasts and bullet holes from the early days of conflict.

He ducked through into a small back garden full of junk; everything of use or value stripped from it long ago. He placed his pack in a cracked bathtub and rested the tin of salmon on top before crouching and poking his head back through the hole.

The noise was closer now. The clatter of six or seven horses approaching along Lillie Road. He guessed he'd have about a minute to find cover. Praying it was a routine patrol and not a dog squad, he ducked back through the hole, grabbed his food and pack and, stumbling over the tangle of scrap, scrambled towards the back of the house.

The door was shut but not locked. He yanked it open and assessed his options. The tin of salmon was precious but the smell of it was like a loudhailer announcing a human presence. Out here where the population was sparse, the Ward would stop and question anyone they saw, just so they'd have something to report at the end of the patrol. Nearer the centre it was busy and they ignored you, saving their energy for dawn searches, breaking up fights over food and lynching petty criminals. There wasn't time to hide the fish and even if he ate it in a hurry, the smell would linger. He grabbed the tin and crept into the house.

Please, let there be some stairs.

Passing through two rooms he found the front hallway and, leading up from it, intact stairs.

Thank you.

Most properties had been raided for wood and a decent staircase could keep a family warm for a week of winter. Two weeks if they used it carefully. These stairs were still carpeted. Three at a time, he ascended.

On the first landing there were two rooms. He passed the damp, mildewed bathroom, its walls dark with colonies of rot. Beyond was what might once have been a bedroom. It was empty now and its windows were gone but it looked out over the rubbish tip in the back garden. If he kept still and hung back, he'd see the Wardsmen pass by on the other side of the wall. Anticipating he might have to run or hide again, he put his tin of food down and pulled his rucksack on. As he completed the manoeuvre and bent to pick up his precious salmon, he felt something hard dig into his ribs.

He froze.

Out of the corner of his eye he saw a woman. Pale-faced, dark haired. That was all he could glean before the most important detail took his attention: a double barrelled shotgun pulled tight into her shoulder. She looked like she knew how to use it.

Outside the clopping of steel-shod hooves approached.

"I don't want any trouble," he whispered. "That's the Ward outside. I only wanted to hide."

The woman glanced through the window and ducked slightly. She backed away still pointing the gun at him; at his head now. She motioned with it for him to follow her.

"You won't shoot me. It'll only bring them to your door."

She smiled without a trace of humour.

"And I'll tell them I shot a thief. Saved them the trouble."

Gordon raised his hands. It was a hundred to one that the gun was even loaded but he couldn't take the risk. Even if she fired and missed, the whole troop of Wardsmen would be off their mounts and through the door in seconds. She probably wouldn't miss with the second barrel.

She sniffed the air and then noticed the tin in his hand.

"Is that… fish?"

"Yeah."

"Where'd you get it?"

"I found it."

"You stole it."

"I found it."

For a moment she had a faraway look in her eye. He could have pounced then, wrestled the gun from her and made a run for it.

But the noise… And if she was faster than he anticipated…

By the time he'd thought it over, his chance had passed. She had the eyes of a predator all of a sudden.

"I haven't eaten fish for two years."

He sighed.

"Fine. It's yours. Just let me go."

Outside the horses had come to a halt. He couldn't see them but they had to be right outside the hole in the wall. If any of them were listening, they could probably hear the conversation.

"Please," he whispered.

She shook her head, backed up and motioned again with the morbid end of the shotgun. There was space for him to pass by her now and that was what she wanted; to get him in front of her. To herd him. He did what she wanted, keeping low. He sensed her crouching too as she followed.

"Up," she hissed.

He mounted the last flight of stairs where there were two more rooms. A ladder led from the top landing, up into a black square hole.

"And again."

Shit.

He climbed the ladder, still holding the tin of salmon. From up here there was no way to see the back garden, no way of telling what the Ward patrol was up to. A single candle burned in the blackness above. He didn't have time to register what it illuminated before he felt the shotgun in the crack of his arse.

"Quick," she said.

He could tell from the strain in her voice that the patrol had entered the house.

She pulled the ladder up and closed the attic hatch with swift, well-practised movements. Like a soldier. She wrapped the fish in a clear plastic bag and pushed it as far from the hatch as possible. Any smell from the open tin was masked by odours of human habitation where water no longer ran. Sweat, urine, faeces. And something else he wasn't able to isolate at first. Something like decay.

Using only gestures his captor showed Gordon where to sit and to stay silent. He didn't require the instructions but accepted them with a nod. On the far side of the attic where the roof met the floor, something wrapped in blankets moved. The woman put her hand on the muffled form and made as quiet a shushing as she could. The shape stilled.

Now the woman let her eyes meet Gordon's over the light from the candle, a light that suddenly seemed very bright and very dangerous.

Indistinct noises and voices came from below.

The woman leaned forward and Gordon noticed that she really wasn't a woman at all but a girl, probably not much older than him. A girl whose face had been worked over by fear and responsibility. He knew the look from his own reflection.

She whispered one last thing:

"If they come up, you'll fight them with me?"

He withdrew his lock-knife and unclasped it.

She nodded once, licked her fingers and pinched out the candle flame.

5

Megan and Mr Keeper walk in silence for many miles. There is nothing unusual in this except that, for the first time, the silence originates in Megan.

Shep Afon is miles behind them and nothing but open country lies ahead. Megan senses the tug of the weave and thinks of her half-finished business with the prostitute. This is the first experience she hasn't shared with Mr Keeper since treading the Black Feathered Path and keeping silent about it fills her with shame. And yet, if she has learned anything at all from him, it is to trust her instincts above all else. An intelligent gravity works on her from the weave, drawing her back to the attic room in Shep Afon. The moment she has a chance, she will go, while the blood of her moon shields her from Mr Keeper's watchful protection. A sudden belly cramp reminds her of her power but she doesn't permit herself a smile; she's certain he would sense it even though he walks ahead of her.

The land spreads to every part of the horizon with such power and presence the sight of it overwhelms her. The land is no different, though. Her eyes are merely seeing it anew; all her senses hum with lush, deep perceptions. Colours and sounds combine so that the landscape sings a song of savage passion at the very edge of her hearing. Smells burst from the feeling of a breeze on her face or the impact of her boots on the path. The air itself has subtle flavours that change each time the wind shifts. The sky is so vast and unfathomable it pulls at her, threatening to snatch her away from the ground. Every rule is broken. Blades of grass are tiny cutlasses of green threat, glimpsed foxes with their jaws clamped over slack prey send her messages of benevolence. A distant dove is a swooping raptor, patches of thorn and bramble promise the sweetest rest.

All the while Megan watches for shadows cast from overhead, listens for the hush of huge wings. She expects a dark figure to step out from behind every tree they pass, his black weeds trailing to the ground or spread wide and sleek, ready to enfold her. And, though she fears his power more than ever, more than the day on which she first laid eyes upon him, Megan knows with profound certainty that the Crowman represents both the darkness of endings and reavings and the darkness of chaos from which births and unions are manifested.

She tries to distract herself with memories of home and the times before she first saw the Crowman; the days of her childhood which she knows are behind her forever. She can visit them now only in reverie or in the weave; those long days spent idly and in wonder, with a trust of things so deep and total there was no space for unhappiness.

On a day like this, so tired and so far away from anything familiar, it feels as though she has lost everything of value. That part of her, the little girl who once ran through the meadows and swam in the Usky river, who danced and sang with the other children of the village, that Megan Maurice has been left far behind. Somewhere, she still sings and still skips, her blonde hair as yet untouched by the feathers of the Crowman; but she is lost to this world and this time, and thinking of her brings Megan only sadness. Even Amu and Apa are closed to her for the moment, and her childhood friends Tom Frewin and Sally Balston seem so distant as to be strangers.

She thinks instead of the old man who arrived in his tiny, almost circular boat – a vessel made of skin stretched over woven slats of split ash – and how he left earlier that day the very same way he had come. He and Mr Keeper had embraced; a long, heartfelt clasping, before Carrick Rowntree had thrown his pack into his boat, pushed it down the sandbank and hopped in like a little boy who couldn't wait to go fishing.

They'd watched him with his single oar, paddling against the current and making headway with no apparent effort. He hadn't looked back and Megan, feeling every nuance of intent and emotion in everything she saw, experienced waves of sadness and longing burst from Mr Keeper. This man, usually so inscrutable it was easy to forget he was her sworn guardian and teacher, loved Carrick Rowntree, would miss him and feel alone without his leadership, knew he might not see the old man again. As suddenly as these pulses of melancholia had begun, Mr Keeper stopped them. It had seemed to Megan like an act of will. They were replaced with a simple joy that came from the inevitably of death and separation, and from the certainty of the cycles of the Earthwalk. They came from the knowledge that in every ending was a beginning and that to be cut away was to be reunited elsewhere. Carrick Rowntree is gone. That neither of them will see the old man again is another certainty living in Megan's water.

What does she have that she can rely on? What does she have that is certain and that can protect her as her abilities increase and her perceptions become more powerful? Only this land and all its gifts and mysteries. Only this land and the feeling of her feet in communion with it as she walks. Only her living heartbeat and the pulse of the world moving through her; the rhythm of her feet and the rhythm of living and dying, beating slow, beating fast everywhere she turns her eyes.

She lets this rhythm lead her footsteps.

The struts and crossbars of their shelter in the woods are untouched, right where Megan and Mr Keeper left them. They rebuild and wrap the bender without a word and Megan can't help wondering if he already knows that she has entered the weave without him. Perhaps he's merely waiting for the right moment to spring it on her.

Mr Keeper makes a broth of dried meat and oats, flavoured with some herbs he has picked as they were walking. They drink it from small wooden bowls, fingering the chewy flesh into their mouths and tipping up the slurry of porridge at the end. Megan is surprised by a hunger she hasn't noticed while passing through the landscape. She has moved like a spirit blown on the wind, seemingly using no energy, but now she eats three bowls of broth and what's left in the cook pot before she is satisfied. The food brings her from spirit into flesh at a plummet and she is so tired she can barely crawl into the bender to unroll her blanket.

"Let me dream tonight," she whispers and drops into the crow blackness of sleep.

The sun is bright directly overhead, much hotter than Megan remembers it being when they left. Shouts and snatches of traders' songs come from every direction. The air is filled with the scent of food both fresh and cooked and a greasy aroma of grilled meat wafts among the crowds of buyers. Megan walks amid the throng of Shep Afon's market place like a ghost. No one sees her but even so, she does her best to avoid contact and its sickening effect on her.

The riverbank where she camped with Mr Keeper and Carrick Rowntree is where she really wants to go, feeling pulled back by the intensity of her experiences there. But she makes herself walk towards the thin house that bulges, the brothel squashed between the two inns. It is the prostitute woman she needs to see.

The door is locked and the building silent – she supposes there will be little happening here until the day's trading is complete and the traders' takings have been added up. Megan passes through the gnarly wood, feeling only slight resistance and no nausea from the inanimate barrier. She slips past the unattended reception booth and trots up the cramped flights of stairs until she reaches the door to the attic room. She raises her hand to knock, shakes her head with a small smile and then passes through.

The room is empty.

There is no mattress on the old bed. The mirror and small dressing table have been removed. No oil lamps hang from the beams. A thin layer of dust coats every surface. Megan crosses to the window and looks down into the market where there is much movement. The heated tones of haggling voices rise up to the glass but her eyes are drawn to the far side of the hub, to the river and its many waterwheels. Something down there tugs at her. She turns back to glance around the empty room again and moves to leave. It is only as she passes back through the attic room door that she notices the crudely fashioned hasp and padlock that have been used to prevent entry.

Frowning, Megan steals down the cramped stairs and along the claustrophobic corridors until she is once more in the market. Urgently now, like an impatient breeze, she flits through the press and noise of the crowds to the wall bordering the river where she and Mr Keeper first rested on their arrival in Shep Afon. Megan hops up onto the wall and scans the riverbank. There is no sign of their footprints or camping place in the sandy expanse of silt. It's as though they were never there. The pull however, is stronger now. It comes from across the river, the quiet side where the outcasts live.

Ignoring the bridges, Megan flits to the water's edge and walks across, the sense of the water buoying her up bringing a grin to her face. She would stop and play here, skipping and dancing over the gentle ripples, if the urge to find the source of the weave's pull wasn't so great. Gaining the far side, she leaps up the same bank her kidnappers forced her to climb when they took her to the hag Bodbran.

Megan surveys the ramshackle huts, lean-tos, tents and benders that make up the loose community of outcasts on this side of Shep Afon's river. The pull is stronger than ever now and comes from the farthest of the dwellings. Megan walks fast, dodging guy ropes, water butts and small piles of firewood. Possessions here are of little worth but many of the dwellings are open and unattended, the few objects within and around each quite visible. Tethered goats munch grass in circular patches and chickens wander, apparently ownerless.

A low, dome-shaped bender takes Megan's attention. It is a little way beyond the perimeter of the dwellings, very deliberately set apart. From the centre of the dome, a pennant of black feathers rolls and flutters to the touch of the breeze. She hurries towards it, glancing around. The whole encampment seems to be deserted, as though, for just a few minutes its entire population has wandered into the hills.

Outside the black bender, Megan halts and the draw from the weave goes slack. No pull. No glow. Silence everywhere. She's been so eager for this, so *committed*, but now that she stands on the threshold Megan hesitates. Maybe this is the wrong thing to be doing. This is no simple dream, after all, no innocent promenade in the night country. She asked for this. She intended it. And she is here without Mr Keeper's knowledge or permission. He has never encouraged her to enter the weave alone; it's as though the idea has never crossed his mind. Does he think she is still too young and inexperienced or is it more deliberate? She senses something like fear in his failure to address such an idea but what kind of fear is it? For her or for himself? Or is it something more far-reaching; a fear for the land?

Megan looks back the way she has come and considers the distance in real time and space. Her body is asleep beside Mr Keeper right now but in her visit to the night country, her spirit is many miles away. She feels both afraid and ashamed. She could still travel back into sleep with nothing further discovered, no transgression committed, and she would wake in the morning able to look Mr Keeper in the eye with no secrets. Surely that is the right thing to do. She turns away from the bender and takes a step back towards the encampment, towards the river.

"I knew you'd return. I could see it." Megan's hand flies to her chest at the sound of the voice. She takes a deep breath and bows her head for a moment. Where's the harm in talking? Or even just listening for a moment? She turns back towards the black dome with its black-feathered flag. The voice of the prostitute sounds mellower now, less strained.

"You don't know how comforting it can be to be right about a thing like this. To see into the weave the way I do now. I owe it all to you, girl. Why don't you come inside?"

It's good to hear how well the woman sounds. Maybe that's enough. Even now Megan could turn away into sleep. This tent and its occupant will be in this place in the weave forever. She's certain she could find her way back. Is there any real need for her to be here now? Once again Megan imagines how it will feel to be around Mr Keeper, but forever be holding something back. Perhaps this is what it means to be grown up; she has seen enough unspoken words behind the eyes of Amu and Apa and many more behind those of Mr Keeper. But she cannot pretend that she is a child any longer.

She tells herself she's strong enough, crouches down and presses through the door flap.

6

Gordon sat cross-legged and calm.

Adrenaline made his heart race and his breathing shallow but he countered the effects with long, slow respiration. Panic would do no one any good. The control he exerted over his body's processes was purely practical; he had become addicted to heightened, excitable states and the natural drugs his body released in times of stress.

As much as he hated being the prey, the attentions of the Ward always gave him a buzz. He knew it was dangerous to be aroused by this. On some level it meant he invited the Ward to find him. Perhaps that was why the patrol had stopped outside the hole in this particular wall and decided to search this particular house. Without them, his pulse would never rise above fifty beats a minute, his hands would never shake, his stomach would never contract and his mouth would never go dry. The methods of self-preservation he had cultivated might never be expressed.

He was seventeen now but he didn't consider himself any less crazy than the boy whose skin he'd shrugged off when he first went on the run. He was crazy in different ways, perhaps, but he was still crazy.

Voices came through the floor as the Wardsmen ascended the stairs.

"What are we doing in here, Walsh? It's empty."

Walsh's voice was weasel high, a northern accent, somewhere east of York, Gordon guessed.

"Goin' wi' me gut, lad. Folerrin' an 'unch."

Another voice, Black Country for sure, shouted from a lower floor.

"It's clear, boss. No one about."

For long moments there was silence. Gordon imagined a small, greasy-haired man engulfed by a uniform far too big for him. He imagined the man staring straight up at the hatch in the ceiling, giving silent signals to his men. They would come with a chair or an old dresser, place it on the top landing and stand on it. Gordon's grip on the knife tightened. He held it in front of him, ready to bring it across the throat of the first man through the hatch. The woman was silent. Even in the confines of the attic he couldn't hear her breathing. She must have hidden like this a thousand times. Her hiding place had served her well until now. He was the one to have brought danger to her door.

More footsteps sounded from below as Walsh's patrol joined him at the top of the house. What were they doing? What were they waiting for?

The whine of Walsh's voice was quieter this time.

"Can anyone else smell fish?"

Gordon swallowed.

"That would be Dixon's cock, boss."

Stifled guffaws and snorts came from below. Even Gordon's mouth stretched into a grin in the darkness. He was glad the girl couldn't see it.

"I'm serious 'ere, lads. I can smell fish."

"Richards is serious too, boss." This was the Black Country voice, the man who'd said the place was empty. There were more sniggers. "Everyone knows Dixon never washes his cock. He thinks it's... manly."

Dixon must have taken offence:

"I never bloody said that."

After that the search lost its priority. Gordon wasn't able to keep track of who was speaking.

"You never said it but we all know it's true. You want everyone to think you're dipping it every night."

"I bloody well don't."

"*I* dip it every night," said another voice.

"Your sister doesn't count."

"No, but yours does."

Walsh's voice was still distinguishable:

"Dixon, is this true?"

"Is what true, boss?"

"That you never wash your ol' feller."

Dixon hesitated for too long.

"That's not 'ygienic, lad," said Walsh. "You're probably riddled wi' disease."

"I am *not* diseased, boss."

"I won't 'ave men in my patrol who don't maintain basic standards o' cleanliness, Dixon. I'm goin' to give you a choice. Either you keep your genitalia sparklin' and sweet smellin' or I'll report you."

"Hold on. What I do or don't do with my cock is my business."

The change in Walsh's tone silenced every snigger. The shouting sounded like it was beside Gordon's ear.

"You'll wash it or I'll cut the filthy article off. Your cock belongs to me, Dixon, and if you think otherwise I'll take the matter straight to Skelton. 'E doesn't like his agents to smell –

especially not of women. You'll be off this patrol and out of the Ward for good. And you know what that means."

There was silence from the top landing.

"I'll see to it as soon as we get back, sir."

Walsh exploded again.

"If I see a barrel o' piss on the way back to the station you'll be washin' it in that. Understand?"

"Yes, sir."

"Right, everyone out. Not you, Richards."

When the footsteps had receded there was silence again from the top landing but Gordon knew Walsh and Richards were still there. Eventually, Walsh said:

"Dixon's got to go, lad."

Richards didn't answer.

"I can't report 'im because it'll bring this patrol into the spotlight. So 'e's got to go. Are you wi' me, Richards?"

"Sir."

"You'll see to it then."

"Yes, sir."

"You're a good lad, Richards. Get this sorted out nice and quiet and you'll be movin' up the chain of command before you know it."

"Thank you, sir."

They didn't move.

"I can still smell bloody fish. Can you?"

Gordon could imagine Richards raising his nose to test the air again.

"No, sir."

Walsh heaved a huge sigh. Gordon thought he heard the sound of a hand clapping a shoulder and a moment later the last two pairs of footsteps receded. Only when they heard the sound of the horses moving off did Gordon allow himself to move. The girl relit the candle and they smiled at each other in the sudden warm brightness.

"Thank God for Dixon's fishy cock," she said.

Gordon grinned.

"Thank God indeed."

The girl reached for the plastic bag with Gordon's tin of salmon inside it. She passed it back to him.

"It's alright," he said. "You have the rest."

"Not sure I want it after all that."

It was a long time since he'd had a reason to smile. It felt good. And seeing the girl smile felt good too.

"You'll manage," he said. He nodded to the shape under the blankets. "Share it."

"Tell you what," said the girl. "We'll all share it."

She nudged the blankets. They shifted as though something were fighting its way out. Then a small face appeared over the rumpled pile. Its hair was tangled and greasy, its skin the colour of an old tusk. But the eyes were bright and intelligent and full of mischief.

"Thank God for Dixon's fishy cock," said the little girl and Gordon was shocked by the noise that burst from his mouth in response. Laughter. Genuine, spontaneous laughter.

"You watch your mouth, young lady. That's not how we behave in front of guests, is it?"

The girl grinned, her smiling eyes fixated with Gordon.

"Soooorrry, mum."

Gordon was very aware of the mother watching his eye contact with her little girl.

"What's your name?" he asked.

"I'm Flora."

It was only then that he realised what would come next. Charmed by the little girl, he'd opened himself up for it:

"Who are you?"

"I'm…"

He'd run for so long, used so many names it didn't seem to matter which one he used any more. At least, when he was out there in the grit grey world it didn't matter. What mattered was that no one knew his real name. And yet here, suddenly, his real name seemed important. A little girl didn't deserve to be lied to whether she knew it or not.

She was already reaching over from her nest of blankets to shake his hand and it was then he noticed how thin her arms were and how crooked her fingers. She could have crawled or stood up to greet him but she didn't and he was very certain it was because she was able to do neither.

He reached out his hand and took hers very gently. The Black Light leapt in his veins at the calling of her sickness but he fought it back; slammed a lid on it.

"I'm Gordon," he said. "And may I say that it is my very great pleasure to meet you, Flora."

7

The prostitute's tent is so thick with spicy, aromatic smoke that Megan chokes as it hits the back of her throat. She blinks until her eyes get used to the haze, wiping tears from the corners of her eyes. The smell in here is immediately reminiscent of Bodbran's tent, and the prostitute, who sits on layers of sheepskin and is wrapped in woollen blankets, smokes a similarly large and conical wrap of herbs. On a low, smooth cross section of oak log, a dozen or more squat tallow candles drip and hiss, creating a small sun, its brightness causing Megan to squint.

The prostitute beckons with both hands.

"Come. Come to me, girl. It's a blessing to see you again."

Stooping, Megan goes to the woman, who unwraps her shroud of blankets and enfolds her like a long-lost daughter. Megan doesn't need to will herself more form; she is here in the weave as solidly as she exists in the day world. The prostitute holds her for a long time and Megan senses a tremor through the woman's tight embrace. When she lets go and Megan retreats to sit down, the prostitute is wiping away tears of her own. Her face has changed; less furrowed by resigned cynicism, the prostitute now looks careworn but content and wears no trace of makeup. She adjusts her position on the skins, wincing, and smiles at Megan.

"You haven't changed at all, girl. How lucky you are to hold your youth so well. Now, after all this time I can't keep calling you girl. What's your name again?"

Megan laughs.

"I'm Megan. And I only saw you yesterday."

"Ah, yes. I remember." The prostitute draws hard on her fat roll-up, holding the smoke in for a long time. As she breathes out she says, "But it's been a sight longer than that for me, Megan. I may see the weave. I can even enter it since you visited me that night. But I can't travel it the way the Keepers do."

How stupid of me, thinks Megan. I should have known that time might have passed for her.

"What's your name?" Megan asks.

"Folk hereabouts call me Carissa."

"Carissa. That's lovely."

"Well, it's better than Annie the Attic Attraction."

Megan blushes.

"How long has it been, Carissa? Since we met?"

"In three months, it'll be a year. I refused my next customer the day I saw you. And the one after that. The next one that came up the stairs was drunk. He had the eyes of man who'd been hurt as a child. Hurt and abandoned. I can see these things. Any road, he didn't understand what 'no' meant. Thought it was a game until I tore a strip off his cheek with my teeth. That just made him more committed, though. He stuffed his wallet into my mouth and broke both my shins with his kicking. Rode me all night after that and then refused to pay because of his face."

Megan sucked at the air in shock and her hands flew to her mouth. Carissa smiled.

"It wasn't so bad. He left enough money for a bonesetter to fix me up but the Mistress didn't want Annie the Attic Attraction any more after that. I knew what I needed to do, though. It was time to cross the river and start again. I do alright now. Folk tell me their pains. They ask me the way forward. Most of them pay. And sometimes, when the things I've told them come to pass, they come back and pay me more. It's tiring at times, but no more so than being on my back all night, and I do a lot more good this way than I used to."

"And you're happy now," says Megan.

Carissa considers.

"No. But I can see happiness in others sometimes. And that's blessing." She leans a little way forward to whisper, "A blessing I'd like to repay."

Megan is ashamed at her misreading of the woman's demeanour. And after everything Carissa has been through, all she has now is her tent and a reliance upon the kindness of strangers. Surely there is something more that she can do for this woman.

As though reading her thoughts, Carissa says:

"Listen, Megan. You don't owe me a thing. You may not understand it until you're a bit older but you've given me a new life. I'll always be grateful for that and I'll always be here if you can find your way back to me."

Unable to meet Carissa's eyes, Megan mumbles a quiet "thank you". She glances around the small domed space. Much of it is taken up with essential animal furs and blankets, protection against the frost that would penetrate the bender in winter. There is no sign that the space is shared with another; Carissa seems to be sitting in the area she uses for sleeping and, apart from a cooking pot and a couple of cracked bowls, she appears to have no possessions. However, near the grease-coated log which acts as a base for all her candles, there is a tiny shelf hand-carved from a single piece of wood. It contains no books, however. Instead, Carissa has made a shrine of it. A crude charcoal sketch of a crow wearing a top hat forms its centrepiece. On either side of it, black feathers have been gummed to the back of the shelf in layers, imitating a black wing. Where the books would sit, Carissa has placed offerings of flowers, grain and polished pebbles from the river.

"I've kept his memory alive ever since you came," says Carissa, noticing what Megan is looking at. "And I see black feathers wherever I go. I used to be terrified of them, you know, but now I take each one to be a blessing."

Megan glances up.

"They aren't always a blessing," she says before she can think better of it. The boy and everything she has seen of his desolation so far are not hers to speak of yet. First she must complete the book. And the path.

Carissa doesn't appear to have read much into her slip of the tongue, though. She shrugs.

"They always will be to me. I'll never forget how you called on him or what he did." Carissa takes a final draw on her almost spent fag, licks her fingers and pinches it out. She drops the dog end into a cup of damp river silt beside her. "Give me your hand, Megan. Only if I touch you can I give you what you've come for."

Megan frowns.

"What have I come for?"

Carissa's smile levels out and disappears.

"Let's find out."

Megan slides closer and reaches towards Carissa. Before their fingers make contact, she senses a radiated warmth that vibrates at some barely perceptible frequency. Carissa takes Megan's hand in both of hers and the cheery candlelight suddenly dims, the flames choked small and blue. Megan finds it hard to breathe. At first, she expects Carissa to begin speaking but it takes only a moment for her to realise that whatever is happening is affecting them both. She glances at Carissa's eyes and sees the trepidation there.

A wind rushes at them and their cosy, intimate surroundings disappear. All Megan can feel is Carissa's hand gripping hers in the darkness as the ground falls away. Megan reaches for the point of contact with her other hand and holds on as hard as she can.

The wind increases, pressing tears from Megan's eyes and tearing at her hair. She becomes aware of pinpoints of light in the blackness above them and a thin band of almost midnight purple that seems very far away. Only then does Megan remember these feelings, even though it can be no more than three days since she last experienced them. She is unable to stop herself from crying out. The tiny dots of light are stars; the ribbon of brightening colour is the dawn horizon. They are flying but there is no feathered breast or black wings to cling to now, no Crowman to guide them.

"What is this, Carissa?" asks Megan. "What's happening?"

There's no reply other than a tightening of the grip on Megan's hands.

"You know how to travel, Megan. And I know the way. Hold me. Hold me tight."

8

Flora frowned for a moment at the touch of Gordon's hand and then sat back grinning and delighted with the little compliment. The girl's mother put out her hand too. Gordon held it as though it were precious.

"Denise," she said, reddening. She withdrew her hand quickly.

This was better than being poked with the shotgun. Better by far than fighting the Ward. Gordon allowed himself to relax. They shared out the fish and he made sure Flora got most of it. In his rucksack was an apple he'd been saving. This seemed like the moment it was destined for. He cut it three ways, again in favour of the sick little girl.

To start with no one said much and Gordon enjoyed that full, mingling silence. To have food, to share it in safety with people who didn't want to rob or rape you; all this was a rare combination of blessings. He let the silence build, happy just to be in company. Flora studied him without any embarrassment and, if that was considered bad behaviour, her mother didn't scold her for it. Denise glanced at him from time to time, assessing him in minute snatches, gathering intelligence with her eyes, processing it and then glancing again. He pretended not to notice.

Flora crawled back into her blankets when the food was eaten. She looked exhausted and moving seemed to cause her pain. Tightly bundled, she lay on her side, peeping out at Gordon and her mother. After watching for a while Flora sat up and reached for a cloth bag. In it was a tablet of blank white paper. It looked very expensive and very clean. Her coloured pencils, by contrast, were either stumpy or broken and appeared to have been gathered from many sources.

"You live up here all by yourselves?"

Gordon's voice sounded like a shout after the quiet they'd shared. Denise nodded, looking around as though seeing the place for the first time.

"Pretty much."

"How do you get food?"

"I've got friends."

Friends.

Gordon nodded, more to himself than her. Did he trust these two? He knew he wanted to. But could he trust their friends? Friends meant uncertainty. Friends meant whispering lips and flapping tongues. And friends weren't always friendly, especially not to strangers.

He moved the conversation along.

"You two should get out of London. Cities are the hardest places to survive. It's less dangerous in the countryside and there's more to eat."

While Denise considered this – not with any enthusiasm that he could see – Gordon glanced at Flora. The girl was busy drawing things she had seen in the street from the attic's tiny dormer window: broken walls, blinded windows and forsaken buildings. Here and there a weed poked through the decaying stratum of damned construction overlaying the land and Flora captured those particularly well.

"I've never been to the country," she said, looking up at him and smiling. "What's it like there?"

"It's green and open. It's beautiful. Not as beautiful as it used to be but it's still a lot nicer than London. There are trees and flowers and–"

He caught the warning flash in Denise's eyes.

"And what?" asked Flora.

"Well," said Gordon. "It's not like that any more, of course. Those days are over."

"I'd like to go," said Flora

"We're just fine here," said Denise.

He didn't force the issue.

"Anyway," said Denise, "if the countryside is so safe and so easy, what are you doing in London?"

This was what always happened when you got talking to people. Tricky questions. The temptation to open up. He ought to have known better. Something about Denise and Flora was safe, though. He could sense the good, the sturdy honesty of good people. In spite of how they'd begun their acquaintance, Gordon felt welcome in their home. For once he wanted to talk. But how to let it out?

"I've got... business here."

"Really?" Said Denise. "What kind of business?"

"The tracking-someone-down kind."

"Maybe I could help with that. Like I said, I've got friends."

The expression made Gordon's stomach tighten. Even so, something made him want to tell them. Something like instinct. He needed any assistance he could get but he usually saved this part of the inevitable conversation for Green Men only. As Cooky had shown him and as he'd done on hundreds of occasions since, Gordon stroked the outside of his eye three times. If Denise noticed it, she gave no inkling. He made the gesture again but she still didn't respond.

"I'll take any help I can get," he said in the end.

"Who is it? Family? An old flame?"

Gordon blushed. Could she sense there was no flame, that there never had been? Was that mockery in her tone?

"Sorry," said Denise. "It's not meant to be an interrogation."

"No, it's fine. I'm just not used to talking about it. People are… you know how people can be. I've been on the road three years now. Folks you can trust are in the minority."

"The world was like that before all this," said Denise.

"I know. But it matters more now. Things are tough for everyone. If we worked together, helped each other out just a little, things would be better for everyone. Seems even crazier to be selfish now."

"People are too busy staying alive to help each other out."

"If that's true, Denise, no one's going to make it through the dark times and out into the light."

Denise looked over at her daughter, colouring by candlelight from her imagination and memory. If Flora had heard what they were saying it seemed not to have made any impression on her. When Denise looked back at Gordon, however, the earlier flash of warning had become a threat.

He inclined his head a fraction to show he understood.

"So," she said, making an effort to get the conversation back onto safe ground. "Who is this someone you're tracking down? Maybe I can ask around."

Gordon prepared himself for the swift descent through the hatch and back down the stairs to the street, one hand already reaching for his rucksack, his eyes roving to make sure he hadn't left anything lying around. Everything was secure and stowed. He took a last look at the young mother and her little girl, a last look before their feelings towards him changed.

"I'm looking for the Crowman."

Flora stopped colouring and looked not at Gordon but at her mother. Something must have passed between them but he was unable to read it.

"Mummy says the Crowman's not real. But I've seen him."

Flora transformed from a kid doing some colouring into a small adult with a mission. Gordon glanced at Denise, ready for her to go into meltdown over this new topic. He gripped the straps of his rucksack, preparing to dart out if she reached for the shotgun. She didn't move. Nor did she attempt to stop Gordon or Flora from discussing this particular taboo. All the power of motherhood had drained from her. Gordon took the opportunity to probe for more.

"I've never seen him," he said. "But he's real. I know he is."

I'm seconds from being kicked through that trapdoor. But she knows something. She definitely knows something.

"I know he is too," said Flora. "He visits me in my dreams and sometimes he lands on the roof or down in the street so I can see him."

"What does he look like, Flora?"

"He's an angel. A black angel."

Not looking at Denise for permission because it would waste precious moments, Gordon pressed on.

"Could you… draw him for me?"

Flora dug into her cloth bag and withdrew a sheaf of papers, scrolled and secured with a rubber band.

"I draw him all the time," she said, handing Gordon the scroll.

With great care he removed the elastic band and opened out the curls of paper. Silence expanded once more in the attic. Denise was tight-lipped but made no move to stop the exchange. Flora's face was anxious.

"It's his face I have trouble with. It changes. Sometimes he's an old man and sometimes he's a little boy. Sometimes he just looks exactly like a crow. I can do a better one if you want."

Gordon shook his head.

"There's no need. You've done a wonderful job. These are the best sketches I've ever seen." He looked up from the drawings. "You say he's been here, Flora?"

Flora nodded big exaggerated nods.

"He comes to see me a *lot*."

The edges of the pictures amplified the tremor in Gordon's hands. So many times he'd been close and so many times the trail had gone ice cold. He tried to control his shaking fingers. He'd never been *this* close,

"Does he ever… speak to you, Flora? Does he tell you what he wants?"

Again came the nods but Flora had become a little girl again and now she looked to her mother for permission to speak. Once more, Gordon missed whatever gesture it was that allowed the girl to continue. Denise let her forehead rest in her left palm and whispered:

"Oh, Christ."

Flora began to speak, softly at first and without much conviction, but as she progressed, her words gathered strength and pace.

The wind makes Megan's eyes sting and blur. She tries to blink away the tears but even in the brief moments of clear vision it is impossible to tell where they might be or where they are going; even though they're racing east towards the dawn, the night is still too dark. Carissa's grip hurts but Megan is glad the woman is so strong. The horror of falling is her whole world now as they speed through the darkness, unable even to see each other faces.

"Where are we going?" Megan screams over the noise of the rushing air but Carissa is either too focussed on guiding them or too terrified to reply.

Without warning the wind from ahead becomes a wind from below. Megan's stomach rises into her mouth and at first she is too shocked to make a sound. The scream is caught at the back of her throat as they hurtle downward. Now the night gives way to morning as though time itself has developed the speed of a falling rock. Dawn breaks, the sun climbs high and Megan sees the ground rise to meet them. She imagines the impact busting open their bodies and smashing their bones to fragments.

All she can do is close her eyes.

Like a child being lowered by a loving parent, Megan's feet are set gently upon the earth. She opens her eyes. She and Carissa, hands still locked together, stand at the opening to a sandstone cave. Its entrance is perfectly round and black, like a mouth pronouncing "O". Megan glances around. Roughly hewn steps lead down and away from the cave into a small valley. An earthquake must have struck the place; fallen rock and clods of mud are everywhere and the trunks of the few trees that still grow there are half submerged in earthy debris.

A noise from inside the cave startles Megan. It sounds like an animal in pain. She and Carissa step back from the entrance. The moan comes again, low and agonised. A ruined human hand appears at the cave's entrance, its fingers impossibly deformed, bulbous scars where some of the nails have been torn off, the skin dotted with some kind of pox.

Megan and Carissa, still holding hands, retreat further, stumbling backwards down a few of the crudely made steps.

"Plague," whispers Carissa.

Megan is shocked to see how terrified the woman is. She places a gentle palm to Carissa's cheek and brings her head to face hers.

"Don't be afraid, Carissa. We're travellers in the weave. Though we can see it and touch it, this is not our world. Nothing can harm us."

The words have barely left her lips and the two of them are flying again. Carissa remains so terrified as to be almost mute, her body rigid with tension. And yet Megan with so much experience of the weave is not the one to lead them. It is Carissa's ability as a seer that has become their beacon.

Night and day pass a hundred times as the wind whips their hair and clothes. The land turns below them, apparently at random, shifting like leaves on water. As another night falls, they descend into the ruins of a city. Carissa is trembling by the time their feet touch the rubble strewn ground.

"This is a bad place," she says. "Terrible things happened here."

Partially decayed bodies line the roadsides. They appear to have been there for years but there is no evidence of rats or flies having eaten their dead flesh. Instead the human remains bear a thick layer of dust. The bodies lie sprawled or slumped where they dropped, the crude weapons lying near the fallen a sign that they died in conflict.

Carissa looks around and seems to take something from shattered scene.

"Food," she says. "They were fighting for food. What is this place?"

"A City. Generations behind us in the weave. They were huge."

"Sitty?"

"Like a big village."

Megan is about to say more when she hears a clatter from behind them. They both spin towards the noise. A bent figure stumbles along an alleyway, using the wall for support and guidance. The person, a man it seems, is staggering right towards them and is only a few paces away. Megan takes an involuntary step back and dislodges loose brickwork from a wall. It thumps to the ground raising dust, the sound echoing into the distance in the deserted streets. The man, who has stooped until now, halts and looks up.

Megan's heart falters.

He seems to look right at them except that can't be possible for the man wears filthy rags wrapped around his eyes. Besides, Megan thinks, he is of this world not of the weave. Megan holds her breath until she hears another sound from the opposite direction, that of wings whispering on the gritty air. She and Carissa glance back and both of them pale. It is this sound the blind man appears to be interested in.

Wings.

Suddenly, Megan is less certain of their safety. She had not considered that other travellers might be abroad among the fibres of the weave. She is a trespasser here, without her guide and chaperone, without *leave*.

"Quick," Megan whispers. "In here."

She hauls Carissa through the open door of an abandoned bus and pulls her along the between the seats to a broken window where they can see out. The sound of beating wings approaches fast and the street grows dark. With a final downthrust of air that whips the dust into clouds, something comes to earth near the entrance of the alleyway.

The stumbling man cowers as a tall, dark figure approaches him. A single caw splits the air, loud as the shriek of storm winds. The cackle reverberates around the entire city. The blind man falls to his knees, bowing his head to the dead ground. A feathered hand extends towards the now foetal figure. In its palm is a lump of dull black stone about the size of a fist. It drops the stone in the cold dirt and the man reaches out for it with trembling, diseased-looking fingers.

Megan and Carissa are whipped from the bus by an updraft that spins them skyward like a tornado. Once again they cling to each as time and space flit past below them like autumn leaves.

9

"I've always seen him. From when I was tiny. Mummy says I used to wake up crying in my cot. And sometimes she would come in and find me talking to someone in baby language..." Flora hesitated, picking at a loose thread in one of her blankets. "Someone she couldn't see. I was always really happy and smiley afterwards because I thought the Crowman was my daddy coming to visit me. But I don't remember very much from back then. Only that I felt very lonely when he wasn't around."

Gordon nodded, knowing that solitude well. His loneliness was created by the Crowman too, even if the reasons for that were different.

Flora's words had aroused some deeply held guilt in her mother, it seemed, because she now began to make explanations and excuses:

"Flora never met her dad, Gordon. He was gone before I knew I was pregnant. There was no work and I needed money for when the baby came along. I did what I had to do. I didn't like having men come into the flat where we lived but I wasn't going on the street. Still, it meant I often left Flora in her cot for two or three hours at a time. I think that's the real reason she was lonely." Denise's eyes filled with tears. She reached out to Flora and squeezed her hand. "I'm so sorry, baby."

Flora couldn't understand her mother's anguish. She was bright in her response.

"Don't cry, mummy. The Crowman kept me company and when he left I was sad. It wasn't because of you." To Gordon she said: "Mummy made men happy, which is very difficult sometimes, and they paid her. She had to work a lot to make sure we had food and everything."

Denise laughed through her tears as she reached for a handkerchief and blew her nose.

"I'm sorry," she said, sniffing and dabbing her eyes. "I'm sure those aren't the details you're interested in."

Gordon shrugged.

"We all do what we have to do to survive. It doesn't make us bad people."

Denise stared at him then, her face frank and her eyes unguarded for the briefest of moments. Gordon didn't have time to interpret what he saw there; having lost centre stage for a moment, Flora wanted it back.

"You asked me if he ever spoke to me. The first thing I ever remember him saying was that I was special and that sometimes special people suffered a lot. But he said that if I helped it would be worth it. He said there'd be a future and I'd be in it. He said I wouldn't suffer any more. He still tells me that now. When I've had a few bad days in a row and... you know. When I feel like I've had enough."

"Yes," said Gordon. "I know what that's like."

Flora looked up, angry for a moment until she saw Gordon's eyes and realised that he wasn't lying, wasn't just saying things to make her feel better.

"Nowadays, he tells me more stuff about other people and

places and what's going to happen. He doesn't talk so much about me any more."

Gordon sat forward.

"He tells you about the future? What does he say about it?"

"He talks about how things might be if other things happen first. And he tells me what will happen if they don't. The Crowman says the future has nothing to do with the future and everything to do with now. What you do now makes the future." Flora closed her eyes for a moment, imagining or remembering something. "You know what you were saying about people needing to work together and help each other? He said something just like that a few weeks ago. He said that's how the present could change the future."

Gordon grinned.

"He sounds like my kind of guy. In three years I've never met anyone who's had as much contact and communication with the Crowman as you have, Flora. He's right; you really are a special girl." He reached over and touched her hand briefly before pulling away with a frown. The liquid darkness awoke once more in his fingers; the gift that had become a curse, threatening to reveal him to the Ward whenever he used it. He blustered on. "I can't believe I'm suddenly this close to him. When was the last time you saw him?"

"Mmm... about three days ago."

"Where was he?"

Flora pointed to several layers of towels folded over a wooden rail.

"Standing down in the street. I saw him through the window."

Gordon moved towards the makeshift blackout but Denise moved to stop him.

"We never open that when there's light in here. Only a few people know we're up here but that's more than enough. Sometimes we look out either at dusk or at dawn. I like Flora to be able to see the street even if she can't actually go outside very often."

Gordon itched to look down and see the place where only three days before the object of his search had stood. If the Crowman visited as often as Flora said, Gordon knew he had to stay here until the next time he came. The Crowman seemed to have an affinity for the girl. If it took a week, a month – even a year – Gordon would wait. He'd never been this close.

An impulse took him.

"You say he talks to you, Flora, but do you ever talk to him?"

"Of course I do, knobhead! All the time."

"Flora!"

Gordon laughed, waving Denise's scold away.

"It's fine," he said. "Would you be able to give him a message from me next time you see him?"

"Yes. Yes, I think so. What do you want me to say?"

Gordon put his fingers to his lips.

What do I say to him? How do I say it?

"Could you just say that… Could you tell him that Gordon Black has come to find him? That I want to talk to him because I… need his help. Can you tell him that?"

"Yes, Gordon." Flora was once more full of her adult importance and it struck Gordon not as precocious or amusing in the slightest. It couldn't have been more appropriate. "I can tell him that. And I'll tell you what he says too."

Gordon slumped back. A deep coil of tension had released inside him and he was suddenly exhausted.

"You can rest here if you're tired."

This was a very different Denise to the one who'd confronted him at gunpoint. Every part of him wanted to stay and sleep. He felt that if he closed his eyes now, he might sleep for three whole days. And up here he would be so much safer too.

"Thanks," he said. "But you've both done more than enough already. I'd like to come back, though, if that's OK. In a few days, perhaps. Maybe by then Flora will have seen the Crowman."

"You're always welcome, Gordon," said Denise. "The least I can do is see you safely off the premises." She shifted onto her knees and reached for the ladder. "Come on, I'll follow you down and show you the safest routes."

When the hatch was open and the ladder down, Gordon waved to Flora across the tiny space. She waved back and smiled.

"It's been great to meet you, Flora."

She waved back.

"Come back soon," she said. "I know he'll be excited that you've come to see him."

Unbelievable. All this time. I'm really going to meet him.

It didn't seem possible. Gordon descended to the top landing and Denise joined him. They made the journey down through the house in silence and she followed him out into the tip that had once been a back garden. The hole in the wall was as far as she would go.

"There are good places all along this road," she said. "Places the Ward don't know about." She gestured out to the front of the house and to the right. "The old swimming baths is a couple of hundred yards down that way. No one thinks of going in there. There are lots of office rooms upstairs but it's damp. If you go the opposite way there's a house with a green door. Number 257. It was derelict long before people started to leave. The garden's so overgrown you'd have to cut your way through but, as far as I know, no one's ever stayed there and the Ward never touch it."

She mentioned other places and Gordon took the information in as best he could, trying to remember one important thing about each bolthole.

"Thanks," he said. He glanced briefly up towards the top of the house. "And sorry."

"What for?"

Gordon looked back at Denise.

"For causing trouble. For bringing them to your place."

"Don't be stupid. It's not mine anyway. Nothing belongs to anyone any more. Well, everything belongs to the Ward. It's the same thing."

"They only came in because of me."

"You don't know that."

"Sometimes they know where to look. It's uncanny. I thought I'd been careful. I don't know why they came in here today but it put you and Flora in danger."

"It wasn't the first time and it won't be the last, Gordon. You can come back here any time you want to. Flora was..." Denise cleared her throat. "It was good for her. She isn't like that with anyone else. The Crowman stuff, it... makes me uncomfortable. But it's all she's got and she told you more today than she's ever told anyone else. She's never said that much about it to me."

Gordon's eyes roved the gritty smog all around them.

"She's like a candle up there in all that darkness," he said. "Bright and spirited and..." His gaze returned to Denise. "What's wrong with her? Do you mind me asking?"

"No. I don't mind." Whatever strength held Denise together, appeared to seep away with what Gordon knew was a huge lie. The hard woman with the shotgun, the woman who was ready to die fighting the Ward; this woman, so much like an animal protecting her young, faltered and slackened. "Everything's wrong with her. She's always been sick. Ever since she was born. She's got some kind of rheumatoid arthritis and her immune system is overactive. She basically destroys herself a bit at a time. There used to be drugs for it but I can't get them any more." Denise let her eyes meet Gordon's. "No matter what I do." She looked away again quickly. "Flora's weak. She can barely walk. She's in pain most of the time – painkillers I can still get sometimes but I save them for when she's really bad. We can't have her crying out because it'll give us away. The Ward kill all the sick and you know what they'd do to me. There's no law but theirs any more. They do what they want and no one can stop them." She wiped tears from her face with her dirty sleeve. "Sorry," she said.

"Don't apologise."

"The point is, Gordon, that Flora's dying. There's nothing I can do about it. There's nothing anyone can do. So you come back and visit us soon because she likes you. You made today a good day for my little girl. I wish there was something I could do to repay you for that."

Gordon's stomach fluttered. He swallowed but kept all expression from his face.

"Flora's already given me more than enough with her Crowman stories." He unslung his rucksack, unzipped it and reached inside. His hand came back with a tin of tomato soup and some vacuum packed crackers. "Here. You two have a nice dinner."

"What will you eat?"

"I'll manage, Denise. I always do."

She took his hand.

"You could stay with us. There's enough room."

He swallowed again but didn't move. Wherever he went, the Ward followed. People got hurt. But he couldn't tell her that; didn't want her to know. He couldn't bear her to wish him gone. Not yet. Perhaps this way, by staying nearby but not with them they would have more time together. Tomorrow. Or the day after that.

He squeezed Denise's hand, grabbed his pack and ducked down through the hole in the wall. He walked away fast, not wanting her to call out to him, not wanting this feeling that was building inside him: the desire to go back with her into the attic and share more food and conversation. The desire to stop running and find a place he could call home. The desire to touch someone in anything other than fury.

10

They are so far into the weave Megan has no idea where they are or when. She feels Carissa's grip weakening.

"Don't let go of me!" she shouts. "I can't get back without you."

If Carissa hears her, she doesn't respond. Her hands slacken and her body becomes limp. Megan holds her tighter. In the half light of an approaching dawn, she sees Carissa's head lolling, her skin ashen. Once more they fall towards the land.

Megan shuts her eyes and presses her face against Carissa's neck. The scent of lavender, aromatic smoke and musky skin distract her for a moment and it is during this tiny absence that they are placed on the ground. Megan thinks Carissa has fainted so she lays her on her front as Mr Keeper has shown her during their healing rounds of the village. Megan checks Carissa's wrist and chest. There's a thready pulse and she's breathing shallowly. For the moment there's nothing more Megan can do but wait for her to regain consciousness.

She stands to try and get a sense of where they are and realises in the gathering light that she knows this place very well. They have landed in the clearing where Mr Keeper lives. Only a few paces away is his roundhouse, with smoke rising from its chimney.

Her sense of relief at being so close to home is short-lived. At her feet, not far from where the path through New Wood enters the clearing, there is fresh blood soaking into the pine needles. The soil has been churned up by many sets of tracks, as though some kind of struggle or fight happened here. The blood is plentiful and its trail leads right to the door of the roundhouse.

"Oh, Mr Keeper," whispers Megan.

At first she cannot approach his dwelling. Her feet won't move. Mr Keeper may not be aware that she has entered the weave alone and he may not be able to follow her. But if he's in the roundhouse, if he's still alive, Megan is certain he'll see her in the weave and then he'll know she has travelled by herself. But when is this? Perhaps she has already completed the Black Feathered Path, in which case to navigate the weave unaccompanied is permissible. But what if, in this time, Mr Keeper has been hurt? Great Spirit forbid it, what if she is being shown the last moments of his Earthwalk?

Instinct tells her none of this is a mistake. If she has been brought here then she must find out why. Tiptoeing, even though her footsteps through the weave make no sound at all, Megan approaches the squat hut. She notices Mr Keeper's longbow resting beside the front door and glances back at the plentiful blood trail.

An animal. Surely just an animal. Please don't let it be him.

She creeps around to the wind-eye and, pressing as close to the wall as she can, peeps inside. It is too dark, at first, for her to see properly, but the roundhouse is definitely occupied. One figure kneels, rocking very slowly as though in trance or prayer. Another figure lies unmoving on the rush mats.

Megan wills her vision to adjust and stares hard into the gloom. By increments, the tallow candles and the light spilling from the iron stove appear to brighten. She cups her hands around her eyes and sees the dried flowers and dried herbs that surround the body on the floor.

The kneeling figure is Mr Keeper, though he appears emaciated and old. The supine figure is her, Megan, face almost chalk white and her body utterly still. Too still. Megan puts her hand to her mouth and backs away from the wind-eye before Mr Keeper can sense her presence.

In the clearing, Carissa is sitting up. She looks sick and confused. Megan hurries back and kneels beside her, distracted for a moment from what she has just seen.

"I'm so glad you're alright," she says.

Carissa can't meet her eyes at first. Megan frowns.

"What is it? What happened to you?"

The woman stares into the trees for a few moments. She takes a deep breath before speaking.

"The Crowman. He snatched me away from you." Carissa looks at Megan now. "I thought he would... I don't know. Not kill me but peck out my spirit and wear it in his hat like a feather."

Megan shakes her head.

"He would never do that. Not to you."

"Maybe not. But he's capable of it." Carissa heaves an exhausted sigh. "He wanted me to give you a message. He said he can't show you everything that's coming because he doesn't know every outcome. He said the time of the Keepers is coming to an end. They've done their best to keep him alive in their retelling of his story but none of them has been skilful enough to tell it right. He says only you can do that and that it's up to you how the future turns out."

"Why couldn't he tell me this himself?"

"He knew you'd ask that. He said that you must do it, not for his sake but for the sake of the world and for the sake of the people. He doesn't want to influence you because every effort you make must be for the good of all, not because you feel it has been commanded. He says you're the first to have retold his story plain and true thus far and that he knows you'll retrieve the rest of it just as well. But he wanted you to know that there is a way for you to record his story which will keep it safe for more generations than you can imagine. If you discover this it will make you the last Keeper to write his story down. After that, things will be different but he didn't say how." Carissa places a hand on Megan's shoulder.

"Is that everything?" asks Megan.

Carissa shakes her head.

"He said…"

"What?"

"He said you and I can't see each other for a long time."

Megan shakes her head, feeling her face redden.

"But why?"

"You must work alone for your work to have real power." Carissa pushes her windblown hair back from her face. "There's one other thing. He was very specific about it. He said: In all things, find the balance. If you can do this, his presence in the world will no longer be needed and he will return to the blackness that bore him."

Megan buries her face in her hands. This foray into the weave has brought her nothing but fear and new burdens to carry.

Why did I come here unaccompanied? Why did I take part of any of this?

She begins to weep tears of frustration and anger. After everything she's done, everything Mr Keeper has taught her, she still knows nothing. She still has no power over this world and nothing but uncertainty in her heart. Through her tears she looks back at Mr Keeper's roundhouse.

"Did he tell you…"

"What, Megan?"

"It doesn't matter."

Megan's sobbing worsens. Carissa reaches out and enfolds her in a protective embrace. Through bubbles of tears and mucus Megan blurts:

"I just want to go home."

"This is as far as I can take you," says Carissa.

Megan notices a change in the light. She swipes at her tears to find that she is sitting on furs in the candlelit black tent. Carissa's embrace is comforting and wonderful, the embrace of a sister, but Megan is torn away from it, hauled out through the canvas flap and backwards across the land at a speed she is unable to control. Back through the dwellings of the outcasts and through Shep Afon. Back across the landscape and into darkness.

11

Gordon preferred hunting, but prey was scarce in London –
in any city – unless you counted rats. He didn't mind eating
rat if it was unavoidable but he preferred a nice, plump
country rat. The rats living amid the broken buildings, piles
of refuse and overflowing sewers had fed on all manner of
filth. Sometimes it was more prudent to hunt in the larder or
fridge of a deserted house and survive on a tin of spam.

He checked out some of Denise's suggestions first, almost
choosing to stay in one of the administrative offices above
the disused swimming pool. It was warm up there for some
reason but the mouldy air tasted bad. What attracted him
most was the idea of a green door and an overgrown garden.
After a cursory glance at some of Denise's other ideas, he
set out for number 257, already set on finding a way in and
making it his temporary dwelling.

Half a dozen steps led up to the front door. Like many of
the neighbouring abandoned houses, it had been boarded up
years before; however, this job was more thorough. Someone
had fixed a steel grille over the front door and padlocked
it. The padlock was rusted shut. A glance over the steps
confirmed the windows on the lower floors and below street
level had been covered with sheet metal. There were dents

where someone had taken a swing or two with something heavy before giving up. Around the outside of one metal sheet, small curls in the metal suggested a failed crowbar attempt.

Number 257 was part of a short terrace of sizable Victorian houses and there was no way through to the garden from the front entrance. To the left of the row, there was a line of long abandoned business premises. To the right was an area of parkland. Gordon trotted along the deserted main road, heading for the open ground. Grass that must once have been thick and green was now knee high and parchment dry. It rustled and crackled making it impossible to tread silently.

The edge of the park was walled but the brickwork had provided cover in some forgotten fire-fight and there were many collapsed and shattered sections. He chose a solid-looking vee in the wall and scrambled to the apex. From there he spotted the alleyway which he hoped led to the rear of number 257.

He walked along the top of boundary wall until he was looking down into the alley. From there he could see the back gardens of the entire row. The garden of 257 was a jungle; too dense and thorny for him to climb down into without shredding his clothes and skin. At regular intervals there were doors set into the wall of each back garden, giving the properties access to the back alley. He could see the one which corresponded to 257 – its paint was the same colour green as the front door, reminiscent of the half-broken door in the garden wall of his home; the door Jude had shut on him the last time he saw her.

He pushed the memories away, dangerous reminiscences that would only weaken him, and dropped the ten feet to the alley floor. Broken glass further disintegrated under his boots as he landed in the dark, walled passageway. Rats scattered at the sudden intrusion, fleeing from the maggot-ridden carcass of a fox. The alley was just wide enough for him to pass through without rubbing his shoulders against the brickwork; more like a trench than a walkway. He moved fast, not wanting to spend a moment more than necessary in that vulnerable compressed space.

The paint on the green door was flaking away and the wood at its base was exposed and rotten. The round bulb of its handle was made of pale china, almost luminescent in the gloom of the alley. He turned it and pushed. The door moved but didn't open. As he'd done with their own garden door so many times, he put his shoulder to it and tried again. This time the door gave way, opening a six-inch gap. Through this he could see the wilderness on the other side had formed a second layer of protection.

When he took his body away, the springy growth pushed the door closed again. A second shoulder-barge created the space he needed to squeeze through. He let the door shut behind him. To his right lay a haphazard pile of old floorboards now fungal with decay. He kicked the upper ones away and found stronger ones below. He took one of these and wedged it under the door handle, bracing the other end against the roots of a sapling; it was no lock but it was better than nothing.

The mess of growth looked impenetrable and much of it was bramble. Now that he was safely within the boundaries of the property, he could take his time. He leaned back against the wall and studied the knots of weed, tree and shrub. Close to the boundary was where the growth was thinnest. To reach the back of the house, he'd have to skirt the perimeter.

The garden was long and some of the bramble had bunched against the wall like coils of barbed wire. Scratched but not seriously harmed, Gordon made it to the rear of the property and assessed his options. The windows on this side were nailed shut with chipboard and much of it looked weakened by the elements. Steps led down from the jungle to the basement windows. To his right a flight of stone stairs rose to a boarded-up back door. He ran down the basement steps for a closer look.

From the street at the front and the alley at the back, number 257 looked impregnable. People needing shelter in a hurry would have disregarded its steel hoarding and impenetrable thorns in favour of an easy bolthole. Perhaps that was why there were no signs of previous break-ins at the rear of the house. And yet, the edges of the chipboard were soft and damp under his fingers. He unclasped his knife, using the tip to chisel away the disintegrating flakes of compressed wood. It didn't take long to expose a glimpse of window frame beneath, its green paint bright and undamaged by sun or rain. Pulling the board away was easy. Most of it came off in a single tug, leaving only the top left hand corner of the double window covered. However, the wrenching and cracking was conspicuous in all the silence and he stopped to listen for a long time after the board hit the ground.

Breaking the window was noisy too. He listened again for several minutes before reaching into the darkness and opening the latch. The window swung out and Gordon swung in.

The next thing Megan is aware of is the smell of wood smoke, tobacco and cooking oats, and a cold ache in her nose when she breathes. She wraps her blanket around her shoulders and crawls out through the bender's flap. The frosty morning turns her breath to fleeing ghosts. Autumn is kissing winter.

Mr Keeper stirs their porridge with one hand and smokes his pipe with the other. Any sadness he may have walked with is gone and his face is kind, half-amused as it so often is. There's not much frost in the cover of the woods, just a dusting of white on the most exposed, extended branches and the outer leaves of smaller plants.

Beyond the trees, though, the land is stiff and unmoving. Tiny rainbow coloured points sparkle in the ocean of white. Megan starts as dozens of raucous calls echo from a distant stand of tall, skeletal trees. Black shapes detach from the black branches and flap into the air by twos until perhaps a hundred crows are in flight, flowing like ink across a page.

She stares at the blank landscape long after the crows have gone, able to think only of empty pages.

"I've so much work to do," she says.

Mr Keeper nods.

"I won't forget it, will I?"

"You won't. You *can't*. It's in you now. In your blood."

"But what if I make a mistake? What if I only almost remember it right?"

"Then the book will always be wrong and the story forever untrue. The generations to come will misunderstand the teachings and the world will end soon after."

Megan sees all this as she looks out over the frozen land. Then she glances at Mr Keeper and sees him grinning. Her lips flatten white against each other. Why does he never take anything seriously?

He chuckles.

"Listen, Megan, the writing is the easy part. All you're doing is recording what you see. You've done it right so far and you'll keep doing it right until you're finished. Don't give it another thought. What's difficult is walking the path, trusting in it when everything screams at you to turn away and give up. You have to be strong to move through that."

Does he know something, she wonders?

He smokes his pipe and watches her, serious for only a moment before his eyes crease at the edges and he is smiling again, cheerful and mischievous.

"There's no point in me trying to convince you that you're strong enough, Megan. That you're worthy. You can only do that for yourself. And the only way you can do it is by walking the path." Mr Keeper shrugs. "You're already doing that, so you might as well stop worrying about everything. Here, have some oats."

She takes the proffered bowl and crouches on her haunches to eat it.

"Carrick was your teacher, wasn't he?" She asks. "When you walked the Black Feathered Path."

"Yes. He was."

"Why isn't he still in Beckby?"

"Keepers move around. Our group of villages only needs one Keeper because it's quite small. Other places need more. Sometimes, a Keeper will make the world his village and move from place to place giving his knowledge and checking all is well. That's what Carrick does. He uses the rivers to move from place to place. He makes sure the Crowman is alive everywhere and he keeps an eye out to make sure people keep the balance."

Megan stops eating for a moment. Surely, Mr Keeper must have been there with her, must have seen and heard it all. Or is it simply that the Crowman foresaw all this? As though she's never heard of it, she asks:

"What balance?"

"All of it. You've experienced the dark and the light of the Crowman, so that's one example but mostly it's the balance of giving and taking. Keepers make sure no one falls into the beliefs that first brought the Crowman into the world. In times gone by folk believed the land owed them its life, not that we owe ours to it. That is the opposite of balance. It almost brought the world to an end."

"Is that what the people who lived in that city believed?"

"Not all of them, perhaps but certainly most."

"I saw them."

"I know you did. I was with you."

"They looked desperate. I didn't know so many people could be so unhappy."

Mr Keeper shrugs.

"You shouldn't be surprised, Megan. We all have it in us. Just as we have the capacity for joy. We can live anywhere we choose; in the depths of the blackest midnight or in the heights of the brightest dawn. And the Crowman soars through all of it. He has been everywhere and knows everything. Because of this, he cares not what is right or wrong but what is simply *true*. He knows how this world must be lived in, in order for it to flourish or to die. He shares that choice with each of us."

"Most of us live in the light, then."

"Most of us live with a foot in the darkness and a foot in the light. Or we stand at dusk moving into night or we stand at dawn moving into light. No one, no *thing*, is purely one or the other."

"But can't we all just be light and good?"

"No. We have to remember where we came from. Before light there was blackness. Blackness is where the light came from. And now we follow that light through time until it returns to blackness."

Megan's porridge is cold. Her mind whirls. She believed the path would bring answers. She believed her training would make her calmer and wiser. But for each door of knowledge she throws open, two more appear on the other side.

"You're saying that no matter what we do, everything will fall and die and be swallowed into the dark."

"Yes."

"Then why should we bother to *do* anything?"

"Because we have the honour of existing."

"Huh! Not for long."

"Life is a wonderful opportunity to be alive, Megan. We should all take it. Look at Carrick, skipping around like a boy, full of light even in the twilight of his years."

Megan is crying.

"It's so... sad."

"Perhaps. But it's also very, very beautiful."

She wipes her eyes and nose on her sleeve.

"But if this is all true, I just can't understand why it's worth *trying* to achieve anything when everything will be taken away."

Mr Keeper sets down his bowl, unfinished.

"If you ask the question 'why' to every answer, eventually there's only one answer left. That answer is: 'I don't know'." He turns and stares into the cold, leafless trees for a moment before looking back at Megan. "I know in my heart that the things I'm telling you are true enough for me to live by, even if they're not exactly correct. No one has all the answers, Megan. All I know is that by being alive, we've become part of something greater than ourselves, something vast and mysterious beyond our ability to understand. This life, this energy, instils us with natural passion and drive. It makes us seek things out and ask questions; questions much like yours. That, to me, is a sign that you, Megan Maurice, are very much alive and walking the path that was created for you.

"Life brings with it a sense of duty and honour and you should listen carefully whenever those things call to you. Listen to what's inside; watch the land and all its creatures for clues. Everything you need to know, you already know and all the things you're learning are nothing more than a rediscovery of those things. I promise you with all my heart, Megan, that all is right with the world, even in its darkest manifestations. This is what the Crowman wants you to know. He needs you to be strong enough to hold that idea, not as a belief but as knowledge, housed in your very flesh. In your bones, in your blood and in your heart. If you can do that, not only will you have walked the Black Feathered Path to its endpoint – and therefore to its beginning – you will also have lived a beautiful, magical and full life. You will have been worthy of the gift of it."

Megan is silenced by the enormity of it all, by its great simplicity and the responsibility it places upon her shoulders. Without a word, she helps Mr Keeper pack up their camp and clean away their breakfast. She waits for fear to rise in the aftermath of Mr Keeper's words but it does not. Instead she finds the hard granite of resolve that anchors her through every uncertainty and danger, a foundation rock that grows more firm and stable with every day she walks the Black Feathered Path.

Her tears dry quickly. By the time they strike out for home across the brittle, white landscape she is calm again. Empty but calm.

12

Gunshots.

Gordon opened his eyes to darkness. Blinked. The darkness remained.

Where am I?

More gunshots.

No. Wait.

The noise seemed to come from somewhere below. Not gunshots but rapping. Stone on glass. Beneath his body was a soft surface, so comfortable his sleep had been dreamless and profound. A mattress.

I'm indoors?

Then it all came back: the girl with the shotgun, the Ward's mounted patrol, the sick child who talked to the Crowman. He swung his legs off the bed, rubbing his face as he tried to remember the way back downstairs. Whoever was out there was hitting the glass with panicked urgency. He heard the glass smash, shards falling inward and hitting the basement's stone floor. His knife slipped into his palm like an old friend. He opened out the blade and ran down the stairs, his left hand interpreting the shape of the house in the darkness, leading him to the basement.

Before he reached the last flight of stairs the noise began

again; this time a stone knocking on the wood of the window frame. Gordon edged down into the cellar. The din continued, whoever was making it unaware he'd arrived.

"Who's out there?" He called.

The knocking ceased.

"Is that you, Gordon?"

He recognised Denise's voice.

"Yes."

"Oh, thank God. Thank God you're in here. Flora's… she's really sick. Can you come?"

He was already climbing out of the window. He set off in the direction of the green door in the back wall but Denise yanked him back.

"This way's quicker."

Using an old sofa as a step, she climbed over the property's side wall and dropped into the next-door back garden. Gordon followed. Denise's footsteps led him across a rubble-strewn expanse to the opposite wall, much of which had collapsed. They stepped over the bricks and she ran to the back gate in the next garden. The door had long before been torn off for shelter or firewood. She stepped through into the alley, able to run faster now. The alley opened out onto a street and a hundred yards further on Denise ducked through the blast hole in the wall that led to her own refuge.

As they climbed the stairs she said:

"I went to the old swimming pool first but I should have known you'd go to 257 after what you said about the countryside. All the greenery in London's in that back garden."

"What's the matter with Flora?"

"I don't know. I've never seen her this bad before."

She let Gordon ascend to the attic first, pulling up the ladder and closing the hatch after her. A candle burned on a saucer near Flora's untidy rumple of bedding. Denise lit several more and placed them near the girl's head so Gordon could see her better.

"I'm not a doctor, Denise."

"There are no doctors. None that I know anyway."

"What about your… friends?"

"You were closer."

Gordon knelt beside Flora and pulled back the blankets so that he could see her better. Her hair was dark with sweat, her teeth chattered and the tendons of her neck were tight. He didn't need to touch her forehead.

"This is a fever. Has she ever had one before?"

"Not like this. The arthritis sometimes sends her temperature up and her joints get hot and inflamed but this is different."

"How long has she been like this?"

"When we went to sleep she was fine. I woke up because her heels were drumming the floor."

A surge of guilt hit Gordon.

"You don't think it was the fish, do you?"

Denise shook her head.

"I thought about that but you and I are fine. This is something else."

Gordon watched the rigors shake Flora's tiny, bent frame. The lids of her eyes rippled as the orbs swivelled beneath them. Once again, the Black Light expanded from the core of him to pulse behind the skin of his fingertips.

No, he thought. I mustn't. All it ever brings is trouble.

He pressed his hands together, forced the living darkness back inside himself, shut it off. His stomach bulged and clenched with sickness. He chewed the nausea back, held it down.

And yet, there had to be something he could do.

"We have to cool her off, Denise."

"But she's shivering. Look at her. It's like she's freezing to death."

"Her temperature's sky-high and we've got to get it down. Fast. Take the bedclothes away and get her pyjamas off."

Denise didn't move.

"We have to do this."

"OK. Alright."

Denise shouldered him out of the way and stripped Flora of blankets and clothes. Gordon saw how crippling her arthritis was. Her knees, ankles and elbows were swollen and red her feet and hands already misshapen by the changes the disease had wrought inside her. Her skin was thin and waxen. Below it her veins and capillaries were visible. The bones of her pelvis jutted and her stomach was concave. Her whole body shuddered with fever.

Gordon sighed inwardly. I could make all this go away, he thought. The fever; all of it. But I don't know these people. I can't trust them. Not yet.

"Have you got some water?" he asked.

"Some. Not much."

"You need to wet a towel or blanket and cover her with it. The dampness will draw the heat out of her skin. It should bring her core temperature down too."

"I thought you said you weren't a doctor."

"I've been around a lot of sickness since I started travelling. And I had a fever like this once."

Gordon sat and stroked Flora's hair while Denise poured water onto an old towel, trying to soak as much of it as she could. Gordon helped her lay the towel over her daughter's trembling form. Flora sucked in a hiss of breath at the cold contact and Denise flinched, not allowing her end of the towel rest on Flora's body.

"Please, Denise. You have to do this."

Denise draped the towel down as softly as she could, not softly enough to prevent Flora from crying out at the touch of it.

"Baby, I'm so sorry." She put her face in her hands for a few moments, then wiped away her tears and pushed her hair out of her eyes. "OK. What do we do now?"

"We wait," said Gordon. "That's all we can do."

After an hour or so, her shivering had lessened and Gordon was sure the fever had receded. Heartened by this and obviously exhausted by the worry, Denise sat back against a cushion and allowed her eyes to close. Gordon checked Flora several more times, noting the heat in her skin much reduced. He too made himself a little more comfortable and soon his eyelids drooped.

They both woke at the same time to the sound of choking.

Gordon sprang across the attic space colliding with Denise and knocking her onto her side. He was first to reach Flora. In her flailing, she had thrown off her towel and it lay in a dry, stiff mould beside her. Gordon recoiled when he touched her head. The heat was too intense, more than a human body could sustain. His hands froze in response, Black Light surging in painful beads from his fingertips and palms ready to do its work.

OK, he thought. *Alright*. I'll do it.

Denise was so focused on her daughter, she didn't appear to have noticed his moment of crisis. He moved to Flora's side, opened his hands and stopped opposing the Black Light. He placed his palms on the girl's emaciated chest.

He took a deep breath and let it go in a long, silent stream. As suddenly as it had arrived, the cold energy of the void was gone. His hands were frail, weak. He closed his eyes and sought the darkness within himself, the power at his core. A sinkhole had opened up within him and the Black Light had been swallowed.

Please, he whispered to himself. Come on. Not this. Not *now*.

Denise took hold of his arm.

"What is it?"

He didn't answer; *couldn't* answer.

I'll never resist you again, he thought. I swear it. Come to me, please. Come to me now.

There was no moisture left in Flora's tiny, crooked body; only this arid, impossible heat. Her leg muscles rippled with cramps and spastic twitches, her arms alternately hooking closed and extending in sudden snaps. Her wasted body arched and bucked. The noise of her battering the floorboards was thunderous. Cuts and grazes opened up with every bony contact but Gordon's attention was drawn to the gurgling rasp in her throat.

Denise drained sallow with fear.

"Jesus, Gordon, what's happening to her?"

"The fever's back. It's a convulsion."

"What can we... Oh my God, is that... blood?"

A watery, pink-tinged discharge dribbled from Flora's left ear and nostril. Her shaking and thrashing sent droplets left and right. The flow increased and thickened, turning cherry red. Blood smeared her face, dirtied itself on the floorboards, blackened her hair like a slick of oil. Her struggles decelerated from frantic to slow motion, the frenetic energy draining suddenly from her limbs. The tension released completely then leaving her cut, bruised body slack.

Gordon looked at her chest and saw no movement. Concentrated urine and a thin gravy of faeces darkened her thighs and groin. Her face was masked and tacky with blood and mucus. The smell was one Gordon knew from every scene of devastation he'd passed through. If they were outdoors now, if it was daylight, the carrion eaters would already be landing, blinking their obsidian eyes, fluffing their coal-dark plumes, shuffling closer.

As he thought this the strangled cry of a raven exploded in his head. The call, loud both in the distance and in the space around them, was clotted with grief and regret. Gordon chanced a look at Denise. She had heard nothing. This was a voice meant for him. Was it the Crowman? He'd never heard the corvid voice so strong, so encompassing. Or was it Flora's soul, a bold crow spirit if ever he'd known one, cursing him as it left this world?

"Thank God," said Denise. "Oh, thank God. She's sleeping now. I'll get her cleaned up."

Denise busied herself finding a rag and soaking it with the last of the water.

"She's gone," said Gordon.

"She'd be so embarrassed to know you've seen her like this. She's quite proper, really. I don't know where she gets *that* from."

Gordon took Denise's wrist and pulled her towards him.

"She's gone."

"Don't touch me like that. Don't you think you can come in here and touch me... and talk to me like..."

Gordon pulled Denise close and held her tight. She struggled and whispered *no, no, no*. He rocked her the way his mother had rocked him when he was a child. When her weeping finally came it began as a howl. After a time, he didn't know how long, the howling became a whimper. Gordon could have cried too. He wanted to, felt the tears needling the backs of his eyes, but knew he had no right.

After a time, he couldn't tell how long, Denise pulled away.

"I really must clean her up. She wouldn't want to be seen like this."

"Of course."

"Can you... come back in a while? I need to talk to her and it's..."

"I'll come back when it's light."

It was dark outside, the night thick with tainted, smoky mist. Gordon stood in the back garden for a few moments and listened to the sound of the broken capital of England. The silence of abandonment, the silence of fear; that was all he could hear. One thing Gordon knew with absolute certainty. He would not sleep tonight.

He returned through the smoggy midnight to number 257, treading quietly along Denise's route. Unwilling to enter the property yet and still feeling the knot of swallowed darkness in his guts, he sat on the cold stone steps leading to the boarded-up back door. In a few hours, dawn would give him a view of the wild garden and over the wall into the next-door plot.

When the stomach contraction came it was a rush he could not control. Vomit erupted from his mouth as he hung his head over the steps. He didn't need to see it to know it was darker than molasses and just as viscous. Nor was he surprised that it hit the basement level without a sound. Tomorrow there would be no sign of it, except perhaps a puddle-shaped patch of stone or concrete, scalloped and paled by its touch.

When the spasm had passed he whispered into the night.

"I'm so sorry, Flora. I could have prevented this. I could have made you a healthy little girl, given you the future he promised you."

The tears he could not shed in front of Flora's mother found their vent then, and Gordon pressed a fist to his mouth to stifle them. But who would approach such a sound in the night, the sound of weeping so desolate it was laughter, the sound of laughter so twisted it was tears?

13

Apa is away in the fields when Megan arrives home.

Amu opens the door and hesitates before drawing her over the threshold and clasping her to her breast. In Amu's eyes, in that pause, Megan sees what she has suspected for some time now. She is changing. For a moment even her own mother did not recognise her. Both of them shed a few tears, just for themselves, and then step back to look at each other again, both pretending they are tears of happiness.

It is only days since Megan saw her but Amu has changed too. She has more lines at the corners of her eye and the skin of her neck is a little slacker, a little drier. Her full dark hair appears less lustrous than Megan remembers it, and thinner perhaps, if such a thing is possible in such a short space of time. As she appraises her mother, though, she realises that all these tiny differences, and they are tiny, are incremental, not sudden. Megan has been noticing them for a while without ever acknowledging it. It has taken some time away from home for her to return with honest eyes and see the truth. Her mother is ageing. She is still beautiful – she will always be beautiful – but time is working its slow magic on her, holding her hand and taking her gently into decay, guiding her to that final winter.

Megan looks into her mother's eyes and sees her own eyes there. This is where she came from; out of the very meat of this woman, out of her bliss and agony from chaos into form, from the perfect nothingness of the beyond into the imperfect beauty of this world. It is impossible to conceal her sadness and wonder and she steps forward and hugs Amu again. Tighter this time, not ever wanting to let go of yet knowing all chalices will be cast down in the fullness of time. Her mother is surprised by the fierceness in her cling. She returns it and this time they both cry without pretending joy.

"I've missed you so much, Amu."

"We've missed you too, Megan."

They stand away from each other again, as mother and daughter and as women; drawn equal by nothing more magical than the inevitability of time.

Amu goes to her stove and places a pan on the hot plate. Megan takes her place on a stool at the table.

"You've lost some weight, girl. Gone from bonny to boyish in a matter of days. Is Mr Keeper starving you now?"

"He's a kind man, Amu, and he's for the good in all things. But we walked a long way this time."

Amu folds her arms across her chest.

"Well, I can't deny you look stronger. I see the granite in your eyes. You look like you could wrestle any man in the village."

"I hope it doesn't come to that!"

They both laugh but only a little.

Amu steps close and touches Megan's face.

"You're more of a woman too." Amu's face creases; a smile of pain. Her voice falls to a whisper. "I'm so proud of you."

She turns away and busies herself at the stove, pushing away tears with the back of a shaking hand. She changes the subject, finding cheer where, for a moment, there can be none.

"We'll have some hot goat's milk and powdered dandelion. That'll keep the cold out. Winter's here all of a sudden."

Megan nods. She too feels winter's touch. On her skin and in her heart. Amu's bright tones are brittle on her ear.

"And when Apa comes home we'll eat hearty. This feels like a special day. I'll take one of the geese."

Megan stands up.

"I can do that."

"You can sit down, girl. You need to rest yourself. No doubt you'll be locked away in your room for the next few days, scrawling in that book of yours."

Megan half laughs.

"No doubt at all. Let me help with the cooking, though."

"Stay where you are. In fact, bring your stool over to the fire and get some warmth into you. We can talk while I prepare the meal and before you know it, your father will come through that door just as surprised to see his daughter become a woman as I am. Who'd have thought such a thing could happen?"

"I've only been away four days."

"Well, it was long enough for you to grow up, Megan Maurice." Her mother turns and catches her eye. "And it seemed an age to me."

Megan smiles. She has so dreaded the moment at which she must begin writing again that she has forgotten how good it might feel to be home. It's better than she could have imagined. She promises herself that for the few hours she has before the work begins again, she will not think about it. She will not tread the Black Feathered Path and she will not invite the Crowman to dine in their home. Not tonight.

Apa's return is muted by comparison. He walks in, ducking through the door the way he always does – as though the low crossbeam is an obstacle he's seen for the very first time. When he sees Megan, the first thing he does is heave a sigh. And when he has let this long breath go, he is a smaller man; sad in a way Megan does not understand.

Has she disappointed him?

Never before has she been so acutely aware of the difference between the way she sees the world and the way her parents see it. She wonders if this is true for all children and their parents or just for her because she has become such a different kind of child, such an unusual and somewhat peripheral creature. For a moment she has the bottomless terror of believing that it has taken that one single moment for her father to stop loving her. And then he looks at her and smiles.

She runs to him and tears wet every face.

Grinding the ink and opening the book does more than merely dispel Megan's fear of this moment. Gordon's story rises up inside her, forgotten until this very moment, and her hand trembles, aching to be at the page. Her writing is deliberate and steady in the instant the raven quill touches the parchment and she writes with firm, flowing strokes. The story does not overwhelm her; it comes in a continuous thread, arriving just ahead of the words she is writing and in this way it draws her on.

She is cleaved by the act of telling; she exists now in two worlds: the boy's and her own. One Megan sees and remembers every detail of the boy's journey, his growth and pain. The other Megan sits, utterly still but for the whispered journey of her hand across each page and the slow sway of her head from one side to the other as the tale comes through.

What she has been told is true. She forgets nothing, not a single aspect. Not the shape of the clouds or the cast of the light. Not the expressions on the faces of those who travel with or oppose the boy. Not the sensation of the powerful muscles moving beneath his skin. She feels his strength and is astonished by it; even more astonished by his uncertainty. Even if he does not know it or cannot yet believe it, Megan knows that this boy will find the Crowman for that is what he was born to do.

The language comes to her also, fed by this same thread, not of memory exactly but almost of reconnection back into the boy's world. She has the feather which gives her understanding of the language, but now she is convinced that even without it she could access his idiom and vocabulary and comprehend it totally. There is a joy in this realisation. Without questioning or judging, she writes, and the tale comes to her both as recollection and as myth. In telling his tale, she brings the boy and his world back to life.

She lives beside him in that world.

They buried Flora in the wild garden at number 257. It wasn't easy but Gordon didn't care about that.

He used his knife to clear a tiny grotto, carving it out of the bramble, weeds and overgrown shrubs. The position he chose left enough space between the roots of better established, woodier shrubs so that he could dig. A scout of the neighbouring gardens didn't yield a shovel as he'd hoped but there was a workman's pick leaning in what remained of a garden shed a few doors down towards the park. It turned out to be the perfect tool for breaking the ground and cutting through the tangle of growth which was almost as thick under ground as it was above. Such flowers as there were among the weeds and thorns, he picked and placed around the graveside. By the time the space was cleared, his palms and the backs of his hands were bloody.

He didn't return to Denise until the grave was prepared. It must have been close to noon by then. The ladder was pulled up and the hatch closed. He hadn't seen it like this before. If he hadn't known the trapdoor was there he'd never have spotted it. He called up to her.

"Denise? It's me. Gordon."

He heard shuffling and a click. The hatch dropped open. Her face was puffy.

"I thought you weren't coming back."

"I wanted to make a place for her," he said. "A good place."

"I need more time with her."

"There's no hurry. Do you want to see it, though? Get out for a while?"

Her face disappeared and the ladder slid down. She descended without her usual confidence, her hands shaking. When she reached the landing she looked as much a little girl as Flora. Denise's life, what little she'd had and everything she'd lost: Gordon felt responsible for all of it. He felt responsible for the world and everything that was wrong in it too. That was the price of knowing you had the power to make things better.

Fully expecting her to shake the contact off, he took her trembling hand and led her down the stairs. She didn't seem to mind his touch, though, and as they descended her grip tightened. She appeared to take some strength from touching him and for that small thing Gordon was very glad. And yet, their touch was risky too, like striking a match near petrol. Part of him wanted arson.

14

Denise wept for a long time when she saw what he'd done.

Gordon sat at the top of the steps to the back door again, giving her space and time. She rearranged some of the flowers he'd picked and found a few more: foxglove and comfrey among them, framing the grave with dainty touches of colour. The sky had brightened and in places the clouds seemed weak enough that they might let the sun through.

Denise came to the bottom of the steps.

"It feels a lot better knowing she has somewhere... safe to go."

"That's good." He rose from the top step and came down to her. "Do you want to go back now? Spend a little more time with her?"

"No. I want you to bring her here now. I'm ready."

Gordon thought about it for a moment.

"Have you got anything to... cover her with?"

"I've dressed her and she's wrapped in her blankets. I've put all her stuff in a bag. I was going to see if I could find a child to give it to but I've changed my mind now. I want everything buried with her."

Something must have shown on his face. He regretted his lack of inscrutability.

"Don't worry. I've kept all the Crowman stuff separate. She would have wanted you to have it."

Looking down, Gordon said:

"Thanks."

"Can you manage everything?" she asked.

It wasn't a serious offer and he was glad to see her reluctance. Even if she'd wanted to, he wouldn't have let her come with him. It was a weird time, the separation immediately after death. Denise probably would have taken one look at Flora, snug in her blankets, and decided to keep her a little longer. This way was better.

"I'll be fine. And I'll be gentle with her, Denise. You don't need to worry. Stay here and enjoy this light while it lasts."

He walked away before she could change her mind.

Flora could not have looked more comfortable or peaceful in her place of rest.

Denise had cocooned her in blankets, swaddling her like a tiny baby. Only Flora's cowled face met the weak rays of sun as they laid her down. Within her grotto, she was soon encased once more in shadow. Denise placed Flora's belongings beside her and put a daisy beside her head. Gordon placed a large black crow feather on her chest.

"Do you want to say anything?" he asked Denise.

She nodded but it was a long time before she spoke. The words sounded weak and hollow at first

"Flora… you had a short life. Not what anyone could call a good one. I often thought it might have been better if I'd… got rid of you before you were born. I wasn't fit to be a mother. But now you're gone, knowing I won't see you again makes me realise how good it was, our time together. This world has got bad enough, God knows, but it's going to be a lot darker without your little light shining. I hope you can forgive me for all the ways in which I could have been a better mum and for all the times I didn't say I love you – the times I just thought it instead. And, wherever you've gone to now, I hope it's paradise compared to the life you had. I love you, Flora, and I don't know what I'm going to do without you."

Gordon let a few moments pass.

"Do you mind if I speak?"

"It's OK."

He was quiet for a moment, gathering the right words, wanting to speak only truth. There had to be a way to address the earth and sky and whatever power lay beyond their physical lives. It came to him then, like a whisper:

"Great Spirit," he began, knowing the words were correct. "We mourn the loss of our little sister, Flora, but we know her spirit has flown back to you. Grandmother, we place her body inside your body, where it belongs, where it came from. Flora, I only knew you for the shortest time but I came to love you and your fearlessness. Thank you for telling me so much about the Crowman." Gordon paused, his mouth dry. "I... I'm sorry I didn't... *couldn't* help you. I tried. But I know your departure from us is a homecoming for you. May your spirit be peaceful and fulfilled until it returns to walk the earth again."

Gordon took a few grains of dirt and sprinkled them onto Flora's blankets. Denise knelt and did the same thing. She stayed crouched there and Gordon knew a few more silent words were spilling forth. He waited until she stood again. He caught her eye and she stepped back from the graveside.

"OK?" he asked.

"OK."

He used the pickaxe to push the excavated earth back over Flora's body. It was only when the earth touched her cheeks and eyelids, caught between her lips and fell into her ears without any flicker of a response, that Denise began to cry.

Moving Denise out of her attic and into 257 was a swift job. So quick it was like some obscene desertion. When the burial was complete, Denise had come to Gordon and rested her head on his chest. He'd held her.

"I don't think I can be in that room without her now. The silence would drive me mad."

"We can find you somewhere else. There's places everywhere. It just means a little searching."

Denise had become frantic.

"No. I need to get out of there now. I can't go back. I can't wait up there while you look around. I never want to see that room again."

She'd been close to hysteria, weeping and pushing her forehead into his chest, as if to burrow away from the light.

"Hey, hey. It's OK, Denise. I'll get your gear down for you. You can stay here until we find you somewhere else. This place is huge."

She was crying too hard for her words to make any sense by then, so he'd walked her to the back steps and sat her down before making the first trip to the attic. She'd already packed everything she owned into a couple of suitcases and a few cloth bags. The attic was featureless now, but for the dark stains on the bare wooden boards where Flora had passed away.

He made three trips back and forth. On the last, he pulled the ladder up into the attic and sat there in the quiet for a while. The little light coming up from below seemed not to belong there.

"I'm so sorry, Flora. I don't know how or even *if* you could ever forgive me for what I've done but, like the fool I am, I still hope you will. And I hope wherever you are now, you're happier than you were down here. I know it's impossible to repay you but I'm going to try. Somehow, I'll make sure your life wasn't wasted on my stupidity."

Gordon took a feather from his pocket, a magpie feather he'd kept for years, and placed it near the bloodstained floorboards. He leapt down through the hatch and found the pole for closing it under a pile of mouldy wallpaper in a room off the top landing. He pushed the hatchway into position and the latch caught, holding it closed. Once again, it was almost impossible to tell the trapdoor or the attic it led to existed. Gordon snapped the pole over his leg and threw the pieces into the back garden as he passed the bedroom and its broken window.

15

"See you when the work is done."

That's what Mr Keeper always says.

This time Megan fears the work will never end. She writes all day and late into every night. But on the seventh day, some time in the afternoon, the thread of telling ends – very suddenly and without any warning – and Megan is spent. With the story up to date, her duty is to return to Mr Keeper. But she needs to rest first; to be in her own world for a while and put a cushion of time between writing and furthering her training.

She lays down the raven quill and stands up. Her buttocks are numb from so many days of sitting. Her lower back aches with stiffness and her shoulders are hoisted high with tension. She takes a few deep breaths and performs some of the exercises she has seen Mr Keeper do to keep himself strong and limber. After a few minutes, the life begins to seep back into her muscles and the stagnation drains from her lungs. Nonetheless, her eyes are hot and strained and her right hand is hooked into a claw. She has lost count of how many times the blister on her right middle finger has filled and burst where it made contact with the shaft of the quill. She spends some time massaging the rigor from her writing hand, pressing the fingers back and the thumb open.

Through the bedroom's tiny wind-eye she can see how winter's touch has hardened and stiffened the land. Everything is either dying or sleeping. Even the animals are quiet. Smoke rises in straight shafts from every chimney into the still, icy air. The gathering of harvests is complete and all that remains in the ground are the overwintering crops for which her father carries the greatest responsibility. Every day, he inspects the rows of cabbages, sprouts and parsnips, making sure they're healthy and protected from rabbits and pigeons. Those animals that come too close find themselves integral to the harvest.

Every tree is bare and bony, but for the distant pines of New Wood among which Mr Keeper lives. Tomorrow, or perhaps the day after, when she feels rested, she will return to him but for now she feels only two sensations: hunger and fatigue.

Amu is not in the house but there is half a wheaten loaf on the sideboard. Megan cuts it into two pieces and takes a cup of milk from the stone ewer. She sits beside the stove chewing, sipping and staring into nothingness until the food and drink are gone. Resisting a great weight, she stands again, rinses her cup and turns it upside down beside the others.

In her room she takes off her shoes but keeps all her clothes on and slips into her bed. She pulls the blankets and skins right up to her nose and turns onto her right side, curling tight.

She dreams of a girl.

Megan is in his world, the world of the Crowman, Gordon's world.

She is in a cramped, dark room with a cocked ceiling. It smells of sickness and human waste. At first she thinks the room is empty but then Megan notices something moving under a pile of dirty blankets. She assumes it's an animal until a tiny crooked hand emerges. The shock causes Megan to draw a sudden breath. From the blankets emerges a little girl, grubby and deformed by some cruel disease of the bones. Her hair is unwashed and tangled and there is dirt under her fingernails. Her face is thin, the skin stretched tight over hot, fragile bones.

The girl struggles to sit up, in obvious pain. She reaches for a pile of blank pages, takes a pencil and begins to draw. Intrigued now, Megan creeps a little closer to the girl. Despite her crippling illness, the girl has a gift. Her drawing is a simple but unmistakable reproduction of the Crowman in flight. Megan gasps and the little girl's pencil stops moving. Megan holds her breath. The pencil begins to move again.

When the girl's work is done, she pushes the page away and studies it. Megan studies it too. A simple yet arresting image of the Crowman swoops out of the paper. There is something so lifelike about it that he is almost more real than when Megan sees him in her visions. The girl has simplified his image though – whether deliberately or not, Megan can't tell – and the result is iconic, so that not only is he alive in the art, he is also somehow eternal in it, a symbol of something.

The girl picks up the piece of paper and holds it out to Megan.

"I knew you were coming," says the girl. "I made it for you."

Astonished, Megan tries to back away quietly. The grimy, twisted little girl looks up and makes eye contact with Megan, smiling the way only a child who has suffered years of pain can smile. She has much power for one so young, if she can see a traveller in the night country.

"He said you'd visit me. And he told me what it meant." Suddenly the girl looks like she will cry. "I'm so glad you came. It means everything is going to be alright. It means everything he's told me is true. I don't have to be afraid anymore."

Hesitantly, Megan reaches out for the piece of paper, finding it as solid as any object she has ever touched. She brushes the graphite markings very softly feeling powdery smoothness and tiny granules under her fingertips. With perhaps less regard for the poor child sitting in front of her than she ought to have, she tears it very slightly near one corner just to be sure. It is real. She rolls the paper into a scroll and puts it inside her tunic.

Still wary of the child and repulsed by her sickness, Megan kneels down on the bare boards a safe distance away.

"I'm very grateful. It's a beautiful drawing."

The girl is delighted by this. Her masklike face opens into a broad grin to reveal receding gums and loose, yellowing teeth. At first bold, now she is shy.

"Thanks."

If the room smells bad, the girl's breath is worse. Megan detects rampant decay in her teeth and pestilence in her lungs and stomach. Living in cramped darkness can't be doing anything to help the weakening child. What she needs is the clean air of the hills and the dawn sun in her eyes, the touch of pure flowing river water against her parchment skin. She needs to run and tumble in meadow grass and wild flowers, to hear the language of wind spoken through the leaves of trees. She will experience none of this, though, Megan is quite certain.

"You say he told you I'd visit. Who do you mean?"

The girl points at the pocket in Megan's tunic as though she is stupid.

"Him of course. The Crowman."

"You know him?"

The girl rolls her eyes now, with adult impatience.

"Oh, please," she says. "He's my best friend. He visits me all the time. More than you can say for mum's *friends*."

Megan looks around, suddenly nervous about being discovered in here.

"Where is your mother?"

"I don't know. Out. Maybe with Gordon. He seems really nice. I think he'd be a proper friend."

Megan shivers to know how close she is to the boy. The focus of her visions varies from telescopic to microscopic. Sometimes she watches all from high above, as though borne by wings. Other times she looks out through Gordon's eyes, makes his search and keeps his vigil with him. This trip to the night country is not mere observation though; she is on his level, in his time. He could arrive here at any moment and they would come face to face.

The girl is watching her, intrigued.

"Do you know him?"

Megan smiles.

"I know him the way you know the Crowman."

"Oh." The girl looks disappointed, as though Gordon is someone she could keep just for herself and her mother. "He never mentioned you."

Megan understands without even having to think about it. The girl simply loves Gordon Black. Perhaps her mother does too. Megan tries to keep her feelings for him pushed to the horizon but spending so much time in his world, watching the boy grow through failure and successive trials, makes it hard not to want something more than just watching, merely studying his life. What more she can't say but when she isn't in his world, she yearns for visions of him, constantly wonders how he is faring and whether or not he is safe. It has been a little like having a brother who has travelled to a far land, and waiting for his letters. A brother or perhaps something more.

This little girl is already possessive about Gordon and yet she is willing to share her best friend, the Crowman, as easily as she might pick a daisy and hand it to a stranger. Something the girl said a few moments before brings Megan back to the moment.

"You said you were frightened. Why is that?"

"The Crowman told me I was going to die. Very soon."

Megan is aghast and unable to hide her shock. Why would anyone ever say such a thing to a child?

"It's alright," says the girl. "I told you. I'm not afraid any more. I'm ready."

Megan can do nothing but shake her head. Tears well at the corners of her eyes. The little girl puts out one hot, crooked hand and places it over Megan's.

"He told me everything would be fine if you came. He said it was a sign that I wouldn't disappear forever into blackness. That's what I was afraid of. He said if you visited me it was a sign that I would live again. In a strong body. In a bright day."

Megan folds the girl very gently into her arms and rocks with her, though it is Megan who takes comfort from the contact rather than the child.

She is still rocking like this when the temperature drops and she opens her eyes to find herself in almost complete darkness. She is sitting in her own bed swaying back and forth with tears coursing down her face. Waking makes her cry even harder.

After a while, she wipes her face and blows her nose on her bedside handkerchief. She slips out of bed and lights a candle. She puts her hand into her pocket and cries out when her fingers touch a scroll of paper, the likes of which have never been made in her world, in her time.

She draws it out and unfurls it with reverence. The paper is torn in one corner and there upon it, by the flickering glow which makes his wings beat and his head turn from side to side as he flies, she sees the Crowman, as magnificent and powerful in art as he has ever been in her visions. She watches him move by candlelight for a long time, losing herself in his grace and splendour and menace.

Her head begins to nod and she places the paper on her table. To flatten it she places the drawing underneath the black book, inside its box where it rests in the soil beneath her bed. She collapses back onto the mattress. Sleep draws over her like the shadow of his wings.

While Denise slept, Gordon spent much of his time at the top of the back steps, enjoying the proximity and impenetrability of the wild garden. Being next to it was enough. He was surprised to find he was comfortable watching over Flora's grave too. Perhaps it was some combination of imagination and wishful thinking but a great sense of ease and peacefulness radiated from her resting place. Far from activating his guilt, knowing she was nearby gave him a sense of continuity. It was in this place, sitting quietly, that Gordon entered a state of absence. He welcomed its arrival.

The brave sun, so strong that morning, so nearly visible through whatever combination of dust and vapour cloaked London, had lost its bid for freedom. Once again it was obscure, at best bringing gloom to what would otherwise have been darkness.

Nevertheless, some sense of power and strength had been bestowed by its brief struggle to break through; Gordon felt it in the air and in the ground. He felt it in his muscles and his resolve. He hadn't come this far to falter and give in. As much as he had felt for Flora, hers was only one more death among the millions who had already claimed by the Black Dawn. Darkness, that of the Ward and mankind's own hand, was still falling across the face of the Earth. The Black Dawn's influence had not yet run its course. There would be more death. More sickness. More evil; man against man and against their mother, the land. The Crowman knew how to counter all of this and he was close now. Gordon could hear the whispered beat of his wings each time he slept, woke always to the caress of a downdraft as something resembling a black angel departed from his dreams.

In this comfortable trance, he was well aware of the presence of the Crowman and trusted him both to guide and stay his hand. There was never any doubt about his existence as a physical being, as a man. The Crowman was real but only in his dreams and daydreams was Gordon truly able to accept this. On this day of farewells Gordon was able to sit uninterrupted on his step and go very far away to that nearby place, a place where he could sit beside himself and see, really see, how things were in the world. Remembering these absences wasn't really important, when he was there he knew this, what mattered was that he carried these times in his heart, in his very organs and bones, long after he had returned to the world and become once more a sceptic, a young man with little but fear and doubt for company on the long nights.

Today, even the sight of the earth moving in Flora's grave was not enough to make him start. At first he thought she would rise up. She didn't. Something was touching the bare soil. Dainty fingers. A girl's fingers but not Flora's. These fingers were straight and soft. Their skin was tanned and healthy. These were fingers which, though small and shapely, had worked the earth and knew it well.

The fingers smoothed the soil, caressed it. The owner of the hands appeared.

Gordon stopped breathing for a moment, afraid the sound of it would scare her away. Yet, in not breathing he risked coming out of his reverie and losing the vision of her totally. He allowed his chest to unlock and let himself relax. The girl became solid and he watched her, awestruck.

She was a ghost, for sure. Her clothes were simple and looked handmade, the fabrics rough and sturdy. She crouched by the graveside, her peasant weeds disguising her shape. Still, Gordon was able to see that she was both slim and strong; a hardy country girl a little younger than him. Her blonde hair brought light with it from wherever in history she'd lived and there was a brightness around her, an aura of dusty sunshine.

Not yet able to see her face, she was still the most beautiful creature he'd ever encountered. Gordon could feel her wholeness and goodness radiating outwards. Without speaking a word to her he knew that she was honest and trustworthy, generous and kind. Had she not been a spectre from the past – some golden age of simplicity and rural living – he would have spoken to her, pursued her. This was the young woman he wanted to spend the rest of his life with. Other than in this vision, however, he knew he would never meet her. Nor was it likely he would ever see her again. Ghosts, and he had seen a few these last three years, must be left to their business.

Knowing all this and heartbroken over everything that would never be, he watched as the girl drew out a white lily from her tunic and placed it on the recently turned earth. Beside this she laid a magpie feather, its deep, lustrous turquoise shimmering in the warm summer light of a distant era.

What the connection between the ghost girl and Flora was, he didn't know and trying to think about it now would be to lose this trance and this vision. But the ghost girl knew something about Flora and her passing – she had chosen to leave the same feather as Gordon had. All he could do, all he wanted to do, was watch this girl and be captivated for as long as she was willing to stay.

That turned out to be a very short time.

She appeared to make some gestures and he thought from the tiny movements of her head that she might be speaking to Flora or saying a prayer for her. When she was done, she stood up. Watching her move set fire to his groin. In his searching and travelling he'd always pushed feelings like this aside. Getting close enough to be intimate meant opening up to danger. Since his first terrified escape from the Ward, when the Palmers had nursed him back to health, his rule had always been not to let that happen. This was different, though. He was drawn to her the way a falling man is drawn to Earth.

When she turned to him, everything stopped.

No breath.

No heartbeat.

He was right, of course, her face was as beautiful as her movements and aura had suggested. She was tanned and her cheeks were touched pink, as though by a frosty morning. Her green eyes glittered in the light from that other time. Her voice was so sweet it anguished him to hear it.

"I see you, Gordon Black. You are loved by many, and more than you know."

He wanted to answer but time had stopped. His body would not respond.

"Flora's time had come. It was signalled by your arrival and it was right that she passed – no matter what you believe. She recognised you and she loved you. And so do I. Never forget that everything you need will come to hand in the very moment of its requirement. No matter how dark the world may seem to you, everything is as it should be and can be no other way. Keep searching, Gordon. Keep fighting and never give up. If you can do this, if all people can do this, there will always be a future."

Surely he would suffocate now. Surely his heart would not restart.

"I see you, Gordon Black. I see you."

The girl began to withdraw into her light and her light began to shrink. When she was gone time began again. He breathed, and his heart continued to beat – both as though nothing had happened. Gordon wept at the loss of her, as though she were the world. Where her light had been, London's gloom gathered like something intelligent, drowning the memory of her, erasing her presence in this time. The sky descended, closed in over the abandoned houses and empty streets, wrapped his head in shadows. Darker and darker until he thought the world was ending.

When he finally roused himself from his fugue, the darkness finally made sense to him. He'd been drifting for a long time. It was night.

16

Dear Gordon

I'm sorry I couldn't say more last time. The scrap of note paper Bossy got for me was too small and I ran out of space. I was so desperate to tell you things. To tell you everything. Bossy couldn't get me any more paper before his trip into the woods to deliver the letter to one of his friends. He's very fair, really. Promises not to read a single word as long as I keep him company sometimes. The one thing I really wanted to say was please, please write back to me. Even if it's just a word or two. Knowing we can talk to each other will make all of this OK. I told you, didn't I, that there was a small price to pay for paper and a pencil? Bossy likes to sit beside me for that. On my bunk. I suppose I don't mind if it means I can communicate with you. Afterwards, he tells me things about what's going on outside the substation. He seems to know a lot. He told me you're searching for the Crowman and helping the Green Men. He says you're tough – well "brick-hard" he calls it. It's good to know. I was so worried after I shut the green door on you that day. You seemed so small and terrified and I had so many nightmares about what they would do if they caught you. Never mind that now. I know you're alive and I don't have nightmares any more. Well not so many. I don't know where I am or I'd tell you to come and get me. Bossy says if he had some help he could get me out of here. As wonderful as that would be, I'd settle for just seeing your face and knowing you're OK. You must have grown so much since I last saw you. You must be a man by now. Silly me. Running out of paper again. Be safe. Write very soon. I love you, Gordon. Jude.

Long before the daylight made a target of him, Gordon raided several houses around the property where Denise's attic now stood abandoned. Most were already cleaned out but one boarded-up basement flat had been ignored by looters. It yielded more tins of food than he could carry, some dried pasta and even some plastic bottles of water. The use-by dates had been exceeded on almost everything he could scavenge and he longed for the land, where he could trap or gather food he trusted. In the cities you had to be thankful for whatever you could steal. He made several trips to transfer the goods to number 257 and lit a fire in one of the many fireplaces the old Victorian house boasted.

Resting pans on an oven tray over the coals, he cooked penne and a couple of tins of tomatoes. By firelight he ate as much as his stomach would hold. Rather than making him sleepy, it renewed him. He mixed the leftovers into one pan and put them to one side, ready to reheat when Denise woke up.

Though he was ready to start searching for the Crowman again, to make forays into the heart of London, he was reluctant to leave Denise in the house alone. When she came round and he was sure she was OK, that would be the time.

Gordon returned to his vantage point at the top of the back steps. By comparison to the almost complete darkness of number 257's interior, the murky light of dawn in the garden seemed bright at first. The lily and the feather remained where the girl from some long ago summer had left them.

He didn't know how he was going to explain them to Denise.

With nothing to do, he let himself drift again, hoping to recapture the vision of the previous day. Agitation in his limbs prevented him from slipping through the moment into the fluidity of time. He knew this restlessness. Even when his mind was not searching his body was itching to pursue his singular and elusive quarry. The chase was programmed into his muscles and his blood. Resisting its call created discomfort in the very hollows of his bones.

A movement at the periphery of his vision drew his attention. Beyond a fence, several properties along, heads were visible. It was the back garden of the house where Denise had lived. The heads belonged to three men. That was about all he could make out at this distance. They seemed to know where they were going and soon disappeared through the back door. These must be Denise's friends, the ones who brought food for her and Flora. They'd be back when they got no response from the attic and then they'd start looking around.

Gordon considered his options. If they saw him sitting up here, they'd approach and then the sanctuary that was number 257 would be open to all comers. If he slipped inside now, there was every chance they wouldn't even come in this direction. He retreated down the steps into the garden and down again to the basement window. If they were decent friends, they'd be back to search another day. By then Denise would have decided whether she wanted to share her new address. For now, undisturbed rest was what she needed most.

Ruing the interruption of what little daylight he could enjoy, he slipped back into the darkness of the house.

••••

Gordon slept on a mattress in a room across from Denise. He wanted to be close in case she woke in the darkness and was disorientated. When she eventually rose it had been light for a while. He was cooking in the fireplace when she shuffled in.

"That smells good."

He could barely see her face by the firelight but she seemed calm.

"This is chickpeas in tomatoes. I've got pasta in tomatoes from yesterday. What do you fancy?"

"Yesterday? How long have I slept?"

"Two days, near enough."

"God. I've never slept that much in my life."

"How do you feel?"

"Sleepy, believe it or not."

They both laughed a little.

"You hungry?"

"Now that you come to mention it, I'm ravenous."

He gave her the steaming pan and a spoon and heated up the pasta in the other pot while she ate chickpeas. There'd been a time when he'd missed herbs, spices and salt and pepper. All food tasted good now. After a while, Denise handed back the first pan and he handed her the pasta. She seemed to prefer it and he was glad to see her eat it all.

As he stacked the pans, one inside the other, a noise came up from the basement. The sound of glass underfoot. Gordon unclasped his lock knife and motioned for Denise to follow him. Together they descended to the basement. By the light coming in through the exposed, broken window they both saw two men. A third was climbing in. Gordon squeezed her hand.

Before the third figure was through the window he said:

"Didn't your parents teach you to knock before coming in?"

The man framed in the window froze and the other two spun towards the sound of Gordon's voice. Both men held out weapons into the darkness in front of them. One, a crowbar, the other a machete. For the moment, Gordon's eyes were more accustomed to the gloom than theirs.

"Why are you breaking into my house?" he asked.

"It's not yours," said the man with the machete. "No one owns anything any more."

"I'm the current occupier. You are the current trespasser. What are doing here?"

"We're looking for someone. A friend."

"Does this friend of yours have a name?"

The man with the machete took a step forward in the darkness. He could see Gordon now, that was clear. Gordon pushed Denise back up into the obscurity of the stairs. The machete man edged forward.

"Listen, shithead. It's none of your business. You should leave before you get carved up."

"Carved up? By three of you? That's quite an assumption. Especially as you have no idea how many of us are in here."

The man tensed. His machete quivered. The man with the crowbar couldn't keep his eyes still. Gordon saw the sheen glistening across his dirty forehead.

"Ah," said Gordon. "Nerves creeping in a bit, are they? Well, it's your own fault – you know what they say about piss-poor planning..."

The nearest man adjusted his grip on the machete's plastic handle.

"Don't drop it now, will you?" said Gordon.

"Listen..."

"I'm listening."

"We've seen the grave."

"And?"

"We want to know what's happened."

"Of course you do. Your... friend."

The man with the machete nodded, swallowing.

"Here's what I suggest," said Gordon. "You go back out into my garden. I'll stay here while you do. Then I'll pop out and we can talk. How's that sound?"

The man swallowed again, glanced back at his accomplice and the man stuck halfway through the window.

"OK," he said. "Alright."

"Good."

No one moved.

"I'll stay right here," said Gordon. "Promise."

The man with the machete adjusted his grip again. The tip of the blade wavered. He took a step back and glanced behind. He nodded to the crowbar man and together they reversed towards the window. Seeing this, the third man dropped back into the garden. More light came in through the window but Gordon retreated up the stairs so the raiders couldn't see him.

When they were outside he took Denise's hand, led her down to the basement and across to the window where they crouched, out of sight.

"Nice friends," he said. "Supportive. Strong sense of community."

"They're dangerous, Gordon."

"Sometimes a dangerous friend can be a good thing. Right?"

"They've always brought us food. Kept our place a secret. Protected us."

"But there were costs. Compensations to be made. True?"

Denise couldn't hold his stare.

"Yes. There were."

"Hey," he reached out and raised her face with gentle fingers. "I'm no one to judge. Understand? We've all done things we wouldn't have done in other times. What I want to know is how much you want these people to continue being... friendly."

"They've got connections. I'll never get away from them."

"You will if you come with me. My connections are bigger than theirs."

He grinned and watched her calculate the options. It was a decision based on the need to survive, not on feelings – people made cold decisions like this every day now. If they were going to be friends that could come later. If they weren't, he'd make certain Denise was safe before he moved on.

"I want to get away from here," she said. "From *them*. I've got no reason to be here any more."

Gordon squeezed her hand and smiled.

"Good choice." He stood up. "You stay right there."

"I thought we were both going out."

"Now, that *would* be dangerous. Don't come into the garden, whatever happens. No matter what you see, OK?"

"But what if you don't... I mean–"

"Don't come out unless I call you, Denise. Do as I say and you'll be fine. Alright?"

She didn't respond.

Gordon pressed her back into the darkness and stepped into the pool of dull, wounded light seeping through the broken window. Out beyond the steps leading up to the wild garden stood the three survivors. Hungry, lean men with simple appetites and little patience. They must have been tough to have survived this long. Through earthquakes and disease, civil unrest and the unceasing round-up of suspects.

Perhaps they were in the pocket of the Ward. That made more sense; Denise had hinted that they had questionable connections. Whatever the case, Gordon had no regard for them. They'd used hard times as an excuse to live off other people's misery – certainly they'd used Denise for their own purposes. The fact that they'd given food and medicine in return for favours made her their possession, not a friend. He'd seen people like this all across the country, seen what they'd done in the name of "survival".

He felt a gathering within himself. Jolts of energy burst up through his feet into his belly and exploded out to his arms and hands. His vision went black for a moment as the obsidian fire ignited behind his eyes. An updraft pushed at him, sending broken glass and dust whirling. To the sound of a thousand pairs of black wings, he leapt up and out through the window.

17

Gordon pushed me back, away from the window and out of sight. But I saw it all. I don't know if I'll ever understand what happened next. I can only tell you how it looked to me. How it felt.

Before he moved, something happened around him; *to* him. The air in the room altered. He was framed in the dim light coming through the smashed basement window and in the space all around him there was this, I don't know exactly, call it restlessness. Agitation or something. The air *fluttered*. That's the only way I can describe it. It was like there was this energy all around him. I could feel it like a push from a strong wind. It made me take a step back.

The air around him blurred. The nearest thing I can compare it to is the movement of a flock of birds. Before all the changes, there used to be thousands of starlings around our block of flats. They often congregated on the pylons and then take off as one. They'd whirl and wheel in the sky, turning fast and coming around, blackening as they blocked the light and then spreading out and thinning as they changed direction in long sweeps. A murmuration; that's what it's called.

The way they flew always reminded me of nature programs about the ocean. They were like shoals of fish, flashing light and dark as they darted away from prey in the ocean. The air around Gordon Black was like that, invisible wings shimmered through it, flashed and darkened in a dozen directions. All I could think at the time was that the weather had suddenly changed. That the wind had blasted through the window and kicked up all the dust in the basement. But I knew it wasn't that really. It was something freaky. Gordon's murmuration. One of Flora's dreams coming true, God rest her sweet soul.

He didn't climb out through the window like the three Ds did – that's Darren, Dean and Danny, by the way – and he didn't jump either. He *flew*. I've never seen anyone move like that. He leapt forward and he took off and he sailed out into the garden like a cat with wings. The three Ds couldn't believe it either. I rushed to the window and I saw the looks on their faces as he landed.

He hadn't gone far; he still had to climb the steps from the basement up to the level of the garden. He didn't try to make it look fancy but something in the way he moved was beautiful and wild and they could all see it. I would never even have thought anything like this before meeting Gordon but all I can say to make it clear is that it was like an animal spirit had gone into him. He moved like something lithe and free, not like the chancers and deadbeats who lived in the city. He'd been on the road for three years by then but Gordon was strong and agile. It came off him in waves.

The three Ds were scared. I was scared too, truth be told. It wasn't like magic or anything but it was the strangest thing I'd ever seen. It wasn't what you'd call normal. Gordon Black wasn't what you'd call normal.

He walked up the steps to get on their level. They backed off until they were up against the thorns and weeds of the wild garden. He had his little knife in his hand. It's not much more than a penknife. Pathetic really. But it didn't look pathetic in his hand. It looked like a single, deadly claw. The three Ds all had their tools held out in front of them but they suddenly looked more like shields than weapons. I think they just wanted to keep him away.

"So," says Gordon, casual as anything. "What did you want to ask me?"

Darren must have had itchy feet or something. He had his machete held out like an accusing finger and he couldn't stand still.

"Who's in the ground?"

"That's Flora."

"What did you do to her?"

"She died of a fever."

"Bollocks."

"Don't take my word for it. Ask her mother."

"You've got Denise in there?"

I put my head up through the window at that point so Darren could see me. I've never seen him so angry. But he didn't know what to do about it.

"Did he hurt her, D?"

I was the fourth D. That was the nearest we ever got to a joke about the arrangement. It wasn't very funny. I shook my head.

"There was nothing anyone could have done," I says. "It was her time." And that made me cry, of course. And that pushed Darren right to the edge.

"Let her go," he says. "I want her out of there now."

"She can leave if she wants."

I didn't move. I just stood there crying. I wasn't going anywhere without Gordon Black.

"Look," says Gordon. "Denise doesn't want to be... associated with you gentlemen any more. I think she deserves a little dignity after all she's been through, don't you? I'm going to give you the opportunity to say your goodbyes but you must never come back to this place. Not to this house. Not to this garden and certainly not to this grave."

"Or what?" says Darren.

"I think it's a pretty fair deal as it stands. All you have to do is leave and not come back. That's it."

Darren looked at Gordon and then at me. He looked up at 257 and finally one small penny dropped.

"There's no one else in that house, is there? It's just you and her."

"I never said otherwise. What does it matter?"

I'm not sure he would have let them go, even if they'd turned around and walked away when he gave them the chance. I don't know if he tricked them into attacking or just pissed them off so much he knew they would. It's another one of those things I'll probably never know.

What happened was that Darren made the first move. He went on the offensive and Gordon took him to task. In these times, someone else making the first move is full justification. Always. I'm not sure it warranted the savagery of Gordon's response, though. All I can say is, at least it was quick. And I knew one thing for certain then. While Gordon Black was alive, I'd always be safe.

Yeah. That's what I thought I knew.

It took Gordon the rest of the day to inter the men Denise referred to as the three Ds.

He didn't do it to hide the bodies. Nor did he do it because of the smell they would make soon enough. He did it because shit was good for the ground. They would be food for the wild garden and perhaps this place would survive and thrive in the years to come. Gordon had visions of the plants bursting the brick walls on both sides and spilling into the neighbouring properties. As the years went by they would spread and ramble, joining with the plants in the park, taking root there and flourishing. It was a pleasant fantasy; something to counteract the knowledge that in many parts of the country nothing would now grow. Gordon buried the three Ds as his gift to the Earth and he prayed for his wild garden to spread and multiply. He prayed for a future.

That night he and Denise dined on tinned potatoes, tinned mushrooms and beef stew, sitting in armchairs Gordon had manoeuvred from other rooms and placed near his preferred cooking hearth. They ate from plates Denise had found in the kitchen cupboard, used bone-handled cutlery and drank water from glasses. She waited until Gordon had finished his meal before she spoke.

"Where did the lily and the feather come from?"

"Hm?"

"On Flora's grave."

"Oh, those. I found them."

"Where? I mean, the feather I can understand but where did you find a single white lily?"

"On the other side of the park there's a pond. It's stagnant but there was a patch of it that still had some life in it. The lily was there."

"Only one?"

"Just one."

"It was very thoughtful."

"She was a lovely child. I wish I'd done more."

"What do you mean?"

Gordon cleared his throat.

"I just wish there was more I could have done."

Denise was quiet for a time.

"Listen," said Gordon. "We can talk about something else if you want."

"No. It's OK. I don't want to pretend it hasn't happened. I don't want to act as though she was never here."

"I don't want you to be upset."

"The whole fucking world is upsetting. As if the disease and poverty and starvation isn't enough, there's violence everywhere. You killed three men today, Gordon."

"You've seen plenty of killings."

"Yes. I suppose I have."

"I had no option. If I'd done nothing they would have killed me. And then they'd have–"

"I know."

"And if they'd left, they'd have come back with others and we'd have had no chance."

Denise took a sip of water.

"No one ever stood up to them like that," she said. "They had a reputation."

"Did they operate alone?"

"No. They were muscle for a bigger fish."

Gordon clenched his teeth.

"We'll have to move on then. Those bigger fish will come looking for them."

"I know. I'm sorry."

"It's not your fault, Denise. But I'll miss number 257." Gordon stroked the worn fabric on the arm of his chair. "This is the nicest digs I've had in any city."

"What about finding the Crowman?"

"I can't find him if I'm dead. We'll have to get away from here. First light. Earlier if you can manage."

"Where can we go?"

"Into the countryside. Just for a while. If they don't find us in a few days, they'll give up. Revenge is a low priority when no one knows where their next meal is coming from."

Denise pushed her food around her plate with her fork.

"There's one other problem, Gordon."

"Uh huh."

"The group they were part of has links with the Ward. That's how they got some of their food."

Gordon massaged his temples with three fingers of each hand and took several deep breaths before looking up. He'd hoped his hunch about them was wrong.

"We need to leave."

"Tonight?"

"Right now."

It took Gordon a few minutes to choose what they needed most from their supplies. He went to find Denise. She was kneeling between two open suitcases and a few bags, crying in the candlelight.

"You need to decide quickly, Denise. Please."

"This is everything I own. Flora's clothes and some of her toys too. Things my mum gave me. I can't just leave it all here."

"You don't have a choice."

"Gordon," she looked up at him. "This is my life. I can't abandon it."

Gordon pushed his fingers back through his hair.

"Alright. Take out only what you need to survive. I'll look for a hiding place for everything else. You can always come back here and collect the stuff when things have calmed down."

"What if they find it?"

"This is the best I can do, Denise. If the Ward had anything to do with the three Ds, we'll be lucky to get away with our skins, let alone all this clobber."

Taking a candle, Gordon tore through the house, mounting each flight of stairs three at a time. None of the rooms had anything secure or unobtrusive to offer. When he reached the highest floor of the house there was small landing with an attic above. A small brass ring hung from the access hatch. Held against the wall by brackets was a boathook. When he hauled on the ring, the hatch opened and a set of aluminium pull-down stairs slipped into view. He hauled them the rest of the way down and climbed into the highest level of the house.

This was where Denise and Flora ought to have lived. It was vast. Loose boards overlaid thick insulation. The entire space was empty. He held his candle up into the gloom. Below the apex of the roof were sections of board resting on crossbeams. They looked like they'd been there since the house was constructed. If he could climb up, that was where Denise and Flora's belongings would be safest.

It took him three trips, two with each suitcase and one with two bags. When it was done, nothing could be seen from below except the old boards. He shut the hatch with the boathook and stashed it up the chimney of the fireplace in the nearest room while Denise looked on.

"Thank you," she said.

He smiled.

"Let's go."

As he slipped through the basement window and Denise handed him the bags, he heard the sounds of iron-shod hooves on tarmac.

"Quick," he whispered, putting his hands through and helping Denise out.

When she was standing beside him, she heard it too.

"Oh, Jesus."

"We can't go through the back gardens," said Gordon. "We'll run right into them. We'll have to try for the park. Come on."

He shouldered his pack, grabbed Denise's hand and pulled her up into the garden.

"We'll never get through all that," she hissed.

He drew her to the side wall and prayed to the spirits in the wild garden to let them pass easily. Though the thorns and brambles still plucked at their hair and clothes, they were able to edge around the perimeter with only a few scratches. When they reached the door in the back wall, Gordon mouthed a silent thank you to the garden and then yanked the door open. The hinges creaked in protest and they both cursed the noise.

"That way," whispered Gordon, urging Denise along the rat run of an alley.

At the dead end, he boosted her up onto the wall and handed up her bag.

"Can you see anyone in the park?" he asked.

She was quiet for a while.

"I think it's clear."

"OK. Move along a bit."

Gordon leapt high, grabbed the top of the wall and heaved himself up.

"That way," he said, pointing.

Behind them, the clatter of men on horseback was loud. The patrol knew exactly where to go. Before they'd even crossed the park, Gordon heard the Ward smashing their way through the back door of number 257. He knew it wouldn't take them long to realise he and Denise weren't coming back. At best, they had minutes to find their next refuge or lose themselves in a crowd. The Ward were getting smarter and quicker all time; it was almost as though they were anticipating him.

"Come on," Gordon whispered, taking Denise's hand and holding it tight.

"I'm going as fast as I can," she hissed.

"You have to go faster," he said, and, breaking from a jog into a run, he drew her on into the night.

18

The bed is warm and Megan is tangled tight in her clothes, blankets and furs, woven into them like a pupae in its cocoon. Scant grey light seeps around the edges of her bed-hood – a tried and tested combination of pillow and bedspread designed to prolong the night.

The scent of wood smoke is a subtle harbinger of morning by comparison to the knock and clang of Amu preparing breakfast for Apa in the kitchen. Megan wants only to close her eyes again and sleep all winter long. She would like to travel back through the weave, wake up the previous spring and somehow make that season last forever. That was a time before knowledge had made a mule of her, when magic was present but unspoken in everything she saw rather than the stone cold reality and vocation it had now become.

Sometimes the smell of eggs cooking in goose fat can overcome all world-weariness, and this is one of those times. After flailing around weakly, like an animal in a trap, Megan manages to free herself from her cosy prison and sits up on the edge of the bed. The air creeping in through every crack in the doors, windows and walls has pincers and its nipping wakes her further. She begins to recall her journey in the night country: the brave, dying child trapped in darkness until death; a girl who need do nothing to find the Crowman but wait for him in her stinking sickbed. Even so, the little girl's illness seemed a terribly high price to pay.

Megan slips to the floor, looks under her bed and puts her hands on the box, remembering the gift the little girl gave her. She hesitates. The loss of that gift will be like a cut to a trusting, outstretched hand but she must check.

"Megan! If you want any breakfast you'd better be quick. Your father's got an appetite this morning."

The voice from just the other side of her door makes her jump. She hadn't heard her mother approach.

"I'll be right through, Amu."

She readies herself for what she knows will be a disappointment and lifts the lid. The book rests where she left it. She peeks underneath. Nothing. She raises it up to see if somehow the paper has stuck to the leather of the back cover. It hasn't. Megan dumps the book back into its box and mutters a small curse. Even though she knew nothing would be there, she is weakened by the truth. The girl's gift, so powerful a symbol, so beautiful a piece of work, has not survived the journey through the weave. Now it is nothing more than a half-memory; not real in the first place and even less so now.

Something about the girl and the obvious tragedy of her tiny, painful existence touches her still. It's as though Megan herself were once a prisoner of darkness and disease, sometime long ago, and as hard as walking the Black Feathered Path can sometimes be, she knows that this life is a beautiful reward, an existence most folk can barely imagine, such is the depth of its passion and beauty.

She can't help but release a sigh of loss, and what little enthusiasm she has for the day ahead rushes away with her expelled breath.

"Portions are dwindling, Meg!"

"Coming, Amu."

Her father is at the table eating with great concentration and enjoyment. A thick slice of bread, heavily buttered, with a still steaming fried egg laid on top. This he accompanies with Amu's spiced gooseberry and apple chutney, the afterburn of which is not to Megan's taste.

"Morning, Meg," says her father through a mouthful.

"Morning, Apa."

"Sleep well?"

"Not bad, I suppose. A few dreams."

"Thought so. I heard you muttering at some strange hour."

"Sorry, Apa."

He leans across the table and pats her arm with real affection.

"Don't you worry about it. We know how important it is, what you're doing. Not just for you but for everyone hereabouts. And we're proud of you, Meg, in case you didn't know. Very proud indeed."

Surely that isn't a tear in the corner of her father's eye.

Is it?

He's already back into his eggs and when Megan looks at her mother, she has turned away to the stove. A few moments later a fried egg, on a thinner piece of bread with less butter, arrives in front of her. She eats it slowly and long before she finishes, her father is up and out of the door to check the fields and animal traps, pecking her mother briefly through his yolk-stained beard as he rushes to be away.

Megan thanks her mother for breakfast and takes a cup of lemon balm tea with her back into her room. She sits at her table, staring out of the window at nothing in particular. To remind herself of the work she has done, she withdraws the black box from its resting place. Placing it before her on the table, she opens it, removes the book and flicks its thick, luxurious pages. Somehow she has filled up two thirds of the volume with her neat handwriting.

It's strange. She's unaware of how and when she's done all this work but there it is right in front of her. And though the Crowman somehow speaks through every page, he has not yet made a genuine appearance in the boy's life. He is always a tantalising step ahead of Gordon. But Megan knows, if only from the dwindling number of blank pages left in the book, that the moment in which he'll discover the Crowman is finally within Gordon's reach.

She turns to the last page she wrote and there she stops, frozen, not breathing.

The little girl's drawing of the Crowman is there. *Inside* the book. Not on a separate page inserted among the existing leaves but on the page following the last one she wrote.

She stares.

It is the same drawing, exact in every detail. Megan covers her mouth to stifle a small cry. She turns over the page, expecting nothing more but unable to prevent herself from checking the other side of it. There is another drawing, by the same artist.

It depicts a small mound of freshly turned soil, surrounded by tiny flowers and hidden amidst a thicket of weed and thorn. Megan knows instantly whose resting place this is. The little girl who was so alive in spite of her sickness has been dead for generations, but to Megan, who only met her for the first time a few hours ago, her sudden loss is like a kick to the solar plexus. For long moments she can't breathe. Worse than losing the little girl is the thought that perhaps her own journey through the weave, back to that dark, dirty room, was the catalyst for the girl's demise.

Even as she has these thoughts, Megan can see the stupidity and confusion she's allowing to rule her mind. Both the girl and her drawing are part of the Crowman's story now. They are in the book. And that must mean there's some reason for it that she isn't yet able to see.

Megan feels an absence coming over her as she tries to make sense of it all but she rebels against the feeling, knowing the weave will draw her back if she lets it. For now, she must be alert. She folds the black book shut, stows it in its box and pushes under her bed so she can prepare for her return to New Wood.

19

Gordon led Denise north.

Once they were on the main roads out of London there was enough foot traffic that they were almost anonymous amongst it. People arrived en masse, still believing London was the place that would save them. Greater numbers, educated by experience, were leaving. But even here among the itinerant masses, Gordon sensed the Ward's eyes everywhere.

Humanity looked very different now. Nothing anyone wore was new. Those with the skills and the materials patched the clothes they had or made new ones out of what they'd found. People still wanted to look like they cared, though, and their clothes, no matter how shabby with dirt and wear, reflected this. Fashions developed as people travelled, sleeves long enough to cover the hands or act as gloves were popular. In their hair, many people wore strips of colour-coded cloth in remembrance of loved ones lost to disease, starvation or the violence of the Ward. Memorial ribbons were often cut from the clothes of the departed. The numbers of ribbon wearers and the variety of colours they wore spoke silently of how many had died.

A hat was a practical item, and everyone seemed to wear one these days. They kept off the dust and they kept off the rain. Battered, peakless baseball caps and sombreros bought as a joke on a holiday in a past that might never have existed. Bleached-out fedoras. Torn bobble hats. A fez. Feathers often adorned both hats and lapels. Some people wore them hanging from bands at their elbows and knees. The feathers were grey mostly, either from dead pigeons or white feathers grimed by the dirt and dust of the road.

Many of the men wore bi-colour coats or jackets, really one half of two different coats sewn together. Shoes were the greatest indicator of luck or status. Many walked barefoot. Others wore plastic bags over layers of newspaper. Gordon had learned to resole and repair his own boots with animal skin but there were few others who had the knack of it.

Like many others, Gordon wore a cowl – the simplest of head coverings – but in his case it was to disguise his head and face. The Ward turned up regularly along the roads, watching the travellers struggle under the burden of their most valuable possessions. Those were the ones who were most often stopped. The Wardsmen would rob them in plain view and either send them on their way or take them into the nearest substation. No one resisted or protested. They merely walked faster and kept their heads down.

Sometimes, mounted patrols came along the road, right through the ranks of itinerants. It was the patrols coming out of London that Gordon and Denise did their best to avoid. When they heard the sound of hooves, they would move to the edge of the thoroughfare and huddle into the thickest stream of departing traffic. Sometimes they turned and headed back into town; the mounted patrols weren't watching the incoming tide. Once a patrol had passed, they'd rejoin the northbound streams. In this way, they made it to the M1.

Denise seemed to think that was enough of an achievement.

"My feet are killing me. Can we find somewhere to stop?"

"Not yet."

"I can't keep going for much longer."

"Yes you can. Set a new target."

"Like what?"

"Like the first service station."

"That's miles away."

"The first exit, then."

"When we get there you'll just say we have to keep going."

Gordon laughed.

"Yes, I probably will."

"I'm serious. I can't keep walking like this. If I do, I won't be able to walk at all tomorrow."

Gordon looked at her. She did appear to be suffering.

"Do you have blisters?"

"Yes."

"How bad?"

"They've all popped. It's really sore."

Gordon looked around. The foot traffic had spread out and, though he hadn't really noticed it before, many travellers were resting or sleeping on the grass verges. Further up the embankments people were relieving themselves in the cover of the roadside shrubs and bushes.

"Come on," he said, leading her to a space at the bottom of the grass verge.

He got Denise to sit down and squatted in front of her. She winced as he unlaced her filthy battered trainers and put them beside him. The fabric of her socks, no telling when they'd last been washed, was damp with fluid from the blisters and there were several watery bloodstains. Her feet were crusted with grime and smelled bad. If he didn't do something, she ran the risk of infection.

"How do they look?" she asked.

"Oh, not too bad." He left her socks on. Already the Black Light was swelling at his fingertips. He shut down all but the tiniest beads of it. "I think you could do with a bit of a foot rub, though."

"Don't do it hard, Gordon. They really hurt."

"Relax. I've done this before."

He stroked rather than massaged her left foot, nauseous with the power of the Black Light but keeping it almost totally staunched. Her foot jerked away from him and he looked up.

"Tickles."

"Sorry, I'll be firmer."

It took only seconds for the Black Light to do its work but Gordon continued with the "massage" to make it convincing. He did the same with her right foot before replacing her trainers.

"We need to get you some new footwear," he said. "These aren't going to last much longer. That's probably why your feet are so sore." He stood up. "See how you are now."

She rose to her feet without much enthusiasm and took a couple of experimental steps.

"Wow. They feel great. What did you do?"

"Uh, acupressure."

"Really? Where did you learn that?"

"I... read about it in a book."

"Well, you missed your calling, Gordon. You could set up a booth right here and make a fortune. I could drum up trade for you. We'd be rich in no time."

"Yeah. And we'd be stuck here in Brent Cross forever."

Denise turned away from him.

"I wasn't being serious."

Gordon went to her and reached out but at the last moment didn't touch her. He didn't know where to put his hand, didn't know how to make contact. His hand fell to his side.

"I'm sorry," he said. "We have to keep moving."

"Yes. I know."

She set off, her pace faster than it had been all day, real power in her footsteps. Gordon rubbed his fingers against his palms, made fists and then shook his hands out. The Black Light was gone again, leaving him a gut full of sickness. At least he'd let some of it through this time – it wouldn't do to puke a cascade of dark, evanescent oil in public. He hurried after her, knowing she'd have enough energy to walk until nightfall; beyond if necessary. As soon as they made it into the broader countryside, he'd get them away from the road and onto the land. Then things would be easier.

Before he caught up to Denise, Gordon looked back, certain he was being watched. There was nothing untoward in the faces of the dispossessed that stumbled from the capital; nothing but the look of hopelessness and defeat they all shared. And yet, Gordon couldn't shake the sense that someone among the travellers was following them.

20

Somewhere above the smoggy clouds a full moon glared down. The thick vapours cloaked and a diffused much of the light but it afforded Gordon and Denise the ability to see a few steps in front. Long before darkness fell, everyone else on the motorway had stopped walking in order to find a place for the night. Prime locations were the level ground nearest the hard shoulder, away from the open latrines that the higher verges had become.

Gordon and Denise kept walking until there was no one else travelling the motorway, their footsteps loud in the night. All around them people snored, grumbled and whispered. The fortunate ones lit camping stoves to brew tea or cook soup, but most slept without the luxury of supper or a hot drink. When all the portable fires were out and the only sounds were of exhausted travellers breathing deeply or whimpering in their sleep, Gordon began to look for a less populated place to stop.

"I'd rather keep walking and get off the motorway at first light if we don't find anywhere safe," he said. "It's impossible to know who else is out here."

Denise didn't answer him. She just kept walking.

About an hour later, Gordon saw a break in the hard

shoulder: not an exit to a road or a service station, something else. They stepped carefully between the sleeping bodies and walked away from the motorway. They were on some kind of road but Gordon couldn't tell what it was. Soon they came to a steel gate designed to stop cars. There were signs on either side of the gate and across it. Gordon could just make out the words:

No Entry for Motorway Traffic. Motorway Maintenance Vehicles Only.

They ducked under the gate and walked on until the road widened, bringing them into a vast forecourt. Gordon could see the faint shapes of abandoned diggers, bulldozers and other road repair vehicles parked around the perimeter. Right in the centre stood a lorry. It looked relatively clean and new, as though only recently parked.

Gordon glanced around before approaching but stayed at a cautious distance while he did a complete circuit of the vehicle. The trailer was open on both sides where the curtains of plastic had been pulled back on their runners. There was nothing in the back. Leaving the driver door shut, Gordon climbed the two steps to the cab to peep inside. It, too, looked empty.

He turned to Denise who stood with her arms folded.

"What do you think?" he asked.

"I think it's a bloody joke."

"This is probably the safest, most comfortable place to sleep on the M1. Do you want me to open it?"

She didn't answer.

"Listen, Denise, you're exhausted. I know it looks rank but this is your best bet of a decent night's sleep."

When it was clear she wasn't going to speak to him, he tried the door. It opened easily causing him to lose his balance and jump back down. No alarm went off. He stepped back and put his head inside. The air was old. No one had opened the cab for a long time and there was no one inside. He saw litter on the floor: an old paper coffee cup and an empty packet of cigarettes. Some screwed up fuel receipts. That was all.

"It looks fine," he said. He leaned down and held out his hand. "Come up. We'll get you comfortable and then I'll leave you in peace."

After a few moments Denise climbed the ladder without taking his hand and pushed past him. Above the seats there was a simple bunk. Gordon found a couple of blankets tucked into a small storage space. The cab smelled of stale cigarette smoke and the blankets smelled of sweat and diesel. But they were in better shelter now than anyone else and relatively protected too. Denise pulled the curtains across the windows but Gordon stopped her.

"You need to be able to see what's happening out there."

She pulled her wrist away.

"Is there anything else I can do?" he asked.

She didn't speak.

"Alright. I'll be nearby and I'll keep an eye on you. Tap on the glass if you need anything. Anything. Got it?"

For a while he thought she would simply ignore him. He reached for the handle.

"Wait. Don't go."

"What is it?"

"Look, I'm sorry. OK?"

"There's nothing to be sorry for."

He opened the door and stepped down.

"Seriously, Gordon. Don't go yet. I have to say something."

He let the cab door swing closed but didn't shut it. Denise looked at him, her eyes wet by the cab's dim interior light.

"I'm grateful for everything you've done even if I have trouble showing it. I'm not angry with you and I don't hate you. It's just that…"

"What?"

She met his eyes.

"Everything was fine before you came along. The first moment I saw you there was trouble and there's been trouble ever since."

"I know. I'm sorry, too, Denise. Let me get you somewhere safe and then I'll leave you alone. I promise."

"Oh, Gordon, that's not what I mean. That's not what I'm saying at all. I want to travel with you but you have to understand that I… can't help being freaked out sometimes. Since I met you, I've lost everything."

What could he say to that? No words existed. No apology was appropriate enough. In the end he said only:

"I hear what you're telling me, Denise. I'll see you in a few hours."

He turned to go and this time she grabbed his arm.

"Don't leave me alone. Please don't ever leave me alone."

From so far within her came all the tears she ought to have cried but never could in front of Flora, the same tears that wouldn't come when they laid her little girl to rest.

"Don't leave me, don't leave me, don't leave me…"

The chant went on and on, mumbled and blurted through fresh cascades of tears as the grief poured from her. The shitty past, the hopeless present, the non-existent future; her tears for all of it came rushing forth.

Some time later – it felt like hours – he lifted her into the bunk, pulled the cab door properly closed and locked them in. He crawled in beside Denise and pulled the blankets over them while she wept herself to sleep. He wanted to caress her then, to stroke her and put his hands underneath her clothes. It was fear that paralysed his hands; fear of their association causing her yet more pain, fear of losing control of his emotions, fear of trusting. He held her tight, instead, praying she wouldn't know his thoughts through the language of touch and wondering if he could even trust himself.

The two men sat in their cramped accommodation on the top floor of the Fulham Substation. Skelton held a recently drawn map of the country in one hand. It showed the areas where the Ward was supreme and those where the Green Men controlled the population. The spread of territory was vastly in the Ward's favour; grey now covered about seventy percent of the land.

Pike sat in a threadbare, coverless armchair staring into space; as though somehow on hold. Unable to concentrate on the map, Skelton admired him. Somewhere inside that chiselled cadaverous head, wheels and gears were in motion; the tiny engine of will which powered the huge, living automaton that was Mordaunt Pike. Whenever that fire of that will was ignited, Pike became an engine of destruction. Absently, Skelton touched himself at the groin for a moment. As soon he became aware of it, he took his hand away again.

There were other things to think about. Their change of approach had already paid some dividends. Gordon Black had been making his mischief across southwest London and now Skelton knew, almost exactly, where he was. All they had to do was maintain contact from a restrained, unobtrusive distance. The boy would lead them where they needed to go. And after that, well…

Skelton's left eye itched – or rather the place where his

left eye had been itched – giving the fingers of his right hand something better to do than dally at his crotch.

He'd used a glass eye for a few months until supplies of the lubricant which stopped it sticking to his eyelids ran out. For a while he tried cooking oil and then gave up. On a day when Gordon Black had been off the radar so long they thought they'd lost him forever, Skelton had almost thrown the eye into a canal in disgust. Then a piece of news had come in linking the boy to a flood and subsequent outbreak of typhoid.

Where the Crowman had walked; that was where they always found him. A couple of their agents within the Green Men had then been able to follow Gordon south towards London. Instead of throwing his glass eye away that day, Skelton had it set into the handle of a walking cane and gave it to Pike, whose limp had worsened steadily in the three years since their tangle with the boy.

He scratched the sunken membrane over his left socket but the itch was deeper inside than that. The eyelids had fused together over time, their lashes knitting into an ugly, spiky mesh and the lips of skin behind them melding. The muscles around the orbit were still alive, however, and the eyeless place twitched and flickered whenever Skelton was agitated or vibrated like a loose drum-skin when he was deep in thought.

Sometimes Skelton closed his good eye. With it shut, he was convinced he could still receive visual messages through the empty socket. The physical eye was gone but the energy of the eye persisted and it saw only energy. When he was calm, he could sense things about people and, very occasionally, the eye showed him where to send his men for Gordon Black. It had been almost right on a number of occasions.

Now, of course, the cat and mouse game had altered somewhat. Direct confrontations had proved costly and unsuccessful. Nor was questioning the boy of any real importance any more. What Skelton needed was to be aware of Gordon Black and his movements until the boy led them to what he'd described to Pike as "a suitable location". This time, any confrontation – if that was what it came to – would be a very different affair. The change of tactics had angered Pike. It had come close to driving a wedge between them but Skelton knew it was the best operational decision he'd made.

"This is the prudent way to eliminate the Crowman, Pike," he'd said on the day of the policy change.

Pike had rumbled a wordless disagreement.

"Subtlety's the way forward, my man. And patience," Skelton had said. "We'll have our retribution all the same, believe me."

"If I held his head between my palms..." Pike had demonstrated, making a vice of his hands. "...I could crush it very slowly. I'd be patient *then*, Archibald." He'd mouthed the sounds of bone splintering and then eased off the pressure. "I'd certainly take my time." Pike had pretended to look into the eyes of his imagined captive. "You can still think, can't you, boy? You can still hear your own skull rupturing, eh? Good." He'd looked up at Skelton. "I should like to watch his lights go out very slowly. I should like him to be acutely aware that I am the one who's putting those lights out, one hairline crack at a time until his head..." Pike had slammed his palms together in a thunderclap.

Skelton had jumped a little but permitted himself a grin before saying:

"I'm sure the anticipation will make it all the more satisfying."

And now that day might suddenly not be very far away.

Pike's hollowed-out eyes stared forwards. There was no hint of what ideas he harboured inside that ironclad cranium. Skelton was sure the thoughts were simple enough: plans for destruction in the name of the Ward, in the name of a future for all humanity. What would their positions be in that new world? Skelton had often imagined it. Their part in the tracking of Gordon Black and the subsequent capture of the Crowman, their prevention of the end of the world; all this would be rewarded, he was certain, with even greater power than they already possessed.

Except, of course, that Skelton didn't believe in the Crowman any more. Three years of pursuing Gordon Black, and many more spent studying the so-called prophecies of thousands of ordinary people, had taught him a few simple truths. The Crowman was nothing more than a ideological figurehead, a phantasmal icon revered by those with nothing left to hope for.

Nor did Skelton believe that the Crowman would trigger Armageddon. No, responsibility for that would remains squarely upon humanity's shoulders. The only real significance the Crowman possessed related to the morale of the people. Without their black-feathered champion, they would be broken. They would no longer resist. All Skelton had to do was use the people's imaginary hero against them. And he was fairly certain that he'd discovered the way to do it.

His greatest satisfaction, though, would be in seeing Gordon Black finally brought to justice for his crimes and in seeing a new world ruled by the grey hand of the Ward. Skelton had no doubt that he and Pike would be kings in that new world. They would be kings because without them the new world would not have had the chance to exist.

He leaned across to his giant companion, still lost in the dim circuitry of his own head, and placed his plump, pale hand on Pike's bunched thigh. The massive, skull-like head turned towards him. As always there was a moment of hesitation and discomfort written in those grey and otherwise unreadable eyes. This thrilled and terrified Skelton in equal measure. While their eyes remained locked, a vast, cold palm sank onto the back of Skelton's hand.

He stiffened at the power of Pike's dreadful touch, his heart stuttering as it accelerated.

21

The mood amongst travellers on the M1 was completely different as Gordon and Denise continued north the following morning. For a while it was enough to distract him from the sense that someone, somewhere, was watching him. On the opposite carriageway, they noticed people smiling and throngs on both sides of the central reservation buzzed with excited whispers.

He put his hand out to Denise and slowed their pace a little as he tried to catch the gist of what people were saying. Voices were muted, though, and hearing what was said was close to impossible.

"What is it?" asked Denise.

"I don't know exactly. Can you tell what everyone's talking about?"

She shook her head. Before Gordon could say a word to stop her she was talking to a member of a group of skinny teenage boys walking just ahead of them. Gordon hadn't considered it too carefully – it was one of the things that sometimes made him feel like he was a visitor from another planet – but Denise was very pleasant to look at. The lads in front of him welcomed her into their group and she soon had them laughing.

Gordon hung back. If they realised Denise wasn't travelling alone, they might not be so cooperative. Their chatter became raucous and lewd and Gordon felt his cheeks scalded with sudden anger. It shocked him.

Hell, I'm jealous of them.

He shook his head and laughed at himself but the anger didn't leave. Even when Denise's fact-finding operation was complete and she fell back to walk with him again, even when the lads up ahead had looked back and realised she was already accompanied the sensation didn't pass.

Gordon couldn't listen to what she was telling him at first. He was too busy staring down any of the boys – probably his age or a little younger – who looked back. Everyone was an opportunist now. Everyone was desperate. Under the Ward, the country was more lawless than it had ever been. Ahead the boys gestured and joked amongst themselves. Gordon set his face against their derision and kept walking.

Beside him Denise had gone quiet.

"What?" he asked.

"Have you heard anything I've just said to you?"

"Sorry. No. I was… miles away."

She gave him a look he'd seen many times in the days since they'd met. Some mix of disapproval and mistrust. It passed quickly but it left him wondering if they'd ever get past the experiences they'd shared or find any comfort in travelling together. He came to the conclusion he always came to, the one that had made a hermit of him: he was better off alone.

"There's talk of war," said Denise in the end.

"There's always talk of war. It gives people something to cling to."

"No. This is different. Not so much a war as a battle. People are saying the Green Men are going to march on one of the Ward's strongholds."

"If the people on this road know that, you can be certain the Ward know it too. It's not the first time this has happened."

"I know it isn't. But there's a real energy to this. Can't you feel it?"

He shrugged.

"I suppose so. But does that really mean anything? I'd rather keep my mind clear of maybes than have hope and lose it. I've been through that too many times."

"Do you think I haven't? I'm telling you, Gordon. There's something different about this."

"Alright."

They walked in silence for a while. Maybe what Denise was saying was true. Maybe there would be some kind of decisive blow against the Ward. As much as people seemed to be divided over the Crowman, they hated the Ward more; the Ward were a real danger to everyone, every day. You could see them and their brutality with your own eyes. There was no need for rumours. Gordon guessed most of the people walking on this road had been hurt by the Ward in some way or another. And even though the Ward were the sworn enemies of the Crowman and even though they promised to stop the world from ending, it wasn't enough to make anyone love or trust them.

Thank the Great Spirit for that, thought Gordon.

My eyes only,

Travelling north now with Denise. Someone's "with" us, I'm sure, but I haven't seen them yet. Almost worse than that, though, is all this talk of war. This is not the way to rid our world of the

Ward. The Green Men, even though they form the beating heart of our nation – its true heart – are a limited force. They must work in secret and are constantly infiltrated by Ward agents posing as dissidents. Sending out counterpart spies into Ward Substations is far harder and comes with much greater risk to the movement. The Green Men are poorly equipped, starving, badly organised and often divided in their ideologies. the Ward are well fed, have the best weapons and even a few vehicles. They are also organised into a hierarchy and share one simple belief – that they must find and destroy the Crowman. Do that and they've destroyed the hope of the people. They may say they're saving the world by killing the Crowman but I don't think they really believe that for a moment. He's nothing more than a threat to their plans of total control. If anything, they seem to understand the Crowman better than the Green Men who, like me, still can't decide if he is a real person or some kind of "force" that exists in nature.

And to cap all this, every wild-eyed man – young or old – who suddenly has something to believe in because war is the only thing that makes sense to them, all of them ask me:

"Will you fight?"

As though I haven't fought the Ward since the very first time they hurt me and my family with their twisted, power-hungry intentions. As though I haven't parted their spirits from their bodies more times than I can count. When I find them bumbling so loudly and stupidly through the woods, thinking they're using the land as cover. Or when I see one in a town somewhere, walking alone; as though I haven't dragged him into some broken alley or smashed building and cut his throat so that his blood can leak down through the shattered concrete to feed the ground. As though I haven't breached a dozen Substations in the dead of night, just to claim a couple more and do my bit. As though I haven't faced them down, four or six at a time when they've caught up with me or come across me by accident. These ragged starveling boys and husks of men, suddenly joyful and wet-eyed at the idea of battle, they ask me this as though I ran away whenever I was outnumbered.

But there's no explaining such things to people in times like these. Perhaps such things can never be explained. Saying "I've killed more Wardsmen than you've got fleas" won't go down too well. No one would believe me anyway.

So I say:

"Yes. I'll fight."

And they clap me on the shoulder, believing another man has come to swell their now unbeatable, unstoppable ranks. It's easier to say yes than it is to fight the people who you hope will inherit the earth. It's easier and smarter to say yes and not be branded a coward by the ignorant.

Denise smiles when they ask and each time I say I'll fight. I say it the same way everyone else does even though half of them don't really mean it. What they mean is they'll be there in spirit even though this isn't really their fight. They'll support it. They'll cheer from the sidelines. People, even the most well-meaning, are all about subtext. You'll never know what they really mean until you learn to read their eyes. Walking the highways of this land has given me that much skill if not much else.

But I want Denise to be happy. Especially now and for as long as it's possible to hold such a feeling in her heart. The truth is, I'll never stop owing her. Her daughter brought me as close to the Crowman as I've ever been and I let her die. The debt is not one I'm able to repay – whether I'm telling the truth about fighting alongside the Green Men or not.

When he could stand the questions no longer from almost every stranger on the motorway, and the very moment there was true countryside on both sides of the road instead of disused logistics terminals and decaying, abandoned suburbs, Gordon took Denise's hand and led her to the hard shoulder.

"What is it?" she asked.

"We're going bush."

"What?"

"We need to get off this road, get some food and find some shelter."

Denise looked across the landscape, frowning.

"There's nothing to eat out there. And there's nowhere to sleep."

Gordon placed his hands gently on her shoulders and looked into her eyes.

"Yes," he said. "There is. And it'll be easier to shake whoever's following us."

Denise glanced down the embankment, back the way they'd come.

"I haven't noticed anyone," she said.

"Neither have I. If we head into the countryside now, we may not have to worry about it any more. the Ward don't do so well off the beaten track."

He hauled her up to the edge of the grass verge where the shrubs and open latrines began.

"I'm not walking through *that*."

"Fine."

He picked her up and she shrieked in surprise.

"Put me down."

But Gordon was amid the shit already, picking his way between turds historic and modern.

"Don't you dare drop me."

He broke a rare smile. It felt good.

They reached a low fence and Gordon placed her down gently on the other side before climbing over. The land was

not as green as it once was and there were patches where
it appeared utterly grey and dead. But Gordon knew better.
He knew the soil underneath was waiting. Biding its time.
The trees were leafless; mourning it seemed to him, and the
expanse before them was silent and still.

"There's nothing out here," said Denise.

And he found himself wondering how many people
believed that, even before everything started to go downhill.
Maybe that was the real reason it had happened.

Gordon didn't bother to answer her this time. He just
started walking and pretty soon he knew she was following
him; like a kid who doesn't want to walk but doesn't want to
be left behind alone.

He thought again about the "war". It wouldn't be a war.
It would be a battle. Perhaps there'd be a few. And when the
Ward had slaughtered a couple of hundred thousand more
weak, ill-disciplined Green Men, they'd finally have the
nation in a total stranglehold. Because one more defeat was
all it would take to completely destroy the will of the people.

And the people were walking right into it.

22

Mr Keeper isn't in the clearing nor is he in his roundhouse so, having knocked a few times, Megan sits down on a log outside the door to wait for him. Whilst this has become more of a home than her parents' cottage, she is wary of entering without her teacher present.

After a few moments of shivering in the frosty morning air, she rises and checks the wind-eye. It's open, as always, and she peeps into the darkness. She can see where Mr Keeper usually sits, and the space is unoccupied but it's impossible to see much of anything else. She supposes he might be sleeping or deep in one of his trances. He probably wouldn't want her to disturb him in either case. Still, she wants – needs – to talk to him.

She calls through the wind-eye in a soft whisper.

"Mr Keeper? It's Megan."

There's no reply.

"Are you in there?

Still nothing.

Sighing, her breath lingering in the cold air, she walks away from the roundhouse and inspects the perimeter of the clearing. No movement. Looking back she notices a thin updraft of almost colourless smoke rising from his chimney.

Mr Keeper always seems to know when she's returning; as though he's watched her through the weave the whole time. She's sure he can't be far away.

With nothing better to do, she saunters around the edge of the clearing. There's nothing to take her attention and no sign of Mr Keeper among the nearest pine trees. A few minutes of leisurely walking brings her back to where she started. She sits on the log again and a few moments later tuts a few times, rises and lets herself into the roundhouse.

The heat is delicious around her and she takes her usual place on the mats, not feeling any real guilt about trespassing; this is a place she can call home as much as her mother and father's cottage and she knows Mr Keeper won't mind her being here.

She sits, soaking up the warmth and relaxing. The many days of writing have taken more of her energy than she realised and soon her head begins to nod. With nothing to do but wait she lies down, pulling one of Mr Keeper's woollen rugs over her.

Just for a little while, she tells herself. Just until he gets back.

Megan wakes with a start knowing it isn't minutes but hours that have past. The cast of the light through the wind-eye is different, the feel of the day much altered. For some reason she can't understand she feels guilty sleeping like this and her heart is beating too fast.

The temperature in the roundhouse has dropped and she checks the stove. Only a few dim embers remain in its round black belly. Unnerved by the way she has allowed the day get away from her, Megan scuttles out to the wood pile and returns with fuel. Small slivers of wood and bark to catch the flame and larger pieces to re-awaken it to its previous heat.

Within a few minutes she has the fire roaring and she uses the crooked iron bar to close the stove's little hatch. She adjusts the draw, slowing the rate of burn. It doesn't take long for the roundhouse to come back to a comfortable temperature.

She looks around. The place is untidy and dirty. It's unlike Mr Keeper to leave things like this; he tends to clean everything up as he goes along and messes don't happen in the first place. She moves around in the warm gloom putting things in their proper positions by remembering where he reaches for items. It's a small space and tidying it takes no time. Next, she takes a straw brush and sweeps the tightly woven mats until she has a pile of dust and other tiny leavings. She brushes them into a pan and hoists them out of the wind-eye towards the tobacco-stained cairn of debris where Mr Keeper spits and where animals, worms and birds forage for discarded nutriment.

She inspects the hanging bundles of drying herbs, taking down those which can now be stored in hessian pouches, and when there is nothing more she can do for the upkeep of the roundhouse she takes a mixture of sage and pine needles and sets fire to them in one of Mr Keeper's small ceremonial bowls. The smoke rises in thick clots. With a large black feather, she wafts their scent around the inside of the roundhouse muttering blessings and asking for purification. She passes the bowl around her own body too, incanting and inhaling, cleansing herself and the space. When the bowl is spent and its ash cold, she adds a pinch of it to a drinking bowl and throws the rest out of the wind-eye. She pours water over the grains of ash in the bowl and drinks the resultant grey tea.

Finally, she slips out of the roundhouse to gather mushrooms for their supper.

Some of the fields were so dead-looking the earth was grey.

Gordon knelt from time to time to hold the dust of it in his hand. He let it fall from his fingers, sometimes like ash, sometimes like sand. Either way, nothing would grow in that earth. Not every part of every field was dead, though. Some strips and corners remained green and had long since turned to meadow. There the grass was long and interspersed with all manner of wild plants and weeds. There too, Gordon knew, small animals had made their homes or taken shelter. Seeds waited there for a spring that had taken too long to come. Whether the people survived or not, those seeds would still be waiting in a generation, ready for the seasons to return. Each time Gordon touched the long grasses that grew in those islands of life, a thrill of anticipation ran up into his chest, quickening his heartbeat, quickening his pace.

Denise, who had dragged her heels from the moment they left the motorway, fell further behind at those moments. These were the times she would call out to him.

"Where's the bloody fire?"

"What?"

"Why are we *running*, Gordon?"

"We're not running, we're just…"

And he'd be off again before he could put it into words.

After a while, though, it became clear that Denise really couldn't take the pace. The land had been flat when they first left the motorway. Now it was beginning to roll a little. She would catch up on the gentle downhill slopes but the inclines were wearing her down. Gordon scanned the landscape for what he wanted and saw it about a mile away.

He turned back and shouted to Denise.

"We're nearly there."

She struggled for enough breath to respond.

"Nearly where?"

"Somewhere we can stop."

"I don't need a special place. I can stop right here."

"I mean a place where we can camp."

"Camp? I hate camping."

Gordon watched Denise puff her way up a hill he'd barely noticed was there.

"Well, what else would you call sleeping and eating outdoors?"

She caught up to him.

"I don't know," she said. "When you mentioned food and shelter I just assumed there might be… I don't know, an old farmhouse or something."

"Buildings attract attention. Everyone's looking for buildings. They're not safe."

"Are you saying we're just going to lie down and sleep on the ground?"

"No. But we're not staying a in a bloody hotel either." Gordon turned and set off again. She didn't follow. "Come on, Denise, there's a lot to do before we can eat."

"I'm knackered. I can't walk any more."

He looked at her face. She believed what she was telling him. The truth was, she *could* walk farther. A lot farther. If their lives depended on it, she could probably run another five or ten miles before collapsing. This didn't strike him as the time to be proving a point, however.

"I'll carry you," he said.

"No way."

"It's not far."

"That's all you ever say, 'it's not far'."

He pointed.

"It really isn't. See that bit of woodland down there?"

"Yeah."

"That's where we're going. Can you walk that far? If you can't, I'll carry you."

"Ha. You might be able to pick me up, but you couldn't carry me fifty yards."

Gordon's smile was sly.

"What will you bet me, then – that I can carry you the whole way?"

"I've got nothing to bet with."

"Fine," said Gordon. "Make it a sportsman's bet."

He held out his hand. Denise shook it.

She was in his arms and off the ground before she could resist.

"Hey! I'm not ready."

Gordon didn't answer. He ran. And Denise screamed.

The world fell silent. All he knew was the joy of the power in his muscles and Denise's fists battering against him in mock terror. He felt the wind rush past his ears and the thumping strength in his heart. A mile away, the distance shortening to the flying of his feet, the trees called out their quiet beckoning. No sound came in through his ears; their voices were already inside him.

Return, brother, to sit among us once more.

He grinned.

It could have been the wind in his face forcing tears from his eyes.

How he'd missed the land. How he'd missed the trees.

••••

Denise stopped struggling and clung to his neck, watching the brightness behind Gordon's eyes grow stronger. She'd been certain he would drop her – worse, fall on top of her – but she could feel the raw power in his arms and legs. He was thin and tall but his ragged clothes hid a strength unlike any she'd known. She'd never touched a man with this much life in him. He was elemental.

His delight at running free through the open land spread into her. By the time they reached the trees, with Gordon barely out of breath, she was smiling as broadly as he.

He dodged through the trunks and over fallen logs and branches, feeling the coolness of wooded shadow darkening his blood, enlivening it with the life of the land. The Earth was not dead, she merely slept; reserving herself for those that were true, those who would love her.

At the far edge of the trees, he found what he knew would be there; a small river. There on the bank he let Denise down, let her feet engage the living land. He inhaled the clean breath of trees and the clarity of the air above the water. His feet seemed to grow roots.

Denise's kiss – warm, soft lips pressed like a boon to his cheek – came as a surprise.

"I underestimated you," she said.

Gordon managed to smile but the kiss had made a boy of him once more. He didn't know what to say.

"How did you get so fit?" she asked.

"I don't know. Three years on the road… you know, it's… kill or cure."

"It certainly cured you. It's like you've been training for something."

He looked across the river.

"Perhaps I have been."

Out here, he could enjoy being next to Denise. It felt alright. Within the gaze of the trees, it felt honest. In this moment of simplicity, he knew he enjoyed being next to Denise. When he felt her fingers reaching for his hand, though, he moved away.

"I'm going to build us a camp," he said. "And I'm going to get some food. You can sit and rest if you want. Drink some water. If you get nervous, call out to me. I won't be far away."

Their eyes met and he smiled, but he walked away before she could do or say anything else. There was a lot to do, after all.

23

Megan makes no sounds when she returns to the clearing, her footsteps as silent as Mr Keeper's when he hunts. This human wild-thing that she knows herself to be is the most incredible form of life. It is close to divine in its abilities because not only does it move through this land, it shapes the land as it goes. It can form the world around for good or ill merely by passing through. If its thoughts are wrong, if it is disrespectful or even simply ignorant, it creates destruction at every turn. And yet, with the mind and body attuned to the landscape and the rhythms of the earth, this human wild-thing can enhance creation, give rise to more beauty, elicit the sacred in all things and live in moment to moment rapture. The line between the two states is so very fine, it is like silk from the tiniest spider. One side of this line leads to destruction in all things, the other to exponential abundance.

Megan steps into the clearing, shy of the sudden space and lack of cover, skittish as a fawn. She recovers quickly, finding the hunter within herself. This clearing is a place where she belongs. She walks with bold, purposeful steps towards the door of the roundhouse, ready to take her position as guardian of this space for the night, to play the role of Mr Keeper for as long as is necessary.

When she is only a few steps away from the roundhouse door, her mind full of the little details of the evening ahead, she hears something behind her.

She stops walking but does not turn.

Her awareness flings itself out behind her as she senses the space. Something else is here with her in the clearing. She knows this even though there is nothing to see or hear or smell that is any different from just a few moments ago. Something *breathes* behind her; something powerful and primal.

The moment she begins to think about what it might be, her new sensitivity locks up and she is left as weak and humanly ordinary as she has ever been.

All she can do is turn. Slowly. Very, very slowly.

Before she is even halfway around her peripheral vision is picking up everything it needs to know about this thing that now shares the clearing with her. A dark shape, low to the ground, muscles bunched and quivering under thick black fur. For just a moment she considers not turning any further and continuing to walk, pretending the thing isn't there. Just as swiftly she adjusts her thinking. To turn her back on a creature like this is no better than suicide.

She has heard of these beasts, everyone has. But no one ever sees them. Megan faces the thing fully and meets its pale green eyes. The cat is enormous and stands less than six good paces away; a bound or two for the animal if it decides to pounce. Its presence is overpowering. Waves of strength and streamlined aggression expand from it. Its spirit fills the clearing, obliterating any presence Megan might have felt she had. Its face is so broad and the jaws so well-muscled it looks almost bearlike. Long silky whiskers poke downward from either side of its mouth and its small ears are angled towards her.

It is sensing her, appraising her. And Megan knows what it perceives: tender, easy meat.

Its eyes lock with hers, mesmeric and intelligent. All the strength and power she felt only moments before drain into the earth and her legs begin to quake out of her control. Even though she has urinated only a few moments earlier, she now has the strong urge to do it again. So strong, she isn't sure she'll be able to stop herself. She tries to swallow and can't. Her heart gallops loud and fast, her breath catching high in her chest.

She hears a low rumble and it takes several seconds for her to realise it's a growl eliciting from deep inside the creature's chest. The growl gets louder, the threat in it enough to make her want to run and never stop but Megan knows that to run is to die. Her body screams its desire for flight; her mind reins it back. The huge black cat opens its jaws and the growl becomes a roar. Megan takes a faltering step backward. The cat advances one stealthy pace and that single, oily motion shortens the space between them. Their auras mingle in the piny evening air.

Lost for a moment in the spell of its green eyes, Megan remembers her windswept journey with Carissa, a journey that brought them to this very clearing, the ground slick with fresh blood. A whimper rises in her throat and she stifles it with a clenched fist to her mouth.

The cat advances again but now Megan locks up, her body overloaded with fear. The cat's mouth draws back from its long white teeth. Its ears flatten against its head and it hisses. The hiss ends in a screech as its mouth opens to reveal the full terror contained in those jaws. Megan sees the tightening and rippling at its shoulders and haunches; it retreats towards the ground momentarily and then it leaps straight for her.

As the black cat glides towards her through the silent air of the clearing, she sees its talons extend from the coal-dark moss of its paws. Each claw is as big as one of her fingers. Its mouth is stretched wide in a roar and in readiness for the bite which she hopes will end her life. She prays not to be alive when the creature tears off chunks of her flesh, chews it and swallows it.

Great Spirit, spare me that...

Her knees collapse easily as she dives low, making her bid for a few more seconds of existence. She hears its claws cutting the air, smells its foul breath and feels the heat of it like steam. The cat passes right over her as she hits the dirt with her hands clasped over the back of her neck. Its landing is almost totally silent but she hears its breath huff out as its weight reconnects with the earth. She waits for the searing of its claws and the finality of its bite. Nothing happens. She rolls over quietly.

The cat has ignored her. It paws at the door of the roundhouse, trying to claw it open, a softer growl now coming from its throat. Its tail flicks and snaps from side to side in irritation. Finally, a couple of claws snag a decent grip on the soft wood of the door. The cat tears it from its housing, sniffs the threshold cautiously and then disappears inside as though into a cave.

Any moment now the cat will come out of Mr Keeper's roundhouse and realise what it's missing. She could run. Now, if she is quiet, she might make it back to the village and raise the alarm. The men would come out and drive the beast away. She rolls into a crouch, ready to spring up and pad away as silently as she can.

The cat's head appears at the door, rising and falling with its rapid shallow breathing. Its regards her calmly and then it is gone again, back inside. It's only now that Megan notices the blood trail. She looks back in the direction from which it came; the gory traces extend to the edge of the clearing. Does this animal know Mr Keeper? Perhaps it knows it can come here to have its wound treated. It wouldn't be the first time Mr Keeper had taken in an injured wild animal and nursed it back to health with herbs and poultices.

With Mr Keeper still absent, the responsibility for this creature falls to her. She knows he would want her to step into his shoes and help the animal if she's able. After all, healing is a major aspect of her training.

Can I really treat a wounded black panther without getting myself killed?

Megan has no answer for this.

Nor does she have any choice now about her actions. To run away would be to end her training and step off the Black Feathered Path forever.

She edges towards the doorway of the roundhouse, unable to see inside. The light is seeping away fast with the approaching dusk. At the entry, she hesitates. There's a huge presence within. She can smell it and she can feel it. Listening hard she can hear the gentle rumble of purring. Perhaps it's this sound which encourages her to enter. She picks up the door, and leans it as best she can into the space it has been ripped from. It takes time for eyes to adjust to the gloom within. Some of the failing daylight enters through the wind-eye and the stove throws out a few flickers of orange through the crack in its door, but even after her eyes become accustomed to the darkness, the roundhouse seems to be empty.

She moves as quietly and carefully as she can towards the stove in the centre of the murky space. Once there, she scans the inner walls. There's nothing to see. Nor does anything appear to have been disturbed. There's only one place the animal can be: the place she has never seen.

At the far side of the roundhouse is the blanket strung across the low ceiling, making a fragile, flat inner wall. This is the private area where Mr Keeper sleeps and as he has never shown her the tiny space, she has known never to enter it. Now, though, things are very different. She hopes that when she explains all this to Mr Keeper, he will understand and judge her fairly.

She moves towards the curtain, quietly at first but then, not wanting to startle the hurt creature, she lets her feet rustle on the matting to telegraph her approach. Even now she is fearful that the cat will erupt from behind the flimsy blanket, knock her down and tear out her throat. This is enough to make her freeze as her hand reaches for the edge of the grimy fabric. She sees that her fingers are trembling.

Unable to breathe or swallow, her heart fat in her chest and her neck throbbing with the beat of it, she watches, detached, as her hand pulls the thick veil to one side. The form lying on the matting is not an animal but a man, a naked man. His whole body shakes. His thin limbs are tightly muscled and sinewy. His pale and dirt-spattered ribcage expands and contracts as he labours to breathe. The skin at his knees and elbows is wrinkled and leathery. His hair is long and matted; leaves and tiny twigs are caught up in it. His lively green eyes watch her but he either cannot or will not speak. Along his flank is a deep-looking cut and many other parts of his body are scored or scratched. Thorns are embedded in his hands and feet.

Megan begins to breathe again. She takes a couple of folded blankets from beside the bed mat, opens them and covers his shivering form. She rushes from behind the blanket, grabs the black kettle and puts water on the stove to boil. She lights several tallow candles and by their glow collects the herbs and other medicaments she thinks she will need, along with strips of clean cloth which she will use as bandages. She pulls the blanket to one side, exposing the man to the light and places everything she has collected beside him.

When the water has boiled, she pours some into a wooden bowl and takes it to the man's side. With suddenly very steady hands, she begins to wash and tend Mr Keeper's wounds.

24

Working as fast as he was able, Gordon made and set his traps first. Snares were easy enough; he carried those with him everywhere he went. All he needed were pegs to secure them, fashioned in moments from fallen branches. For his river traps, he needed to cut some new wood. Twigs of hazel were the best for weaving into an oval shaped cage. As bait he placed inside the cage a dead crow that he'd discovered beneath the trees, its feathers sleek and oily black, its body warm and pliant, as though it had fallen in response to his need. He hoped the slow-moving water in the bend of the river he'd chosen would prove fruitful. When everything was in position, a good distance from where he planned for them to spend the night, he returned to Denise.

She'd fallen asleep sitting up against a tree. Her mouth hung open, such was the depth of her slumber. Without any consciousness to animate her face, Denise looked many years older than her age. Sitting there like that, her breaths coming long and slow, her jaw slack, he could imagine her dead. Everyone was tired of this world except him, it seemed. How many people lay down at night praying not to wake up, he wondered? It happened on the motorway everyday. Come the dawn, there were always figures who didn't rise from their narrow resting places by the side of the worn and shattered highway. He hoped Denise would have a reason to keep waking up in the mornings even though her child was dead. There was nothing wrong with this world that people hadn't done to it. It could have been such a beautiful place.

Gordon left Denise to sleep and looked elsewhere in the small wood for what he needed. Thin branches of ash, longer poles of hazel, the pliant yet strong ends of birch boughs. All this meant taking living wood and Gordon spent time with each tree he chose, touching the bark with his palm, asking for forgiveness, explaining his need.

Removing his lock knife, he tested the blade and found it dulled. He sat beneath a healthy, many-limbed hazel tree, where his boots had already crunched and crushed dozens of spent and rotten nutshells. He took a whetstone from his pocket, spat on it and began to work it against the blade. Its once-convex profile had become a sickle shape. This constant sharpening and use, Gordon knew, was shortening the blade's life but that didn't seem to matter. The knife had extended his life more times and in more ways than Gordon could reckon. The whetstone was a gently rounded pebble about the size of his palm. He'd taken it from the River Usk while the Palmers had sheltered him. In comparison to the blade, there was barely any wear at all on the stone. He loved how it warmed up to his touch, returning to his pocket charged with heat each time he finished honing his blade. He replaced the pebble now, smiling a little at the comfort of that warmth beside his thigh.

Removing his boots and socks, Gordon placed them near the river so he could enjoy the kiss of the land on his bare soles. When he returned, he began to strip the wood he needed from each tree, laying out poles by type, length and thickness.

Near Denise he cleared a space of leaf litter and fallen twigs, cutting away any brambles and nettles before building the shelter. When the structure was complete, he slung a lightweight olive green flysheet over it and tied the edges into the framework. If he'd been alone he would have slept rough and open to the elements. He'd done it hundreds of times and found it renewing in ways he couldn't easily explain. But he couldn't expect Denise to live like that; not after she'd been used to sleeping indoors, and not if he wanted her to travel with him even a few paces farther.

He stood back and walked around the outside of the shelter one last time checking everything was secure and watertight. This was as good as it was going to get without better equipment. Inside he laid many layers of birch fronds on top of each other until they were springy enough to sit or lie on. Once they lay down to sleep, the air trapped beneath them would warm up, keeping them insulated. With everything double-checked, he watched Denise for a few moments to make sure she was alright. She still breathed. She still slept. He realised how hard he'd pushed her over the last couple of days.

For a while he scanned the area around them, stretching out with his senses. Even though he could see no evidence of it, he still had the suspicion that someone knew exactly where they were. But that had to be paranoia this time, didn't it? He was absolutely certain that no one had followed them from the M1. Either way, all he wanted was to keep moving but with Denise here, it would be difficult to keep their momentum going. As the light began to fade, Gordon moved silently away, barefooted and stealthy, loving the wildness that leapt in him at the touch of the earth.

••••

The bounty was modest but Gordon knew it would be good eating.

He took his catch back to camp, resetting his traps and snares before leaving. What he couldn't use – the guts and offal – he buried beside the trees whose branches he'd cut to make their shelter. The rest he laid by the river. Only one of his catches was dead; the rest of them still struggled. A plastic bag that had been caught in the branches of a bramble secured the living prey for long enough that he could start a fire.

It was the crackles of wood burning that woke Denise. In the dim light of evening, she looked wide-eyed and spooked.

"How long have I been asleep?"

"I don't know exactly. A few hours."

She looked around.

"You've made... an igloo."

"It's a bender. Well, sort of."

"What's a bender?"

"It's the nearest thing to a hotel we're going to find out here."

This seemed to satisfy her. For a moment.

"Why is that bag moving around?"

"That's dinner."

"Dinner's... alive?"

"It's best eaten fresh."

"I'm not eating anything that's still trying to get away."

Gordon laughed.

"Don't worry, I'm going to cook it first."

"What are we having, anyway?"

"Poor man's surf and turf, I guess."

"I haven't a clue what you're talking about."

Gordon added more wood to the fire, building it into a glowing pyramid. Sparks flared upwards and winked out.

"Well, it's going to take a while yet because we need a really hot bed of ash but we're going to eat char-grilled crayfish and rabbit."

"Yeah?"

"Yeah."

"That actually sounds quite nice."

"You have no idea."

What little warmth there'd been during the day was sucked away quickly with the disappearance of the sun. Gordon and Denise sat close to the fire which was now a heap of coals, glowing almost white in places. Their knees burned if they got too near but the warmer the fronts of their bodies became, the colder their backs felt. From time to time they faced away from the fire to warm their stiffening spines.

The filleted rabbit spat and sizzled on skewers of hazel resting over the fire. When the meat was blackening Gordon dropped the crayfish into the fire where they hissed, their carapaces turning apple red in seconds. When they were done, he placed them on the grass to cool and handed Denise a skewer of rabbit. He showed her how to break open the crayfish shells to get at the red and white flesh within. All was quiet while they ate but for the succulent sounds of chewing and murmurs of appreciation.

"Oh my God, Gordon," said Denise, licking her fingers. "This is the best meal I've had in years."

Gordon grinned.

"There's nothing like wild food. It keeps you strong."

"Maybe that's why you're so fit."

"It could be. I was puny when I first left home. After living close to the land for a few months I started to..."

"What?"

"*Fill up*, somehow. It's hard to explain. Just being out here now makes me feel alive and energised. If the Ward were coming after us, I could run all night and still take them on in the morning."

"God, I hope that won't happen."

"It won't. They're not around right now."

"How do you know?"

"I just know. We'll be safe here for tonight. Maybe a couple of nights if you need to rest up."

Gordon looked at the pile of shells beside Denise.

"You finished?"

"I'm stuffed, thanks. It was lovely."

"Told you."

Gordon gathered up the remains and walked into the darkness amid the trees to bury them. When he came back Denise was gone from beside the fire. He frowned for a moment until he heard a rustle from inside the shelter. Checking around the edge of the fire, he kicked in a couple of stray coals and squatted beside it for a while.

In a silent prayer he thanked the land for its bounty and the trees for their wood. He thanked the animals for their flesh. Feeling the intimate touch of the night on his back and smelling smoke and soil and the damp air off the river, he gave thanks for that thing he so often felt was a curse: his life. In the quiet and dark, he found contentment for a brief spell. Why it came to him in that particular moment in that particular place, he had no idea, but he wasn't so hurt and jaded that he couldn't accept the gift. The feeling he had as he ducked down to enter the shelter was unfamiliar and he could not help but be wary of it. Happiness was a fleeting, dangerous thing.

••••

Gordon used their bags to cover the entry. They had one sleeping bag and a couple of blankets. They unzipped and spread out the sleeping bag as a mattress, wrapped their coats around themselves and placed the blankets over the top. Even so it was cold and the air beside the river was laden with moisture. There was no option but to press close together for warmth. Gordon lay on his right side, turning his back to Denise and pushing close to her. She put her arm over his chest and pulled herself in. He could feel her shivering.

"You OK?" he whispered.

"Yeah. Apart from freezing my tits off."

Gordon chuckled.

"It's not funny. I've never slept anywhere as cold as this."

"This is as cold as it's going to get tonight. Now that we're in here, the shelter will preserve our body heat. If you don't move around too much, the insulation underneath us will warm up too. In a couple of hours it'll be toasty."

"Toasty."

"Right."

After a while her trembling stopped and her grip on him loosened. Her breathing slowed and levelled. Only then did Gordon allow himself to slide towards sleep's cliff edge.

And fall.

He dreamed of the girl who'd come to visit Flora's grave. She of that past time when the world was youthful and bounteous, unscarred by humanity's avarice and lack of respect. The girl was dressed in her simple, unflattering clothes and she lay in the bright sunshine on the grassy banks of a river.

Gordon longed for the world she lived in. He could see the connection between the girl and the land, how deeply she loved and understood it, how her life and the lives of those around her kept the land healthy. So different from how it was in his time, where the people, separated and lost to the land, were the cause of all the its sickness. To live in her world, to live his life with her in that benevolent sunshine by that peaceful river and to be in her arms each day, to touch her face and smell her hair, the yearning was enough to make him weep.

The scene remained unchanged though, the girl on her back, warm in the sunlight, the river sighing by, its water so clear he could see each rounded stone and pebble, follow each flash of a darting fish between the rippling reeds. Gordon felt the warmth from that sun and because the vision was not taken away from him, he relaxed and allowed himself to observe.

Something permitted Gordon to approach more closely. He floated nearby, wanting to touch the ground of this other world with his bare feet and know its power but unable to manifest there fully enough to do so. Instead he watched the girl's face tighten to some dreamed concern. If anything, that extra expression, the wrinkling of her skin, made her even more beautiful and real. She was not some perfect creature untouched by the cares of life, she was a living girl – a woman, really –with her own challenges to face.

He drifted closer.

The heat of the day was pleasant but intense. The sleeping girl had begun to sweat, the seeping at her hairline and temples darkening the blonde to brown. Something about this wet hair changed Gordon's fascination with her from an appreciation of beauty to a physical need.

Before lying down on the river bank, she had loosened her rustic attire to allow her skin to breathe in the rising heat. She'd opened the simple ties of her smock at the neck and beyond.

His urge to see her breasts revealed shamed him at first until he realised that this was his function as an animal. He was built to desire a woman in this way and, he assumed, the stronger this natural desire was, the more likely it was that he and the woman would produce strong healthy children. Before he could be too taken with the idea of her uncovered breasts, he saw the scar which occupied the flat territory directly between them. A white ridge of tissue, healed after branding. A pale, shiny lump of skin that would never be erased during her earthly time. It was in the shape of a crow's foot.

The tanned skin of her chest rose and fell in gentle rhythm. Hypnotised, he stared at the mark for a long time, knowing this dream was not merely his wish for companionship and escape. There was some real and actual connection between him and this girl, some strand or fibre that bound them together through time, to which they both clung. He wanted to stay here forever. Even if she never woke up and never spoke to him again, just to watch her breathe, here in this pastoral, sun-drenched bliss. It was a simple need, made wounding and terrible by its impossibility.

He scanned her face. In her sleep she reminded him of someone. The lines of concern deepened, squeezing more expression from what should have been her young, smooth face. Pain and death. In an instant he knew who she resembled: an older, robust and healthy Flora. She could have been Flora's older sister if she hadn't come from a time so long before. Yes, take away the crookedness of Flora's limbs, the swelling of the joints, let the sun ripen and fill her face and grow her straight and tall and this could be the young woman she might have become.

He watched, imbuing himself with an indelible memory of this unattainable creature. She was a true woman of the land, the human female to his human male. An animal woman, woven into the fabric and mind of the earth.

The sweat beaded on her forehead and ran back past her temples, staining more darkness into her sun-honeyed hair. Gordon felt the heat from the sun drumming into his back. He began to sweat too. The girl's hands moved and he started back, terrified of being caught watching her; standing so closely by, so lustfully. If she woke, she would scream to find a ragged man like him standing there, tainted as he was by the darkness of his own dying, broken world.

But she did not wake. Her hands went to her tunic, drawing it open so she could breathe more easily. Her fingers worked the ties of a simple, rough blouse below, parting more of them until a broad stretch of skin was exposed from her throat to below her navel. With slow, soporific movements, she found the ties at her skirt and unwrapped it from her legs. Her hands fell to her sides in the soft, lustrous grass and Gordon stared, no longer breathing, at her partially revealed body. Though smooth, her entire body was sheened with a down of the softest, finest peach fluff. How exquisite it would be to touch the velvet of her skin.

Somehow, he moved closer to her, knelt at her side, impelling his dream body by will alone. His stomach trembled with longing and the beat of his erection was hot and deep like the touch of the sun. Her groin was covered by cotton undershorts the colour of risen cream but the rest of her legs were bare. He was unable to swallow as he studied them. Her muscles were strong and well-used, her knees prettily scarred by dozens of childhood scrapes and falls. Despite the musculature of her legs, they were slender, containing the power of the deer to run and leap. This girl – no, this woman – she was fast and strong but as the curves of her belly and the kindness of her fingers proclaimed, she was gentle and yielding. Still unrevealed, yet more visible than before, he could see the mounded flesh of her breasts to either side of the keloid crow's foot. His hands were drawn to them, his mouth to hers. Unable to stop himself he leaned over her. Before his lips touched hers, before his hands slipped under her open, parted blouse, he closed his eyes.

The world turned to darkness.

The world grew cold and turned over.

He lay on his back now. Warm lips met his in this darkness. Cool, insistent fingers drew his hands upwards and pressed his palms against heavy, tender softness. A weight settled on his thighs. The cool fingers, frantic now, forced down his trousers. His own fingers explored the body above him, touched its face, its long hair. He stroked its neck and followed the outlines of its shoulders, slipped under the arms and along the slim flanks to its spreading hips, hips that pinned him to the ground. Everywhere he touched he found naked skin. Soon, he too was denuded and anticipation crackled in every part of him.

Her lips returned to find his. Her breasts flattened and spread against his chest. She settled back and in one single, succulent movement, engulfed him.

Gordon cried out, wild and ecstatic. He reached a sensation beyond which there was nothing more and his body released, casting itself into the body of this woman. He howled and she howled with him and he was glad to be this animal, to know his humanity through this new language of flesh. He crushed her to him, and she clung like ivy to a ruin. Head rushing, groin pulsing, Gordon died a little.

He was awake. He knew where he was now. The cold touch of reality and the cold touch of the air were daggers to his senses, glory to his skin. He held Denise tight, glad he didn't know the name of the girl in his dreams, the name he would have screamed. Denise stroked his hair and the feathers woven there. He could not see her eyes and he was glad she could not see his. The love they shared was meant for others but had no others to go to.

Touching her naked skin raised gooseflesh beneath his fingers. She held him tighter. Gordon hardened again. They did not sleep until dawn.

25

Once Megan has dressed his injuries as best she can and he is comfortable, Mr Keeper takes her hand and thanks her.

He holds her hand in his for a long time. This contact between them is unprecedented, as is her tending him unclothed, as a patient, as a man who until now has been invulnerable and impossibly beyond her reach. The skin of his torso, though pale, is that of a younger man. His day-to-day appearance, she now realises, is a kind of act or smokescreen; one that implies age and experience beyond his years. She has feelings for this wounded, denuded and vulnerable man. Feelings she ought not to have. It is with a gentle will that she puts them to one side. The Path must come first. Walking it, and walking it well, takes precedence over all other things.

"You're welcome," she says after far too long. "I hope I've done it right."

"You couldn't have done it any better."

As usual, there are two ways of taking a comment like this from Mr Keeper. She hopes he means she's done a good job.

"Are you going to tell me what happened?" She hears immediately how bad this sounds. "I mean, am I allowed to know?"

Mr Keeper pushes himself up on one elbow and gestures with his chin towards a box near the wind-eye.

"I want to smoke. Could you bring me my pipe?"

She does as he asks, waiting as she always does for information and not expecting to receive any. Once his pipe is primed she holds out a tallow to him and he lights up from its greasy flame. The first draw makes him cough and he collapses onto his back, his face creased in agony. After a while the spasm passes. Pale, he rises onto his elbow again and nods for the candle. Megan holds it out and he relights his pipe. This time there is no cough but she can see the dark seepage through the bandages around his waist.

He blows aromatic tobacco smoke all around himself, relishing the clouds with the satisfaction of a child. Finally, he remembers her question.

"Much as I hate to share this with you, Megan, the time for you to know has come. It is your duty to listen very carefully to what I have to say."

She nods, ready for whatever Mr Keeper will tell her. She has all the training he has already given her, some of her abilities even beyond his now. And yet, there is a flutter of fear in her gut; that, and a growing sense of the magnitude of a Keeper's responsibility.

Mr Keeper must see some of this in her face.

"Listen, Megan. I know how you feel, whether you believe that or not. I was once where you are, learning the things you're learning and fearing the future. What we do isn't easy and it never will be. For a while, maybe a long while, your duties may seem like some kind of curse. But, and I promise you this from the heart, one day you will wake up and see that it has all been worth it. You'll see the wider significance of what it is you've been doing all the long years.

From that day onward you will wake with a smile, knowing another day of Keeping is ahead of you and that what you once thought was a curse is, in fact, a gift.

"Without us, everything would swing out of balance again. Every Keeper has an awakening when this knowledge rises in their blood. You'd think that sense of importance, of vitality, would make a person proud. Arrogant even. But it never does. You'll never meet a Keeper with anything other humility at his core. When your moment of awakening comes, Megan, you will feel nothing but a deep sense of honour that you, among so many, are strong enough to walk the Black Feathered Path. You will understand your place in the world and you will know you are blessed."

Mr Keeper taps out the spent bowl of his pipe and refills it. Megan helps him light up.

"There are still people in this land, men mostly, who yearn for the past; for the days before the Black Dawn. These men know there was vast power back then, technologies that made gods of us all. These men believe there is a way to recreate that power and still maintain the balance. The simple fact is, they're wrong."

He draws deeply on his pipe.

"They don't understand the difference between a tool and a machine."

"What does that mean?"

"People use tools, Megan. Machines use people."

She thinks about this. She's not even sure what a machine is.

"I don't think I understand."

"By the end of your training, you will. For now, all you need to know is that it will be part of your responsibility to make sure others do not confuse the two."

He smokes with commitment, his gaze untethered, and Megan assumes he has finished speaking. He is a shapeshifter, an elemental force, and she doubts she'll ever know the extent of him. Yet now, here he is, bleeding, pale and weak on his bedroll. What if she had taken longer over the writing? Perhaps without her he might have died. Even now, he may not survive. What will his power amount to then? How can Mr Keeper not be powerful enough to save himself? She notices his pipe hand is shaking, and his pallor is more profound; a bleaching out of his skin as though his limbs are shafts of dead wood, abandoned in the sun for years.

She doesn't know what more to do for him. His trembling worries her. The roundhouse, since she has seen to the fire, is hot. There's no explanation for his unsteady hands.

"Are you hungry?" she asks, on a whim.

He shakes his head.

"I think you ought to rest," she says.

"You're probably right." He looks at her and his eyes, always so youthful and mischievous, look beaten for the first time. Their whites are yellowy and fractured with tiny rivers of blood and his skin seems to have loosened. His hair has lost its colour at the temples and below the felt-thick locks at the back of his head. "But there's no time for rest, Megan. That's what the world after this one is for."

She points to his bandages.

"You're still bleeding. You'll exhaust yourself."

"Even without the bleeding, I'd feel as bad as I do now. That's the price of power. Such… gifts are costly and rightly so."

Megan's fear for him must show in her eyes. When he asks for water, she knows it's only to make her feel better. Still, she pours it and tips the drinking bowl for him and it has a rallying effect on both of them. He puts out his hand and holds hers again, just for a moment. There's such kindness and knowledge in his touch that she almost cannot stand the exquisite surety of the contact. In a thousand years, though, she could never pull away from such a touch, so it is Mr Keeper who withdraws after an appropriately short communion.

"Everything's going to be alright, Megan. Give it time. Give *me* time and you'll see."

He's talking about her walking the Path now, as though today's events are already forgotten.

"But what about this… What's happened to you? Are you going to explain it to me?"

"I've been trying. But it's difficult. You weren't meant to see it like this." Mr Keeper sighs deeply, appearing to have run out of clever ways to explain his condition. "I went to check on a group of men whose… activities have come to my attention. They're very suspicious and they know all about Keepers. For men like these, there's so much at stake that they would risk killing a Keeper to make certain their work remains secret. The safest to see what they were up to was to accept another form."

He smiled then, remembering, and tapped out his pipe ready for an unprecedented third bowl. He lights up from the tallow and blows generous puffs of tobacco smoke out through mouth and nostrils like some reclining, ailing dragon.

"Using the stealth and speed of the black panther I tracked these three men to a cave about fifteen miles east of here. When they left, I went inside. They must have spent years and travelled the length and breadth of the country to gather their equipment. They'll have entered the dead cities to recover artefacts from the old times. The fact they're not afraid of the ruins of our past is a bad sign. That boldness is the awakening of the same thirst for dominion that awoke the Crowman and brought the Black Dawn. It's the same mistake we made before: seeking knowledge outside of ourselves, when the root is of all understanding is within.

"These men feel an emptiness inside themselves. We all know that hollowness – it's natural. It makes us yearn in a language we don't understand for things we cannot conceive. And yet, if we settle down and watch quietly within – as I've shown you, Megan – that space fills up with tranquillity and blessings and simplicity. Then we see and can be content; for our very incarnation in this world is a gift beyond our reckoning.

"But these men have wandered so far from that knowledge that they have stepped back through time into the ignorance that almost ended creation itself. They want hold knowledge and power in their hands and wield them like weapons. They want to control what they do not understand because their very existence terrifies them. And the more they search outside and the more of this outer power they create, the smaller they become, and the farther they shrink from the Great Spirit – who would give them everything they could ever wish for in return for nothing but a little trust and little love."

Megan is shocked to see that Mr Keeper is crying.

"Everything we've done, Megan, all the abundance and goodness that Keepers have opened the world to could be overturned by men like this. Stupid, frightened men filled with nothing but want. Men who cannot see the magic all around them. I fear for the Earth, Megan." Mr Keeper smokes and knuckles the tears from his eyes. "I've seen similar things a dozen times in my years as a Keeper. But I've never seen such commitment, such suicidal single-mindedness, as I saw in those three men."

The effort of the telling has cost Mr Keeper much of the little strength he had remaining. Megan sees him begin to sink down and she crawls to his side to help him lie back. The pipe falls from his hand, the half-smoked bowl still sending up curls of spicy vapour. When he is comfortable and covered up, she takes the pipe and empties it into the belly of the stove. Returning, she finds Mr Keeper either asleep or unconscious, breathing in short, painful-looking spasms. She puts her hand on his forearm and then moves it down to take hold of his hand. His grip is soft and loose.

His eyes flicker open and he smiles.

"I'm alright, Megan. I just need a little time."

"I know," she says, though behind her words there are doubts. "I'll be here. We'll get you right."

He nods and Megan can see that he believes in her. This is the greatest weight she has ever carried. He is not only the Keeper, *her* Keeper, he is a man she loves. They are of the same family now, the family of the Earth, and, somewhere above, their spirits are twined together in the weave.

"Mr Keeper?"

"Yes?"

"What were the men making in the cave?"

She watches his sleep-bound eyes remembering what he saw.

"I… don't know what it was. I've never seen anything like it before."

"Do you think they'll come after you?"

"Whether they do or not, we'll have to go back there." His eyes brighten for a moment. "The Path demands it, Megan."

26

Gordon woke first and moved Denise's arm away from his waist. He turned to look at her in the thin morning light, stained green by the flysheet.

She was not unattractive. She was, in reality, a beautiful woman even if the world had left its ugly marks upon her. As intense and prolonged as it had been, the wonders they'd shared in the total blackness of night felt like a bad secret now. He did not love Denise and she did not love him. She needed him in order to stay alive and she knew it. He, in turn, owed her the protection and care that he ought to have given her child.

Everything about Denise was a reminder of what was wrong with this world and only made him wish harder for the world he saw in his dreams. But there was no going back in time, no return to the girl in the sunshine. Everything that happened between him and Denise from now on would only heap more weight on his shoulders. More dissatisfaction. More despair. More hopelessness. Denise was wrong. The world was wrong. They were wrong.

There was a time when he'd cared about the people he met. He'd done his best to help those who needed it whenever he could. He'd harried the Ward with his blade and his cunning. He'd led them across the land, wasted their time, eroded their morale and taken the souls of their agents.

Something had changed; he had to accept it. Though his parents had promised him the Crowman was the only way they could be liberated, he had seen enough substations and watched enough of the Ward's brutality to understand that they had made a very deliberate and informed sacrifice. They'd known that while he might – *might* – succeed in finding the Crowman and making a difference for the land, he would never do it in time to save them.

His parents and sisters had to be long gone by now. They'd probably been killed within days of him leaving the house – while he was feverish with blood poisoning in the disused railway tunnel. Why this realisation came to him now, he didn't know. Perhaps he'd finally grown up. After all this time, it felt more like an acknowledgement than a revelation. Much in the same way that, though it mimicked love, love was not what he shared with Denise. That was nothing more than animal necessity.

Such, he now understood after these three years of searching, was the case with his quest for the Crowman. It was a necessity. Not for him. Not for his family. For the world. There was nothing else left for him to discover now. No love for Gordon Black. No bright future for him. No bucolic tranquillity at the side of a woman he truly loved. The world would not heal during his own short span. He would not find joy in his lifetime. Only one thing worth living for remained. A thin bar of hope pointing through clouds of despair. Find the Crowman and the world had a chance, even if he did not. He would lead Denise to safety as he'd promised and then he'd finish this.

He sat up, cold with determination, moved their bags from the doorway and crept out. No sun penetrated the clouds. It was hard to say what time of day it was. All he knew was that the time to move on had come.

He slipped into the icy river to wash himself.

27

Dear Gordon,

*I've got a whole sheet of lovely white paper this time! Bossy got it
because I kept him company a little longer and a little better than
usual. No one else knows except you, Gordon. It's our secret and
I know that when I finally see you, you won't ever talk about it.
Anyway, it doesn't matter because Bossy's so good to me. There's no
other way I could get these messages to you. He said there'd been
a number of unavoidable issues with the postal delivery service
recently. That was how he said it. And then he laughed. I think it
he was joking with me. When I asked what he meant he said there
are some weak links in the chain and that not every communication
is successful. I really hope you're getting these letters. I know quite
a lot about how you are from Bossy. About how you're trying
to get to the Crowman before the Ward do. How you're always
fighting them. But you don't know anything about me, Gordon.
I thought I'd tell you about a day in the life of Jude! They wake
us up really early every morning. You have to get up or they come
in with their whipsticks and well, you know. It's best to do what
they tell you. Always. Anyway, then they give us barley gruel. It's
like a watery soup with a few grains at the bottom of the plastic
cup. Sometimes it has a lump or two of meat in it or a few greens*

211

*but mostly it's plain. At least it's easy to eat. After what they did
to my teeth, consommé is about all I can manage! You wouldn't
believe how thin I am. I can see all my bones. But I feel OK. After
"breakfast" nothing happens until exercise time. I usually think
about things until then. Good memories and things that used to
make me laugh. I think about you a lot but I try not to think about
what will happen in the future. I don't think any of us do because
it can make you feel really low. Some of the others have got so low
they've hung themselves with their trousers or used a smuggled-in
blade to cut the arteries in their wrists. So you know I always think
about the past. A lot of people sleep during the day. I can hear them
snoring. But I try not to otherwise I can't sleep at night and that's
much worse. Exercise is the only time I see the others apart from the
guards and Bossy of course. It's also the only time I get any fresh
air. I can't tell you how much I miss our garden and the walks
we used to go on. Up the bridleway or out to the Faraway Tree.
Even just across the fields. That's what I dream about most. Being
outside. Feeling the wind in my hair and the sun or the rain on my
face. Every time I dream about being outside I always cry when I
wake up. But anyway we walk around this concrete quadrangle for
twenty minutes and I get as much air into my lungs as I can. We're
not allowed to talk to each other but even just seeing someone else's
face, someone who isn't a guard, makes it easier to keep going until
sleep time. In the afternoon they make us work in our cells. Mostly
sewing grey uniforms or knitting grey gloves. Sometimes they get
us to sort through piles of clothes looking for valuables or things
that can be used again. It's tempting to keep the things you find.
Wallets, photographs, pairs of glasses, nail files, coins. Even food or
lipstick or matches. But you can't keep anything. There's nowhere
to hide it and even if there was if the guards found it they'd come
in with their whipsticks. It would be worse than the punishment
for not getting up in the morning. Much worse. At night they give*

*us a kind of dried bread. It's so thin it's like a cracker. It's hard
to eat with my mouth like it is. I have to get a lot of saliva going
for each bite and wait until it softens before I can swallow it. I
really try to make mine last and I pretend I'm eating sausages
or roast chicken. You know, a big cooked meal like mum used to
make us. After that there's an hour or two to wait before they
blow out the oil lamps. If you're lucky you get to sleep quick and
go right through without waking. If you have a hundred worries
on your mind or have a dream that wakes you, the night can feel
like it goes on forever. Oh! I forgot to tell you my cell is en suite. I
have my own bucket and bowl right in the corner. OK. Not funny.
But you have to find a little reason to smile every day. I've found
that helps a lot. Otherwise well, you know. Did I say I love you
in the last one? I can't remember. I'm sorry if I didn't. I love you,
Gordon. Be safe. I know you must be having a tough time out
there but please, please write me a letter when you have a chance.
Jude.*

In the morning, Denise was different with Gordon, her gaze
all over him like oil. Each time she tried to meet his eyes, he
had to look away. He hoped she'd interpret it as shyness.

Eager to be moving on he said:

"How are you feeling?"

"I haven't felt this good in a long time."

Gordon cleared his throat.

"Uh, I meant do you think you're ready to travel?"

She frowned a little but it passed.

"No. I like it here." Her eyes flicked to the shelter. "It's
comfortable. It's warm and," she grinned, "the food is great."

Gordon clenched his teeth and looked away again when
her gaze sought his. As he stared out across the quiet, almost
comatose land, he thought of the night before. What they'd

done. The things she'd shown him. Already he wanted her again but what about afterwards? Would it always feel this forced, this *untrue*?

"We can't stay here. We'll lose what little advantage we have."

"I know. But don't spoil it, Gordon. One more night won't hurt." She reached out and took his hand. Gordon flinched but managed not to snatch his hand away. "It'll do us good," she said.

He swallowed down his frustration and stood up. He wasn't sure he could delay another twenty-four hours to be on the move again; the Crowman wasn't going to wait for him. Yet neither was he sure he could wait until nightfall to touch Denise again.

"One more night, then. But we leave at daybreak."

"What's the matter, Gordon? You seem really… tense. I haven't upset you, have I?"

"No. No, of course not. I'm just… I can't help thinking about this 'war' everyone's on about." It wasn't a lie. Not exactly. But the thought had also crossed his mind that he could grab his pack and leave Denise here; a thought followed swiftly by the shame that he could think such a thing after everything that had happened. He tried to concentrate on his wider concerns. "I can't help feeling like everything's coming to a head. That this will be the final clash between the Green Men and the Ward. I don't think it's going to go well."

"How can you say that? Look at the numbers of people ready to fight."

"It'll never be enough, Denise. They're not an army. They're a rabble. They're lit up by passion and desperation. When they meet the Ward in battle, those lights will go out like that." He clicked his fingers. "They'll falter."

"They will not. How can you say that? These people would die to end the Ward's choke on them."

"And die they will, Denise. I promise you that. They will die by the tens of thousands. There has to be a better way."

"What way?"

"I don't know."

"Then you shouldn't criticise."

"I don't know *yet*, Denise. But I will. They need a figurehead. They need the Crowman. If he could lead them into battle, I think they'll have a chance. But most of them don't even think he's real. Some people even believe he was invented by the Ward as an ideological enemy; that if they could get everyone to believe the Crowman will bring the end of the world, they'd be as good as allies to the Ward. I've got to find him. I've got to prove he's real and powerful, that he's not just an idea." He looked at Denise and managed to smile for the first time that morning. Everything had been so different in the darkness, so magical and correct. Physically, their union had been perfect but out here in daylight, the two of them just didn't fit together. "Sorry if I've been a bit distant," he said. "It's really worrying me."

"It's OK," she said. "It really is. You'll find him before this war begins. I know you will."

"Thanks."

He leaned down to grab his pack. In his haste to be away he knocked it over. From the top spilled out his carefully wrapped sheaf of feathers. He scrambled to replace them but Denise was too quick.

"What are these?"

"Nothing. Just some old crow feathers."

"Like the ones in your hair."

"Yes. Like those."

"Why have you got so many of them?"

"Listen, Denise, give them back. I really need to go and check the traps so we can eat."

Her voice hardened off.

"No. You're not going yet. Tell me about this."

Now, finally, he could hold her gaze. No one challenged him like this. Who did she think she was? What right did she have to know so much about him? Without any warning his bubble of defiance burst and all his indignation went with it. He felt weak. Of course, this woman whose child he'd allowed to die, the woman he now led across the dying land, of course she had a right to know about the man she was travelling with.

He slumped back down to the ground.

"Open it up," he said.

"No. It's OK, Gordon. I'm sorry. I shouldn't pry."

"Open it."

Denise unrolled the cloth wrapping and the breeze agitated its contents.

"Don't let them blow away."

She laid a stick over them.

"How many are there?"

"I don't know. Hundreds."

"Why do you keep them?"

"I've been collecting them most of my life. When I see a black feather, I always pick it up. It's like a sign that I'm on the right track. It makes me feel... God, I don't know... supported somehow. Does that just sound totally crazy?"

Denise stared at the feathers in silence for long moments. She touched them with her fingertips as though they were sacred objects. When she didn't speak, he began to regret giving in to her demands. Then he saw Denise was crying.

"What's wrong?"

She looked up, liquid crystal spilling over her cheeks.

"Flora had these." She tried to wipe her tears away but they kept coming. "Not as many as you, but she had plenty. I never understood where they came from because she never went outside. She said the Crowman left them for her and I didn't argue. It didn't seem fair to take away what little joy she had. But I always thought she'd discovered an old nest up in the attic and pretended the feathers were gifts."

"What do you think now?"

"I think he gave them to her." She overrode her tears and wiped her face again. "I'll tell you what else I think, Gordon Black. It was no mistake that you came to us. I think you're destined to find him. I think that's what you're here to do."

Gordon found his own cheeks wet with tears.

"You have no idea how good it feels to hear that. I used to think finding these was a curse, you know. Because never in my life have I found a single white feather. But the longer all this has gone on, the more I came to realise that I was walking the right path." He laughed without much humour. "A black-feathered path."

"It's no curse. It's a blessing. It gives your life meaning and purpose. I don't know anyone else who has that. You should be thankful."

Gordon sighed, shamed by her words.

"Yes. I think you're right."

Silence gathered between them. Gordon didn't know how to prevent it, hadn't he already shared more with Denise than was safe or wise? The sudden sense of exposure, knowing something below his surface had been revealed, caused a ripple of vulnerability and dread through his solar plexus. He squatted by the feathers, laid the stick aside and gathered them back into their bundle. Denise's voice breaking the wall of hush between them did little to resolve his misgivings.

"I'll look after them," she said, placing her hand over his.

Gordon froze, unable to look at her.

"Don't you trust me?"

No.

But Denise had trusted him first, hadn't she? With her attic hideout and her daughter's life? Even with her own. If he couldn't show a little faith now, in another human being in the harshest times, perhaps he had no faith left.

"Of course I do," he heard himself say.

Denise smiled and he was able to look at her then, to let her see his eyes.

"Good," she said, taking the wrapped feathers and giving him a soft, lingering kiss.

When he stood up, she stayed where she was, wrapped her arms around herself and shivered.

"Cold?"

"I'm fine," she said.

"I could get the fire going again."

"I'm OK. Really, Gordon. Anyway, I wouldn't want anyone to see the smoke when I'm here on my own."

She was right, of course.

He shrugged off his coat and gave it to her before pulling on his pack. She hugged the material but didn't put it on.

"Thanks. Now, go on," she said, grinning. "Off you go. And don't come back without a sackful of meat. I'm already starving."

Gordon spent the day out of camp.

Checking the traps and snares only took minutes. He spent the rest of the time wandering the landscape and staying clear of Denise. Here and there the land had been torn open by tremors and quakes but there were no rifts as great as the one he'd first seen on leaving the sandstone cave. The earthquakes that had torn England open had quietened over the last few months.

At the crest of a small hill a couple of miles from their camp he surveyed the terrain around them, planning the first part of their continued route north. They were far enough from major roads to remain unnoticed but it was always a good idea to stay away from the smaller towns and villages. People still trying to survive in those places had fallen very far from civilisation and Gordon didn't want any extra conflict. What was coming would be bad enough.

He'd told the truth to Denise. If they'd had a head start over the Ward, it would have been eroded by now. They needed to move soon. The Ward would know he was travelling across country too – they knew his modus operandi well enough by now. With this alleged war coming, avoiding the Green Men would be impossible too; not without being hunted down as a coward. The simplest thing would be to go to one of the Green Men's strongholds and act like he was part of the uprising until he could get back to London.

From the top of the hill he could see a few miles in every direction. The grey swatches of dust where nothing grew and no animal had any reason to forage were like streaks of leprous tissue, spreading across the body of the world. He could see the long black rends left by earthquakes. They passed through land both living and dead, resembling claw marks, as though some vast bird had swooped and dragged its talons across the earth, trying to tear pieces of it away. The wires carried by pylons no longer crackled and hummed with power. In the villages and hamlets visible from his vantage, houses and cars still burned; whether from a Ward attack or because of looters, he couldn't tell. It seemed as though destruction begat destruction, no matter what the cause. People – the kind of people he wanted to avoid – burned things because they could now, just to see another piece of the world laid waste. When there was no law, when nothing beyond survival seemed to matter any more, there was a savage logic in violence and ruination. He half understood their feelings:

If this is the end, then bring it on...

But what if, as Gordon still believed, it wasn't the end? Wasn't it worth trying to keep the world alive, to maintain the simple trust that one person would neither harm another nor take from them just because there was no one to punish their actions. Surely, such trust was a *natural* law, part of the order of the universe.

He couldn't even be sure of that. Perhaps a handful of the folk he'd met on the road had remembered that trust in spite of everything, put kindness and care before hunger and rage. Most had not. It was as though the entire population had been waiting for a time when lawlessness would give them freedom from morality. If such a motive existed in just one person, it existed in all of them. It existed in him. But if that was true, and he was sure it was, then the capacity for honour and trust existed in equal measure. Humans were demons and angels, and everything in between. They were free to decide how they behaved. The trouble was that Gordon had learned one indisputable thing in all his searching, trusting people was the riskiest thing anyone could do. Sometimes he wondered if he even trusted himself.

He returned with more meat than the previous evening. Three rabbits and a similar number of crayfish. Denise sat with her back against a tree, facing the river. His coat was in her lap.

He allowed his footsteps to announce his approach and she looked up.

"I was beginning to think you'd left me here to fend for myself."

It was so close to the truth he didn't know how to respond at first. In the end he shrugged as though time was the last thing on his mind.

"I found a high place to look out from and thought about where we'll go next. I also did a full circuit of this area, just to be sure there's no one else out here." He held up his catch. "And there was nothing in the snares for most of the day. These guys all got caught within the last hour or so."

Denise looked at Gordon with his bounty of food and any tension that had been in her face disappeared.

"You're the ultimate hunter-gatherer, aren't you?"

"You said you were starving."

"I'm even starvinger now."

Something in her smile tugged at him. His groin warmed and swelled. He tried to ignore the sensations and moved between the trees to gut and skin the rabbits. When he'd buried their offal, he returned to wash his hands in the river.

"I've been working hard too," said Denise. "I found your needle and thread."

When he turned she was standing up, holding out his coat. It was unrecognisable.

"What do you think?"

The coat was almost invisible beneath a layer of black feathers. She'd sewn them in from the end of the coattails and from the ends of the sleeves so that they lay over each other as they would on the body and wings of a bird. She'd put a lot of thought into which size of feather went where and at the lapels, cuffs and tails, feathers hung and fluttered from frayed strips of black cloth. A breeze moved the coat in her hands and it shimmered blue-black in the evening light.

"I cut up my best top for the ribbons but it'll turn some heads next time we're on a major road," she said, grinning. "This'll be the new fashion. I was thinking about what you said. Something like this could be a uniform for the Green Men; something to bring them together."

He stood and shook his head.

"I don't know what to say."

"Don't say anything yet. Come and try it on."

"I'm not sure I can."

"Please, Gordon. I've worked on it all day. I'm glad you've only just come back or I wouldn't have had time to finish. Just put it on and see how it feels."

Gordon was paralysed.

"Look, if you hate it, I'll unpick it all and you can keep the feathers wrapped in their old bit of rag. I haven't damaged them, I promise you."

He didn't move, couldn't even swallow.

"Oh, come on, Gordon. You've done so much for me. All I wanted was to give something back to you."

…give something back…

The phrase went right to his heart. That was all anyone had to do to make the world better. He couldn't refuse such a sentiment.

He stepped forward knowing he would never forget Denise's smile of gratitude and relief. He put both arms out behind him and she place the armholes over his hands. In one movement, he shrugged into the coat. The sensation that the coat had *leapt* onto him would have been disturbing if it didn't feel so good to wear it. It was a new skin and it felt right.

"Turn around then."

Slowly, arms out to either side, feathers dancing at his wrists, he faced her.

"Wow. That's looks even better than I thought it would. It suits you so well. How does it feel?"

"It feels amazing."

"You know what, Gordon?"

"What?"

"It looks like a bit like armour. Maybe it'll protect you." She put her face up to his and kissed his lips. "But not from me."

She stroked her hand down his arm, enjoying the silky bounce of the feathers. Then she looked away.

"What is it?" asked Gordon.

"I put Flora's feathers in with yours. I wish she was here to see it. She'd have loved you like this." She turned to face him again, her eyes shining with tears. "She loved you anyway. As soon as you left the attic that first time she told me how special you were. It was like she knew all along that you were going to come into our lives. Like she'd been passing the time until you got there."

Without much confidence, Gordon put his arms out and around Denise. The fierceness of her returned embrace set him off balance and he stumbled backwards a step. She didn't let go. He knew this hug. He'd seen it many times in his childhood. The hug of a daughter seeking solace in the strength of her father; Jude hugging Dad.

Gordon held Denise as tightly and fully as he could and they stood rooted that way beside the river as darkness took the shine away from his feathers. She was the one to pull away and he sensed a sudden hardness in the movement, a severance. Whether she'd had what she needed now or had simply found no answer in his arms, he couldn't tell. When she looked at him, her eyes seemed once more as guarded as when he'd first met her.

"I need some poor man's surf and turf," she said.

It could have been the failing light, but to Gordon, Denise's smile looked grim.

As night fell, Gordon grilled everything he'd caught. Leftover rabbit meat would last a day or two longer and keep their strength up as they walked. Sitting beside each other, they spoke very little as they ate. Denise went into the shelter as soon as she'd finished her food. He listened to her rustling as she moved around, preparing the bed and covers.

There was no reason for him to remain outside. Even though he wasn't tired, he followed her into the shelter and covered the entrance with their bags. Denise's hand was on his shoulder as soon as he scooted onto the bed; she pulled him down towards her and kissed him hard. He reached out in the dark to find her already naked and she stripped him with frantic, insistent tugs. Once again the night brought forth their animal spirits; a dark fire in the blood. They mounted each other again and again, sometimes sleeping in between, sometimes only resting. Gordon thought about the burning houses and cars he'd seen from the top of the hill. Maybe their frank, uninhibited unions were nothing more than acts of destruction inspired by the brevity of their future. Though each coupling was ecstatic, for Gordon the loneliness that followed was crushing. It was easy to believe that the world was out of hope and out of time.

If this is the end, then bring it on.

Let it burn, he thought. There is no future.

Let it burn.

28

This morning is the coldest of the season so far.

Megan's ears ache and redden at the touch of the air as she searches for the right place between the pines. She has slept nearby Mr Keeper, waking each time she heard him stir or cough or groan, which was often. Even when his sleep and breathing seemed untroubled she woke and checked on him. Now she is stumbling with fatigue.

Wrapped in furs from the roundhouse, she walks between the silent trees looking for a space that feels right. She finds what she wants in an area where two pines have fallen, leaving a gap that stretches up to the sky. She sets the snares and places scraps of rabbit meat around them. This is one of the many things Mr Keeper has taught her how to do but she didn't think she would need the skill; especially not so soon. Three should do it, she thinks, though she does not look forward to dispatching the creatures the snares catch. No matter how willingly they come, killing is never without its price; somewhere it is noted, remembered.

When everything is ready, she disguises the snares and kneels a short distance away, incanting the prayer Mr Keeper taught her for this kind of hunting She repeats the simple invocation about fifty times, barely whispering the words into the breath of the woods and yet knowing with total certainty that they have been heard.

She leaves quietly and returns to the warmth of the roundhouse.

Rather than a trembling act of bloodstained terror, the slaughter is quiet and sacrosanct. Megan talks to the three rooks, strokes their feathers and thanks them for their sacrifice before she breaks their necks one by one. She dismantles their bodies right there beneath the trees, where the sky can watch her hands working. She separates the usable meat from the bone and feather, the sinew and claw, placing it in a wooden bowl; warm vapour rises and fades into the silent, still air above it. What remains of the rooks she buries, adding a little of her own blood from a nick she cuts into her forearm.

Back beside the stove in the roundhouse, her fingers still creaking with cold, Megan puts the meat in a black cook pot with quick-bine, ale and some seasoning. Worrying about Mr Keeper's many external wounds, she adds a whole head of crushed garlic to ward off infection. For most of the morning, the mixture cooks on the stove, bubbling gently, its aroma filling the warm air of the roundhouse. When it is ready she wakes him.

The canal's surface was speckled with unmoving debris. Paper, plastic and half-submerged pieces of waterlogged timber. Here and there, the partially decomposed bodies of birds and other animals. Twice Gordon noticed bloated human carcasses, filled with gas and breaking down but as yet untouched by carrion eaters. Perhaps the water was poisoned. It didn't matter; this wasn't water they were going to drink. The canal formed a clear, relatively direct path, sheltered by hedges and trees and a good distance from the roads for most of its course. It was the perfect route north. And, if his hunch was right, the Grand Union Canal led all the way to the Midlands. If they hadn't have left the motorway, if Gordon hadn't climbed his hill the previous day, he would never have thought of it.

The narrowness of the path also meant Denise couldn't have walked beside him even if she wanted to. It wasn't so much that he wanted to lead and her to follow; he just didn't want to have to talk. His excuse to himself was that she stopped him from concentrating. The real reason was harder to accept but that didn't make it go away; this kind of closeness, with anyone, was dangerous.

He'd never travelled with anyone before. He'd always avoided friendships and kept moving to stop himself from growing roots it might be painful to cut later on. But if the end of everything was so close, why didn't he want to spend as much time as he could with Denise, enjoying her company in every way possible? Even if he couldn't hold it in his mind for more than a few moments at a time, the answer was simple. He didn't love her. He didn't even like her particularly. He didn't want to play his last days out in a lie – a thought swiftly followed by:

But they're already a lie, though, aren't they?

This was all an act. To travel together, for him to provide for her; he was doing out of guilt. The one thing that didn't feel false was their sex; not until the clashing waves of tristesse which swiftly followed every coupling. He wanted her and yet being with her hollowed him out somehow, left him barren. How long they could go on like this he didn't know but he couldn't just leave Denise out here alone. He'd get her to somewhere safe. Get her among the Green Men.

And then he'd move on.

The only thing that felt good was his coat of black feathers. She'd made a flippant comment about it looking like armour but it was true: the coat made him feel safe and strong. After years of hiding all the black feathers he'd found along his path, he now showed them to the world. Black was his true colour and the crow was the symbol he sought in everything. It was right that he wore this coat for the final part of his search. He was close now; there wasn't any doubt in his mind. There were only two possible outcomes:

If he didn't find the Crowman or didn't find him fast enough, the land was done for. Everyone would perish, even the Ward. But if he could track down the Crowman, and quickly, the chances were that the Green Men would someday triumph over the Ward. Once the Crowman had reconnected the people with the land, the Ward wouldn't have the strength to stand against them. Gordon would have completed his sworn duty. He would dismiss himself then, find a secluded spot where he could live out his days. He had grown to love the chase, he had become it. But when the chase was over, what then would he be?

Denise's footsteps catching up to him made his shoulders tighten.

"Hey," she said.

"Hey."

"What are you thinking about?"

He'd lost track of how many times she'd used this opener since they left the M1. In the end he said:

"Why do you keep asking me that?"

"I don't know. I mean why wouldn't I? You're always so quiet and intense. You seem so angry."

"I'm not angry."

"Well, you seem it."

"I'm not."

"So what *are* you thinking about?"

Fuck, he thought, why didn't I leave her in London?

"Listen, Denise. There's a reason why brains are encased in a shell of bone; it's because they're private."

"Don't you want to talk to me?"

"Sure. Of course I do, but… you can't just ask people what they're thinking like that."

"Why not?"

"Because it's not a real conversation. Why don't you tell me what you want to talk about and then we'll talk about it. It'll happen naturally. You don't have to do it this way."

"I want to talk about what's going on inside your head."

Gordon stopped walking and turned around. He needed to know how Denise looked in that moment; whether she was winding him up or if she was serious about the question. Either way she was being incredibly stupid. From the look on her face, she seemed genuine.

Fine.

"I'll tell you what I'm thinking about, Denise. I'm thinking about how the Ward took away my family and turned me into an outlaw. I'm thinking about the people I've killed while I've been searching for the Crowman – I lost count a long time ago. I'm thinking about what people have done to the world to make the land turn against them. I'm thinking about the millions who've died and the ones I could have saved. I'm thinking about all the things which have been lost already and I'm wondering if it's even worth *trying* to carry on when things are this messed up. I'm thinking of the hundreds of thousands more people who will die at the hands of the Ward and I'm thinking about what will happen to this world if I don't find the Crowman. I'm thinking about the things that need to happen if this land is ever going to heal and I'm wondering if I have the strength to keep searching and keep fighting. Most of all, Denise, I'm wishing that this wasn't the life that was handed to me. I never asked for this, I don't want it and I never have."

His face muscles were twitching as he turned away and continued to walk, faster now; the pace he would have used if he was travelling alone. A mile or so later he slowed down and looked back. There was no sign of Denise.

"Shit."

He retraced his steps, running.

29

Denise was where Gordon had left her but she was sitting down now and staring across the canal.

He stopped running when he saw her, approaching at a fast walk. If he hadn't argued with her, if he'd just found her sitting like this, he'd have said she looked half-amused and half-bored. When he reached her he knelt but he didn't have the strength to take her hand.

"I'm sorry," he said. "That's been brewing for a long time. It wasn't fair to aim it at you."

Her eyes drilled some distant point.

"I'm glad you could trust me with it."

"What do you mean?"

She turned to him.

"People who never fight aren't being honest with each other. My mum and dad used to argue a lot. But they were happy. Comfortable with each other. Know what I mean?"

Gordon nodded but he didn't. Not at all. The only person he'd ever been able to talk to honestly was Jude and there were some things he hadn't even told her. His parents had always seemed happy together but they'd argued only occasionally. Here was Denise using his outburst as a way of building even more into their relationship.

Wrong, wrong, wrong.

He had to look away.

"It does beg the question, though," she said.

His neck prickled.

"What question?"

"Why are you being like this?"

There were many inconsequential but fascinating things to see on the other side of the canal. The way empty beer cans had rusted. The way the rushes had died. The way–

"Gordon, look at me, will you."

Heat rising into his face, he forced himself to meet her gaze.

"You seem more than content to fuck me into exhaustion for half of every night. You do it with more passion than I've ever known. Like you love me. And then, when daylight comes, you barely speak a word to me. Why?"

He found he hadn't breathed for almost a minute. He let his breath go in a stagnant sigh.

"It feels wrong," he said.

"What does?"

"Us being together. I wouldn't have... chosen it."

"Neither would I."

"Really?"

She nodded without a trace of doubt.

"Really. You're not my type. You're too... *good*. Well, most of the time you are – when you've taken what you want you're like all the rest of them."

"No. Don't say that. I'm not like other men."

"Oh, you're depressingly similar, Gordon Black, no matter what you might think."

Stung, Gordon looked away again.

"I know what your problem is," she was saying. "You're an idealist. You want perfection in an imperfect world. You want things to be clear cut and simple. That's not how life is."

He nodded, unable to disagree even though he wanted to. "I know."

"Me, I can live with imperfection. I've done it all my life. I've made the best of a bad family, a bad home, bad relationships, bad times." She took his hand. Her fingers were cold and desperate. "The world's so screwed, so damaged. There's so little left that feels good in it. I know what you're feeling. I really do. But, you and me, we're not as bad as you think. We're alright. And I'm going to make the best of this, Gordon. I'm going to make the best of you. Of *us*." She squeezed his fingers. "Do you think you can do the same?"

He even managed to smile, though it was weak and fleeting. He looked into Denise's eyes and knew they had stepped closer to one another in spite of everything. There was nothing in those eyes for him to fear.

What scared him was himself.

"Yes," he said. "Of course I can."

He stood up and held a hand out to her.

"Are you ready to move on?" he asked.

"Are you?"

He nodded, almost smiling again.

"Come on. Let's get going."

For a while they walked hand in hand, Gordon negotiating the crumbling edge of the canal towpath and Denise dodging the brambles and thorns of the overhanging hedge. It made more sense to walk single file and soon their fingers slipped apart. Denise took up her customary position on Gordon's six and tried to keep up as his pace increased. From time to time he glanced back and smiled and Denise smiled back.

She didn't ask him what he was thinking about.

●●●●

As the day began to wane, Gordon kept his eyes open for somewhere they could stop for the night. While it was a great way to make progress north, the towpath afforded no place to pitch camp. Denise fell further and further back and, though she didn't complain, Gordon could tell her feet were sore again. Their cooked meat was gone and they were down to a couple of cans of tomatoes and one small can of sweet corn; it was hardly worth opening them just to eat them cold. The lack of food made Gordon clear-headed and light of foot but he knew that wouldn't continue indefinitely. They needed rest and he needed time to hunt.

In the late afternoon he spotted a thickly wooded area on the opposite side of the canal; so dense were the trees that they formed an almost black wall of wood. If they could find a small clearing among them, it would make great place to shelter. At the next bridge they came to he squeezed up through the gap between the hedge and the brickwork. A couple of minutes later, Denise limped up after him.

"You OK?" he asked.

"Fine."

He knew she was lying but he appreciated her perseverance. Travelling, living outside, was making her tougher. They crossed over and walked back a few hundred yards to the edge of the woodland. It was only as they came amongst the tightly crowded trees that Gordon smelled smoke and the unmistakable aroma of flame-roasted meat. His stomach rumbled. The fire must have been well-established and carefully tended – he hadn't seen any smoke from the towpath. He turned back to Denise.

"Someone's beaten us to it," he whispered.

"What do we do?"

Gordon weighed it up.

"We can either introduce ourselves and ask to share their space and their fire or we leave. Walking into someone else's camp is never easy, though. No one likes intruders."

He looked out through the trees. The light was already failing. Their chances of finding another place before dark were slim. Though he wasn't averse to sleeping under the overhang of the trees lining the canal towpath, he didn't think Denise was quite that wild yet.

"There's one other thing we could do," he said.

"What's that?"

"I could take a peek. See if the natives look friendly or not. We could decide what to do then."

Denise's eyes were wide.

"I'm coming with you."

Gordon shrugged off his pack and left it at her feet.

"There's nothing to be worried about, Denise. It'll be quieter if I go alone. I'm used to this and I won't make a sound. Worse than walking into someone else's camp is getting caught sneaking around outside it. Sit here and rest your feet. If you don't make a sound, no one will see you."

He squeezed her hand and turned to go. She tugged the feathers at his sleeve and he looked back.

"Be quick," she said. "I don't want to be alone out here."

"Ten minutes. No more. OK?"

"OK."

30

Gordon let the trees and the earth fill him with the spirit of the hunter.

He drew stealth and strength from the air. His breathing slowed, his heart rate dropped; he became still. He knew which way to go and he could sense presences at about ten o'clock from his starting point. Half a dozen people, he guessed.

Silent and swift, he flowed between the trees more like a shadow than a man. He heard the hiss of red-hot embers, the spit of grease falling into flame. The waft of cooking intensified. It could only have come from a large fire and a sizeable catch. For a moment he lost concentration. The aroma made his stomach grind against itself. Saliva burst beneath his tongue. In the next instant, discipline overrode his hunger.

He advanced.

The wall of trees between him and the camp thinned until he began to see figures ranged around a broad fire pit. It looked as though the clearing had been forced by the cutting down of trees – there were low stumps everywhere. A couple of them formed seats for the clearing's dwellers. Judging by the way things were laid out, this crew – at least eight strong that he could now see – had been living here for some time.

The fire pit was well looked after and much used. Several longbows leaned against a tree. The shelters were good-sized ex-military tents with a few patches but the way they sagged in places was a sign they'd been up for more than just a few days. The camp had a permanent feel about it but Gordon still couldn't decide whether it was a safe place to ask for shelter. If things got unfriendly for some reason, they were certainly outnumbered.

He tried to get a better sense of the individuals.

They could easily have been Green Men. They seemed to understand outdoor life and they all wore the drab browns and greens that made hiding and hunting in the countryside easier. Of course, much of that drabness came from dirt and constant usage. Spare clothes were harder to come by with each passing month. Secondhand often amounted to peeling garments from a corpse approximately your own size.

Many of them seemed to have learned about sewing skins together to make hats and jerkins. A few wore fingerless gloves, some of leather, others knitted from untreated wool. They must have been living outside for a good while because, although they weren't outwardly dirty, Gordon could smell their bodies even from this remove.

What they all had in common, man or woman, was their shaved heads. This suggested not that they held some common ideal, but that they were suffering with lice. The spread of lice happened easily in closeknit communities – not necessarily through unhygienic practices but through people sharing beds and being in close physical contact with each other. It meant this could be a loose family group; the beginnings of a tribe.

He would have acknowledged this with a smile if it hadn't been for one detail. There were no children. He'd come across several groups like this in his travels – Brooke and her father had been the first of many he'd spent time with. There had been plenty of others too wild or too strange to keep company with, but children had featured in every family setting. Perhaps this group had been childless before the Black Dawn and that was the common ground that had kept them together. Whatever the case, there was nothing about them that frightened him. They could walk into this camp and announce themselves as harmless passers-through.

He stepped back, ready to turn and retrace his steps. At the same instant, two of the group standing around the fire pit moved away, giving him a better view of the blackened spit and what lay beyond. Hunks of meat rotated and smoked over the scorching coals as a man turned the handle of the spit. The meat was ragged and pale but the portions dangling nearest the fire were charred black. Blue-grey smoke rose from the huge skewer.

Forming the backdrop to this and rippled by rising heat was the place where they butchered and prepared their meat. Two carcasses hung from grimy ropes slung over an A-frame of newly cut logs. One was whole. The other, partial, was divided into cuts. The skin was ash pale and had been hanging for some time. Now that he could see the raw meat, he could smell it too. Fatty and a little high, the scent of it reminded him of meat left too long on the butcher's counter on a hot day. At every cleaving and division, at every exposed joint, the flesh was grey. Of the partial carcass, all that remained was one handless arm, hooked at the wrist, half a ribcage and a footless calf snagged through the ankle. They swung and turned gently to a breeze Gordon couldn't feel. Perhaps it was the heat from the fire that pushed them back and forth, spun them lazily first this way and then that.

The complete carcass had undergone only the preliminaries of the process. The skin was pale but very hairy. Its genitalia were missing and its abdomen had been opened neatly from pubis to sternum. This cavity was empty. The cheeks and eyes were also gone; delicacies were always the first cuts. He'd been a big man and a fit one too by the look of him. Whether these were his friends who had turned against him in hunger or whether he and his, likely female, counterpart had been hunted he couldn't guess. None of the people in the camp looked undernourished so perhaps it was not necessity that drove them to this. Perhaps it was simply choice. Itinerant humans were far easier to hunt than wild animals and their meat yield was greater. Not only that, their bodies were made up of the exact nutrients other humans required.

Gordon's anger was tempered only by his responsibility. He moved away, as much the shadow as he'd been before. Only when he was out of sight did he turn his back on the clearing and make faster progress back to Denise. As he crept, he unclasped his knife.

Denise had not moved. She was still crouching beside a tree, hugging it for support though it looked like she took comfort from the contact too. Her eyes were wide and unblinking. As soon as she saw him she began to beckon with quick flicks of her hand. She looked from side to side as he approached, close to panic.

When he reached her she lunged upwards to meet him, almost knocking him over.

"Thank God," she said. "Thank fucking God you're back."

"What happened?"

"A group of men came past. They had a... girl. She was tied up with rope and they were carrying her between them on a pole like an animal. She was bucking and trying to scream but they'd gagged her too. Gordon, she couldn't have been more than ten years old. She was terrified."

Gordon closed his eye for a moment.

"We have to leave," he said. "Now. As fast as you can run."

"I can't run. I'm exhausted and my feet are in agony. And what about the little girl?"

"She's got no chance and neither will we if we don't move. There's too many of them."

"You have to do *something*. I can't even think about what they're going to do to her."

Gordon wasn't about to reveal the full inventory. He took hold of her hand.

"Listen, Denise. This has happened to me more times than I can count. It's already too late for the girl you saw. If it had been just me and I'd seen her, I'd be doing something about it. But if I see to her, I'm going to lose you. If you want to stay alive, we must go." She didn't move. "Right now, Denise."

She shook her head, scattering her tears.

"I'm not going to lose another child."

"She isn't…"

What? He asked himself. What exactly wasn't she? Wasn't every child their responsibility in a world like this? Now that he had left childhood behind, wasn't it his place to protect it for others?

He saw the anguish in Denise's eyes. She hadn't stopped being a mother just because her own child was dead.

"Alright," he said. "Which direction did they come from?"

"Across the fields."

"You're certain? Not from the canal?"

"From the fields. I saw them."

"OK. Take the pack and get back to the towpath. Go as far along as you can and hide – somewhere you can still see this wood." He pointed back the way they'd come. "A little bit farther than the bridge should do it."

"I'll come with you. I can help."

"No, Denise. You can't see this and you need to stay safe. Wait for me and I'll find you. I promise. If I don't, it's because I'm not coming. OK?"

"Shit."

"Do you understand what I'm telling you?"

"Yes."

Denise couldn't fathom him. In some ways he was still a little boy. In others he was more a man than any she'd known. She thought, perhaps, she really might be able to love him if they were together long enough, but she doubted they had much time left.

The boy who was a man turned and moved away, his black coat melding with the trunks of the trees.

"Gordon."

He didn't look back but Denise thought she heard him whisper:

"What?"

"Kiss me." she said.

Perhaps he hadn't heard. He kept moving, silent and fluid, until the wood claimed him. Despite the pain in her feet Denise found she was able to run very fast.

31

The trees darkened around him.

Out of sight but somewhere nearby a coven of startled rooks took flight from the trees, their wingtips slapping the branches as they hoisted for the sky. Their cawing was like knowing laughter in the twilight. Gordon felt them, circling high overhead, far above the tops of the trees, watching as the humans below made their awful mischief. Their strength descended to him, though, filling him with raw black power and rage. His own coat of feathers seemed to sing with the voices of crows, the rattle of magpies, the chawk of jackdaws, the chuckle of ravens. The short blade at his hand was just another feather, sharp and silvery.

By the time he reached the camp he was a trembling silhouette, a man-shaped pool of darkness. Four other men had joined the group now and meat was being passed around. They ate it with their hands, burning their lips and fingers as they tore into the roasted flesh.

The girl lay in the dirt near the fire, bound in rope at her ankles, knees, wrists and elbows. She was gagged with a filthy remnant of corduroy, also held in place with rope. They'd dropped her within sight of the fire and the butcher's workplace and her eyes flicked, wide and unblinking, from horror to horror and thence to the faces of her captors. Tears made dirty rivers on her cheeks. He wasn't sure if she reminded him of Jude or Flora. Perhaps she represented all that was precious and innocent and full of the future. Perhaps he was just looking for a way to deepen his rage.

These men and women who, perhaps only two or three years ago, had jobs and families, went to work in the mornings, slept in beds at night in centrally heated houses, made love to their spouses in the safe, private warmth of those beds, drank wine and ate food and chatted to their friends and wept at the passing of their loved ones; these people who had so recently been human were now not fit to be considered animals.

Their voices and laughter came to him in snatches:

"–don't have to kill her yet, do we?"

"–so sweet I could eat her *before* I eat her."

"–meat we've got will keep us going for a few more days."

"–keep her alive for a while? Pass her round, eh?"

Gordon pressed the knife flat to his wrist and stepped out of the trees. Only the little girl saw him at first. He winked at her. He walked among them, tall and calm, his manner so assured they didn't notice him for several moments. He took the time to turn to the girl and raise his eyebrows in mock surprise that he'd got so far without detection.

Then one of the bald men said:

"Who the fuck are you?"

"I'm the law of the land."

He slipped his arm around the nearest head and opened its neck with his knife. The woman, trying to seal the wound with both hands, stumbled away and fell face first into the fire pit. Her blood boiled and smoked. She didn't get up. The closest man tried to run when Gordon's eyes fell upon him.

Before he could even turn, Gordon lashed out backhanded, cutting his throat so profoundly both his trachea and oesophagus were severed along with his arteries. The man collapsed to his knees, lungs and stomach filling with his own blood. Gordon stepped back to avoid the spray.

Around the camp, skinheads were finally pulling out their weapons but none of them advanced, the shock of their losses plain on their faces. Gordon walked up to the nearest of them, a huge man who would have been even heavier in the days of plentiful food. The man flexed his knees ready to counter or avoid a slash. It didn't come. Gordon stood in front of him, arms folded, casual. The man, apparently unarmed, backed away to a safe distance. On all sides the skinheads had either found something to fight with or taken cover.

Gordon waited. He glanced at the girl. She lay abandoned near the fire pit. He caught a movement on the far side of the fire, saw a shimmering and heard something spin through the air. He stepped to one side. The meat cleaver hit the ground where he'd entered the clearing, kicking up black dirt before coming to rest. The burly, unarmed skinhead ran to retrieve it and advanced on Gordon.

"Get around the back of him," he shouted to the others.

The stunned skinheads began to pull together, some circling around the far side of the fire, others coming straight for Gordon. The burly man lunged while Gordon was assessing the advance. His cleaver came down from on high in a heavy butcher's stroke. Gordon's left hand stopped the descending wrist mid-swipe, leaving the man unguarded. Gordon moved in, his blade hand flashing momentarily in front of the man's eyes. The cleaver fell from his hand. Uncomprehending, he stared at his empty hand and the fallen weapon. A moment later, blood began to course from his upper arm, just below his armpit. When he clamped his left hand to the gushing wound, Gordon turned to face the others.

Once again, his eyes flicked to the girl. This time one of them saw the glance and Gordon knew his weakness had been revealed. He and the skinhead who'd caught his look lunged for the girl at the same time. The skinhead was closer. As the skinhead grabbed the girl's feet, Gordon struck out with his boot catching the man right on the chin with his toecap. The skinhead flopped to the ground beside the girl, unconscious and quivering; a deep snoring vibrated in his throat. Gordon knelt beside the girl and picked her up in his left arm. Bound like this, she was a dead weight. He only had time to cut her elbow and wrist restraints before two more of the skinheads, spotting his moment of distraction, came at him together empty handed.

He spun at the attackers, both women, knife hand arcing out as he stepped directly between them and the girl. The blade caught the upper arm of the first woman, parting stained fabric like tissue, slicing toward bone and exiting below her collarbone. Much of the momentum of the strike was gone but the sweep continued, opening the second woman's right breast and tearing through her nipple. Of the two, she was the one to squeal loudest. The damage was enough to discourage them for a few moments but four more skinheads pushed through to take their place. Three wielded machetes, the fourth a hatchet.

Gordon had enough time to glance at the girl again. Unconcerned about her gag, she was working the knots which held her knees and ankles. He could see how easy it would be to slip the bonds free but in her frantic desperation to release herself, the girl was merely pulling them tighter. Her breath rasped fierce at her nostrils, forcing mucus out and sucking it back in again so fast Gordon thought she must be close to suffocation.

Movement drew his attention to a new attacker – the man with the small axe. Mid-arc, the hatchet cut through the air near his neck. He shrank from the blow and the blade whispered across the feathers of his jacket. There was no time to use his knife but Gordon stepped into wake of the blow, trapping the hatchet against the man's body as it reached the nadir of its swing. He smashed the point of his left elbow into the hatchet man's exposed throat and felt the cartilage collapse under the strike. He let the man drop at his side to asphyxiate in the dirt.

As the weapon fell from the man's hand, Gordon grabbed it in his left hand. Backhanded, he let the hatchet fly as though he was throwing a Frisbee. It was a poor throw, coming as it did from his weaker side. Rather than sinking blade first into a neck or head, the flat, heavy back edge of the hatchet caught one of the three as yet unharmed skinheads on the ear. The sharp-cornered lump of steel cut through the ear and scalp, making solid contact with the man's skull near the mastoid bone. It wasn't enough to rob him of consciousness but it put him out of the fight.

The rest of them stood their ground, unwilling to tangle with a man who'd more than halved their numbers. Then he saw them grin at something behind him and he turned, wishing he'd held on to the hatchet. At least then he'd still have had something he could throw. The girl had managed to release her knees but the skinhead he'd kicked in the chin had regained consciousness and crawled on top her. He had her pinned down. Even as Gordon watched, the skinhead retrieved a small penknife from his pocket and hauled the girl to her feet. He made himself small behind her and put the blade to the girl's throat.

"This what you came for, birdman? Eh? Is it?"

The skinhead sawed at the girl's neck opening her unprotected skin. Blood flowed freely but it wasn't the death stroke. Not yet. Her captor leaned down and licked the wound, coming away red-chinned. Now the girl's wide eyes were squeezed shut. Her entire body shook and Gordon could see a dark stain spreading at her groin.

He stepped toward them.

"Oi! One more step and she's meat."

Gordon raised his blood-tainted blade and held it high. He showed it to those who still stood ready to attack, turning it like a talisman or an object of mesmerism.

He moved another step closer to the girl.

"What are you going to do *after* you've cut her throat?" he addressed the question to all of them. "Have you thought about that? Do you think I'm going to walk away? And do you know," he asked, letting his eyes meet every gaze in the group, "do you have any idea how many lives I've already ended? What makes you think I'm going to leave a single one of you alive?"

He took another steady step. The skinhead tightened up ready to snap.

"No closer, man. I mean it."

The hand that held the penknife was shaking now, gradually sinking deeper into the flesh of the girl's throat.

"Let her go," said Gordon. "I'll have to tend that wound of hers. It'll give you a head start. That's the best offer I can make."

Each of those still standing looked around, took in the carnage wrought by the single interloper. They looked at each other. There were still six of them. Together they could run, get away. Survive a little longer. But if they killed the girl they would have to face this tall, dark man right now.

"Shit, Malc. Let her go," said the man with the head wound. He had his hand pressed to his ear but blood had already soaked one half of his jacket.

The women agreed.

"Do what he says, Malcolm. Let's get out of here while we still can."

"What? Leave because of this bloke? This feathery fucking queer?"

The rest of them backed away.

"Fine, you stay if you want," said the one with the blood-soaked jacket.

"You fucking cowards. We're meant to work together. That was the agreement. Not fucking disappear when things get difficult. That was the whole *point*."

Without his support group, Malcolm was out of options. He let go of the girl and backed away. The girl slid slack-bodied to the ground and lay there pale and limp. The wound in her neck flowed freely but she hadn't lost enough blood to make her faint. The stress and shock of her ordeal had caused it. When Malcolm was far enough away, Gordon knelt beside the girl. The skinheads were grabbing items they felt they couldn't live without and running out of the camp.

Gordon inspected the cut in the girl's neck. The blood flow had stopped. He checked her pulse at the wrist. There was no movement beneath her skin. He listened to her chest. No breath. No heartbeat. He prayed for the Black Light, willed it to his fingertips.

Nothing came.

"Why?" he whispered.

There was no time for wondering. He thumped her hard on the chest and breathed into her slack mouth. Neither action revived her. He began heart massage, pumping down hard and fast and then breathing for her again.

"Come on, kid. This isn't the end."

Pressure and breath, pressure and breath. Her body remained doll-passive beneath his ministering hands.

"There's a future for you, I promise. A bright future. I'm working on it."

He pumped faster, working himself into a sweat.

"I'm working on it. It'll be there. All you have to do is breathe.

"Just breathe.

"Breathe!"

The girl died as the sun went down. Of terror; that was all Gordon could think. Perhaps her heart had been weak to begin with. Or maybe her mind had been strong enough to end her life before the skinheads did it their way, with gang rape and butchery.

As darkness gathered he cleaned the girl as best he could and made a resting place for her at the centre of the skinheads' clearing. Once she was buried he used a pair of steel tongs to break the circle formed by their fire pit. He used the hot stones to build a cairn over her body so that her grave would always be visible. He buried the remains of the man and woman hanging from the timber A-frame near the girl and placed a single stone at the head of each of their graves.

When he was done, he strode into the night.

Before dawn, Gordon had tracked and captured all of them by ones and twos, returning them to their camp. Some stumbled at knife point, hobbled by ankle ropes. Others came back slung over his shoulder. He bound them the way they'd bound the girl, like animals restrained for slaughter, and staked their ropes to the ground.

They were all alive and conscious when he strung the first of them up on the A-frame at first light. Alive, bound and facing the workplace where they'd turned other humans into meat. With a deft act of surgery to their eyes, akin to circumcision, Gordon ensured none of them would miss a single nuance of his performance.

He used the one with the injured ear first – the wound had swollen and suppurated and the man had begun to run a fever. Gordon cut his clothes away and hauled him up, feet first, to hang from the A-frame. Whilst those who waited were gagged, the hanging man was free to plead and scream all he wanted. Gordon stripped himself naked. Then he went to work on the hanging man, whose watery shit ran from his buttocks to the top of his head and whose piss dribbled into his own face.

Gordon whetted his knife blade against his river rock for all of them to see. He tested it on the man's thigh, a single delicate stroke opening his flesh deep into the quivering muscle below and sending streaks of blood from his groin to his shoulder.

He addressed his audience and fellow player:

"What you do to this world, to its people, you do to yourself. You do to *me*."

Blade-led deconstruction of the human form absorbed Gordon utterly. He lost count of the hours but the direction of the light had changed considerably by the time it was done. The hanging man was alive until the very end. He managed only one more that day before using one of their tents to bed down for the night. He was exhausted.

The work took two more days. Malcolm, last to be lifted from the earth, was insane with waiting by then. When it was complete Gordon washed himself in a nearby brook, dressed once more in his coat of black feathers and walked back to the canal.

He left the pieces for the rooks.

PART II

THE COMING OF THE CROWMAN

"There is no death. Only a change of worlds."

Chief Seattle (1786-1866)

"An individual may walk many paths but all paths lead to the self; and the true self is greater than any individual can ever be."

Aaron Alwin, Keeper of the Crowman,
Guardian of the World

32

Half propped up against folded skins and blankets, Mr Keeper looks like an ancient sack of bones, older than Carrick Rowntree and nearer to death. At first he shakes his head when Megan shows him the food but she pushes a spoonful of hot broth into his mouth and he has no choice but to take it. Brown juice trickles from his lips and she wipes it away with a rag. A little spark ignites deep within his eyes when the warmth of the stew hits his stomach.

She gives him a second spoonful and this time he makes a small nod of approval at the flavour. Now she gives him a third bite with a chunk of meat in it. He chews and swallows with gusto and pushes himself into a more upright position. He holds out his hand and she gives him the bowl. In a few minutes he hands the bowl back empty. She refills it.

After three bowls of ricky pot he is a different man. It's hard for Megan to say exactly what it is that is different about him. He still looks old and scrawny. He is still wounded. But the light that glows in his eyes has expanded into his skin and beyond. He exudes the powerful aura she remembers from the very first time she met him face to face in her parents' kitchen.

"Is there more?" he asks.

"I think three bowls is enough, isn't it?"

"I meant for you, Megan."

"I'm fine. I don't need it."

Mr Keeper reaches for his pipe and baccy.

"Actually, you do."

Before he says another word, a chill passes through Megan because she knows what is coming.

"You want me to go there, don't you?" she asks.

"You're the only one who can do it, Megan. No other Keepers live near enough. I never imagined something like this would happen before your training was complete but even so, you *are* ready. You have the understanding and strength to do what all Keepers must do: preserve the balance. Those men must be prevented from pursuing their work. For all we know they might have finished it already."

"Won't they be expecting more trouble?"

"I doubt it. As far as they know, they came to work and found a black panther in their hideout. Those with a hankering for technology from the old times have usually lost touch with the land already. I doubt they'll even suspect that they've been visited by a Keeper. They may have put some kind of deterrent or barrier up in the mouth of the cave to keep out wild animals, but that, I think, will be the extent of it."

"What will I have to do?"

"You must destroy everything in that cave with fire. I'll give you what you need for that."

"What if they catch me?"

Mr Keeper lights up and smiles, his irritating good humour returning far too rapidly for Megan's liking.

"Then you must educate them."

"What if they don't take kindly to my instruction?"

Mr Keeper's grin broadens at this.

"Well, Megan Maurice, I would suggest you impress upon them the importance of your knowledge. A Keeper has the final say in any matter such as this."

"I'm not a Keeper."

At this, the old man shrugged.

"It's true, the book isn't complete yet, Megan. But it will be soon and then you *will* be a Keeper. I have no doubt about that. In the meantime, you're acting under the auspices of one and you carry my authority. These men and their meddling must be stopped. By any means, Megan. Any means at all."

Megan sits back, quiet for a moment. This is her opportunity to show Mr Keeper what she can do, to prove herself. She knows she has abilities beyond her teacher's already, but will it be enough?

"I may have your authority, Mr Keeper. But I don't have your power. I can't take the shape of an animal."

"Little good it did me in the end. Anyway, Megan, you have no idea what you're capable of yet. You're only limited by what you don't yet know and your view of the world. The broader your perception becomes, the more possibilities the world will hold for you and the greater will be your power."

Nothing in her walking of the Path has been easy and none of it has been fair. It is disorganised and random with no clarity of beginning or end and no recognisable signposts along its way. It would be easy to fall into frustration as she so often has when he talks like this but Megan can already see herself searching for the secret cave and confronting the men who dare to forget how delicate this land is.

And yet, what does she really know of being a Keeper? Truly, in her heart, how certain is she of herself? What weapon does she possess that can defeat such determined men?

She is surprised to hear herself voicing her doubts.

"I don't need perception. I need training. I need to know what it is I'm meant to be doing." She gestured beyond the walls of the roundhouse. "Out there I'm just a girl, Mr Keeper. If those men catch me, they won't listen to a word I say. And who knows what they'll do to me?"

Mr Keeper closes his eyes for a moment or two and takes a pull on his pipe. I've gone too far, she thinks. When he opens his eyes again he will send me home. Why can't I learn to keep my mouth shut?

"I'm sorry," she says, knowing it's too late. "I'm... frightened."

His eyes open again but his expression is kind.

"You've every reason to be frightened, Megan. Do you think I wasn't? But you're not a child any more and you can't pretend to be. The things you've done, everything you've learned and all the thinking you've had to leave behind to come this far – all this has brought you out of childhood. You're a woman now. I ask you to do this because I believe in your ability to achieve it–"

"But even you couldn't do it."

"No. I couldn't. But I trust you to succeed where I have failed, Megan. If I didn't, I wouldn't ask you to do this. It's too important." He takes a final suck on the pipe and tips the remnant ash into a bowl beside him. "The age of male dominion still pulls our world out of balance. The energy of woman, the Earth Amu, must now rise. It's time for you to step into your power, Megan. See it, embrace it, use it."

There is always a choice; it is implicit in everything Mr Keeper says. Megan knows she could leave the roundhouse now and go home. It would be to forget she ever walked this path, ever knew this man the way she has come to know him. It would be to draw a thick curtain over her life and smother its potential. But at least it will be safe. At least it will be *knowable*.

And safe.

She realises with a tiny snort that these are things she is no longer interested in. She is interested in the wild nature of the land and its creatures. She is interested in pondering mysteries she may never penetrate. She is interested in living in the fullness of magic that exists between the great fatherly spirit above and the bounteous motherly earth below. She wants to keep it alive and give it everything she has so that its mystery will continue for those who come after her. She did not come into this world to stay coddled at her family's hearth, nor for her life to be anything other than the most ecstatic mystery.

"When should I go?"

"You must go now. Eat some ricky pot and I will make you a map."

33

Denise had made far more ground than Gordon could have anticipated. Two days of near-running pace didn't bring him close to her. In her fear she must have fled.

As he travelled he caught sight of small bands of men and women moving north with him. He tried to stay out of sight but there were others who, like him, had found the Grand Union towpath a road they could be safe on.

He began to come upon trains of people walking in single file. Many of them carried longbows. The rest were armed with weapons which belonged in tool sheds, workshops or farm outbuildings but they walked with purpose, these people. Perhaps understanding that this war might signify their final act in the world, that it might decide the future. They weren't raucous or overconfident. They walked with quiet determination, saving themselves for whatever lay ahead. Gordon began to believe that with a mindset like this, they might have a chance. They'd be lost without the right leadership though and this made him push the pace even harder after he'd spoken to as many travellers in each group as he could.

They all asked him if he would fight, of course. And he always answered that he would. But he had questions for them now: had they seen a dark haired girl with two packs? Had they heard tell of the Crowman? Many of them had seen a girl who matched his description of Denise. It seemed that she had fallen in with a group of the Green Men's First Guard; as near to an elite force as a civilian army would ever get. Some of these forces travelled on horseback and the group she'd found were such a one. That explained her speed.

All those who'd seen her said Denise and the First Guard were heading to Coventry where Green Men from all over the country were massing. Everyone who made it that far would have their place in the war; everyone who chose to fight now could consider themselves Green Men. As to the Crowman, the stories were as jumbled as ever; some versions of stories he'd heard years before, others more recent.

From a white-haired, stooped old man armed with a pick-axe handle:

"I heard he was spreading the flu all over London like a cloud of poisonous gas, hoping to take out the Ward bigwigs. Ended up killing the likes of us mostly."

From a man, two sickles in his belt, whose brown beard almost reached his belly:

"Crowman? You're joking, aren't you? That's a story we used to tell our kids to stop them misbehaving or get them up to bed. It's not real, mate. My advice? You want to keep your mind on killing Wardsmen. If there's hope for the future, it's in the destruction of the Ward. They're *real*. And they're bleeding this world to death."

From a woman, so gaunt she looked like twigs in a paper bag; a woman whose weapon – a baseball bat with barbed wire wrapped around its head – was the fattest thing about her:

"I've never seen him but my sister did. Said he fixed her broken leg after her house collapsed. Got rid of her piles too…"

The woman smirked. "She'd suffered with them for years. He got her whole family out of the rubble and he healed them." The woman shrugged, the points of her shoulders jabbing upwards. "That's what she told me, anyway. You never know who to believe these days, do you? You think you're talking to a friend and then you find out you're talking to the Ward."

From a boy who was obviously older than Gordon but was not yet a man:

"I'm from London, mate. I know all about your Crowman. I've heard the stories. He's not some superhero. He's a fucking psychopath. I've heard he kills for pleasure. He doesn't care whether it's a Wardsman or Green Man like you and me or just some poor scavenger out on the street. He's using the chaos to do whatever he wants. Rape. Murder. Torture. You name it. When you come across the worst misdeeds, it's probably him that done it." The boy had a replica samurai sword tucked through his belt. People walking behind had to take care not to cut their knees and whenever the boy turned around, the tip of the sword spun with him, sending those closest scattering. Gordon himself almost fell into the canal when the boy was startled by a bird in the hedgerow. He beckoned Gordon closer and whispered, "I'll waste him myself if I catch him."

From a bald man wearing dirty orange robes and mouthing silently as he passed a string of beads through his fingers:

"Look within, brother. That's where you'll find him." The man, whether he was a real monk or not was impossible to tell, thumped his own chest twice with a clenched fist. "This is where I keep the Crowman. He's with me all the time."

The only stories he heard that made any real sense were those eyewitness accounts of Denise passing through on horseback. Frustrated, Gordon moved past each new posse of ragtag fighters without further questions, cursing himself for the time he'd lost chasing rumours.

Megan's pack is light this time and she walks with urgency, eager for this to be over, eager to be pursuing Gordon in his search for the Crowman.

She senses his journey will soon be over. In his world the Black Dawn has risen over the land and thrust it into darkness. Gordon has become a man and the clash between the Ward and the Green Men is imminent. That conflict, she believes, will signal the culmination of Gordon's long quest. She is not certain of this but it is something she feels within; there is a natural sense of conclusion arising from everything she sees in Gordon's world, an inevitability about the turns his path is now taking.

Whilst it is her duty, this journey to the cave is a disruption to her completion of the Black Feathered Path. The sooner she can put whatever is in the hideout to the torch, the sooner she can return and continue her own quest for vision. When the book is complete, her training will be all but finished and she will officially take the responsibilities and powers of a Keeper. Though this terrifies her, neither can she wait for it to be so.

The morning crackles and creaks with frost. The soles of her boots meet knobbly, unyielding ground with each step and the air is powder dry. Though she is well wrapped up in furs, the cold bypasses every layer. Perhaps it is merely nerves causing her to tremble inside. She walks faster to build up some heat.

A couple of hours into the journey she realises that she can't keep up the pace. Another simple lesson she has failed to learn from irritatingly sensible Mr Keeper. She brunches on wheaten loaf and sips water as she walks, allowing herself to ease off for a few miles before putting the pressure on again. By mid afternoon, assuming Mr Keeper's map is correct, she is two or three miles from her objective.

Once again, she slows the pace, eats and drinks to keep up her strength. A mile or so farther on, she checks the map again. This area is more detailed, showing a coppice where she can rest and prepare out of sight. The cave is on the far side of a small valley between two gentle hillsides. Its position is marked by a windmill on the top of the hill opposite the coppice. According to Mr Keeper the three men are using the wind's energy, not only to mill grain but to operate the machinery in the cave directly beneath.

It isn't long before Megan spots a thick knot of woodland up ahead. Relieved that the map and her reading of it is correct, she hurries on releasing a sigh as she disappears from view among the trees.

The coppice is comprised mainly of pines, with a few deciduous trees struggling to survive between them. It is dark and sheltered and its shadows are wild. Megan revels in the comfort and sanctuary it provides. She couldn't have asked for a better place to prepare.

Near the lower border of the coppice, she shrugs off her pack and collapses onto the soft cushion of brown pine needles. She massages her calves and thighs, takes off her boots and kneads her aching feet. When she has eased the tension from her lower limbs and replaced her boots, she wraps her travelling blanket around herself, lays her head on her pack and allows her mind to drift away from her body so that both may rest.

34

Two branchings from the Grand Union brought Gordon onto the Coventry Canal.

Here the stream of human traffic was almost constant and the sense of excitement, of being part of something important, grew. Many of the groups sang as they marched: old rugby songs and football chants, hits from the days when everyone had music at their fingertips. Some of the rabble carried instruments – anything from guitars to recorders – and when they played in unison even Gordon felt something new and vibrant dance in his heart. He hurried past, singing or humming with each group as he came into the city of Coventry.

The canal passed through an area of new residences that had once been a desirable place to live. Now they were shells, their glass smashed, smoke stains rising up from balconies and windows. He climbed the steps leading up from the towpath and crossed a black footbridge spanning the ring road. On the other side, he descended into the city. Near the disused bus station, beside a vast car park where every vehicle was no more than a carapace of rust, Green Men had gathered in their thousands to make a new city of tents, shelters, cardboard boxes and lean-tos. The flimsiest of these were underneath an overpass to give them a little shelter from the elements.

This was not like London. Here there was no threat of roving patrols. The Ward had failed to hold this city, though they'd tried many times to take it back by force. Coventry, one of the hardest-hit British cities during the Second World War, had a proud, flinty heart. The people here, some born in the city but many more having recently arrived from elsewhere, appeared uncowed by their circumstances.

Gordon hadn't witnessed such simple joy of spirit since his childhood. He remembered now how children had played together in break time, sung songs and chased each other in breathless, laughing circles. He remembered how grownups had gathered around tables to eat and drink and tell stories.

For some reason, this scene of ramshackle chaos and camaraderie reminded him of Christmas. The colours of Christmas were so bright in his memory they were like the intense, individual flavours of boiled sweets. Sweet indeed, those recollections, when hereabouts all was dirt-grey and charcoal-drab, when the clothes of every person were stained with the grime of the road and the touch of the land, when the smell of people was reminiscent of the smell of animals. Yet Gordon was happy to walk among them, for their spirits were as bright as Yuletide, as pure and as innocent as any rejoicing human could be. He relished it all. This was a time before bloodshed and such times might not return, neither soon nor ever.

As he walked, dislocated and spectral amid the cheer, people noticed his coat of feathers, glancing at him a moment longer than they looked at anyone else. But none made comment. Black feathers, Gordon noticed, were common here. Woven into people's hair, sewn around the knees of their trousers and elbows of their sleeves, worn as necklaces and charms. Black feathers even decorated many of the weapons resting on shoulders or worn through belts or hanging in decorated slings from backs and chests.

Gordon laughed to see it.

Oh, yes! He is here!

How it could be, Gordon wasn't sure, but the Crowman no longer walked the streets of London. The promise of war had brought him north. Gordon could feel the Crowman's presence both in the minds of the people and out here among them. The Crowman walked here, somewhere nearby; Gordon knew it. Reaching out, sensing that presence among the throng, Gordon picked up his pace.

The Green Men were here in vast numbers. Everyone who had journeyed here to fight the Ward, they were all Green Men now, whether they cared for such a title or not. Yes, there were a few among them who only partially understood and plenty who misunderstood, but the wearing of black feathers by so many who now banded together; that was a sign of change. There was a chance. Right here, right now. If the Crowman could carry these ordinary people into battle and if they, in turn, could carry him in their hearts, the days of the Ward and the years of the Black Dawn would have their end. There would be something beyond it all. A place for children; a future.

As daylight began to wane, Gordon continued to search, among the people yet somehow soaring above them; appreciating their numbers and the strength of their combined will. Beneath the tarmac and concrete of Coventry's city centre, the land thrilled at the touch of thousands of faithful feet, feet that longed to walk barefoot in wild meadows and wade carefree in cool rivers and unpolluted lakes. These people yearned to come home to the land, to listen to its silent song, to sit upon the bones of great Grandmother Earth and accept her wisdom instead of imposing their own upon her.

The people around him grew greater in number and navigating between them required more skill. Many of them had stopped moving and were straining to hear a man speaking somewhere up ahead. Curious, Gordon pushed his way through the now almost static crowd.

At the base of a broad pillar supporting the overpass, standing on the roof of a double-decker bus, a man addressed the throng. Gordon glanced around. Green Men still arrived from every direction, all of them pushing forward to hear the speaker's voice as though it were a popular show – either that or some strange outdoor benediction. In the gathering dusk, Gordon stepped between the people of the crowd like a man stepping between reeds, or stalks of corn. People grumbled as he passed, some of them trying to stop him with their elbows. Unfazed, Gordon pressed forward, coming almost to the front of the multitude.

From here he could see the speaker clearly and make out his words.

Atop the bus – once red, now wheel-less, rusted and hollowed out by abuse and neglect – it was a ragged man who held court with such magnetism. He wore not clothes but woven twists of rag. The filthy ropes of cloth were draped over a gnarled and knobbly frame of bones, secured with knots here and there and a belt held the mess together at his middle.

Each time he moved, the man's grimy flesh appeared between the plaited strips of remnant fabric and Gordon saw he was pocked from head to toe, the survivor of some skin virus perhaps, or a victim of some gradually consuming pox or cancer. He was blind, this man, and a rope around his waist secured him to a bolt driven into the concrete pillar behind him. Thus he could walk in an arc on the roof of the bus without falling.

Walk he did, like some wild animal recently captured and imprisoned in a cage; searching for an exit along a few feet of barrier, an exit which did not exist. The angles of his jaw and cheek bones were so sharp his head appeared barbed somehow, and his matted hair hung in clots about his face.

He raved, this blind skin-sick man, and the people cheered to hear the rasp and rattle of his shattered voice.

"Beneath this concrete and tarmac, beneath the very foundations of this city the Earth is gathering herself. She waits for you!"

The crowd raised up its hands and voices in a cheer.

"She does not sleep, my good people. She does not die. She lives! And she will take you any way she can. She will take your hoe and your shovel and she will welcome your return. She will take your snares and traps and place her bounty within them. She will take your blood, the blood you go to give in battle, and she will thank your children for your sacrifice.

"She lives, I tell you! She lives the way only a blind man who has sinned against her can see. She is not dead. But without you, good people of this land, without you, be assured the Earth will die and every creature that depends upon it will die too. The world will cease to spin and the spirits that have always called this place home will go elsewhere in the universe to weave their magic. And every soul that ever lived or died on Earth will be lost to oblivion.

"She lives and she demands to live!"

The man staggered as he walked, afflicted in ways Gordon could only guess at. He looked as though he had been beaten by an army of men, his limbs broken and the bones badly reset. Every finger on his hands was crooked. When he pointed into the crowd, his fingers were the snapped branches of dying trees.

"I see you, good people! I see your proudly worn black feathers and I know what they signify." The man's voice fell to a hiss. "He is here…"

And rose to a roar.

"HE IS HERE!"

He threw his broken arms heavenward and then pointed once more into the crowd, his bent fingers sweeping the ranks as though he was searching for something, following his broken fingers with his blind eyes as he scanned.

"The Crowman walks among you. You've seen the visions. You've heard him in your dreams. You've told his stories and in doing so you've kept him alive. I've heard the rumours, we all have. He's a killer of children, a bringer of pestilence and war, a god of earthquakes and storms. The Ward would have you believe the Crowman's arrival signifies the end for all of us."

The man slumped forward as though exhausted. He fell to his knees. His head hung to his chest. His filthy, tangled hair became indistinguishable from his rag robes.

The crowd fell silent, waiting.

His head came up. His eyes, wide and white, showed the cracks and punctures and rends which had blinded him. He held his broken hands out to the crowd in supplication, shaking his head, as though at *their* blindness, their ignorance.

"The Crowman is the future, good people. The Crowman is the heart of the world. He is here. He is alive and that heart yet beats, deep beneath our feet and in the chest of every true Green Man and Woman."

The Rag Man knelt on his scarred, bony knees and nodded.

"Yes. It's true. It's all true. I have seen because I have eyes no other man has. It was the Crowman who gave me these eyes, my true eyes. And he sent me out into the dying world tell you all what only I can see."

The Rag Man struggled to his feet.

"Do you want to know what I see?"

People in the crowd nodded. Some even said "yes". The old man raised his voice.

"Do you want to know what I see?"

All around came shouts of "yes" and "tell us what you see". It wasn't enough.

"DO YOU WANT TO KNOW WHAT I SEE?"

"Yes, yes, yes, yes, yes, yes, yes, YES, YES, YES!"

Gordon found his own voice adding to the chaos of answers. He believed it more than anyone here, he wanted to know what the Rag Man saw. He wanted to know everything. Most of all he wanted to find the Crowman. The Crowman was here among them, somewhere in this city. Somewhere in the crowd perhaps. As though a cloud had cast a shadow on a warm day, Gordon shivered. He spun, scanning the multitude for the figure he longed to see. There was nothing but dirty faces, faces upturned to the Rag Man and screaming for his answer.

The crowd's pleas died down when the Rag Man used his ravaged hands to calm them, patting down the noise with gentle movements. When there was silence, utter silence, he spoke, weeping.

"I see nightfall in the morning. I see the Black Dawn! You will say it is the end of everything but there is light in that darkness, good people. A light that will carry us into the Bright Day. Men and women of this land, I see the future. The Crowman has come. He is here. Find him. Let him lead you."

The silence gathered and rose like a spell. The Rag Man bowed. Only then did the assembled masses break the hush with rapturous claps, whistles and cheers.

35

The crowd dispersed slowly, back to their tents or canvas shelters or into cardboard-covered sleeping bags beneath the overpass. Many walked back towards the old bus station and some sought sanctuary a short way up the hill in the cathedral. A few of the listeners stayed where they were. Like Gordon, they wanted a more intimate audience with the blind prophet.

Daylight was replaced by the weak glow of flickering lamps and small fires. The Rag Man would have been lost without his helpers, a trio of boys somewhat younger than Gordon and dressed in similar ropes of reclaimed fabric to their master. They unhooked him from his tether in the concrete column and led him to a hole cut in the roof of the bus. From there he descended a ladder into the upper deck and took a seat in the back row.

While he waited his turn, Gordon shinned up a lamppost nearby to get a closer look. One by one, those who wished to speak with the Rag Man were ushered in by the boys and climbed the steps to the upper deck. Gordon could hear murmurs of conversation from the back of the bus but nothing distinct and it was too dark in the candlelit gloom to clearly see what took place. The Rag Man appeared to bestow blessings, often touching the heads or faces of his visitors with his broken fingers before they left him, but more than that, Gordon couldn't make out.

He was last to enter. Coventry was falling into darkness and all around flames lashed upwards from oil drums and fire pits made of brick and breezeblock.

Candles, flickering in the breeze that pushed through the bus's glassless windows, lit Gordon's way up the stairs into the top deck. The limbs of the boy who led him appeared and disappeared through the ropes of his garment as he walked and Gordon couldn't help but think how cold such a uniform must be. On reaching the upper floor, the boy and his two fellows retreated to the front of the bus and waited, as though vigilant for trouble.

"You can leave us," the Rag Man said, waving a crooked hand at the boys.

Gordon looked back. They were hesitant.

"No harm will come to me, boys. What more harm can there be? Go now."

The three rag boys, barefoot and sullen, descended the stairs but Gordon was sure they waited just below, their ears cocked upwards to catch every word.

There was an upturned plastic milk crate in the aisle. Gordon took his place there. The Rag Man sat in the middle of the back row of seats. His face didn't look real in the wavering glow of the candles, nor did his broken body. This form he'd taken was merely a vehicle, a hermit-crab's shell. In trying to see beneath his hideous armour Gordon missed the evidence that was right before his eyes.

"You've been searching for him for quite some time now," said the Rag Man, his voice seeming to pass through broken bottles to exit his lips.

"How do you know that?"

The Rag Man laughed; shards and tinkles, hobnail boots stirring gravel.

"Have you found him yet? That's the important question."

"No."

"But you're close."

"I think so," said Gordon. "You said yourself he walks among us. You said he was here."

The Rag Man's blind eyes stared and flickered as though trying to catch a glimpse of something moving fast inside the bus. Gordon couldn't help but look over his shoulder. There was nothing there.

"Yes," said the Rag Man when his sightless orbs had ceased to scan the inside of the bus. "I do my best to speak the truth these days. The truth as I see it. As near as I can get."

Gordon ignored what appeared to be the beginnings of a digression. He'd searched too long too waste time on an old man's stories.

"Can you help me find him?" he asked the Rag Man.

"Help you? You don't need any help. It's your destiny to find him. No matter what you do, you cannot escape that one simple fact. You and the Crowman will be united."

United? As friends? As brothers in arms?

"What does that mean?"

The Rag Man began to cough, his throat clattering like a wood chipper. The spasm went on for a long time and when it finally stopped, the Rag Man was breathless and shrunken.

"It means," he said in a cracked whisper, "that your search is almost over."

"When, though? When *will* it be over?"

The Rag Man grinned, exposing a few broken, blackened teeth.

"You haven't changed all that much, have you?"

"What?"

"Still impetuous and impatient. Keen to be moving on…"

Gordon's skin chilled. Did he know this man? Had they met on the road sometime?

"I've never been too far behind you, you know. Never too far away. And even when I wasn't really looking I heard a little morsel of news here and there about your travels through this half dead land of ours. It seems you go by many aliases."

Gordon stood and backed away, stumbling over the milk crate and catching hold of the back of a seat for support. He did know this man. He had tried very hard to forget him.

"Grimwold."

He'd drawn Gordon to this place somehow, knowing exactly what it was he wanted to hear. And now, lured into the bus, he was about to suffer the man's retribution.

"Sit down, please, Louis Palmer. Or don't you use that name any more?"

In the warmth of his coat pocket, Gordon's hand found the comfortable shape of his knife. He heard footsteps on the stairs. In an instant the blade was free and he'd turned to face the three boys.

Behind him the Rag Man stood up.

"Please! No more bloodshed. There's been too much already and there's so much more to come. Louis, put away your weapon. Boys, I want you to leave us alone. Go into the city and don't come back until morning. I mean it."

No one moved at first. Gordon didn't see anger in the eyes of the rag boys, only concern for their derelict master. Gordon brought his breathing and heartbeat under control. He folded away his lock knife and slipped it back into his pocket. The rag boys retreated down the stairs. Gordon looked out into the night and only when they'd passed between a dozen fires and were out of sight did he turn and face Grimwold.

"My name is Gordon Black."

"Gordon it is then." Grimwold gestured towards the milk crate. "Please, Gordon. Sit."

36

There was silence between them for a long time and Gordon thought:

Thank fuck he can't see me.

By the flickering of candles, he watched Grimwold. He studied him. The pockmarks were the scars of a thousand blackthorn needle wounds. The bent limbs and fingers were the result of dozens of broken bones; none of them set back into their natural forms. Grimwold's eyes looked like milky glass, hammered until it shattered and then painstakingly reassembled.

"Sometimes I'm glad I can't see myself," said Grimwold. "But most of the time I don't care."

Gordon wanted to apologise but there were no words that could make amends for this. All he would be doing was salving his own rotten conscience.

"And don't ever say sorry to me, Gordon. There's much more to this than action and reaction, crime and punishment."

Is he reading my mind?

"Meeting you brought the Crowman into my life. That night on the river bank, my world changed forever. I met him, Gordon. He came to me as I lay smashed and bleeding under the thorn trees and he gave me a kind of sight. It's like radar for the future or something. I have visions and I share them with the people. Everywhere I go, people come to me and I tell them the things I've seen. Sometimes a droplet of the Black Light awakens within me and I'm able to do something for the sick or the wounded. You made me, Gordon. You fashioned me this new body and the Crowman saw value in it. He gave me an opportunity to make a difference. So here I am."

Grimwold made it sound inconsequential, like the story of a hitcher who'd ended up in the wrong town and then decided to stay because he liked it. But Gordon had made Grimwold pay for things he hadn't even done, he'd punished him for all the pain in his own life; all the pain he had space to comprehend on that particular night. Such had been his rage. Such had been his... insanity.

There were no words.

No words.

"I followed you across this land, Gordon. Touched the hedgerows, woods and caves where you'd slept. Walked in your footsteps through cities living and dead. As I followed, I was healed. Slowly my new sight came to me. After a while I had no reason to follow you any more. I could see you whenever I wanted just by thinking about you." Grimwold chuckled to himself. "The things you done, boy..."

Gordon stared through the glassless window into the night for a moment, remembering; weighing up the dark deeds against the light. Grimwold, however, had concerns too pressing to afford him the luxury of such reminiscences.

"I have something for you, Gordon."

Grimwold reached between the twisted ropes of rag covering his torso and brought out an object, held in both hands. For a moment Gordon glimpsed more scarring behind the torn curtains of cloth and then the old wounds were hidden once more. Grimwold seemed to be quivering with excitement.

"Put out your hand."

Gordon hesitated.

"Do it."

Gordon extended his arm, his palm upwards.

Grimwold placed something cool and black in his hand.

A jolt leapt from the object and seized his arm in a coil of icy current. The surge spread through his chest and into his entire body, paralysing him as he sat on the milk crate. The Black Light rose within him like a tide, more powerful than ever before, blinding him utterly. In the cannibals' clearing, trying to save the unnamed girl, he thought its force had deserted him but here it was again, stronger than ever.

Grimwold! He could use it to repair the damage. He reached forward with both hands but the Rag Man backed away.

"Don't you touch me, Gordon Black. Don't ever touch me again. There is no remedy for the deeds of the past. I have no regrets for the changes you wrought upon me. You moulded me like clay, like a creator. You brought the Crowman to me. There is no undoing his will."

Gordon sat back, trying to blink away the blindness. Whatever charge he'd received from the black object in his hand, the flow now reversed and the tide of raw Black Light was drawn into the artefact, filling it up until he thought it would explode into a thousand fragments. The reaction ended and the black stone warmed to the touch of his hand, as any stone would left next to the skin for long enough.

Gradually, Gordon's sight returned and he inspected the object resting in his palm. It shone under the candles, reflecting dozens of pinpoints of gentle ivory light. It was a crystal of some kind, black as obsidian but carved with symbols. Two crows facing away from each other in a stylised tree and one crow with its wings spread over the whole image. The tree's roots met the uppermost crow's wings, forming the circle which encompassed the motif. A black feather had been bound with thread to each of the four compass points of this outer circle. From the top of the stone extended a black leather thread.

"You need to wear it, Gordon."

Gordon gazed at the thing, entranced. Grimwold became agitated.

"Put it on. Put it on!"

Gordon kept staring at it, turning it in his fingers, tracing its fine workmanship. It almost felt as thought the stone were the Black Light made solid. He placed the necklace over his head and let the stone rest against his chest for a moment. Within seconds his fingers were exploring it again.

"Where did you get this?"

"I made it."

"Made it?" Gordon looked at Grimwold's crooked fingers, many of them without nails, his blind eyes. "How?"

"The Crowman gave me the design in a vision. Not long after, he gave me the stone too. Told me it comes from somewhere near the heart of the world. It was just a lump of cold crystal when I first held it in my hands but day by day I worked it, cracking away the crust which hid the design. It was as though the shape of it already existed inside the crystal. All I had to do was take away the dross without breaking it. Easier said than done. It's taken me two years to make it."

"It's incredible."

"It's more than that, Gordon. It's alive. The Crowspar is conscious. I guess you'll find that out for yourself soon enough."

"What am I supposed to use it for?"

Grimwold slapped his knees with both palms and sat back.

"Ho! Well. Now you're asking. It's a compass. A focal point. An oracle. A doorway. A talisman. An icon. A chronicle in crystal. I could go on and on. It's whatever you need it to be, Gordon. But it's much more than that too. No matter how long you hold it for, you'll never understand everything about it. It's a grail but it's absolutely real; more real than you or I perhaps. Long after you and I are gone, the Crowspar will live on. And yet you are able to hold it in your hand. It's a gift, Gordon. From the Crowman to you. It will take you the rest of the way."

With the Crowspar resting against his heart, Gordon felt serene. There could be no firmer sign that he was in the right place at the right time, that everything he'd done and all that had happened along his way was somehow correct and unavoidable. He'd made all the right choices so far and they had kept him on the path. But then...

"Grimwold?"

He knew his voice sounded like the voice of a boy, a boy with so many questions he'd bring a smile to the face of any adult.

"What is it?

"Do I... have a choice? In all of this, I mean. Can I change it? Go against it? Can I back away?"

Grimwold scratched at something within his rag robes. Whatever inhabitant he liberated with the tip of his finger went into his mouth before Gordon could spot what it was. Grimwold chewed and something tiny crackled between his remaining teeth.

"Well, I hoped you wouldn't ask me that. But then, I suppose, I knew you would. You do have a choice. We all do. But to shy away from what you know you were born to do is to spend the rest of your life asleep."

"That doesn't sound so bad."

"It is bad. It's terrible. Imagine if the Earth decided not to spin. If the trees and flowers decided not to grow. If farmers decided not cultivate the land. If lawmen decided not to keep the peace. What do you think would happen?"

Gordon shrugged.

"Isn't that a bit of an oversimplification?"

"It's a serious question, Gordon. A relevant question. The least you could do is consider it."

"Well… I suppose everything would stop?"

"Life would be pointless. It's the path to uncreation, Gordon. Worse than Armageddon, it would be the unmaking of the world. Our lives are a gift and they come with responsibility, not only to ourselves but to the land, to everything that has life around us. We must be ourselves with great commitment and energy. It's our privilege and our duty."

Grimwold reached out with unexpected speed and accuracy, seizing Gordon's hands in his. The touch of his pitted skin and unnaturally angled fingers was repulsive.

"Look at me, Gordon Black. See what you did with your rage, with your need for justice and vengeance. You made me what I am. But I chose the path that led me to you, and you chose the one that converged with mine. So, in a sense, I created you. We adhered with great energy to who we were born to be and it has brought us both a long way. A terrible path it was, yes, but the correct one."

Grimwold let go and Gordon found he was sweating even though the air swirling through the bus's upper deck

THE BOOK OF THE CROWMAN

was almost freezing. Where Grimwold's hands had touched his there was a lingering sensation, a burn like frostbite. Grimwold sat back against the damp, ruined upholstery of the back seats.

"You could choose to avoid all this, Gordon," he said. "You could go back... or at least go no further. You could hope that someone else would take up your cause and find the Crowman so that he might be brought to the people, so that he may guide them. But it is not another man's job to do. It's yours. Even so, you could make yourself scarce in some valley somewhere far away where no one would ever find you or even bother to look. And perhaps the world would survive without you fulfilling your purpose in it. Let's face it, Gordon, this isn't just about you. There are others out there trying to do what's right to protect the future. So you could just say 'no' and forget about all this. But you would live the rest of this life in uncomfortable slumber and one day you would return to this world to finish what you started. And you would return and return until you fulfilled what you first came here to do."

Gordon laughed.

"So, you're saying that ultimately I have no choice."

Forlorn and without humour, the laugh died the moment it left his mouth. Grimwold leaned close and pointed a crooked finger in Gordon's face.

"You have the same choice we all have. And you should be grateful for it."

Grimwold sat back again, his breath seemed to come in laboured gulps now, his shoulders rising and falling with the effort of each gasp.

"Are you alright?" asked Gordon.

Grimwold shook his head.

"I've done all I can for you, Gordon Black. I think you should go now."

Gordon's body wouldn't obey the command.

What more do I want from this?

Despite Grimwold's assurances, perhaps no words would ever absolve him. Gordon stood from the milk crate. He took a breath ready to speak but Grimwold cut him off.

"There's enough between us now, Gordon. Enough for a lifetime. Our paths have converged twice and now they split forever. This much I have seen. So don't say any more. Not another word. Not even goodbye. Leave me in peace. Go and make your choice."

Gordon stood in the aisle for a long time. The sounds of voices from outside the bus were indistinct murmurs. Fires flickered in the darkness in every direction. Grimwold's head lolled back against the grimy cushion of his seat. His eyes were open but for all Gordon knew he could have been asleep already. He could have been dead.

Gordon wanted to speak. He truly did. But his mouth would not open. He had no words for this. Gordon ran from the rusted double-decker; home and pulpit to a Rag Man of his own creation.

37

Dear Gordon

Are you OK? God, I wish so much that you would write back
to me. It seems like so long since I started sending you these letters.
Bossy says you will have got some of them by now, even if they
didn't all make it through. In spite of everything, he's always very
nice to me, really. Was very nice, I mean. You won't believe who
I saw yesterday. It was Skelton and Pike from back when... Oh,
heavens, Gordon I still can't think of it even now. If you were here
and you'd seen them and you had Dad's knife with you, you'd
have... well, you know. God, I'm crying now. Smudged my bloody
writing. I'm sorry. They scared me so much when I saw them. I've
never forgotten what they did to us. How they came in and, oh dear
God in heaven, Gordon. When I saw them in the doorway I peed
myself. Skelton was laughing and Pike just looked dead in his eyes
like a statue or something. Skelton's voice was awful. He sounded
more like a girl than ever. He said they're going to move me
somewhere better, away from the other prisoners. He said they're
going to give me some food to fatten me up and find me some nice
teeth so I look like a young lady again and not some old trout. That
was what he said, the bastard. Bossy stood in the corner looking
really angry. When they left he said I should do a little something
for him, give him a special cuddle and a special kiss. He said it

was hard luck because I wouldn't see him any more. He said he
wouldn't be able to send any more letters for me. He came and sat
next to me and I stabbed him in the neck with a tiny screwdriver
I found in someone's old clothes. I've been hiding it in my latrine
bucket where no one would want to check. Stupid Bossy. He looked
so surprised when I did it. I got him again and again before he even
put up a hand to stop me. I even managed to get him in the eyes.
Then I did one in side of his head and it got stuck so I stopped. I
said to him as he sat back on my bunk: "You never sent any of my
letters, did you?" and he shook his head. I know that means you
won't get this one either, Gordon, but it doesn't matter. I know one
day I'll see you again. I know it. And then I'll tell you everything. I
love you, Gordon. Jude.

Needing to be far from the throngs of gathering troops and
their families, wanting the solitude of the countryside and
unable to find it in the city, Gordon fled along uninhabited
streets into the night. He pounded up a hill, passing women
selling favours for food. Without his pack, he had no blankets
or shelter.

When he came to a twin monolith of tower blocks,
he entered the lobby of the nearest and ran up the stairs.
Feeling along the walls of the corridors, he found doors either
hanging off their hinges or missing on every level. Sometimes
he passed silent figures crouching in the darkness – asleep or
dead he couldn't tell. He didn't know what he was looking
for; only that height would give him some sense of remove
from all that he had witnessed. He needed time alone, time
to think.

The farther he climbed the more intact doors he came
across. With the lifts long since abandoned, it seemed few
people had the energy to come this high up when they

wanted a place to sleep. If he'd been in the wilds, it would have been a hill or mountain Gordon would have climbed. In the city, this high-rise was the best he could do.

When there were no more flights of stairs he explored the last, uppermost corridors more carefully. On this level here all of the doors were still in place. A few of them were open. He listened for a long time at every door until he was certain the whole floor was uninhabited.

The locked doors were the ones that beckoned. He walked up and down the passages running his fingers over unopened front doors until he found one that felt right. Pushing off from the opposite wall he smashed the sole of his boot into the wood, as near the handle as he could. The impact sent the flimsy door crashing inwards where it connected with the wall of the inner hall and then bouncing back. Gordon stepped inside and pushed the door closed behind him, finding a chair to wedge under the handle.

There were rooms to either side of the hall, all of them tiny, and at the far end a door led into what would once have been a small living area. The sofas and chairs were still there. Gordon went to the window and looked down. From here he could make out tiny fires in every direction, most of the centred around the old bus station and car park.

The air in the flat was old, dead and undisturbed. Gordon unclasped and opened as many of the windows as he could. The air that came in was smoky and cold but it was better than the stagnant air within. For a while he stood, watching the flickering lights far below. He was high enough that there was only silence to accompany them and the occasional whine of the wind as it swept around the edges of the tower block. Only now did his energy wane as the pace of his journey and the lack of food began to catch up with him.

He found the tiny kitchen and checked the cupboards. Whoever had lived here before had been well-prepared for what was coming. Perhaps when they'd left, they'd been in too much of a hurry to carry anything. Or maybe they'd simply gone out one day and never come back. How many millions of people that had happened to, he could only imagine. Whatever the case, most of the cupboards were stacked with tins and dried goods. The rest were full of glass jars.

In the almost complete darkness, it was hard to tell what the tins contained so he used their shapes as guidelines. Spam was obvious, as was corned beef. Smaller cylinders might be tinned fruit. When he had enough of what he hoped he wanted, he found a fork, two bowls and even a can opener. Near the kitchen window, where a small emanation of clouded moonlight came in, he prepared a main course of cold spam and tinned spaghetti. Dessert was a tin of strawberries.

He took his bounty back to the living area, sat down on the sofa and began to eat, as slowly as he could discipline himself to. Even so, fullness crept up swiftly on his shrunken stomach and the meal was far too quickly over. Hauling himself with great effort from the couch, he returned his dishes to the kitchen and went in search of a bed and blankets.

38

In spite of thick covers and a comfortable bed, Gordon slept badly. It always happened this way when he first came in from the outdoors. Walls and doors and warmth caused him to feel trapped and claustrophobic and he woke many times through the night, flailing to escape the binding of the bedclothes only to wake again later and cover himself up.

He was three-quarters wild now and vowed to himself this would be the last night he ever spent in a building. He needed the touch of the open air on his face, the proximity of the earth beneath him, the night-sounds and day-sounds of the land all around him just to feel like he belonged. Certainly he did not belong here, in this tower block, in this city.

Though he hated to admit it to himself, not having Denise beside him to share this dark envelope also caused him a degree of restlessness. It hadn't taken long to get used to the comfort she gave him in the darkest hours of the night.

When grey light began to bring the colour back to the world, Gordon was still exhausted. He pulled the covers over himself and slept on for as long as he could. Though he woke often, he didn't rise until he felt the strength had returned to his body. He sat once more in the living room, then, eating his fill of corned beef and baked beans, followed by a tin of pears. What he couldn't eat in that sitting he left in the cupboards. He had no way of carrying anything without his pack and finding food for himself would be no trouble once he was back on the road.

Before he left he spent time looking out of the window. Daylight revealed a clearer view of Coventry's massing forces. The car park beneath the overpass, a camp to tens of thousands, had mostly been broken up. The forces of Green Men he'd seen there the previous night were either marching out of the city or had already gone. But more were arriving from north and south all the time. More than he could count. Poorly-equipped, hungry-looking troops thronged every street and, somewhere down there, a command system now directed them through the city and out to meet the enemy.

As high above it all as he was, Gordon could feel the excitement. The people moved as one. Suddenly there was the promise of something decisive happening, a chance to fight back. He recognised the anticipation in the way people moved around. Every woman and man walking with a sense of purpose and possibility. There was hope again. But hope, Gordon knew, was risky. It was the gambler's flimsy conviction; that good things will come against all the odds, a win just around the next bend. This was no simple game, though. No inconsequential turn of a wheel or sequence of cards. If the Green Men lost, Gordon didn't believe they could ever recover.

He turned away from the scenes below, back to his own temporary living space. In here there was only a sense of abandonment and dereliction. The flat had been neatly kept, almost obsessively so. Magazines and newspapers were stacked in a special rack beside the armchair. The few ornaments on shelves and surfaces looked to have been placed with mathematical accuracy. Everything in the space was angular: the television and game console, the DVD player, the stands and shelves, even the furniture. Everything cubic.

Boxes inside boxes inside boxes.

Unable to bear another moment in the flat, Gordon leapt from the sofa and ran to the door. He whipped away the chair and let it fall behind him in the hall. He left the door wide open, hoping someone might find the bounty in the kitchen and survive a little longer. He sprinted along the corridor, between the tightly spaced doors and almost tumbled down the dozens of flights of stairs.

Gasping, he spilled out into the daylight through the ground floor doors. Everything was dirty brick red, drab grey, slate grey, grey black. All he wanted was the whisper of the trees and the breath of the wind through uncut grasses, to see the whole land healed and made green once more. He wanted to see the people walk upon the land as lightly as they would tread their own flesh.

Gordon soon realised it was a mistake to try to get back to the car park where he'd spoken to Grimwold. In spite of everything, Gordon still had questions he was certain the Rag Man could answer.

The whole population was on the move. Most of the shelters had either been packed up or abandoned. Slowly, because of the huge numbers, but with great purpose, a tide of civilian militia was flowing away from the area around the car park bus station. Walking against the tide was time-consuming but he had to find something to guide him. A sign. Anything. Just one small clue to follow.

Those who'd just arrived had no real choice but to join the throng and keep marching. The momentum of the multitudes carried them along. What condition these travellers would be in when they finally met the forces of the Ward, Gordon didn't like to imagine. He prayed there would be time for them to rest and eat before they went into battle.

His own progress, against the flow of human traffic, was exhausting. He went first to the old double-decker bus but it was deserted. Checking inside he found no trace left behind of Grimwold or his rag boys. Perhaps he too was required for war. That the Green Men had allowed him to preach to all these people must have been a sign that the Rag Man's presence was welcomed.

Outside the bus, the masses of troops thickened, their momentum irresistible. Gordon gave up trying to walk against them.

"What's happening?" he asked a group of men armed with axes.

"Heading south," said one of them. "On the M6. Scouts say a huge Ward army is coming north. Wherever we meet, that's where it'll begin."

"What happened to the Rag Man?"

The man shrugged.

"Who knows?"

Gordon worked his temples with agitated fingers.

"Have you seen a woman travelling with a group of First Guard?" he asked.

"They were first to leave. Just after dawn. They're leading us in."

Dawn? thought Gordon. They'll be halfway to Rugby by now.

"Thanks," said Gordon. He joined the direction of the tide now, aiming instead to push towards the front of the column, but it was clear that even this tactic would take hours.

He turned back to the axe-wielder and called out:

"Have you seen the Crowman?"

"Not yet. But he'll be there. The Rag Man says he's with us and I believe him."

Gordon turned away and pushed on. He had to find the Crowman today. Otherwise, he feared the deaths of tens of thousand of Green Men would be on his hands.

39

It's dark when Megan wakes and a fine snow is falling, its crystals barely the size of alfalfa seed. By the light of the half moon, it could be powdered gemstones sifting down from the sky. The sky is clear, but for a haze furring the edges of the moon. Where this snow comes from is a mystery.

Megan sits up and peers through the pines across the valley. The cave mouth is out of sight but if Mr Keeper's map is correct, it will be easy to see once she is nearer. She rolls her blanket up and stows it below her pack. Nerves make her stomach tumble and her bladder demands release. The moment she has finished relieving herself, she needs to go again. She glances at the food and water in her pack and can face neither. The time has come.

The night is utterly silent but Megan thinks she can hear the tinkle of the snow as it falls past her ears. The ground is anvil hard with frost and covered by a dusting of rainbow particles that sparkle in the moonlight.

Midway down her side of the small valley, she feels exposed and turns to look behind herself again and again. There's nothing out here with her, neither fox nor rabbit nor badger. She is the only creature braving the night. Her faint hope is that Mr Keeper has slipped her a fungal sacrament at some point in the last day and that all this is nothing more than a vision. But she knows now, through experience, the difference between the world of dreams and the real world. At least she thinks she does.

This is real. Too real.

She reaches the midpoint, the nadir of the valley, and stops. The night casts its mantle like a net of enchantment. Everything is white or grey or charcoal; lustrous in the moonlight. Megan wonders why terror and beauty go hand in hand and finds no answer. This is just the way it is. She steels herself and walks on, faster now, wanting the job to be over, wanting to make a good and swift retreat when her work here is done.

At the crest of the opposite hill, the windmill is a three-armed giant who has fallen asleep standing up. Still, she can't help but feel that it, or something within it, watches her approach ready to pounce or sound an alarm. She tries to ignore its quiet sentinel stare.

There's no sign of the cave entrance. Directly below the windmill is a thicket of well-established hawthorn, its winter branches twisted with age and bristling with unforgiving spines. Somewhere behind it must be the way in. She approaches and can see the ghost of a track between the stunted, agonised trees. The footprints are well-furred and indistinct with snow. She moves slower now, careful to make as little noise as possible. Her breath quietens, her heartbeat thickens and slows, her footsteps become as light as the prowling, hungry fox.

Ahead of her opens a deeper blackness within the night. She approaches the mouth of the cave. At the threshold, she stops and listens. There is nothing but the hiss of empty space.

She passes the entrance and moves to her left. As the tiny light of the moon is left behind, she uses her fingers on the cold stone to guide her in. Too soon, her fingers meet an angle and she finds herself at an impasse. In the total darkness, she uses her fingers to explore the obstruction. What she finds feels like mud bricks with seeping mortar between them. Someone has erected a rough wall – to keep out animals, no doubt – but there must be a door in this wall. She follows the uneven plane of its surface, her fingers dislodging gobbets of still-damp mortar as she explores. She finds hinges next, the panelling of a door and, with a sinking heart, a sturdy iron chain and lock.

Megan stands in front of this low door in the darkness. A strong insistent voice from within tells her she can't continue. The men have safeguarded their secrets too well. The only option is to go back and tell Mr Keeper she has tried and been unsuccessful. They can always return, together and better equipped, when he is well. This same voice tells her to run right now, back out of the cave, across the tiny, shallow valley and up to the coppice. To keep running until she is far away from here and safe from the men who made this wall. She knows this voice too well. It is the too-convincing whine of fear. She stills it with her will.

There is a way through this obstacle.

She moves back to her left where the rough blocks meet the stone sides of the cave. She unsheathes her knife and begins to rake out the mortar from between the bricks. It is too easy. She scoops out mortar as though it is the jam in a cake. A brick comes loose and she pulls it free.

Too scared to light a candle to work by in case someone sees its light, Megan is unable to see the effect she is having on the wall until it begins to collapse. She staggers backwards from the dull clatter of tumbling bricks. As quickly as it starts, the small avalanche is over and silence returns to the cave. Her heart batters away inside her chest, her animal composure shattered by the racket. How far away will the sound have been heard? Are the men in the windmill above her right now? Will they have felt the rumble of falling masonry?

To run is to lose the advantage she's created. She must go through the collapsed wall and complete her job.

She removes her pack and lights a tallow candle. She can't afford to sprain an ankle on the uneven ground no matter how terrified she is of her light being seen from outside. She steps over the scattered bricks and moves deeper into the cave. The space around her broadens and opens out. A few paces farther on she enters the body of the cave. It's about four times her height at the highest point and about fifteen paces across in the widest place. Around its edges smaller tunnels lead off into darkness. Whether they are used as access or departure points, she can't tell. Many of them are too small even for a child to squeeze through but she supposes some of them could easily lead to other caverns like this one.

The space Megan occupies is full of things she neither recognises nor understands. Strings and ropes hang from a tiny aperture in the roof of the cave. These lines are attached to various collections of items held together with twine, leather bindings, wooden casings and iron sleeves. Some surfaces are black and yet as reflective as the surface of a lake. In other amalgamations, crystals of various hues are bound in reflective threads and woven into concertinaed patterns. Tucked away in a deep recess like a miniature version of the cave, there is a smithy's furnace and forge and all the tools required for making and shaping iron or steel. On every stretch of the cavern's wall hang racks and racks of small instruments and items which Megan knows can only have been recovered from the dead cities; things that have no place or business in this part of the land.

Over all of this is a fine layer of white dust making it appear as though the cavern has lain undisturbed for years. But here and there she sees evidence of hands dabbling in this dust, smears made by fingers and swatches of clear space where an arm or elbow has brushed through the layer of powder. Some of the equipment has been touched so much and so recently there is barely any trace of powder. She holds up her candle towards the hole bored into the roof of the cave and sees a shimmering rain of particles, lazily falling from it. Not snow, not dust but flour from the mill high above the cave.

There doesn't seem to be anything outwardly *wrong* about any of what she sees. This place is a site of industry and study and enquiry. And yet every item has an aura of simple doom about it. These things, if developed, if spread, will separate the people from the land with great efficiency. They will prevent them from hearing the voice of nature and the people will fall out of balance again. Megan doesn't have to know what any of these machines are to know what they will ultimately lead to. They may have brought good things to people for a time but whatever power they bestowed upon their wielders was cold and meaningless without a conscious connection to the land.

Megan doesn't *want* to understand what she sees. She merely wants to destroy it. From her pack she takes out the black oil Mr Keeper has given her in two large water skins. She does as he has instructed her and douses every piece of apparatus with the oil. The cavern fills with a thick but heady smell. Megan uses the last of the oil to run a trail back towards the broken wall. She sets her tallow to the glistening track and fire races away along it. Megan doesn't watch it reach its destination. She turns away and she runs as fast as she can. Out through the throat of the cave, out of its mouth, past the grasping hawthorns and into the frozen night.

40

Neither Skelton nor Pike could ride a horse. With all the remaining fuel required for war machinery, this meant the journey north was made in an open carriage. It was pulled by a nodding, plodding horse, a shire breed if Skelton recognised correctly, and driven by a Wardsman so young and shy he'd barely said a word to them. Occasionally, Skelton would turn and lift the canvas tarp covering their cargo and permit himself a small grin of anticipation. Soon, very soon, their mission would be complete.

Pike and he sat with a couple of thick rugs over their knees to keep off the cold. The pace was slow but the touch of air passing over them was constant, numbing their faces, making Skelton's forehead ache. From time to time, Skelton's hand would move unconsciously beneath the folds of wool and touch Pike's knee or thigh. Sometimes he sought out the giant man's slab of a hand, squeezed his cold, callused fingers. Pike, never a garrulous man in the first place, had grown even quieter over the past months. His face was locked into a grim scowl for most of the hours in a day, except when Skelton used one of the secret keys which revealed some other expression – of tension or release perhaps. In his sleep, the same downturn of his dour mouth hid the flesh of his lips, lips Skelton longed to reveal, to touch with his fingertips. Pike was an unexpected companion but they'd worked together for so long and with such single-mindedness that Skelton could not imagine a time when they wouldn't be together.

What went on in Pike's mind remained a mystery. Since that first touch, which had awakened stirrings and possibilities in Skelton – even the butterfly caress of real emotion, if he was honest – Pike worked as hard and as seriously as he always had. When they were off duty he responded to Skelton, albeit with the same mechanical, dutiful manner he brought to any task. Sometimes Skelton wondered if Pike felt the same way as he did. Sometimes he wondered if the man had any feelings at all other than the drive to accomplish the objectives of the Ward. Hence it was that, from time to time, Skelton could not help but reassure himself that Pike was beside him, not just as a partner in Ward business but as a dearly held brother, a friend for life. But as the slow progress north unfolded over the cracked, long undriven motorway and Pike's physical response remained neutral, Skelton grew hungry for interaction.

"He'll be ours soon. A day. Two at the most, I'd have thought."

Pike may have grunted under his breath but Skelton couldn't be sure. He didn't give up.

"All this effort, Pike. The men we've sacrificed to this cause. I can't quite believe that we'll hold the key to all of it in so short a time." Pike didn't make a sound. "Do you ever wonder what we'll do when Gordon Black has been disposed of and the Crowman is laid to rest?"

Pike's head turned slowly towards him. Such was the length of time Pike had spent unmoving Skelton expected to hear the grind of rust between his bones. Pike's flat yet fathomless eyes looked into his. Skelton was always unsettled by what he thought he saw there. Either a vast, deep emptiness or a total reflection through which no entry could be gained.

Baritone and motorised, Pike's words brought the conversation to a swift conclusion.

"We haven't got him yet."

His head swivelled to face the front again and whatever light had greyly flickered behind the disks of his eyes guttered and was snuffed. More and more these days Pike's engine seemed to stall, leaving Skelton wondering if it would ever start up again. He was overwhelmed by a sudden uprising of grief. He pushed it away as best he could.

Pike's five little words could mean so much. They could mean so little. Was he merely saying that they shouldn't get ahead of themselves? Or, by saying their mission was not yet accomplished, was he implying that he too would be saddened by the arrival at their common goal. And was he also alluding to the possibility that the end of the mission would also be the end for them? Skelton couldn't decipher it. He knew Pike no better now than he had when they were first assigned to work with each other. Though they had risen to the highest echelons of the Ward as a team, it wasn't enough for Skelton. He wanted more. He wanted Pike to love him. He knew he would give up everything else if he could be assured of that one simple requirement. Neither vengeance nor duty would endure. Only love could do that.

The driver sat hunched in front of them, trying not to be noticed, it seemed to Skelton. They moved in the slow lane up the motorway. To their right passed occasional grey troop-carrying trucks. Only elite troops got a ride. The rest made the journey on foot. The convoy stretched onwards beyond view. From time to time a grey tank rumbled past, and behind them, in the slow lane, horses like the one pulling their carriage hauled an array of field guns and heavy mortars. Marching up the southbound carriageway went the bulk of the Ward's infantry; more men than Skelton could begin to estimate.

Non-Ward pedestrians, the country's permanent refugees, had no option but to move to the hard shoulder and grass verges in order to continue their journeys in or out of London. Mostly they stood and watched the endless convoy pass. If these were the kind of people they were likely to do battle with, thought Skelton, they looked beaten already.

In the hours they'd spent rolling along behind their steady Shire and silent driver, Skelton realised he was running out of patience with the endless resistance from the people of the country. They needed to understand that the Ward had everyone's welfare at heart. They wanted a future and they were going about securing it as swiftly and cleanly as possible. If only the people would stand down, everything could move forward smoothly and without more pain and bloodshed. Though he had a taste for cruelty, Skelton was tiring of it.

Perhaps my engine's stalling just like Pike's.

That brought a humourless grin briefly to his lips.

Maybe we're all just tired…

There was a thud. Something bounced off the side of their driver's head – half a brick, Skelton noticed as it rolled off his coat and back down to the blasted tarmac. The silent Wardsman made an inhuman noise deep in his throat as he slumped over to his right. The carriage began to drift into the overtaking traffic to the sound of angry horns and the hiss of truck brakes.

Skelton, sluggish with hours of pondering and boredom, struggled forwards to take the reins from their unconscious driver. He pulled the left rein and succeeded in bringing the horse and their carriage out of the way of the trucks. He hauled on the leather straps and after a few more paces the horse stopped.

Pike reanimated the moment before the missile struck, having seen something come at them from the grass verge – a boy, barefooted and grimy, had thrown the fragment of brick and he had another ready to fly. Pike leapt down from the still-rolling carriage as soon as the driver fell over. He strode towards the boy, who threw his second projectile – a simple stone this time – straight at him.

Thinking the boy was aiming high, Pike ducked but the boy had anticipated this and Pike took the blow on his forehead. It stopped him. He straightened up and put a hand to his brow. It came away bloody. Slower now, he advanced on the boy. A man, the boy's father perhaps, moved into Pike's path. Pike's businesslike backhand knocked the man out. He rolled and lay facedown in the gravel. Pike reached the boy who lashed out at his shins and crotch with his bare feet. He grabbed the boy's head, rotating it hard and fast between his palms. The boy dropped to the almost bald verge. His legs still kicked but without direction.

Skelton watched the unfolding scene with detachment and even disbelief. Something snapped in the starving travellers who'd witnessed Pike's response. Perhaps twenty of them – whether related to each other or merely fellow travellers, Skelton never found out – launched themselves down the verge at Pike and the nearest vehicles in the convoy. The strength in their fleshless bodies surprised Skelton but it surprised Pike more. Four of them took Pike down when they slammed into him. The rest swarmed onto the drivers of nearby carriages.

Taken by surprise, and probably not well prepared for combat, some of the drivers were killed by the travellers who beat their heads and faces with stones held in their desperate fists. It was a full minute before a troop carrier stopped and spilled its men onto the motorway. The two behind it did the same. Quite suddenly a hundred or more elite, battle-ready Wardsmen brought the attack to an end by catching every single one of the skirmishers.

Without a word spoken the Ward troops bound their assailants, knelt them on the hard shoulder and beheaded them with machetes. They let the bodies drop and returned to their vehicles as though they'd done nothing more than stop to relieve themselves. The engines of the trucks had not stopped. They rolled away and the convoy recommenced. Moments later, the first truck stopped again and four Wardsmen trotted back to take over the positions of the slain carriage drivers. Skelton and Pike's driver, too injured to stand, was hauled to the grass verge and left there.

When Pike climbed aboard again his face was half covered by a tacky red mask. There was blood on his hands and coat too. Skelton reached under the seat and brought out one of their travelling cases. From it he took a small first aid kit. As their carriage moved off with a new driver, he cleaned and dressed Pike's wounded head and wiped the blood from his hands and uniform as best he could. Pike looked straight ahead throughout as though nothing had happened. His stoicism caused Skelton to flush with pride and arousal.

41

Denise waited for Gordon on a bridge over the M6 about ten miles south of Coventry.

There were many others who waited with her, leaning on the railings to scan the vast column of fighters walking south to meet the Ward. The bridge provided a perfect vantage spot for people who'd been separated from friends and loved ones in the press of Green Men leaving Coventry.

Of the small company of First Guard riders she'd travelled with since running from the skinheads in the wood by the canal, only peach-faced Jerome remained. Mounted on his pale, spotted horse, she felt his eyes drawn back to her again and again. She smiled to herself. His fellow First Guard had galloped south in readiness to split and organise the Green Men troops before battle. They'd left Jerome, or rather, Jerome had made it clear he should be the one to stay. This amused his more world-weary comrades who gave him a spare horse for Denise to use on the last leg of their journey.

She'd already learned a lot about the Green Men forces; useful information. There were a few simple ranks among them. The Chieftain, First Guard – who acted as commanders and sub-commanders – and the nameless hordes of Green

Men troops; a rabble made up of anyone old enough and willing to fight.

It was clear to Denise that those in the higher ranks knew this was not a fight that would be won with finesse and incisive manoeuvres. All the Green Men had on their side were greater hordes – of a population that had been pushed to its limits in every possible way. If this fight was to be won at all, it would be through sacrifice and determination; a willingness to go all the way, for each militiaman and woman to lay down their lives taking one or more Wardsmen with him. It was a numbers game, nothing more.

While the Ward were far better organised and more accustomed to open combat, they had come to a wall in their ideology. They still had all the power. They still controlled most of the country and most of its cities. But they had separated themselves from the territory they planned to take. They had no roots or mythology to guide them and they sought only more power. Each Wardsman knew, whether he chose to voice it or not, that the Green Men cleaved to something more powerful than dominion; they were fighting for the land and for their lives.

Denise saw all this and felt a thrilling sense of liberation in sharing neither ideology. To survive one had to be pragmatic. She'd always had her own ways of staying alive; if she could leave the fighting to others.

Nevertheless, she knew the land a little better since travelling with Gordon. She could even stretch to saying she understood how worthwhile it would be to protect it. But she wanted to stay alive no matter who won, and that meant playing the game she'd played best all her life; the game of men.

She had no intention of laying down her life in battle, though there were now many women in the ranks of the

Green Men. Perhaps a quarter of the fighters passing under the motorway bridge – fifty or more with every passing second – were female. Women who had nothing left in their stomachs but fury. Perhaps, Denise thought, they were fighting for the chance to bring children into a world that could actually sustain them, or keep alive the children they hadn't already lost to the ignorance that had brought the world to its knees and spawned the Ward.

Whatever the case, Denise wasn't moved to join them. She was a realist and a survivor. The combination meant taking certain liberties with trust from time to time and playing men like slot machines. It was the ones who paid out she was interested in.

Jerome, high on his horse, had been such a one. As had some of his fellow First Guards. Gordon had been another. She found herself genuinely excited to see him again as she waited up here with her current guardian. She appreciated Jerome's puppy-like eagerness to please her, combined with a protective instinct that was half brotherly, half fatherly and a little too much like shackles to be of any real interest to her. He would be the man who kept her safe until after the battle had played out, when a clear victor would step forward from the field and claim her loyalty.

In her hand she held a black top hat which she'd traded for a favour. She'd decorated it with crow and jackdaw feathers. It would finish Gordon's outfit perfectly. Plenty of the fighters had taken to wearing feathers in their hats but there would be no other Green Man to rival Gordon's battle-dress. He would be powerful and unmistakeable. She stroked the hat and placed it on the backpack at her feet.

Jerome's horse fretted and stamped at the concrete of the bridge. He leaned down and tried to quiet the animal.

Whether it was Jerome's nerves or the endless stream of agitated fighters spooking his mount, Denise couldn't tell.

"Will you know him?" asked Jerome.

"Of course I'll know him." She let her eyes meet Jerome's. "We're... intimate."

He coloured and looked away. So readable. So *playable*.

"Can you be sure he'll come with you?"

Denise didn't answer straight away.

She didn't want to make a silly mistake and miss him. Her gaze fell back to the flow of rough and ready troops. They walked fifteen to twenty abreast. Many of them wore black feathers in various arrangements but none of them looked the way Gordon did, resplendent in his shimmering black coat.

There was still no sign of him.

"He'll come," Denise said, speaking into the wind. "He's very dependable."

She glanced up.

The boy in the saddle responded perfectly, knowing he was being compared to another. His rage ascended in rose coloured flashes to mottle his never-shaven cheeks. Though Gordon also reacted to her, though he was similarly innocent, he was no marionette; he'd sooner slice through his own strings than be her dancer. But even innocent, boyish Jerome wasn't as stupid as he seemed. Otherwise he wouldn't be here with her now.

Denise rested her chin on her hands on the railings and let the advance of the Green Men's army hypnotise her.

42

Once clear of Coventry's smaller roads, the column loosened and Gordon was able to trot between the ranks. Their pace was little better than a fast shuffle; none of them had learned to march in unison. Without his pack he made swift progress out to the motorway and once there he jogged along within the barrier of the central reservation making good time.

His pace had an edge of panic and desperation to it. Gordon recognised this but couldn't control it. Somewhere amid these crowds was the one individual who could make the Green Men victorious but Gordon couldn't stop to search every line of fighters and even if he did, he had no idea what the Crowman *really* looked like. All he'd ever had to go on were sketches, poems and hearsay. Even so, Gordon had a sense that he would know him if he saw him.

He had to keep believing that the moment of revelation was coming. He had to trust Grimwold's words and the silent language spoken by every tree and bird and rock he'd passed since his journey began. And he had to get ahead of these troops fast. If the head of the column met the Ward before they had a figurehead to follow into battle, Gordon didn't believe they had a chance. It would be like feeding meat into a grinder.

The motorway bent lazily to the left and crested a rise. On the other side was a long shallow decline and, almost a mile away at its lowest point, he saw the exit for Rugby. At the top of the slip road a bridge spanned the M6 and even from this distance he could see people ranged along the edge of it. With the hill on his side, he picked up the pace.

He saw Denise long before she saw him and, as he'd hoped, she was accompanied by a First Guard. There appeared to be only one but that was far better than her travelling alone. He left the centre of the motorway and moved across to the hard shoulder, slipping lightly between the bodies of the marchers. Many of them already looked weary enough to drop but the combined energy and momentum of the vast column, and perhaps the thought that finally they might be able to make a difference; all this seemed to hold them up and keep them moving. When someone flagged or collapsed, those around them lifted them up. In three years of travelling Gordon had never seen so much cooperation and cohesion between people. He could only wonder why it took the promise of war to make it happen.

When Denise began to jump up and down, waving and calling out to him, Gordon was already running up the slip road.

Megan is halfway up the coppice side of the valley when she begins to hear faint pops and sharper cracks issuing from the opening of the cave and echoing into the night. She turns and looks back.

There's an orange glow behind the hawthorns, making warped black silhouettes of their gnarled bodies. The light from within the cave is enough to reveal thick, black smoke rising from the cave mouth. She hopes she has done enough to destroy everything inside.

As she watches, her eyes are drawn to a bright flash high above the cave. It comes from inside the windmill. Moments later she hears a thump, the sound following the light across the valley. Something inside the mill has exploded and from within there is a brightening glimmer. Megan's hand goes to her mouth as she remembers the hole in the roof of the cave where highly-combustible flour was sifting down. The flames would have leapt up the constantly falling grain dust and into the body of the mill where, no doubt, there are tons of tinder dry sacks of—

Another flash, much brighter this time and the bang that follows it is much louder. The air from the valley pushes her back a step. She notices now, by the light of the fire taking hold of the mill, that there are figures outside it, their hands raised in dismay at the destruction. Three figures. It looks like three men.

Megan turns away and sprints up the final stretch of the hill, wasting no more time on backward glances.

43

The two horses trotted south along the deserted A5. One carried Jerome, the other, Denise. Gordon ran comfortably alongside them on the grass verge. For the moment no one spoke. Gordon didn't mind. He was glad they were making progress. Now that the daylight was waning, he cursed himself for all the time he'd spent trying to catch up on sleep in the high-rise flat.

Their reunion had been mixed and he replayed it often in the silence:

Seeing Denise running to him from the top of the slip road had made his heart beat faster. Her smile, her eyes, her hair, the way she moved; he was very glad to see all that again. And he ached for her too. Even before they embraced, he was uncomfortably hard. Her hug closed tighter around him when she felt it. He was glad his coat was there to hide his condition from the disapproving young First Guard who looked down on them. Even as he held Denise close and his physical need for her prevented him from swallowing properly, he knew it was wrong between them, just as he always had.

And yet, he couldn't pull himself away.

"It's so good to see you, Gordon," she said, pulling back so that she could kiss him. "I thought you might not come back."

"I was always going to come back."

The words sounded trite, almost rehearsed, but he knew they were true. All this was inevitable; it was his calling.

"And the little girl?"

Gordon shook his head. Denise released him and her hands went to her mouth. He took hold of her shoulders.

"Listen... I..." He struggled to find a way to say it. "They didn't... It wasn't a bad end for her, Denise. I did everything I could."

"What about the rest of them?"

Gordon felt the First Guard looking at him but he didn't look up. Not yet.

He shrugged.

"They're gone."

Now he raised his eyes to the First Guard, dressed in his green and brown uniform with a thick leather belt and brass buckle clasped around his waist. The buckle had a simple motif engraved into it – an oak tree. Gordon nodded to himself. It was a good symbol. The horseman was no more than a boy really. Gordon could see from his eyes that he had fought and that he had killed but his innocence seemed not yet to have been entirely rubbed away. There was an ambitiousness to his cheekbones, or was it arrogance? Either way, Gordon decided in that very moment that he didn't trust this boy, with his soft, tanned skin and clamped lips, his resentful jealous eyes.

He held out his hand nonetheless.

"I'm Gordon Black."

"I know who you are."

When nothing further was forthcoming, Gordon let his hand drop. Denise tried to smooth the waters.

"This is Jerome Proctor," she said. And then, catching the boy's eye and smiling she added, "Sub-commander Jerome Proctor."

"It's good to meet you," said Gordon. "Thank you for taking such good care of Denise."

"We should be moving on," said Jerome. "There's a lot of ground to cover if we want to get ahead of this rabble."

Gordon looked down at the passing multitude.

"We'll never manage on the motorway. Do you know another route?"

Jerome's lips thinned further at being told his business.

"It's all planned out. Denise will ride with me. This mount is for you."

Gordon shook his head.

"Denise can have the horse. I'm happier walking. Or running if need be."

Jerome's eyes flashed and he coloured up again.

"Look, we brought this horse especially to make it more comfortable for you."

Gordon was embarrassed for the boy. It was obvious to all three of them that what he really wanted was for Denise to sit behind him and hold on tight. Gordon tried not to smile but he wasn't sure he managed it.

"I'm fine," he said. "Really."

For a moment, Jerome didn't seem to know what to do.

I hope you don't hesitate like this in battle, thought Gordon. You'll get people killed.

"Come on. Let's get moving."

Gordon walked off just to speed things up.

"Not that way," said Jerome.

The First Guard leaned over and made a meal of helping Denise into her saddle before moving off. She could barely ride, that much was clear, but she could hold on while the horse made headway and that would be good enough.

After a few minutes of silence, Gordon said, "So, which way are you taking us?"

"You'll see as we go," said Jerome.

"I'm sure I will," said Gordon. "But I'd still like to know what our plan is in case anything goes wrong or we get separated. Best be prepared, eh?"

For a while he thought Jerome wouldn't answer. He rode stiff-backed and staring straight ahead as though he hadn't heard. Gordon was on the point of getting their personality problems out in the open when a response came back from on high.

"We're following this road to the A5. It's only a couple of miles away. From there we head south. It's a little longer than taking the M6 but it will be clear and a lot quicker. Once we hit the A5 it's almost dead straight all the way."

"All the way to where?"

Again the long, reluctant pause. Gordon knew Jerome had no good reason for not telling him their destination other than the satisfaction of knowing more than Gordon did.

"The original plan was to march on Northampton, take it and move south one town at a time. Keeping that information from the Ward proved impossible." Jerome made a point of relinquishing tunnel vision for a moment and looked directly at Gordon. "Their spies are everywhere," he said, before turning his attention back to the road ahead. "The Ward began to mass their forces in London ready to come north and reinforce every one of their territories. As soon as the Chieftain heard this, the plan changed. Now we'll meet them in open combat. All our fighters will be deployed where the M1 meets the M6. When the Ward arrive, that's where they'll have to meet us. And by then we'll occupy all the most advantageous ground."

"And where are the three of us heading, Jerome?"

"Junction 18 of the M1. The southernmost point. Nearest to the action."

Gordon was silent then, trying to imagine how a battle such as this would play out. Trying to see a way in which the Green Men could possibly come out on top. He looked up at Denise, who seemed to be waiting for his attention. She smiled at him and, in spite of everything that was wrong about their connection, he found he couldn't wait to be alone with her. Perhaps tonight there would be an opportunity to slip away for a while. He winked at her and she looked away, satisfied. If Jerome caught the quiet exchange, he made no show of it.

"The whole thing, this 'plan' of the Chieftain's," said Gordon. "It's suicide. You've seen them in combat, right? They're superior in every way. They have vehicles and fuel. Many of them have guns. I've seen them destroy a village with mortar fire and send the occupying Green Men screaming back into the woods."

"Whose bloody side are you on, Gordon?" asked Jerome.

"I'm on the side of the land and the people who still know how to love her. I'm on the side of the Crowman." Gordon glanced up to see if Jerome would meet his gaze. The First Guard rode on, eyes level and fixed on the road. "There must be another way of doing this."

"I suppose you've got a better plan than the Chieftain, is that it?"

"No," said Gordon. "I don't think I do. I admire what he's trying to achieve and I admire the people even more for being ready to lay down their lives. But I can't help thinking that this isn't the answer. I think all these lives could be put to better use."

The First Guard's gaze had remained on the road when he said:

"I think you should probably shut up."

The three of them had continued in silence from then on.

Can't run like this all night. I've got to rest. Got to stop.

But Megan can't stop because she knows with complete certainty that the men from the mill are coming after her. They probably saw her lumbering up the hill and even if they didn't, her boots will have left a trail in the cold, glinting crystals that seemed to fall directly from the moon. She has to keep moving.

She thanks the Great Spirit for the moonshine above and the clarity of the night all around her. Without these boons she would be unable to travel at all without losing her way or breaking an ankle. It gives her pursuers the same advantage but at least she has a head start on them and at least she knows where she's going. The men behind her will have to work out her route and constantly re-check her trail.

Some time after her sprint has become a run and her run a fast march, the frozen moon dust stops falling. No more footprints for the men to follow. They'll have to use other skills. Another blessing. Only then does Megan begin to believe she might actually make it back to New Wood.

She pushes the pace.

44

Gordon was content to let Jerome lead them. When their horses slowed to a walk, he hung back, strolling beside Denise, making Jerome choose between being in control and travelling alongside the object of his infatuation. The First Guard looked back at them often but his need to show his authority appeared to override everything. Gordon would have smiled if it hadn't been so sad.

"What happened to all our gear?" he asked after a while.

Denise nodded towards Jerome.

"They told me they couldn't carry any more stuff." She mimicked a Birmingham accent. "'You're baggage enough, missus,' one of them said. They made me leave it all behind."

"Everything?"

"More or less."

"What did you do with it all?"

"There wasn't a lot of time, Gordon."

"It's OK. I just want to know what happened. I feel like I've left parts of myself scattered all across the country."

"I found a gap in the hedgerow on the towpath," she said. "A few miles from where we saw the girl. I crawled through and found an upturned water trough. I put everything inside it and turned the trough upside down. If we ever go back, it should all still be there."

Gordon nodded to himself.

"Thanks, Denise. You did well. I was worried you'd chucked it all in the canal."

"Believe me, I thought about it."

As they walked, Denise tried to shrug off her backpack. She couldn't do it and keep control of her horse. She stopped the horse with a long tug on the reins and slung the backpack down to Gordon.

Jerome looked back and stopped too.

"What's the hold-up?"

"It's nothing, Jerome. You keep going. We'll be right with you."

"I'm not authorised to leave you unprotected, Denise."

"So wait there, then."

"We really need to keep moving. There's not a lot of daylight left."

Denise ignored him and slid down from her horse. Retrieving her backpack from Gordon, she said:

"I did manage to save a couple of things."

She unzipped the pack and brought out a clear plastic bag. Inside was a black notebook and pencil. It was Gordon's most recent journal, as yet unfinished. There, too, was the bulging scrapbook of scrawled Crowman imagery and fevered poetry. He flipped it open. Inside were the letters from his mother and father. He slipped the books into the deep inside pockets of his coat, one on each side, before embracing Denise, holding her tight.

"Thank you. You have no idea how much this means to me."

He pulled away and saw Jerome's young face, twisted and aged by envy.

"Actually," she said, "I think I do." She reached into her backpack again. "I've got something else for you."

Carefully, she withdrew the black top hat with its festoon of black feathers and handed it to Gordon. He held the hat up and turned it in his hands. Silky plumes poked up from the band like crooked black teeth. Some of them were long enough to poke up over the rim of the top hat, making it look like some elaborate junk-shop crown. From the rear half of the brim hung feathers dangling from sewing thread, tangling and turning in the wind.

"That is one mental hat, Denise. Where'd you find it?"

"I found the hat on a… fence post in Coventry. The rest I did myself."

"Yeah?" Gordon looked again. "It's brilliant. I couldn't possibly wear it but it's great. Thanks."

"But you must wear it."

"Nah. I'd look weird."

"Like you don't look weird already? Come on, Gordon. It's the perfect Crowman-hunter's headgear. I'm sure he'll take it as a great compliment when you find him. Go ahead. Try it on."

Gordon lifted the hat up and placed it over his head. It slipped down and stopped, the brim a couple of inches above his eyebrows. The trailing feathers mingled with the ones already woven into his hair. To his surprise, the hat was warm.

"What's in here?"

"I lined it with rabbit fur."

"From another fencepost, was it?"

Denise shrugged, her smile a little too convincing.

"Something like that."

What does it matter? he thought. She thought of me. She made an effort.

"How do I look?"

"Distinguished."

"I think I'll keep it on," he said. "It feels great."

Jerome's horse stamped its hooves, perhaps passing on its rider's impatience.

"Mount up, Denise. We need to keep moving."

She widened her eyes at Gordon.

"Yes, sir!"

This time Gordon helped her on with her backpack and boosted her up into the saddle. Jerome was moving away before she'd even taken the reins.

Gordon hung back a little as they walked, taking in the strangeness of the picture ahead of him. Two riders progressing along the white lines in the centre of a major road. Not a car in sight and none expected any time soon. To either side, the hedges were hawthorn, elder and blackthorn, their winter branches spiky and exposed.

There had once been industrial parks and truck-stops on both sides of the road. Over the years people had dumped rubbish alongside the verges and the black refuse sacks were caught forever in the barbed grip of the hedgerows. Shredded by thorns, the ribbons of black plastic fluttered and shivered in the constant wind. They made a sound like prayer flags, though what the words of the prayer might be, Gordon couldn't imagine. The bags would still be caught there, dancing to the touch of the wind in a thousand years, whether the people of this land survived or not.

When he looked straight ahead, letting his eyes defocus a little, the torn black plastic might have been the ragged bodies of ravens that hung amid the spikes to either side as the three of them walked south to battle, and to war.

••••

Night has stretched the distance between the cave beneath the mill and Mr Keeper's roundhouse.

In the daylight, no stretch of land or river bank seemed as long as they seem now. The darkness teases the miles into forever. Megan, whose heart has not yet settled, feels the treacle of fatigue cooling and settling in her leg muscles. She knows she is slowing down – from a walk now to a trudge – but she can do nothing to make herself move faster.

As she lumbers over the frozen ground, Megan notices that she can see a little better. Glancing up she sees a vague lightening of the sky to the east. Without stopping, she removes her pack and pulls out the last of her rations and water. Staggering a little, she replaces the pack leaving her hands free to nibble the crust of the bread and take tiny sips of water.

For a while this dispels the swollen sensation of uselessness in her legs but it doesn't last long. Her body cries out to her for rest and she wants to take heed. Megan is fit but she has never had to move this far this quickly. Soon her pace has slowed again and with every few steps her boots drag.

She hears noise; hooves distantly hammering the hard ground, hounds baying. The shock makes her stumble. They sounds are so faint they seem little more than echoes from some distant place in the weave. But Megan knows they are nothing so benign. They are of this world; right here, right now. It is the sound of her pursuers, the men from the mill, somewhere in the darkness.

She prays it will be far enough.

45

The dawn light gathers strength, enabling Megan to see more clearly, but the thump of hooves is closer now.

She crests a small rise and comes out between two small patches of woodland. On the other side of this natural gateway, the land begins to look familiar and she realises that she can see both New Wood and Covey Wood from here.

Between them is the village where she was born, Beckby, her root in this land. I will not rest, she thinks. I *will* make it home.

The land speaks, its voice silent but vast in the approaching sunrise:

Everything you need will come to hand in the very moment of its requirement.

The gum clogging her muscles drains into the earth and is replaced with simple vigour. She is tired but she can run and the strength of every living thing in the morning twilight will run with her.

Megan gathers velocity down the incline from the gateway between the trees, racing across the familiar landscape. The earth here recognises the touch of her feet and her feet know this earth. A silent wind thrusts her forward. The extra speed is proof of magic but Megan's elation at the wonder of it lasts only moments. That same breeze carries the howling of bloodhounds.

Gordon guessed they'd covered another four or five miles and dusk was coming down fast.

The A5 dipped and rose in long sections. As the sun set, they crested one final hill. The dirty red ball of the sun quenched itself into the dark horizon to their right. Ahead of them the A5 was dead straight for four miles or more – not a single kink in it. It passed between fields and alongside abandoned radio masts, around the bases of which a thick mist now twisted and tangled. The road cut through a distant and crumbling logistics park where trucks rusted in their dozens and vast, once-white warehouses had fallen in on themselves like wet cardboard.

At the limit of his vision, Gordon thought he could see a couple of wind turbines and the place where the A5 met the M1. But as the grimy, bloody light fled from the landscape, the view shrank and it was difficult to be sure of anything. Mist spilled from the fields and closed like a grey sea over the road.

Jerome nodded to their right.

"Looks like there's a farmhouse down there. We'll stop there for the night."

Gordon looked but couldn't see anything other than trees and fields, all becoming obscured by mist as the minutes passed.

"Where is it?"

Jerome pointed. He must have had a better vantage from his horse. Gordon looked again and thought he could just make out a grain silo between the trees. He couldn't see a farmhouse, though. Not even any outbuildings.

"Listen," he said. "It's not far now and I don't mind travelling at night. We should keep going."

"My instructions are to bring both of you in safely. It isn't wise to travel at night. We'll stay here and leave at first light."

"Jerome. Use your eyes, man. We're almost at the rallying point. I need to get down there right now – it's for the good of the cause, I promise you."

Jerome brought his horse around and walked it right up to him. Gordon stood his ground. The horse breathed into his face and nuzzled his shoulder. Gordon smiled briefly and held the animal's head.

"We're stopping here," said Jerome. "I have my orders."

"Fuck your orders. Come on, Denise, let's go. You can stay on your horse or you can walk. It'll take a couple of hours, tops."

She looked from Gordon to Jerome and back again.

"You know, if what the Chieftain says about the Ward is right, aren't they going to have scouts and spies all over the place? I'm frightened, Gordon. I'd much rather travel during the day – like we did before."

Two to one. Proving to Gordon that democracy was fundamentally flawed. He couldn't stand the idea of not being with her tonight, of not being inside her. He had, of course, considered the danger of roving Ward scouts but they usually travelled in ones and twos. They'd have been easy enough to dispatch but Denise's opinion changed things.

There was a compromise, of course. After spending some time with Denise, he could leave while she and Jerome were sleeping. Travelling alone at night, he'd be there as dawn rose or even earlier, allowing him to continue the search without too much of an interruption. And Jerome may have been an idiot, but Gordon knew he'd take Denise safely the rest of the way.

"OK, you win," he said. "The farmhouse it is."

Jerome wheeled his horse away and walked it off the A5 onto a side road just beyond the top of the rise. Denise's horse followed its companion and Gordon walked along behind them. There wasn't much to see; the mist grew thicker by the moment, seeping through the hedges and swirling around them.

Soon he was following the sound of hooves on tarmac rather than the sight of two horses. Considering Jerome had seen the farm from the A5, they seemed to walk a long way before they reached a gate. Once they passed through though, Gordon realised the First Guard had at least been right about something. He could now see the grain silo, outbuildings and the main farmhouse, all ranged around a broken and pitted yard.

He expected the house to be partially ruined or burned out by looters but when he got closer he could see not even the windows had been broken. He reached into his pocket for his knife. The place was in such good repair, the chances were the occupants had defended their territory with some vigour. If this was of any concern to Jerome, he didn't show it. He dismounted and wrapped the reins of his horse over the top plank of a wooden fence bordering the sloping fields. From here Gordon could just make out the tops of a few radio masts poking up through the deepening fog. Other than that there was no sign of the A5 or any other feature of the land. He might have been looking out across a vast, grey lake.

Jerome helped Denise down from her horse and secured it beside his. He was a lot shorter without his mount, Gordon was amused to note, but he was bold; he opened the back door of the farmhouse like he owned the place and walked inside without any attempt to keep the noise down. Denise looked back and held her hand out to Gordon. By the time he'd reached her, though, she was already inside.

Jerome was rifling through the kitchen cupboards, bringing out tins and putting them on the counter. A couple of candles burned on the well-worn pine of the kitchen table. Jerome worked almost frantically in the shadows, releasing food and seasoning it with salt and pepper. Moments later, he handed Denise and Gordon a tin each. The lids had been cut open with a short knife blade he'd found in a drawer. Gordon noticed the cooker was a range, set up for solid fuel. If they gathered some wood they could get a fire going.

"Why don't we eat this stuff hot?" he suggested.

"What's the point?" asked Jerome.

Gordon sighed quietly. All of a sudden he was very tired of Jerome's brash, careless attitude. Perhaps he'd have responded better if an order had been issued to cook the food.

"Never mind," said Gordon. "I don't suppose you found any cutlery, did you? Or are we dining with our fingers tonight?"

A spoon struck Gordon in the chest and clattered to the floor. After a moment, he picked it up and began to eat. His meal was a can of unflavoured butter beans. They tasted bitter.

"Did you check the dates on the cans?"

"They're all fine," said Jerome.

Gordon ate quietly. The quicker he and Denise could find a comfortable room to settle down in for the night, the better. His eyes met hers again and again in the flickering gloom and he saw in them her rising heat, just as he had seen it on every other night he'd spent with her since they'd sheltered by the river. Maybe staying in the farmhouse wasn't such a bad idea.

The moment she placed her empty can on the table, Gordon stood up and reached out to her. This time she took his hand. He picked up one of the candles and held it out in front of them as he made for the corridor leading away from the kitchen.

"Sleep well, Jerome."

The First Guard didn't reply.

46

Megan takes the tiniest, most overgrown routes she knows towards the village outskirts, ducking through gullies, between hedges and along disused farm tracks. This extends the distance she has to run but it will slow the horses if not the dogs. The animal inside her rises to the chase, not like the fox to the hounds but like the wolf. She is leading them the way she wants them to come, knowing the territory is unfamiliar to them. Behind her, already far too close, erupt the curses from riders slowed by thickets and tracks treacherous with loose rock.

She keeps to the edge of the village, all the time making for New Wood. The last section between the cottages and the first pine trees is open and she pounds along through the dawn, the dogs and mounts, though somewhat slowed, still on her trail. As she reaches the edge of the wood, she hears the riders approaching fast and realises they must already have cleared the obstacles she's led them through. Their hooves become a gathering of thunder, a storm close on her heels.

The path through the pines is narrow but not narrow enough to prevent her pursuers from following. The sounds of the dogs is frantic now as they finally close on their quarry.

Their baying is interspersed with snarls and growls. Megan knows they are hungry, that they can sense their prize is close.

She flies into the clearing with the dogs' teeth clashing at the space left by her feet, the snapping of their jaws as clean and neat as river rocks clapped together. With her sanctuary now in view and a cry of triumph about to leap from her throat, it is with disbelief and indignation at first that Megan feels hot, determined teeth take a hold her left calf, closing over the flesh and piercing it to the bone. Wet warmth bursts from every puncture in the blood-rich muscles.

And then she is falling; falling and still trying to run as the second dog's jaws clamp around her right thigh, stronger and more painful than the first bite, its teeth like needles of fire. The weight of two bodies hauling on her brings Megan to a halt and the dogs begin to shake their heads, tearing open the wounds they've made, releasing more of Megan's blood to steam at the touch of the cold morning air. The horsemen surround her, their mounts wide-eyed and snorting clouds of exertion, sweat rising from their sleek bodies to twirl and evaporate in the grey light.

Her strength and animal will leaks away with her freely running blood. Megan falls to the ground on her face. The two dogs, each attempting to claim its share, pull away from each other, opening her legs as they try to tear her in half. All she can do is wait for them to lose interest in the flesh there and go for her throat.

I almost made it back, she thinks. At least I have done a Keeper's work.

She hears a hiss and a dull, wet snick. One of the dogs lets go of her. The same sound comes again, this time followed by series of high-pitched yelps. Megan looks up from the ground. Around her the horses rear and whinny. One dog stands, staring ahead and panting, an arrow directly through its head. The other chases itself in weakening circles, trying to remove a similar shaft that protrudes from between its heaving ribs. Soon the circling dog lies down, its teeth snapping weakly at the arrow.

Megan looks towards the roundhouse. Mr Keeper is naked but for his bandages and a bloodstained sheepskin tied at his waist. His chest is heaving as he supports himself against the door, a third arrow nocked in his longbow. The riders rein their horses in and turn to face him. He looks so thin and pale to Megan that he could be a spirit. She begins to crawl towards him but she can only pull herself with her arms; her legs won't respond. His eyes meet hers for a second and he urges her on, levelling his next arrow at the riders.

She hears a voice from above and behind her but she doesn't turn to see which of the men is speaking.

"This girl is a criminal. An arsonist. She's destroyed my mill and we're taking her back to Nunwych for trial."

"She walks the Black Feathered Path, gentlemen. And your attack on her is a far greater crime than any mill fire she may have caused. She cannot be a criminal because she acts on my orders. No doubt she set fire to what was underneath your mill too, eh?"

There is no response at first. When it comes the man's tone is low and threatening.

"You Keepers do nothing but hold the world back from the glory it could attain. We were close. We could have resurrected the magic of the past, the powers that were every man's before the Black Dawn."

Megan sees the weariness on Mr Keeper's face.

"Those powers were the cause of the Black Dawn."

"You don't know that."

"Oh, I know it," says Mr Keeper. "I know it very well."

"You're nothing but meddling old men with outdated views. You'll all be relics of history within a generation."

"We'll see."

Limping, his breathing laboured, Mr Keeper approaches the riders. The horses rear as he closes the distance, panic making them stamp their hooves. Megan hears him whisper to the horses, though his mouth doesn't move.

No harm shall come to you.

The horses settle. When he is only a few paces away, Megan is able to see Mr Keeper's wounds, bleeding freshly beneath the bandages. He should be lying still and resting.

"You look half dead already," says the miller.

"It was you three who half killed me," says Mr Keeper. "Don't you remember?"

He bares his teeth at them and the growl of a huge cat vibrates from deep within his chest. Once again the horses rear and the men struggle to calm them.

"You?" blurts the miller. "But…"

"Don't talk to me about the power of the old times and the magic that existed before the Black Dawn. Your search for past glories is born of ignorance and stupidity. It endangers us all. I wanted to give you a chance to see things differently, to appreciate the magic that is all around you every day. The decision has cost me dearly. My duty is to this land and its people, not to three foolish men." Mr Keeper uses his longbow to point back in the direction the men have ridden from. "Go back to your homes. Don't return to this village unless you come willing to talk and willing to listen. If you continue your dabbling into the technologies of the past, your equipment won't be the only thing to burn. What you've done carries a death sentence."

There is silence for what feels like many minutes. Megan's vision begins to narrow and dim. She hears the men turn their horses around but Mr Keeper calls them back.

"Take your filthy dog carcasses with you."

After that there's nothing.

47

Denise fucked him with the same fierceness as before, drawing him onto her, into her, not inviting but demanding. There was a frenzy about her; that same desperation for union in the face of total destruction, as though this really was the last time. It roused in Gordon the most primal, harsh desire he'd known. They became animals once more, glad to be alive for another moment, just one moment more.

Their pattern had always been to love and collapse, ride and rest again and again but tonight Gordon was unable to reach climax. His lust built and built but never reached its conclusion. Conversely, Denise cried out in ecstatic extremity time after time, her tones close to screams of pain. At one point, Gordon thought he heard a floorboard creak outside the door but he didn't care whether Jerome was listening or not.

After a while, Gordon felt a great cold quelling his fire. It seemed to rise from the core of him like advancing frost. It took his strength and it bled away his desire until he finally fell unspent and unfulfilled beside her; his skin the ice to her steam. Denise seemed contented though, more than satisfied by their savage dance. She laid a hot arm across his frigid chest. Gordon felt his breathing decelerate until it seemed as slow as the tides. The chill gripped him in its glacial cocoon.

"I don't feel well," he said.

"You're alright. Probably just tired – you ran most of the way from Coventry."

"I think I got a bad can of beans."

"Get some rest. You'll feel fine in the morning."

She leaned over and kissed his cheek. He was so cold, it felt as though her lips and arm were the only warmth he'd ever experienced. Her mouth lingered tenderly and for a long time, as though Denise didn't want their closeness to end. Just before he fell into the arctic seas of unconsciousness, her lips left his cheek and her arm withdrew. It seemed as though she had sped continents away from him in just a few moments. He thought he heard her slip from the bed and dress before leaving the room but he could easily have been dreaming by then.

Denise watched from the doorway as Jerome stripped back the musty sheets and blankets to reveal Gordon, curled and childlike on his right side. His skin bore the scars of dozens of fights and the wounding touch of thorn and bramble. His long dark hair, black feathers bound into it, lay around his head and shoulders, hiding his face. His breathing came in long, deep pulls, the pause after each out-breath seeming far too long.

"You gave him too much," said Denise.

After an experimental prod or two with the sole of his boot, Jerome began to secure Gordon's wrists behind his back.

"He's fine."

"You're not taking him like this."

"It's out of my hands now."

Denise stepped forward and pushed Jerome off the bed so hard he fell backwards, knocking over the bedside table and smashing the bulb in the defunct lamp. The back of his head connected with the wall and he lay dazed for a few moments. She flung the rope and it landed across his face and chest.

"Don't talk such *shit*."

Jerome rubbed his head, his face screwed tight against the pain. He looked more stunned than angry.

"What the hell is wrong with you?" he asked.

"He has the right to some bloody dignity."

The First Guard struggled to his feet.

"Fine. Get him dressed then. But make it quick."

He stood with his arms folded as Denise retrieved Gordon's clothes from the floor. She knew where each item was; she'd been the one to tear them from him. She knelt beside him on the bed and rolled him gently onto his back. The hair fell away from his face and, by the candlelight, she saw the beauty and innocence of the boy he must have been until so recently. She looked up and saw the quiet satisfaction on Jerome's face. He'd bested his rival without a single blow struck.

"Fuck off," Denise said.

"What?"

"You heard me. Leave us alone. I'm not doing this with you gawping over my shoulder."

Jerome left without another word.

When Denise was done, she called out for Jerome. He came back in to find Gordon laid out on the bed as though in a chapel of rest. His hair had been pushed back from his face and his hands were crossed at his breast. His coat of black feathers looked like a funeral suit.

"Very funny, Denise."

"Appropriate though, Jerome. Considering."

"I still have to tie his hands and feet."

Denise stepped back from her drugged lover.

"Whatever."

Jerome crossed to the bedside and checked Gordon's pockets. Denise held up a battered rucksack.

"I've got all his gear," she said.

Satisfied, Jerome hoisted Gordon into a sitting position.

"Can you give me hand?" he asked.

"I've done all I'm doing," said Denise.

Jerome tried to prove his strength but struggled at every step, getting Gordon over his shoulder, lifting him up and then carrying him along the corridor to the kitchen and out of the back door. A horse and cart waited in the mist that swirled in the farmyard. A smart looking Wardsman wearing a helmet and armed with a cavalry sword, dagger and crossbow waited for them. On the back of the cart was a large grey ammunition trunk designed for heavy ordnance. Its similarity to a coffin was not lost on Denise as Jerome dumped Gordon's limp body into it and staggered away with a relieved gasp.

The Wardsman stepped forward to secure the lid of the munitions box.

"Wait," whispered Denise.

She ran back inside and the farmhouse and reappeared with the top hat she'd decorated for Gordon.

"He won't need that," said the Wardsman.

"I don't care. I need him to have it."

The Wardsman shrugged. Denise went on tiptoes, leaned into the box and kissed Gordon before placing the hat beside his crumpled form. The Wardsman screwed the lid into place with six wing nuts and leapt up onto the plank that formed the cart's simple seat. He looked down at them. Denise thought she detected a note of amusement in his voice.

"The Ward thanks you for your loyalty. When the battle's over, your asylum is assured."

Denise managed not to cry, though the price of survival seemed suddenly extortionate. The cart disappeared into the mist. The clatter of hooves echoed around the farmyard and receded.

48

Gordon walks alone through a dead forest. The trees stand dry, barkless and woodwormed, their branches grey. The air hangs thick with the stench of rot and mildew. Distantly, he hears the cawing of a thousand crows – they are calling to him but he cannot understand their language. Eyes observe him from behind every tree but each time he turns to look, there's nothing but the ranks of decaying uprights, stretching their dead bones into a dark sky.

In his right hand he carries a sword as broad as his forearm. The blade is dull green-black but for its edges, honed so sharp it makes the air sing. Whorls, knots and symbols are etched into the matt surface and these too shine as Gordon angles the sword this way and that. Where the blade meets the haft, an exact engraving of the Crowspar drips thick Black Light. Each droplet manifests wings and flits away before hitting the ground, no more than a ragged shadow at first but soon becoming a magnificent raven, soaring fast between the hulking, spectral tree trunks then upwards to add its bright blackness to the sky. Locks of hair hang from the hilt of the sword, hair taken from the head of his father, mother and two sisters. Between these hangs an array of black feathers, twirling and twisting as he walks deeper into the dead woods.

Something hanging among these fetishes catches his eye. He brings the sword closer. There among the black feathers is a single

341

white one; ice bright and flashing. He holds the sword out in front of his face, turning it first one way then another. He tests the blade with a couple of experimental swings and the terrible whoosh as it cuts the air is like the rush of wind over a huge black wing. The blade flies at his will, stops and turns with his thoughts. Never has he seen such a powerful object.

Emboldened, he strides towards the centre of the woods.

The clearing, when he finds it, is the only part of the forest left alive. Each tree that rings it is lush with full growth. Vines, ivy and moss cling to the trunks and branches, the pale green hair of hanging lichens caresses him as he passes. The trees are full of scurrying insects and animals, all of them awaiting his arrival. They are still and attentive as he passes through this ring of life and into the clearing.

The centre of the circle of trees is marked by a standing stone. He advances toward it, a column about his height, and circles it, inspecting the markings chiselled into its surface. The stone has two convex faces and resembles a blunt arrowhead. On one face the symbols match those on his sword, though in the stone they are rendered with less clarity. On the other face there is a crude representation of a man.

As Gordon tries to make sense of the standing stone, a bird flies from the ring of trees that pulse with expectant vitality all around him. He recognises the movements of the bird, the signature and shape of its wings, the attitude of his body, the angle and curve of its head. It lands atop the monolith.

A crow. A crow unlike any other.

Save for its eyes, beak and claws, the crow is as white as polar snow.

Not wishing to threaten the creature, Gordon lets his sword rest at his side. The crow watches him with intelligent eyes, as ancient and wise as the Black Light itself. A great benevolence emanates from it, wrapping Gordon in a sense of comfort and well-being so profound he could weep. It feels as though he has come home somehow, discovering life here at the centre of the dead wood; finally finding his place in a world driven to self-destruction and insanity.

"You've come a long way," says the crow in that silent voice of the land Gordon has come to know and trust. "But the journey isn't over yet. Your greatest challenge lies ahead of you still."

"I know. I haven't found him. I've tried. I really have."

"No matter what you'd done, you could not be any further along the path than you already are."

Gordon trusts this creature. He knows he is dreaming and that it is safe to say what he has never yet told anyone.

"The war isn't going to start tomorrow. Not the way everyone thinks it is. No one seems to understand that this war has been going on inside us all along. Maybe since the first human."

"How right you are."

"When this battle comes it won't be the beginning of anything. It'll be the end of something. I'm frightened it will be the end of everything. Not just us. And not just the Ward if, by some miracle, the Green Men can win. I think tomorrow will be the end of the world."

The white crow hops to the left and to the right. It airs its wings and caws, raucous and irritated, showing the barbed blade of its tongue.

"You can't say what tomorrow will bring but you've every reason to be frightened, Gordon Black. Something will end tomorrow and you must be as strong as you can be to weather it."

"What about the Crowman? I must reveal him – give him to the people."

"Yes. You must."

"But how? Time's running short."

"That's not for me to tell. All I can say is that the land has nothing but faith in you." The white crow hops down and lands on

his left arm. Gordon holds it up in front of his face. "The land has dreamed of you for a long time." The crow's bottomless eyes reflect the emptiness and doubt Gordon holds at the very heart of himself. The crow flaps and takes off, circling the clearing. "Be strong, Gordon Black! The enemy approaches!"

Its pure white wings cut through the darkness above the forest, and, as though having torn a veil, the crow is gone, the gash in the oil black night sealing behind it. The once-silent creatures of the wood, all aloft in the limbs of the final circle of trees begin to chitter and fidget. The ground quakes to the tempo of heavy footsteps.

Lumbering and creaking, Gordon's foe enters the ring at the centre of the forest. The animals and insects disappear behind leaves and branches, into cracks and holes in the bark. Eyes blink and antennae wave in the direction of the intruder.

A grey beast, man and machine melded, smashes through the inner circle of trees, scattering leaves and vine remnants, splinters of newly grown wood and the limp bodies of a dozen tiny animals. Debris, some of it still twitching, rains down and the beast takes up its position facing Gordon. The thing, Gordon now sees, is a humanoid exoskeleton with two humans operating it. One sits inside its head, the other in its chest cavity. The two control centres are heavily protected but open at the front to enable the controllers to see out. Both the men wear the uniform of the Ward, as does the machine that is their slave and their prison cell – they are chained inside the thing and each control centre has been welded closed.

The beast has four arms, two ending in hammers and two in crossbows. Its steel legs are thicker then tree trunks. The hiss of hydraulics and the moan of gears accompany its every movement. Gordon raises the dark-bladed sword in front of himself and advances, looking for a way to slip his blade deep enough to kill the controllers.

The beast stomps towards him, lifting a hammer fist and swiping it laterally. Gordon leaps back, feeling the force of the wind but not the force of the hammer. It is a near miss, though, and before he has time to think about his own attack, a crossbow bolt lances past his head and lodges shaft-deep in the obelisk at the centre of the clearing. A second arrow is flying as Gordon dives to the ground, tucking his sword in and rolling away. A metre behind the spot where he stood, the tips of two flights are all that remain of the bolt. He leaps from his roll, trying to place himself behind the beast. It is far too quick, turning easily with him. The next two bolts from the crossbow also slip wide of him but only because he is sprinting. It's a near miss. He hears metal sink deep into the wood of a tree somewhere behind him.

There has to be some weakness in the beast, but what he can do with a simple sword against projectiles and giant hammers, he has no idea. Nor does he know what effect, if any, his blade will have on the beast's steel carapace. If the controller of the crossbow arms is as good as he ought to be, the next two bolts are going to anticipate his speed and direction. One of them will nail him for sure. In the slim moment of the reload, Gordon runs straight towards the beast, dodging two late hammer blows and diving between its legs. As he does so, he takes as good a look as he can at the workings of the thing. It has only one weakness that he can see.

The column-like legs turn with surprising speed, threatening to crush him. Even as he thinks this, sensing his presence directly beneath them, the controllers make the beast leap up. It comes down feet together in the place where Gordon took a moment to peek up into its workings. He manages to dodge away but the thunder of the landing and the shaking of the earth under its weight throw him off balance.

This time a hammer hits him in the left shoulder. He leaves the ground and as he sails through the air, he feels two more bolts fly past him. One of them slices opens the sleeve of his coat of black feathers, scoring a deep, hot track along his right forearm. When he lands, on his back between the trunks of two trees, he has dropped his sword.

It lies a few feet away, between him and the beast. His left shoulder hangs lower than it should. Shattered bone angles up through the black feathers of his coat. His left arm won't move at all. His right arm is wet with blood but he thanks the Great Spirit the bolt did not lodge in his flesh. Flexing his fingers, he finds the arm is still serviceable. A crossbow bolt slams through his left bicep. The velocity is so great, it passes right through and into the ground, pinning him.

He hears the beast advancing, its footsteps like the pound of falling boulders. The controllers want to be sure of their final shot. Already a crossbow hand is rising as the beast strides towards him in three-metre paces. Gordon tears himself up from the ground, calling on the Crowman and all the forces of the land and sky to muster within him. He hears the tearing of his own flesh wrenching free of the shaft that pins him and the sound of two bolts loosed from the crossbows almost simultaneously.

He rolls to his right, anticipating the agony of tumbling over his broken shoulder and skewered arm. The pain clears his mind like lightning illuminating a dim room. He rises from the roll and one of the bolts opens his calf to the bone as it passes across his shin.

He can still run, and run he does, stopping to regain his sword as he races towards the beast. The distance between them closes fast. A hammer arcs downwards and he sidesteps it, aiming and trailing his sword as it passes by. The blade opens a curve of hosing and grey oil spurts free. The reeking fluid is hot where it spatters his coat but he has inflicted a genuine wound. The hammer arm can flex but it can no longer straighten. Both he and the beast have stopped. He is almost directly beneath it. Now the crossbow hands fire again and this is their last volley; no more ammunition is stored in the arms. The bolts disappear into the earth, one slipping directly between the beast's steel toes. To reach him here the remaining hammer hand will have to smash into the beast's own legs. Once again it leaps up trying to crush him on landing. This time, Gordon is ready. As it comes to earth, he is standing clear with his sword ready. He slices through the cables, first behind the beast's left knee and then behind its right. He has to dodge again as the beast collapses onto its own heels.

For a few moments the controllers are mystified by their hamstringing. Gordon uses this pause to climb onto the beast's knees and deliver an upward thrust straight through the protective bars on the machine's chest. He can just see that he has gut-stuck the thoracic controller. He slips the blade free and a wash of blood and watery entrails cascade down over him. He smells the shit of the controller leaking from a breached and dangling loop of intestine.

As he climbs the chest, passing the disembowelled controller, there is an impact so enormous it knocks over the entire machine. Gordon lies face down across its chest cavity, horizontal now. He cannot breathe. From the cranial controller he hears manic giggles. He tries to lift himself but is unable to. Neither of his arms will work. Nor will his legs. He turns his head, trying to look over his shoulder. All he can see is a huge mechanical arm, its hand seeming to disappear into his own back. No wonder he can't breathe. The beast has smashed a fist into itself, putting a hammer hand right through his upper body and knocking itself into a position it will never rise from. Insane, the cranial controller still cackles to himself from the prison that is the beast's head.

Gordon's world goes dark.

49

Gordon woke into total blackness, sweat slicked, heart galloping. He tried to reach out for Denise but his arm didn't respond. He was lying on his left side. Hard surfaces met him both beside and below. He noticed rhythmic movement. Wherever he was it couldn't be the bedroom of the farmhouse. Trying to raise himself up he became aware of ropes at his wrists and ankles. The side of his head made contact with solid wood. His mouth dried out. The terror of dying at the hands of the mechanical beast was nothing. It was a dream.

This was real. Too real.

Calm down. Don't lose control. Think.

What was the last thing he could remember?

He'd eaten with Denise and Jerome. He'd led her to the bedroom and they'd made love. But something had been wrong with him, hadn't it? A deep coldness like he was getting sick. He'd had to give up. Something in the food? Now he remembered Jerome liberally sprinkling what he thought had been salt and pepper over the cans of food. But by the scant light from the candles, how could he have known what Jerome was adding to his meal? He remembered the bitterness of his beans and the rush Jerome had been in – not even wanting to heat their food on the range.

So, Jerome had drugged him. Was Denise in on it? Something niggled about the way she'd behaved with him. As though she'd known full and well that this was the last time they'd be together. But hadn't she always been that way? There was no point in thinking about it. He needed to get out of this box. This *coffin*.

For a while he listened to the sounds from outside. He could hear a horse's hooves on tarmac and he could a feel a rolling sensation beneath him. He was being pulled in a carriage or cart. He was fully clothed for which he was very glad but it seemed odd. Why would they have dressed him when he'd have been easier to deal with naked? Some sense of propriety on Jerome's part? Denise feeling sorry for him? Or was there some occasion which demanded him to be clothed?

He didn't even know who had taken him prisoner. It was conceivable that he had slept through an attack on the farmhouse in the night and that the Ward had chloroformed him and taken him prisoner then. Or perhaps some faction within the Green Men wanted him out of the way. There was no working it out.

Between his chest and the side of his box, Gordon could feel an obstruction. He bent his chin down and felt the tickle of feathers. They had packed him up with his hat.

But why?

After a contortion that brought on cramps in muscles he didn't know he possessed, he managed to locate the brim of the topper with his chin and grab it in his teeth. Turning his head from side to side, he felt there was some weight in the hat that hadn't been there before. Not daring to hope, he flicked his head forward, launching the hat away towards the middle of his body. It reached no further than his stomach but he thought it might be enough. Wriggling as quietly as he could, he managed to turn his back to the hat and then squirm up towards the top of the box. His hands, tied behind his back, came into contact with the feathers adorning the topper.

It didn't take long to locate the source of the extra weight in the hat, hidden behind the plumes of black feathers. A familiar shape slipped into his palm.

50

The rhythm of the horse's hooves slowed from a trot to a walk. Gordon began to hear the muffled voices of many men. He moved into what he thought would be the best position and waited. The horse came to a halt. He felt the cart wobble as the driver dismounted. Footsteps approached from two directions.

"Did you get him?"

"Yes, sir. He's right in here."

Gordon started as the driver thumped on the box near his head.

"Has he tried to get away?"

"Not a peep out of him. They gave him enough to keep him asleep for a week."

A week?

Gordon remembered his nightmare and how he had called on the land and all its spirits for strength. Perhaps he was already tapping into that current of natural power. His fists tightened in anticipation of bloodshed.

"OK, let's get him out and take him to Skelton."

The name drew a red cloud into the darkness.

Every fibre of muscle in his body twitched to the sound of the nuts being unscrewed. The lid was lifted and his world scorched white.

Gordon Black sprang from his box, black feathers smoothed by the passage of air, his knife blade winking in the sunshine.

Sunshine.

He hadn't been blessed with its unclouded light for months. Its heat charged him further, soaking into his dark clothing even as he rose into the air. Ranged around him in readiness for battle were thousands of the Ward's troops, each man dressed in close-fitting grey uniforms with helmets and visors. Astonished faces turned his way from every direction, none more disbelieving than that of the driver and the Wardsman addressing him. Before Gordon landed, he'd made up his mind. These numbers were too great for him, no matter what power he might have held. Flight was the only option.

He landed on the cart, leapt over the driver's makeshift seat and slashed the leather straps and harnesses connecting it to the cart. The poles on either side fell away from the horse and it started forward, terrified. Gordon dived from the seat towards the startled animal, managing to cling to its neck as it bucked and whinnied. All around him, Ward troops who'd been eating rations, preparing their swords or polishing their boots and buckles were standing up. Some of them had raised crossbows in his direction. A few had rifles. Gordon got his legs on either side of the horse and heeled it hard.

"Go!" he hissed.

The horse bolted forwards as an arrow sang behind his neck.

"Hold your fire!" shouted the Wardsman the driver had been talking to. "Alive! He must be alive!"

Troops rushed in from all sides. The horse bucked again but this time it was half-hearted. What it really wanted was to be away from its passenger. It accelerated accordingly but Gordon clung on.

He whispered now to the creature.

"I won't hurt you. Just go. Go as fast as you can."

He found the reins and squeezed his thighs together to avoid slipping off. The horse reached a gallop. Troops scattered at its approach and Gordon looked for a route into the countryside. There wasn't one. The Ward camp had been pitched across the entire intersection of the A5 and the M1. The fields to the south were occupied by uncountable thousands of grey uniforms. The fields to the north were blocked by hedges. Gordon galloped through the camp towards the motorway junction only to meet more Ward troops pouring out of the underpass. Every instinct told him to avoid the motorway; once he was on it, he would be as good as trapped until he found another junction. The reality was he had no choice. Wardsmen were closing in on three sides. He hauled the reins to the left and the horse overreacted, almost coming to a halt.

The Wardsmen racing towards him from the underpass were almost within reach. He heard someone shout:

"Grab him!"

Frantic now, he ground his boot heels into the horse's flanks.

"Go on!" he yelled.

They clattered up the slip road, gathering speed and joined the northbound carriageway of the M1.

As he came level with the motorway he looked across it. It was deserted.

"Thank you," he whispered.

Behind him, the quickest Wardsmen to react had managed to mount up and were already racing out of the camp. He spurred the horse on with desperate kicks, eliciting agonised whinnies.

"I'm sorry. But you have to go faster. As fast as you can."

The horse's hooves were thunderous on the damaged tarmac and Gordon feared it would break an ankle in one of the cracks. The fall would probably kill both of them. But the horse avoided every fissure in the road's surface. Up ahead in the distance Gordon thought he could see other forces massed on both sides of the motorway, fighters wearing the drab khakis and browns of the Green Men.

Great Spirit, let me make it. I've come this far. Don't let it end yet.

He chanced a look behind. The mounted Ward troops were faster. Much faster. Their horses were bred for galloping and jumping, not pulling carts. But there was still some distance between them. Enough that he could reach the Green Men if he maintained this speed. Gordon, knowing little more about riding than he had to stay on the horse, kept his head down and held on with all his strength.

About a mile from the first Green Men, the cart horse began to tire. He looked back. Many of the Wardsmen were now close enough to fire crossbows and hit him, he had no doubt. He kicked his horse harder but it no longer had the reserves to respond.

"Please! Come on! Just a bit farther."

The horse slowed. Now, over the sound of his own mount's hooves, he could hear the thunder of twenty more right behind him. He glanced back and saw the expression of glee on every Ward cavalryman's face. Their horses weren't even winded. They were enjoying the hunt and they knew they had him.

Gordon could do nothing but look behind and try to anticipate the inevitable attacks. The face of the nearest

Wardsman creased in confusion when a thin wooden shaft appeared at his chest. The man slipped from his saddle onto the tarmac, pulling his mount to an abrupt halt. A second shaft appeared above the foreleg of a chestnut coloured mare. The horse collapsed to the ground, rolling over its own neck and landing on top of its rider. Gordon looked ahead. Green Men were loosing volleys of arrows from the cover of the trees at the top of the grass verges on both sides of the motorway. They came thicker and faster now, thumping into flesh and bringing the Ward pursuit to an end.

Gordon rode on, allowing his horse to slow to a canter and a trot. As soon as it stopped he dismounted and came to the front of the sweating creature, its lungs pumping like huge bellows.

"Thank you," he said. "You saved my life."

In his wake, the Green Men took to the road and finished the fallen Wardsman with blows to their heads and blades to their throats. It was swift and efficient. The unharmed mounts were taken and added to the Green Men's own small band of cavalry, the wounded horses were dispatched and dragged away, presumably for meat. Gordon had walked among the starving foot soldiers. He wondered how many of them had already subsisted on the flesh of their own kind and how many more would do so today once the bodies of the fallen Wardsmen had been stripped of clothing and booty.

A party of four First Guard appeared on horseback, leaving the cover of the fields beyond the southbound carriageway. He held up a hand to them and they hailed him back. He led his winded, sweating horse towards them.

"You must be Gordon Black," said their lead rider as Gordon crossed the central reservation to meet them. "Heard a lot about you but we assumed you weren't coming."

"Oh? Why's that?"

THE BOOK OF THE CROWMAN

"Jerome Proctor said you never showed up."

Any doubts he'd had about his suspicions, any hopes he'd had for Denise's innocence were quashed in that instant. But he wanted Jerome for himself; he planned to give the traitor a special and unique reward when the time came.

"I probably walked right past them," he said. "It was a busy road."

The First Guard nodded to the south and asked:

"So what was that all about?"

"I uh… thought I'd do a little damage on the way in. Didn't expect so many of them."

The First Guard grinned.

"Worked out quite well," he said. "Considering it was totally unplanned."

Gordon relaxed a little.

"I think I owe you an apology," he said. "If I'd had more time to think it over, I probably wouldn't have led them right towards you."

"Well, I can forgive you that this once. But you're working for the Green Men now." He stroked his eyebrow three times in mock secrecy and reached a hand down. Gordon took it. "My name's Dempsey." He gestured to the three men with him. "These are Carter, Finney and Stone."

"Are you the ones who brought Denise north along the canal?"

"That's us."

"That's two lives I owe you, then."

"Tell you what," said Dempsey. "Seeing as you've brought us almost twenty enemy cavalry, we'll call it quits, eh?"

Gordon didn't have time to thank him. In the distance there was a volley of funnelled thumps. Dempsey and his men started in their saddles.

"Get off the road!" he shouted.

Gordon tried to pull the cart horse with him but it wouldn't budge. Dempsey and his crew were already up the embankment and trotting through a gap in the fence. Gordon sprinted up after them as a sudden whining grew loud overhead. As he reached the fence and dived through, six mortar shells exploded in quick succession. The shockwave from the first impact knocked him off his feet. He crawled the rest of the way into the field and rolled down the other side, out of range of the blasts. Hot tarmac and charred hunks of horseflesh rained down around him. His ears ached and sang.

A few yards off in the field, the four First Guard had turned back, waiting for more shells. Gordon hurried over to them, glancing back all the time though no further mortars fell.

When he reached the horsemen Dempsey said:

"You OK?"

"Fine. You?"

Dempsey nodded.

"They're saving as much artillery as they can for the main event. Honestly, I don't think they've got much firepower left."

"Do you really think you're going to defeat the Ward in open combat?"

"The Chieftain's not that naïve. We have to wear them down before they meet us on the battlefield. And once they're there, we'll need a little guile. Right now we've got a dozen skirmishing parties harrying their columns and camps between here and Northampton. They're attacking supply chains and fuel dumps, even poisoning their water – if an army can't drink, it can't fight."

Gordon was impressed. The Green Men had never been this organised before.

"We should find some cover," said Dempsey. "Do you want a ride?"

"I'll be fine walking," said Gordon.

51

A journey across country of about a mile brought them to a small village called Clay Coton. All the way along the route and as far as Gordon could see to the north there were camps of Green Men fighters resting before the call to arms came. Riders threaded among the camps passing out smoked meat and crates of water rations collected in assorted glass and plastic bottles. Everything he saw and everything Dempsey told him gave him hope.

The village had been populated by commanders and sub-commanders but Gordon didn't see any sign of Jerome or Denise. In a way, he was glad. Dempsey and the others had commandeered a small cottage and they offered Gordon the sofa for a bed.

"Thanks," he said. It seemed rude to mention that he planned never to spend another night indoors.

They gave him meat and water and Dempsey explained the battle plan. It involved tempting out phalanxes of Wardsmen with weak-seeming bands of Green Men. Once each group of Wardsmen was out of reach of support, a stronger troop of Green Men would reinforce and attack. They knew this would only work a few times, but if they managed several of these manoeuvres early on and fairly simultaneously, it was hoped they'd be able to weaken the Ward considerably.

The only projectile weapon any of the Green Men carried was a bow – a reinvention of the traditional longbow, Dempsey said. Living wild, as most of the Green Men did, one thing they weren't short of was wood. Even in the places where the land appeared to have died, the trees yielded enough timber both for arrows and bows. Longbowmen had been the ones to save Gordon from the cavalrymen who'd chased him out of the Ward camp. Dempsey doubted his bowmen were quite as good as they'd been in times past but they were improving all the time and almost every man and woman knew how to use the weapon.

Additionally, since starvation had become the most immediate problem people faced, the Ward had lost support because they had no answer to the problem. Everything they did now was short term: steal or extort enough to stay alive, find and destroy the Crowman, kill every Green Man.

At the mention of the Crowman, Gordon interrupted.

"Have you seen him? Grimw… The Rag Man says he's among us."

"I've heard that. And I've also heard of your search for him – from Denise and quite a few others. Stories of your exploits have spread right across the country. Today the story'll be how you slew twenty Ward cavalrymen singlehandedly."

"It was forty at least," said Gordon and they both chuckled.

"Listen, Gordon, can I be honest with you?"

"If you can manage it, you'll be in the minority."

He hadn't meant it as an insult and, as Dempsey didn't appear to take it that way, Gordon felt somehow closer to him.

"I've never seen the Crowman," said Dempsey. "Or anyone like him. I don't believe there is such a person. I don't think he's some kind of earth spirit or messiah, either. I think he's a myth. Something we came up with to keep our hopes alive. Don't get me wrong, I don't think that's a bad thing and I don't want to diminish the value of your search. In fact, somehow, what you've been doing these past few years has been an example to people. You've become sort of a legend yourself."

"I doubt that very much."

"Well, it's true."

For a few moments Dempsey's soldiering mien fell away. Gordon watched the man, trying to guess his thoughts. It was as though Dempsey was trying to understand what could motivate an individual to act as Gordon had acted, to dress as he had dressed, to live so single-mindedly and yet without fulfilment for so long. When he spoke again it was in tones Gordon didn't recognise for a few moments, the tones a brother might use; a brother or a friend.

"I've been assuming all this time that you'll fight alongside us, Gordon, but as I sit here and think about it, I realise that's perhaps callous of me. The war you're fighting seems different to ours. I want you to know that you're at liberty to continue your search. No one will call you a coward or they'll have me to answer to. If only a quarter of what I hear of you is true, you've done more than your share already."

Gordon acknowledged Dempsey's words with a slow inclining of his head, not a bow of self-congratulation but of acceptance. The other First Guards had remained quiet since meeting Gordon. So close to battle and with so many spies on both sides, they were probably suspicious of his odd clothes and odd ways, the fact that he was a loner.

Now Carter spoke up.

"How many Wardsman have you killed?"

Gordon was honest.

"I don't know."

"One for every feather in your hat?"

"One for every feather in my coat. More maybe. I'm not finished yet." Gordon stroked a hand along the plumage on his left arm. Carter almost laughed and then stifled it when he realised Gordon wasn't joking.

"The Ward are men just like us," said Gordon. "They have the same requirements and the same choices. It's too late to teach them that they've chosen the wrong side – we've all had that choice throughout history. It's time for a new history now, based on exactly the same choice. This is everyone's last chance to get it right."

He drew his lock knife from his pocket and unclasped the blade. He turned it in the stagnant, dusty air of the cottage, the dim light from the windows gliding along its edge. He studied its worn crescent of a blade, trying to understand the relationship between it and his hand, how his will had moved this blade, parting the veil to allow death entry, parting the flesh to allow bad blood its vent. This object was all he retained of his father. His father had been an honourable, brave man. He had made the right choice and it had been the ultimate sacrifice. In some way this blade was an extension of his father's will too. Gordon hoped he had acted as his father would have wanted.

"After all this time, after uncountable generations, there are still people who don't understand their reliance on the land. Human mutations, they've not only forgotten her but turned against her. They are the Ward and the Earth cries out for their blood. What can I do other than answer her call?"

Gordon folded away the blade with some reluctance, to find the four First Guard staring at him, Carter in particular looking pale. Gordon slipped the knife back into his pocket. He thought his explanation had been simple enough. Clearly, all it had done was mark him out as a lunatic.

"Listen," he said, "the Black Dawn has made the world a very simple place. Those who, even in these desperate times, can't act for the good must be brought to an end. When they're gone, we can roam the land again. And she'll love us. The way she used to. Isn't that what we're all fighting for?"

Carter, Finney and Stone glanced at each other and then back at Gordon.

"I suppose so," said Carter. "But no one's ever put it quite like that before."

Dempsey was sitting in the corner listening and smiling. He nodded to himself and stood up.

"We should have you making the final speech before the battle, Gordon. You'll rouse the fighting spirit, even in the boys and the old men!"

"I think I'd better save my breath for the wet-work," said Gordon.

"Speaking of which," said Dempsey, "we're going out raiding tonight. Trying to create as much disruption and demoralisation as we can. Would you like to come with us?"

Gordon grinned.

"Absolutely."

"We'll leave here at dusk with about thirty men. I suggest you get some rest before that."

Gordon moved to the door and opened it. An eager wind swirled in around his boots.

"I'll see you this evening," he said.

52

Megan wakes to the pain of her own pulse.

She feels it in her thigh and her calf and wishes she could lose consciousness again. The pain won't allow it and so she opens her eyes. As she had hoped, she is in the roundhouse. She is lying on furs and wrapped in blankets, her legs poking towards the stove. All around her are laid bundles of herbs and dried wildflowers. Mr Keeper kneels nearby. One hand clutches the bandage around his waist, the other holds his pipe. Though she can feel his eyes watching her, she sees his face only as a black oval, silhouetted in the light from the wind-eye.

In that moment, she sees a furtive face peek in from outside. It is there for only a few moments. It puts a shocked palm over its mouth and it is gone. Megan once peered in through the wind-eye just as timidly and she now remembers her journey through the weave with Carissa as her guide; seeing her own body, pale and apparently dead on the roundhouse floor, while Mr Keeper knelt beside her.

Something releases within Megan, the beginning of the loosening of a knot. In spite of the pain, which burns like coals under her skin, she is happy to be here. This place is safe and Mr Keeper is her guardian in a way even her own family can never be. He is her spirit father.

"What a pair we make," he says.

She grins until she remembers the pursuit and attack. The sensation of the dogs tearing at her living flesh remains close, the certainty that she might die still lingers. The knot within her releases completely then. Her body begins to shake and she cries. She doesn't recognise the sound she makes.

Ohooo, ohoohoo, ohooo.

It's a wail of mourning for the life she almost lost. Not yet can she rejoice at being alive. The meat of her is still in the jaws of the dogs.

Mr Keeper's voice is soft and assured.

"It will pass soon enough."

She nods, fast, through her strange tears and even stranger weeping, managing to smile despite her body's unstoppable catharsis.

Mr Keeper moves towards the stove with some difficulty but she can tell he is much improved. The bandage at his waist has been changed and the stain of blood over the wound is tiny now. From the boiling kettle he pours water into a pot to brew. The scent of unfamiliar herbs fills the roundhouse. He waits for the mixture to infuse and then pours a small bowl for Megan. By now her sobs have petered out. Mr Keeper props her into a half-sitting position and she is able to hold the bowl without spilling it when he hands it to her. He pours a similar bowl for himself and retreats to his cushions near the wind-eye.

Megan drinks from the steaming bowl. The liquid is bittersweet but not unpleasant. It leaves her mouth and tongue swollen and insensitive. Within minutes the pain and throbbing in her legs has eased. A thankfulness to be alive rises from the deeps of her and her tears now are tears of gratitude. She does not regret walking this path. She knows her place in the world and she occupies it with a sense of honour and thankful pride. She drinks more of the numbing tea.

"Your parents were here."

Megan is too surprised to respond. Amu and Apa aren't meant to interfere.

"Almost the whole village was here at some time today. They all heard the commotion this morning. Riders went out after the miller and his two accomplices. Your father was among them. I told them to make it a lesson not a lynching."

"Were my parents… angry?"

"No. They were concerned. I didn't tell them exactly what happened but they understand you were out of the village on Keeper's business and that these men chased you back. They know you were tired and hurt – I didn't tell them the details but I assured them you'd be fine. Like you, I expected them to be angry and upset but they surprised me. They thanked me for everything I'd done for you, said you were becoming a fine young woman and that they were very proud of you. Your mother came back later with a pot of roasted lamb and potatoes. It was delicious."

Megan is ravenous and her dismay must blaze like a beacon. Mr Keeper laughs.

"It's alright, Megan. I haven't touched it yet. I thought it would be nice to eat together. Then we can tend our wounds and rest."

She shakes her head, half annoyed, half amused.

"Can we eat it now? I'm starving."

"Of course we can."

Mr Keeper doles meat and potatoes out of the large pot Megan knows so well from her mother's kitchen. He passes her a bowl and sits back with one for himself. They eat with their fingers, silently but for the smacking of lips and murmurs of appreciation.

When her bowl is empty, Megan holds it out for more. As he fills it for her, Mr Keeper says:

"As soon as you're able to walk, I think you should go home for a few days. Take some time off."

Megan is aghast.

"I'm alright. I can carry on."

"I know you can but that's not the point. Whether you feel it yet or not, you're exhausted. You can't learn anything in that state. And you can't open your eyes to the Crowman when you're not at your fittest either. The best you can hope for is to see him in the night country from your own bed – that part of you, at least, should still have a bit of energy left."

"But I want to stay here. With you. I want to keep going."

"I understand. I really do. You're coming close to the completion of the book. I was eager just like you at this stage. The trouble is, Megan, I'm exhausted too. I need some time to rest and recover. I can't guide you like this and I certainly can't give you the protection you need when you journey for vision. Trust me. It's best for both of us if you go home for a while."

Megan is embarrassed to have pushed this revelation of weakness from Mr Keeper. She can't help but see him as indestructible, as a man with endless energy who will always be there to encourage her onward and guide her in her searching. But he is, in reality, a man. A special man with incredible insights and powers but still just a man. And he is wounded and tired.

"I'm sorry. I was too busy thinking about myself."

"Don't worry. I'd have done the same thing. It's just for a few days, Megan. Then we can continue."

She can tell he is smiling, that his face is kind, even though the light hides all this.

"Alright?"

"Yes," she says. "Of course it's alright."

They both eat second and third helpings and their hunger is such that their agreement represents the last words that pass between them. Megan's final memory of the day is placing the empty bowl beside her as Mr Keeper approaches to check her wounds. She is unconscious before he reaches her.

53

Gordon walked among the resting fighters, stopping when he saw people who looked likely to hold similar hopes to his own. Many of the people he talked to, not just men of fighting age but women and young boys too, wore black feathers like his. They stood out like some sort of tribe within a tribe and, once more, he felt the surge of optimism from deep in his chest. These people were believers. They had made their choice and were willing to lay everything down in pursuing it.

He asked them if they'd heard about the Crowman. He asked them if they'd seen him. Time was short so he asked them not to tell him stories from a month or year before. He wanted know: had they seen him among their number today? Had they seen him walking these fields? And all day, though many of the people he spoke to said they had seen the Crowman only weeks or even days before, he found no one who had seen him among the massing ranks of fighters.

The day waned too fast and Gordon began to lose hope. Another day gone and war coming at any moment. Before the battle began, he had to find the Crowman. The people had to see him, all of them at the same time, as they walked across the land to meet the Ward for the final time. Face to face, not in an interview room or the back of a collection van. Hand to hand. As equals for the first time, not outnumbered and unarmed in the middle of the night. Here at last, the rage and passion of the people would be unleashed. And here too, the land would speak through its people with similar rage. This was either their moment of liberation or the end of everything.

It was past midday when Gordon came upon a small group of fighters lying on mats in the long winter grass of a field that still showed signs of life. All of them wore black feathers in their hair and at their knees and elbows. Black feathers hung and fluttered from their longbows and spears. At his approach they all rose to their feet to greet him.

He frowned.

"You're Gordon Black, aren't you?" said one, stepping forward.

There was no reason to deny it here so he nodded.

"Heard a lot about you. What you've done and that." The man seemed almost shy. "Glad to see you here, like."

All of them smiled and he felt not merely their resolution but their love; a thing so rare it was like a gift – especially on a day such as this.

"I'm looking for the Crowman," he said. His approach had become simplified by the lack of time. "The Rag Man says he walks among us. Have any of you seen him?"

There was a boy in the group. He couldn't have been more than nine or ten, thin as a sapling and sallow as belly-flesh. His hair was raven dark and his eyes deep, earthy brown. He walked right up to Gordon and in a voice no stronger than a whisper he said:

"I've seen a dark man. A tall man. Walking alone across the fields. He stopped and put his arms out east and west, like this." He made the shape of a scarecrow and the hairs all over Gordon's body lifted as he shivered. "Then he raised his arms up to the sky."

Gordon dropped to one knee to meet the child's eyes.

"When was this?"

"Today," said the boy in his hushed voice.

Gordon blinked. It had to be a mistake, didn't it? He dared not hope. He dared not.

"Tell me more about what he looked like."

"He was a big man. Not broad but taller than any of us here. His coat flapped behind him all tattered like. His face was pale but his eyes were black. He walked the way a crow walks, head bobbing, sort of."

"What else did he do?"

"He seemed to be talking to himself. Waving his arms around like he was mad. Or like he was talking to the earth and the sky. I couldn't hear him, though. He was too far away."

Gordon snorted a joyful laugh.

"This is unbelievable. How long ago was it?"

The boy shrugged.

"Maybe an hour or so. I'd been asleep and when I woke up, he was the first thing I saw."

"Did you watch him for long?"

"Maybe ten minutes."

"Did anyone else see him?"

The boy glanced back to the rest of his group before meeting Gordon's gaze.

"I don't think so. Everyone was tired from the march. I was the only one who'd woken up."

Gordon almost couldn't bring himself to ask his next question in case the boy ran out of answers.

"Did you see where he went?"

But the boy held no disappointments for him. He nodded, eyes wide, and pointed away over the fields.

"When he was done with his talking he ran to that wood over there." The boy's index finger picked out a small stand of ancient-looking oaks about half a mile east. "He ran so fast it looked like he was flying. I weren't frightened, though. He's for the good, the Crowman. For the good of us all."

The boy looked again to his band of elders and they all nodded their accord. Gordon put his hands on the boy's shoulders.

"You're a good lad," he said. "Strong and true and I'll never be able to thank you enough for what you've told me today. Not in a thousand generations. But here..." Gordon reached into his pocket and brought out his father's knife and the river rock he sharpened it upon. "I don't know how much longer this blade will last. It has done nothing but take life from those who don't deserve the comfort of this land and give life to those who do. In your hands it will do many good things in the name of the earth. Use it well."

The boy took the knife in confusion and wonder. To him and his group Gordon said, "I'll see you on the field of battle. Fight for the land that loves you. Never give up. And keep the Crowman in your heart."

He turned from them and ran for the small stand of oaks, ran with the wind under the panels of his coat, ran, dancing and leaping and crying out in joy and long before he made it to the dark gathering of trees, he saw the crows circling above it in slow, leisurely wheels and knew that his search was at an end.

54

The herbs and broths accelerate Megan's recovery. After a few days' rest, she is able to go home.

She embraces Mr Keeper at the doorway of the roundhouse and is taken aback by the condition of his body. He has never been a bulky man but he feels emaciated in her arms, drained of his essence. He stoops a little as though he no longer has the strength to carry himself upright.

"Go carefully," he says, standing away from her as though she's already gleaned too much knowledge from their contact. He keeps hold of her shoulders. "Don't wander far from home or do too much. Allow yourself to heal. That mother of yours is a wonderful cook and she'll want to coddle you and build you up. Be sure you let her."

"I wish I could be here to do that for you."

"You know the Keeper's way well enough by now, Megan. We can look after ourselves better than most."

Megan nods, a little embarrassed.

"When should I come back?" she asks.

"When the time seems right. You'll know. Meanwhile, rest. And dream, Megan. The Crowman still has more to show you. Perhaps a great deal more."

"You said you thought the book was almost complete.

How much more can there be?"

"It isn't just the book he reveals, Megan. So keep an open mind. If he wants to show you more, go along with it as best you can."

"I will."

Mr Keeper ducks down into the roundhouse and doesn't come out again. This, she assumes, is goodbye for the moment. The opening and closing of his connection always jolts her. She is delighted when he lets his barriers down, affronted each time he slams them closed.

The first few steps out of the clearing are the easiest. She has been practising walking around the roundhouse and was confident of her returning strength and stamina. But before she is halfway along the tightly wooded path, both leg wounds begin to ache and pound. By the time she reaches the edge of the village, her face is creased with the pain of walking and she is sweating despite the cold.

She doesn't notice the two figures approaching along the main track until she looks up between stifled grunts and muttered oaths. Their smiling faces bring back a world she has left behind; it's like seeing the first day of spring all over again instead of being trapped here in the bony claws of winter. Tom Frewin and Sally Balston are two of her fondest friends from the days before she first saw the Crowman. Seeing she is in difficulty, their smiles are replaced by frowns of concern. They run to her.

"Meg!" pants Tom on arrival. He's always carried a decent layer of blubber over his already strong frame. There seems to be more of it now. "What's the matter?"

"My legs. They're... really sore."

"So, it's true then?" asks Sally. "About the wolfhounds?"

"Yes. It's true."

For a moment the three of them stand there in the grey gloom, tiny particles of frozen mist swirling around them. Megan looks at their faces and sees something still alive there, something that has died in her.

She begins to cry.

"It's really good to see you," she says.

"It seems like years since we saw you, Meg," says Tom. "I thought you weren't allowed to talk to us anymore."

"Oh, no, Tom. It's nothing like that. I do have to spend a lot of time... away... but I can still see you. I've just been busy."

"We've been very busy too," says Sally, apparently not wanting to be trumped. "With school," she adds.

A pulse of pain shoots up through Megan's legs as she shifts position. She can't hide it. She puts out a hand to steady herself and finds Tom's chunk of a shoulder.

"I don't suppose you could help me home, could you?"

Neither Tom nor Sally say a word. They are friends still, after all. Each of them drapes one of Megan's arms around the backs of their necks and, thus united, they begin to walk.

"Slowly," says Megan. "That way we can talk a bit more."

"So, what's it like, Meg?" asks Tom. "This thing you're doing. Everyone says you're going to be like Mr Keeper one day. I've always thought he was a bit, you know... paddlewhacked."

Megan giggles despite her pain. What else can you expect from a boatman's son?

"I know he seems odd. But he's lovely really. Something like a teacher and a funny uncle all mixed up together. And the things he's taught me. Well, it's opened my eyes, Tom. Opened my eyes to a whole new world."

Sally makes a face.

"One world's enough for me."

Megan nods.

"Sometimes I feel exactly the same way."

By now they're almost home and Tom seems eager to ask her something else.

"Are you allowed to come to the Festival of Light? Everyone'll be there."

Megan can't believe she's been so totally absorbed as to forget the festival. They're approaching the front door of her parents' cottage now.

"I think so," she says.

Sally stops walking and turns to Megan. Any doubt about their relationship seems to have dissolved.

"It would be great if you can come, Megan. I've really missed you. We all have."

The three of them hug – something they never did when they were chasing through the meadows or swimming in the river but things are different now and they all know it – and then say goodbye. Megan lets herself into the cottage and collapses onto a stool by the stove to rest and warm herself. The cottage is empty but she is happy to sit in alone, listening to the wood spit and crack inside the stove. A little quiet before her parents return is exactly what she needs.

That very night, after she has eaten with Apa and Amu and fallen with great thankfulness into her bed, the Crowman comes to Megan.

Returning to her parents has been bittersweet. She has done her best to hide her pain and the shock of her attack from them. They have done their best to hide their worry and celebrate her safe homecoming – no matter how brief it may be. In this way they all have been less than honest with each other. There is an underlying sadness too. They know Megan's stay in the family home will be temporary and short-lived, for Megan's training must continue. They know also that once the training is complete Megan will leave them. Though their cottage will always be her home, she will find a new place to live; a place from where she can begin her life as a Keeper. That neither she nor her parents feel able to bring these matters into the open causes Megan a good deal of melancholy. As parents, they are meant to be stronger than this. As one who walks the Black Feathered Path, so is she.

It is with a full stomach and a weighted heart that she falls into bed and into sleep and it seems she has been in the night country only moments when the dark figure of the Crowman takes shape in her consciousness.

They are not in her bedroom. She sits up to find herself sitting high in a leafless tree where a strong limb meets the trunk. She hugs the trunk to keep from falling. Beside her, squatting on the same branch, is her guide through these realms. The way he sits makes him look like a bird. His knees are drawn up to his chest and his coat flows down behind him like trailing tail feathers.

For a long time he doesn't speak. Dawn is coming and they are facing east but the light in this land is grey, always grey. Here, cloud and dust and smoke obscure the sun every day, it seems, and so it rises behind a dirty veil, illuminating the land without ever really warming it. Megan shivers.

The landscape around them is dead in many places; the trees, shrubs and weeds rotting in the earth or crumbling to particles to be blown into the sky. There are good-sized swathes of healthy land too, where the grass is long and lush and the trees, though deep in skeletal slumber, still pulse with life. Megan senses that a crucial moment is approaching; the future could go either way. In all her wanderings here, she has never once felt that the outcome was certain. Even though she comes from a time in which the land has flourished, she knows she can be sure of nothing. Mr Keeper warned of that long ago – nothing is as it seems. She can afford to make no judgements.

When the struggling dawn has made what difference it can to the land, the silent Crowman holds out his hand to her. She takes it, grateful for his touch in this forsaken world, no matter how impenetrable he may be. Something in this dark man is benevolent beyond words. That this quality is cloaked in trickery and secrecy is something she has ceased to fear. His cold fingers, hiding a warmth deep within, close carefully and deliberately over hers.

"Come, Megan. There is still much to see."

They glide from the high branches but they land far too soon. Megan opens her senses to whatever is coming, ready to record it all.

55

The leafless oaks stood silent and strong, their roots thick and buried deep. Their trunks were squat and massive and though the trees weren't particularly tall, Gordon guessed they must have been centuries old. That such a patch of oak wood had survived all these years was a miracle. It was no surprise to Gordon that this was the place the Crowman had chosen.

He said a hurried prayer of thanks to the Great Spirit and entered the shadowy forest microcosm. It was like stepping into prehistory. The striated bark of the trees was softened by a pelt of velvety moss as thick as carpeting. Fronds of delicate pale lichen hung from every branch. Above his head the upper limbs of the trees were bound together forming arches and vaults. They let almost no light through and Gordon had the impression he walked in a wild cathedral with woven branches for its ceiling and roof, the mighty oak trunks forming its supporting columns. He glanced back out to the fields. A shimmer like a heat haze made the figures camped in the distance indistinct and unreal. He had stepped into another world, another time.

Finally walking in the sacred space he had so long journeyed for, Gordon passed reverently beneath the protective arms of the oaks, between their sturdy legs. He was a child among giants, safe for a moment in the sanctuary and company of trees.

The wood seemed much larger within than without and Gordon passed through it at an easy pace to begin with. The earthy scent of decay and fertility, the aroma of many fungi poking up through the leaf litter, the dampness of the air as the wood breathed were all the scent of homecoming to Gordon. If he hadn't had to fight this war, he might have made this dark, moist place his home.

After half an hour or more of searching, Gordon found himself back where he'd begun. The first chill of doubt, his constant companion for so long now, caressed the skin of his back and bled into his stomach.

"No. He's here."

He set off again into the cloisters of the oak basilica, this time marking well his route, walking faster and spiralling inwards towards the centre. He made certain not to miss a single tree or space, trailing his fingers across the soft green fur covering every trunk. When he reached the natural centre of the wood, he spiralled his way out in the opposite direction. He found nothing. No footprints but his own. No disturbance to the trees or stunted, light-starved weeds and brambles that grew between them. He looked once more out of the wood, towards the group of feather-wearing fighters.

They were gone.

Were they ever there?

He looked about him. All was silence. The oaks themselves, who would have spoken to him in strange whispers on any other day, made no sound at all.

I'm alone, he thought.

A heaviness seeped into his limbs, a trickle of lead into every muscle, slowing and thickening his movements, dragging him down.

One more look. He has to be here.

Stumbling now with exhaustion and the promise of ultimate disappointment, he followed the tracks of his first diminishing circle into the heart of the wood. Weariness sat around his shoulders like a wet cloak. His head hung. His strong chest collapsed inwards and his shoulders slumped. The circles of his footsteps grew smaller until he reached the very centre of the wood. There was nothing there. Nothing but trees.

One particular oak stood thicker and shorter than those around it, the first split in its trunk quite low to the ground. It made a comfortable looking hammock shape. Right now, Gordon could think of nothing more he wanted than to be cradled in the crook of a mighty tree, to close his eyes and forget about the world, forget about his failure and sleep. He could stay here, hidden among the oaks and no one would find him. No one would even come to look. No matter what the outcome of the battle, he would be safe and hidden. Gordon knew he had done everything he could, given all he had to this search.

He had found nothing.

Another thought now rose in his mind; one that had circled his consciousness a thousand times, one that he'd kept away with a spear of hope. But now that spear was broken.

I'm insane.

He laughed. The sound was muffled and swallowed by the trees.

I've been chasing a story, believing all the time that it was real.

His laughter became weeping.

Gordon climbed up into the oak at the centre of the wood and found it comforting and protective. He didn't bother to wipe away the tears from his face, nor did he try to stop himself from crying. He had no energy left to pretend he was strong. He had no energy left for anything. He curled up in the broad, curved fork of the oak tree and his tears soaked into the moss.

The wood darkened slowly around him and a mist crept over the ground to swirl and eddy over the roots of the trees. The sounds of the nighttime creatures came from all around. Badgers nosed through the leaf litter looking for worms and grubs. Slugs and snails did slow dances across every surface; Gordon heard the wet crackle of their passage as they slid near his head. Nightjars called out their haunted melodies and fluttered somewhere above. The outer branches of the oaks creaked and clattered against each other in a wind he couldn't feel down here among their trunks.

There was another sound. An approach, but not of an animal. Steady, stealthy footsteps. Cloth caught and released by briars. Breathing.

Gordon reached a hand towards his pocket, only to remember there was nothing there that could help him now. His body came alive again. Heat flowed into his muscles. His heart beat hard and loud, strong once more. He put his palms to the mossy bark below him ready to spring up, either into the higher branches or onto the stalker. He raised his head and looked into the deepening dusk.

In the shadows a few paces away stood a dark figure. A man. Tall and thin, his outline indistinct because of the feathers he wore. His arms were stretched out to either side. Was it a gesture of welcoming? Of inclusion? A presenting to

Gordon of the night or, perhaps, the whole world? Or was it simply communicating–

"Here I am."

The voice was deep, sensitive, resonant. Gordon swallowed, unable to speak.

"Do you recognise me?" asked the figure.

Gordon couldn't see its face in the darkness but it seemed to be the face of a man. And yet, the night made his features swim and whirl. One moment he saw what he thought was a man; the next he saw ancient, intelligent eyes shining with the Black Light. A majestic, downward curving beak, gleaming like obsidian in moonlight. The mist gathered and turned at the figure's feet. Were they the talons of a great coal-black bird, or the booted feet of a man?

"I… I don't know."

"Perhaps you've stopped believing."

"No," said Gordon. He sat up in the tree. "Not at all. I was disillusioned. Tired. That's all."

"And yet you are unable to sleep…"

"I was beginning to think I was crazy. Am I crazy? Are you really here? Or am I making this up so that I don't destroy myself with guilt? The things I've done… What if there was no reason? No justification?"

The figure allowed its arms to drop to its sides. The feathers it wore shimmered, pearly black.

"You had to come this far," the figure said. "You had to come this *way*; do the things you've done. And you had to come to the end of your faith. You did stop believing, Gordon. That's why you're hiding in here, crying to yourself like you've never cried before. The search had to lead you nowhere and the burden of it had to break you before I could appear. Do you understand?"

"I don't understand anything any more. Why was I the last one to find you? I've met so many people along the way who've seen you. Heard so many stories about you. And yet it seemed as if I was held away from you somehow. Why?"

"It isn't enough to catch a glimpse of the Crowman, Gordon. It isn't enough to watch him pass by and perform some miracle. It isn't enough to say you've seen him kill a Wardsman or dispatch some evildoer. You have to *find* him. None of those who've seen the Crowman could do that, Gordon, and that's why they were allowed a glimpse. But you had a destiny that called you, and everything you did and everything you encountered along the way pointed you in this direction. If you'd have seen me too early on, it would have done nothing for you. You had to be thwarted. You had to be outrun. Your belief had to be smashed. Only then would you be ready."

Gordon permitted himself a smile. He laughed but stopped; the oaks were grim and the wildlife in the wood had fallen silent.

"You were just in time, Gordon. Tomorrow there will be a battle. Because of you, because of everything you've done, I will be present. It will make a difference. It will change the way things might otherwise have been. There *will* be a future. And the land will one day bring forth its abundance again. The love between humanity and the Earth will be restored. It will be a Bright Day, Gordon Black. A Bright Day indeed."

The figure stepped back into the shadows of the wood.

"Wait!" said Gordon. "You can't leave. Not now."

"I won't be far away. You must sleep now in readiness for tomorrow."

"But the people, the fighters, they need to see you. The Ward need to see you."

"They will, Gordon. And those who live to witness it will never forget me. I'll be there with you tomorrow. I promise."

The figure receded between the oaks and was lost to the night and the rising mist.

Gordon snorted into the empty wood.

"Sleep, he says. "Not a bloody chance."

He turned over onto his back so that he could look up from his vantage into the night. It was almost black above the trees. He should have been out raiding with Dempsey and the others by now. Tomorrow he would make up for it. He would fight alongside the rest of them. He laid his head against the moss-laden bark and watched the turning mist rise like a tide until it was just below his hammock of wood. His eyes fluttered closed.

56

The tree shook. Droplets of dew rained down from the branches. Gordon shifted position. Again the vibration, followed by a distant thud. Gordon opened his eyes, hoping he'd been dreaming.

He hadn't.

The ground tremored in time with faraway sounding thumps. This was no earthquake. He slipped from the embrace of the oak and landed in a crouch on the forest floor, one hand still resting on the warm moss that enveloped the tree trunk. The movement from below came again. Above him the branches of the canopy rattled against each other, shedding more condensation. It was day outside but very little light penetrated the womblike binding of the oaks. He felt safe there. If he decided to stay, no one would ever be able to find him.

Beyond the oaks and across the fields, though, Gordon knew people were already dying under the Ward's artillery fire. Out there somewhere the Crowman walked among the fighters spreading courage and hope. Perhaps he already stood at the head of the Green Men's army, rallying them, telling them to hold fast under the bombardment and then leading them into a battle they now had a chance to win.

He knew if he hid in the oak wood that he would never forgive himself. He may have found the Crowman but he had not finished fighting the Ward. He would fight with the people, under the banner of the Crowman, and he would play his part in this battle. He would make the same sacrifice as everyone else.

Gladly.

He ran then. Between the dark, broad bodies of oak trees whose foundations were thrust into the very history of the land, who had touched the Earth so deeply and for so long with their taproots they knew her better than any human. Gordon let his hands touch their trunks as he passed between them, telling them to send his message into the soil:

I love you. I will fight for you.

And asking them to transmit his prayers:

Send me the strength you gave to these trees. Make my hands your weapons. Give me the power to carry out your sentence.

The light at the edge of the wood grew brighter as he approached. His feet flashed faster until the weeds he passed became whips to his ankles. Somewhere behind him, hidden by the darkness within the maze of oaks, he heard the voices of crows, rising up from the trees all over the land. He heard their wings pushing at the air, eager to attend the battle. He felt that disturbed wind, touched and stirred by their feathers, gathering behind him, pressing him into the world.

Gordon Black flew from the trees. The feathers in his top hat sang as the wind passed over them. The feathers in his hair gathered and rolled behind his shoulders, scattering the light from the grey sky. The feathers of his coat billowed up about him and behind him in a black fury, like the frantic beating of ragged, vengeful wings.

He came to the battle.

57

Megan travels in the night country when she sleeps. By day, she writes.

The Crowman has taken no notice of her injuries. If anything, he unfolds his story with more enthusiasm than before. She knows something is coming. He is drawing her towards it as swiftly as he is able. As the blank pages remaining in her book dwindle, a fear grows within her. The boy has grown cold and grim and relentless as he closes on his objective. Her goal and his are the same and Megan is terrified that his darkness will spill over into her soul.

Great Spirit, let me never become as wounded or as cruel as Gordon Black.

She repeats this prayer more and more often as her convalescence progresses and the boy's history blackens with blood and fury. Outside her window, winter darkens the landscape. The Festival of Light approaches. Only a few days away now, it will take place on the longest night of the year. Megan wonders if she will finish her work before it. If not, she will be unable to attend and that will take her even further from her friends.

One morning, when the writing dries up and no more story will come, she stands from her tiny desk, throws off her blankets and puts on her winter furs. Through her wind-eye she can see the snow flurries thinning and the clouds beginning to disperse. She needs movement and air. More than that she needs sunlight and she senses it will break through very soon.

She prepares a small pack and puts her boots on. She could have returned to Mr Keeper days ago but the pace of the Crowman's unfolding tale is such that she dare not wander far from the book. Her recovering legs can take her far enough from the cottage that she will feel a small sense of freedom today, but she knows nightfall will bring another journey into Gordon's pitiless world.

She sets off through light snow but it soon ceases and the day brightens. The mist floats upwards and away from the land. It unstitches and fall apart, allowing golden swords of light through the rends until unobscured sunshine blasts down from sheer blue. There is no wind, and the sun pushes heat into Megan's face.

Her limp has almost gone and, though her legs still ache, they feel strong again. She doesn't even think about where she is going. She passes through the gate into the meadow, its grass and wildflowers having receded under the crush of winter, and up into the fallow fields where last season the corn grew two feet higher than her head. She walks straight across the exposed, dark earth towards bare-boned trees that would be menacing to anyone who didn't know better. She passes through their boundary and even here among the oaks the rays still penetrate, solid bolts of powerful sunlight streaming heat and goodness into the ground.

She finds the fallen oak and climbs up into the throne formed by its toppled roots. She can't believe she was ever frightened by this place. Being here now is like coming home.

She chuckles softly. Why did such a natural and obvious thing need to be so difficult? In answer, she hears the crows, out of sight in the branches high above, calling down their own good-natured derision. *It's far easier for humans to be stupid than it is for them to be honest,* they seem to say.

She takes a chunk of Amu's oat bran loaf from her pack and bites into it, reflecting on the harsh wisdom of the crows. When the piece of bread is gone, she reaches into her pack for another and stops. She is not alone. Footsteps approach from between the monolithic uprights that are the oaks' ancient trunks.

The Crowman steps clear.

"So, here we are again, Megan."

She is stunned at first.

There has been no warning of his approach. No change in the air, no alteration in her perception. His arrival is similar to that first day all those months ago – as if he is actually here, in person. As flesh and blood.

He is beautiful to behold. Taller than any man she knows with dark, silken locks falling around his shoulders. Pristine black feathers are woven into his hair and there's one she hasn't noticed before – a single white feather as stark in its whiteness as all the others are in the purity of their black. One grey eye regards her in the way a curious jackdaw might, its head slightly tilted for a better view. The other is covered by a patch made from the down of raven chicks. On his head is a black top hat, its nap brushed and gleaming, feathers poking up from the band at various angles and hanging from the rear of its brim. His plumed coat shimmers like charcoal, catching the sunlight. His hands are covered by the length of his sleeves. He seems to absorb the sunlight and radiate it as blackness. His smile is touched by the same black light. It is knowing, compassionate, generous, wrathful.

Her heartbeat quickens.

"Are you frightened, Megan?"

"No. Not this time."

"Good."

He glances around at the quiet, steadfast oaks. An air of sadness takes him for the briefest moment, dimming his radiance like a small cloud passing between the earth and the sun.

"My tale is almost over, you know."

Megan nods.

"I can feel it coming," she says.

"I wanted to be there when you discover the last part. Not to guide you through the weave as I usually do in spirit, but to accompany you, to show it to you in my own way. To take part in it, if you will. Are you agreeable?"

Megan can't imagine a reason why she wouldn't be.

"Of course. I'd like nothing better."

"And afterwards…"

Again the dark cloud.

"And afterwards?" she prompts.

"Afterwards you and I must part for a time."

"Part? Why? I… don't understand."

"It's difficult, Megan. You must learn to have faith in me. For that to happen, I need to go away for a while. Remove myself from your sight. You must find me then in other ways, in the whisper of the wind when it makes tongues of the branches, in the darting of the wren after she catches your eye, in the way the light shatters when it touches the river. You must watch for me a while and listen for me a while and I must not be there, except in spirit. Do you see?"

She shakes her head but only because she doesn't want to admit it. She doesn't want to accept the truth.

"Yes, Megan," he says. "I can see that you do. And that was why I picked you." He hesitates for a moment and then appears to decide on saying more. "Besides, we've met before. A long time ago and I… Well, we will meet that way again some day. Souls do not die. They are reborn until–"

"Are you saying I must *die* before I see you again?"

"No. I'm saying that part of me knew you once, in physical human form. The part of me that is Gordon Black. He has always waited for you to return. One day that part of me will reunite with you in this realm."

Megan looks down, frowning, trying to remember who it could be in Gordon's brief history that he might long to meet again. She looks up very suddenly, her expression bright.

"You're talking about the little girl, aren't you? Flora?"

"Yes."

Megan accepts this knowledge with a small nod. It makes perfect sense now. She was there. She saw the Black Dawn through the eyes of the girl who died in the attic. The little girl was *there* in his lifetime and met Gordon Black, touched him. In spite of his power and all the people he healed, Flora was one he dearly wanted to save and couldn't. But they will meet again some day. The mingled sense of comfort and melancholy this causes is hard to bear and Megan resolves in that moment to go back through the weave and pay her respects at the little girl's resting place. When the book is written. *If.* That's when she'll return.

The Crowman holds out his hand to her. This is their last journey together and she will not see him like this again for a long time. From the way he talks, she senses it might be many years. She looks into the Crowman's single slate-grey eye and sees only love there; though behind it she sees the burden and pain of his vast knowledge.

"Are you ready?" he asks.

She gives him her hand.

"Yes. I'm ready."

58

Through a battered and scratched pair of binoculars, Dempsey watched the storm of the Ward's barrage with dismay at first. The Green Men stood to lose thousands of men.

They had dug no trenches: the predominantly civilian troops were too tired on arrival and they'd had neither the time nor the equipment. There was no cover other than drainage ditches, hedges, sparse stands of trees and the depressions between natural rises in the landscape. But the fighters were ranged so far and wide across the countryside that the shelling from the Ward could not be concentrated effectively. Green Men cowered in the places where they'd woken, able only to pray for survival.

The bombardment ended within half an hour. As their scouts had reported, the Ward were throwing all their stockpiled weapons into this conflict but their ordnance was limited. Following the raids and skirmishes of the previous forty-eight hours, much of that ordnance had been destroyed or sabotaged.

Dempsey's own raid had been a more subtle affair. Armed only with bows and knives, his twenty men had come to an encampment of Ward troops two miles south of Junction 18. Reconnaissance had shown this camp to be heavily defended. It was a mobile ammunition station, complete with horses and carts to transport rifle bullets and tank shells to the front lines. His group had found most of the guards asleep – exhausted by their own journey, probably. Those men woke into death by the blade. The rest of the watchmen were silently dispatched by longbowmen.

Dempsey's men surrounded the camp and began to steal the horses. At some point a Wardsman raised the alarm and two dozen sleepy, terrified troops struggled from their tents and bivvy bags. There was no close quarter confrontation; every Wardsman was taken down by arrows. A couple of rifle shots came out of the Ward encampment, killing one of their own horses. Dempsey's men piled the ammunition they couldn't use – everything but shotgun shells – together and set fire to it as they left, destroying everything. No one followed them back to the village.

Dempsey's only disappointment was that Gordon Black had not made good on his promise to join them. His opinion of the man – well, the boy if truth be told – had plummeted. Yet he'd known from their first meeting that Gordon was wild and untameable. Such an individual didn't really fit with the Green Men's operations, even if they were only quasi-military in nature. Despite Gordon's weird personal agenda there'd been something about him that Dempsey liked. Wherever his search for the mythical Crowman had taken him, it had given him a depth that most of Dempsey's brothers in arms didn't possess. And Gordon had killed many men along his way. That much was clear in his stark grey eyes, eyes that spoke silently of sights seen and deeds done that would never be uttered by his tongue.

As Dempsey rode to the head of his sub-command, a body of two thousand infantry and longbowmen, he hoped he'd see the boy again. He raised his field glasses once more to survey the land, checking positions and weak points but always on the lookout for a singular, black-clad figure.

Between the village of Clay Coton and the M1 was a mile and a half of open fields. Conglomerating into ranks out there now, in the aftermath of the shelling, were a good fifty or more sub-commands of similar size. From this distance, to see so many troops coming into formation made Dempsey feel strong and proud. This may not have been a trained army, in the main, but it was vast and it was committed to this fight by the utter extremity of its circumstances. If they won, there was a chance they could rebuild their lives. If they lost, they lost everything. The Ward offered no hope any more, only tyranny and blind consumption of every resource. They would rape the world to death.

A mile or so to the south the first physical engagement of the battle had begun as the Ward advanced into the first scattered forces of the Green Men. Some of them were ready, others were not. Those nearest ranks of Green Men were not longbowmen. They were the simplest, most poorly equipped infantrymen. Dempsey could see columns of Wardsmen leaving their formations to chase these swiftly routed troops. Once each blood-hungry Ward breakaway was free of the main columns, the Green Men's longbowmen, waiting in cover, stepped clear and loosed their arrows, cutting down swathes of grey uniforms at very little cost.

In this manner the early part of the plan was more of a success than Dempsey could have hoped for but the Ward quickly learned not to chase weak-looking troops other than with tanks. Within minutes of defeating five or six rogue Ward units, ten grey tanks accelerated away from the Ward columns and into the Green Men's weakling infantry. They didn't fire their guns. They merely chased down the larger groups, crushing as many troops under their tracks as they could. It was a grim dance to watch, almost grotesquely comical, as the tanks pursued small groups of tiring runners, scattering them like sheep and mowing down the slowest of them.

This action sparked a genuine retreat of the Green Men's infantry. They ran stumbling and staggering back towards the now ready ranks of sub-commands. As they fled, volleys of rifle fire from the front lines of Wardsmen brought hundreds of them down. Figures both grey and camouflaged lay dead and dying on the grass. Dempsey couldn't honestly tell through his binoculars which side had come off better in the first part of the engagement.

It was then that Dempsey glimpsed a singular figure sprinting through the massed units of Green Men, his black coat flicking around him like wings of rag, his top hat still firmly on his head. It could be no other person and seeing him there, moving with such unnatural speed and energy, sent a charge of eagerness and pride through Dempsey's heart. He wanted nothing more than to follow that dark figure into combat, to release the souls of the enemy and anoint the earth red with their blood.

Something happened as Gordon passed through the vast ranks of Green Men. From this distance it was as though he were a tiny magnet moving between iron filings. His passage sent ripples of attraction through the columns of his comrades. The mounted sub-commanders seemed drawn by him and they trotted off after him. Behind each sub-commander came two thousand starving troops, armed with axes and flick-knives, shovels and gardening forks. Some of them carried sawn off shotguns, others wielded pieces of martial arts equipment – nunchuks and katanas, throwing stars and wooden staffs.

All of them followed Gordon down towards the enemy.

The tanks had returned to the head of the Ward's vast cohorts. Now they turned and led the entire army further into battle. Ten unstoppable chunks of grey metal, their phallic guns pointed into the unprotected ranks of the Green Men. Despite the power of the attraction to join Gordon on the field, Dempsey held his own sub-command back.

At some invisible command, the tanks opened fire simultaneously sending ten explosive shells through the marching columns of the Green Men. The angle of firing was so flat, each shell killed fifty or more men before impacting, exploding and taking at least twenty or more. Pale smoke billowed from each grey carapace and, at the site of each blast crater, black smoke and a mist of obliterated dirt and flesh wafted down over those still marching. Hundreds of fighters taken out in a single volley. Not yet engaged with the enemy, the Green Men faltered. Ranks piled into the backs of the stalled, stunned troops in front of them.

Between the first lines of the Green Men and the tanks was a distance of only two or three hundred yards, closing all the time as the Ward advanced. At the centre of this body-strewn no-man's-land, facing the entire Ward army alone, stood Gordon Black.

His figure, tiny even through Dempsey's binoculars, now ran back to the faltering Green Men. At his mere gestures, ripples of force passed through the hesitant troops. Dempsey couldn't hear what Gordon was saying but the fighters could. They stiffened and closed rank. Once more Gordon faced the enemy and began to cover the space between them at a run.

A noise from the field swept back towards Dempsey and his horse bucked at the strangeness and power of it. The sound buffeted Dempsey's troops. It washed over the other sub-commanders and their columns ranged to Dempsey's right and left. The battle-cry of a hundred thousand men, women and children passing a psychological point of no return. No matter what happened, he knew they'd follow Gordon Black into glory or death.

Dempsey nudged the flanks of his horse and moved forward. He caught the eyes of the sub-commanders to either side of him and they nodded their assent. The remaining columns of Green Men followed marched down towards the field of battle.

59

It was a long run from the wood to the place where the fighters had gathered but Gordon felt no cost to his muscles or energy along the way. If anything, his entire being had filled up with power as the battlefield beckoned. His desire to savage the foot-soldiers of the Ward became almost sexual in intensity.

As he approached the rear of the Green Men's ranks of civilian troops he was choked with pride. They *could* win but many of them were going to die today. Some because they were too weak to fight well, some because they were too inexperienced to do anything more than poke a hoe at a Wardsman before being shot, cut down or disabled. Thousands would die by being in the wrong place at the wrong moment and still more would exhaust themselves to the point at which death would be nothing worse than a release from pain. But they were here and that meant something. It meant the heart of the land was still beating in each and every one of these people. They would bleed and die for her. They would do whatever was necessary to win her back from the choking grasp of the Ward.

Beyond these nearest formations, Gordon could hear the sounds of battle already begun – shouting, the clash of weapons, the swoosh of arrows flying and the grumble of tank engines – and he ran through the ranks to join those who'd engaged the Ward.

As he passed between the columns he shouted what he knew each fighter needed to hear:

"I've seen the Crowman! He's with us! Pass the word!"

Even as he spoke the words he could feel the effect they had on the people nearest to him. Risking a glance behind as he ran, he saw the shining behind the eyes of the fighters, how they clasped each other, how some unrealised force rose up within them at the sound of that name.

"The Crowman fights with us today! The victory is ours!"

As he burst forth from the front ranks, Gordon saw the carnage wrought by the roving Ward tanks and the Green longbowmen. Bodies, some pierced or cut, many crushed, others showing shafts of hazel, lay all over the shell-cratered fields.

Gordon stopped for a moment, watching the tanks retreat back to the front of the Ward's lines. A few feet in front of him was the body of a boy. His legs and lower abdomen were flattened into the dirt and bore the prints of caterpillar tracks. The weight of the tank had caused his limbs to split under pressure and blood had sprayed outwards to darken the already dark, exposed earth. The force had pushed the boy's innards through his mouth. His eyes stared upwards, his lips stretched wide around his reversed stomach and one lung which bore the scrape-marks of his own teeth. Clutched in his right hand was a lock knife, its worn, curved blade unmarked by the blood of the enemy. Gordon knelt, closed the boy's shock-wide eyes and retrieved the weapon.

He rose up, held the blade high for those behind him to see, and ran forward towards the enemy, drawing the army of the Green Men in his wake.

••••

When the tanks fired, the air to either side of him superheated briefly, screaming protest at the passage of the low-flying projectiles. He turned and saw the corridors of blood and bone they'd torn through the forwardmost columns and the depressions in the earth where dozens more fighters had been vaporised by each ensuing explosion.

The entire Green Man army stopped in its tracks, stunned into terror by that single volley of tank fire. Halfway across the space between the two front lines already, Gordon had no option but to go back for his people. If they turned away now, both the battle and the war were lost. Every death since the Ward had taken power would be in vain. He sprinted back to the heads of the stalled columns, near enough that they could hear, far enough that most of them could see him. He drew breath and gathered power from where his boots met the earth.

His voice carried out to the petrified fighters.

"The Ward have always had more power than we have and that's no different today. Many of us are going to die right here in these fields. We'll die because we believe in something greater than ourselves. We believe in this land and we believe in its future. To turn away from the Ward now and save your skin will be to do nothing more than die slowly and take the future with you. If you don't fight now, there won't be another chance. Today is either the end of everything or the beginning of something beautiful beyond your ken. What you do now, right now, is all that can decide whether the land lives or dies. The land has sent us a leader, a man who has fought for us all along. She sent us the Crowman. He is not a myth. He is not a rumour. He is a living breathing man. And I tell you this, he fights alongside us today. He is here. I have seen him. With the Crowman among us WE CANNOT LOSE. Let us march forward and lay down our lives together."

Gordon raised his knife hand high.

"For the land!"

The Green Men raised their weapons to the sky and responded:

"FOR THE LAND!"

Gordon raised his blade again.

"For the future!"

The Green Man army replied as one:

"FOR THE FUTURE!"

Gordon faced the enemy and walked forward. United under the power of the Crowman, many of them wearing his wondrous black feathers, the last of the land's faithful marched into battle, howling for the blood of their enemies.

Gordon's body quaked with rage and power.

The Ward's tanks fired again, ending hundreds more lives in seconds. The columns marched through the destruction, steadfast behind Gordon Black. When he leapt onto one of the central tanks, those in the front ranks came forward and did the same. The Chieftain had expected armoured vehicles to form part of the Ward's assault. They couldn't stop the tanks and they certainly couldn't destroy them. But they could stop them from firing. A few of the Green Men carried sacks of stones small enough to fit inside the barrel of each turret gun. A few of these inserted and held in place with tar and a simple plug of hessian sacking would cause devastation when the gun was fired. If any of the tank crews tried to get out and clear the blockage, they would be swamped by Green Men.

Gordon now initiated this process, though it was costly. Many of the tanks fired as Green Men shinned along the barrels or before they'd pushed their stones inside. Rifle fire from the approaching Wardsmen picked off dozens of fighters from each of the ten tanks. Two tank commanders tried to fire. Their guns exploded, killing them, their crews and those assailing their vehicles. The other eight tanks managed one more volley before their guns were disabled. All the tanks were good for now was cover for slowly advancing Wardsmen. Chasing the Green Men into their own ranks was too costly to their rapidly diminishing fuel. Gordon watched with pride and satisfaction as the tanks retreated from the field to clear their guns.

The ranks of Green Men flowed forwards and Gordon took up his position at their head once more. Following him were the mounted sub-commanders, leading the first much-depleted columns. Behind them, more sub-commanders and their vast units were also moving forward. The Ward army began to spread to the left and right, stretching the line of imminent contact. The Green Men's sub-commanders responded. Rifle fire was already cutting down swathes of the Green Men's front ranks but now each sub-command split into infantry and longbowmen. The bowmen began to loose volleys of arrows over the heads of their own fighters and into the deeper ranks of Wardsmen in the distance.

Finally, the Green Men and the men of the Ward came among each other.

Gordon was first to sweep into the enemy lines. Those nearby him saw the young man become a furious warrior and they were inspired. He didn't engage any of the Wardsman singly; he slashed at arms and legs and faces and moved on before any soldier could retaliate. Those who saw him coming raised their swords or their crossbows but Gordon anticipated every attack. He swooped between the grey uniforms, a black figure leaving a wide red trail behind him. His rage and energy spread from Green Man to Green Man and Ward troops began to fall like dry stalks to the scythe.

60

Ranks of Wardsmen broke away in various flanking manoeuvres.

Dempsey and the other sub-commanders who'd held back near Clay Coton met each of these attempted incursions with longbow volleys. This tactic even proved successful in repelling cavalry charges along the sides of the Green Men's main attacking force.

What amazed Dempsey most was the battle's direction. The Ward were being pushed backwards towards their rear position in the village of Crick. He'd long since lost sight of the black-coated figure that was Gordon Black. He prayed the young man was still alive – if not for him, this battle might have been lost before it really started. Dempsey's suspicion, though, was that Gordon, fighting as a lone unit, would have tired and fallen within the first hour or two of the battle. No one was capable of that expenditure of energy – running and fighting, grappling possibly – for very long. The troops at the front of the attack had been reinforced twice now and Gordon had not come in with either of the waves of fighters returning to rest and eat.

Now that they had pushed the Ward so far back, Dempsey had no choice but to march his forces along behind the main columns in support. When the daylight began to weaken, Dempsey watched in astonishment as the Ward signalled a full retreat into the village of Crick. The Green Men, still fit to fight and still winning the battle, did not follow. Sub-commanders brought their ranks back to the fields north of the village and those of higher rank took shelter in the abandoned farms and houses of the village of Yelvertoft.

Dempsey searched for Gordon among the returning, exhausted troops but couldn't find him, though he asked every tenth fighter he passed if they'd seen him. None had. Yet the looks on the faces of every Green Men he saw were triumphant and somehow serene. There was a sense of certainty that he had not seen on any face since the Ward slipped into power and began to crush the life out of the country and its people. Where had it come from, this sudden self-belief from those who, only the day before, struggled to draw breath with the Ward's boot crushing their windpipes? Simply from taking up arms, from having the courage to face up to the enemy and say "enough"? Dempsey didn't think so.

A group of smiling, bloodied Green Men walked past his mount and he called down to them as the dusk spread its blanket over Yelvertoft's small main street.

"How did it go out there today?"

The front man of the group stopped.

"It was like the prophecies. All those visions from before the Ward took over."

"What do you mean?"

"It was like being part of something... awesome. For the first time in my life, I felt like I was doing something right."

Dempsey nodded. Fighting the Ward made him feel the same way. But the man was right, there had been so much more to it today. Dempsey noticed the man's face was wet with tears. Everyone in the group was crying with him. The man spoke up again:

"This'll never be forgotten, you know. They'll be telling this story for the rest of time. This was the day the Crowman showed himself to us. This was the day he fought alongside us as a brother. Not an idea or a concept or a piece of propaganda but a real man. Flesh and blood." The man looked to his comrades in arms. "We all saw him, didn't we?" Every one of them nodded, solemn and rapt at the thought of what they'd done. "Three or four of us at least owe him our lives, I'd say. That's how close he was to us. And tomorrow, we're going to end this war and set the land free. We'll see you out there, brother."

"That you will," said Dempsey. "That you will."

Dempsey awoke troubled from a dream. All he could remember was the image of a twisted black tree high on a hillside, outlined against a setting sun. In the tree, there were three crows. The crows were talking to him and whatever words they'd uttered had terrified him into wakefulness. Now, as he rubbed the grit from his eyes, he was glad he couldn't remember what it was they'd said.

No one he'd talked to after the success of the first day had seen Finney, Carter or Stone. Dempsey had searched for them until the darkness made it impossible to walk. By then he was on the outskirts of Yelvertoft near the overgrown country road leading south to Crick. There he'd found a short row of minuscule houses, all of them deserted. Smashing the window of the last property in the line, he'd climbed through. A very brief fumble in the dark confirmed he was in a tiny bungalow that would once have housed someone elderly and alone. The single bed was musty but otherwise clean.

Now he was awake and it was still dark outside. He knew there was no chance of weaving his way back into slumber. The nightmare faded so fast, all that remained was a sense of unease. Beyond this, the only emotion Dempsey felt was the desire to get back into battle and win this thing today. In years to come, they would call it the Two-Days War. He gathered his pack, let himself out through the front door and went in search of his horse and some breakfast.

The thump and whine of a mortar made Dempsey dive to the ground. The shell struck about twenty yards away, blowing a hole dirt deep through the tarmac of the nearby T junction. More shelling followed, the explosives landing deeper in the village. He heard people screaming and the terrified whickering of the stabled cavalry mounts. The bombardment did not peter out as it had the day before. As if they'd been saving ordnance for a moment like this, the Ward now laid down a heavy barrage, dispelling the quiet and dark of the early hours with screeching hellfire. Green Men ran confused in the darkness and brightness, searching for their comrades in arms or a safe place to rally. They found nothing but destruction.

Dempsey, knowing what would come next, began to crawl the periphery looking for survivors and gathering them into a force. It took valuable time but he managed it. Once he'd formed a substantial group of fit fighters, he sent out others to do the same. His simple order was for all remaining troops to meet beside the canal bridge at the eastern limit of Yelvertoft. If they made it that far, there was a chance they'd live to take a few more Wardsmen down.

Because it was mostly populated by commanders and sub-commanders, Dempsey knew the sudden loss of Yelvertoft probably signalled the end for the Green Men. What would their fighters do with no one to lead them? The Ward had known this was where most of the Green Men's top brass were encamped. Even after today's victory, there were those who still believed in the Ward enough to spy for them.

Dempsey cowered by reeking canal with his tiny troop of survivors and held his head in his hands. They'd been too cautious the previous afternoon. They could have pursued the Ward into the village of Crick and ended the fight right there while they had the advantage. Now the cunning Ward officers had mounted their devastating counter-manoeuvre. Whether these attacking troops were Ward reinforcements or men held in reserve for exactly this purpose, Dempsey didn't know. But he had to face the facts; they'd been outsmarted and outplayed.

Jerome and Denise crept out of Yelvertoft as soon as the Green Men's victorious fighters had fallen into an exhausted sleep. They didn't have long to wait.

Jerome had found ways to keep his sub-command out of trouble for most of the battle, only sending them into a full charge when the Ward appeared to be routed at the end of the day. He'd been among the first to return to Yelvertoft, where Denise was waiting in the cottage they'd picked out that morning.

A couple of hours before the mortar attack began, he took Denise and their two horses and led her through the village of slumbering troops to a small, densely overhung country lane. This byway would take them the three miles to the Ward stronghold in Crick quicker than going across country. The wild hedge growth had created a low tunnel. Instead of riding, they had to lead their horses all the way and the tangle of rampant vegetation made for slow going; this was one part of the landscape that remained full of life.

Jerome had known all along that, no matter what happened on the first day of the battle, no matter how good things might have looked for the Green Men, the victory would always go to the Ward. They were well organised and had better training and equipment. They had planned for this event longer and more carefully, and they weren't starving to death. They also had greater numbers of troops and had managed to keep that one piece of intelligence secret long enough for it to make a difference. He knew he'd made a sensible and well-informed choice about who to serve. It had resulted not only in his survival thus far, it had also netted him Denise.

Last night, knowing she too had made her choices and had to abide by them, Denise had finally given him what he wanted. It was better than he could have imagined. He'd had some grubby fumblings with the leftovers of humanity's womenfolk but none of them compared to Denise. And she'd shown him how much more there was to come. For the moment, for as long as he could claim her as his, Denise would remain at his side.

They entered Crick through a small checkpoint and Jerome had to wait while a young Wardsman ran to an officer to verify his story. A few minutes later, they let him through the barrier. Jerome installed Denise in the vicarage, placing a small ring of guards outside, not to protect her but to keep her from running off. He knew she was wild and alert to every whiff of opportunity. If he was able, he wanted to hang onto her just a little longer.

Around that time, a force of fresh-looking Wardsmen, horses and carts set out across the fields to take up their positions around Yelvertoft, ready for the predawn bombardment. Jerome didn't give them a second glance. Once they'd entered the vicarage, he took Denise to the bedroom and continued from where they had left off, the distant thud of mortar shells unnoticed.

61

At some point in the afternoon, Gordon began to tire. By then the Green Men had all the forward momentum and the Ward were in a controlled retreat towards Crick.

His knife, held so tight for so long, was fused in his right hand. The feathers of his right sleeve were blood-soaked from cuff to armpit. He was wounded on his shoulders and torso where blows he'd only partially evaded had opened his skin. Much of his body was bruised – when the fighting had become so close quarters that enemy and friend alike were crushed against each other, knees and elbows and heads had become weapons of desperation.

Wherever Gordon found himself on the battlefield, the Green Men around him became his temporary units. His life had been saved by the swift reactions of strangers on more occasions than he could count. Why the troops cleaved to him with such faithfulness he didn't know but he was deeply grateful; more Green Men than he could count had died keeping him alive.

The spirit of the Crowman had been with him throughout the battle, giving power to his right hand and making him swift and strong, but Gordon had not seen the dark figure since their encounter in the oak wood. Now, with his strength waning and his limbs becoming leaden, Gordon began to doubt the Crowman again.

As the Green Men pushed the Ward to the outskirts of Crick, Gordon glanced to the east and saw a hill which rose from behind the nearby tree-lined horizon. The hill was grassless and pale in the late afternoon light. A single gnarled tree sprouted near the hill's highest point. Gordon's heart lurched as he recognised it from his dreams.

To the west, and much nearer, as he pushed forward in pursuit of the Ward's last stragglers, he could see enormous, squat buildings – warehouses or logistic units perhaps – now long abandoned and beginning to collapse. Towering over the crumpling structures were two wind turbines. No longer marking time in lazy spirals, they had rusted to a stop. He'd seen all of this before in his scrapbook but from another angle.

If he was finally here, in the place that had been the subject of so many prophecies, why hadn't the Crowman done as he'd promised and fought with them?

Have I done something wrong? He said he'd be here. He *swore* it.

For a moment everything stopped. Gordon came to a halt and those that still followed him stopped too. He glanced again towards the barren hill.

In front of the scorched, twisted tree stood a figure Gordon could recognise even from half a mile away. The figure, all in black, was as still as a monument. It held its arms outstretched to either side, as though to encompass the world. Gordon's strength returned. The power of the land flowed once more into his limbs. With his left hand he felt the shape of the Crowspar beneath his clothing and the Black Light pulsed there as though it were a living organ, a black heart.

Gordon pointed so those Green Men around him would see; so that they too would be lifted by the sight of their dark messiah.

"The Crowman!" he shouted.

As if in response to his words, the Ward's retreat became frantic. They turned their backs on the Green Men and ran for the shelter of the village. The Green Men seemed uncertain what to do. Even the commanders and sub-commanders hesitated as their enemy fled the field.

"He's giving us the victory," shouted Gordon. "Let's finish it."

He ran after the routed Wardsmen. Those nearest ran with him, still caught in his influence. After a hundred yards, his entourage began to fall away. When he looked back he saw scattered Green Men standing, panting and spent. Behind these strays, the main body of the army was turning away under the orders of their commanders. Why didn't they follow him? This was the people's moment; everything they'd struggled for, everything they'd *died* for, they could claim right now if only they would fight on.

When he looked back at the enemy, most of them had made it to Crick. The rest were scrambling to leave the open fields that had formed the day's battleground. He ran on alone a little farther, the urge to end the war making his legs move even though he knew full well that nothing more could be done.

Behind him, the distance between him and the triumphant Green Men seemed suddenly very great; they were pulling back and wheeling to the east. By comparison, the space remaining between Gordon and the outskirts of Crick was tiny. Perhaps only a hundred yards now. Anyone with ammunition left in their rifle could drop him in a heartbeat.

Even an artfully aimed crossbow bolt might do it. Regaining his sanity, he turned away.

There was a shout from the road skirting the village.

Gordon stopped and looked back. A horse and carriage emerged from the hedges. The driver trotted the carriage a short way into the field. There were three occupants and he recognised them all. Two grey-coated figures disembarked. The first was unnaturally tall and moved with a pronounced limp. The second was almost as wide as the first was high; he oozed from the carriage like a slug.

The third figure, a starveling, was pulled roughly from her seat. Her hands were bound behind her and her dirty hair fell across her face as they yanked her into the field. Her clothes were little more than rags and she was barefoot. Even so, Gordon could see her eyes peeping through her filthy, thinning locks; the same eyes that had once stared out at him from the crack between a garden wall and a broken old green door. These eyes were different, though; educated by brutality. All this time they'd had her. All this time he'd been so certain she was dead.

A tiny light shone now in those beaten-down eyes. The spark of hope fulfilled, the brief flicker of joy.

"I propose a simple trade-off," shouted Skelton in girlish tones.

There wasn't much that needed to be considered, as far as Gordon was concerned. He already owed Jude his life; she was the one that had ensured his escape the day the Ward took his family away. His life in return for her freedom? There was nothing to contest. Even if she hadn't given him his freedom that day, he'd gladly give his life for hers. He loved her. It was as simple as that. He glanced up at the hill for guidance, for a last burst of strength, but the Crowman was gone. Maybe he'd never been there.

Jude tried to run then but Skelton's plump fingers caught her frail, fleshless arm and held her easily.

"We could have done this years ago, if only you'd come to us. What you've put her through, Gordon..." Skelton chuckled to himself. "Well, it's despicable."

Skelton's taunting aroused a tidal wave of self-doubt in Gordon. He should have been angry but he was too tired. The search had gone on too long. What had he been doing all this time other than chasing a phantom? He should have gone back. He should have got Jude out and saved her from whatever the Ward had done. He was strong enough, smart enough. If only he'd known he could have done it.

And yet, his parents had been adamant, hadn't they? He still had their letters to prove it. Since their separation everything he'd felt, from his deepest core and from his connection with the land and all its miraculous life, everything had told him the Crowman was real. A real man. Flesh and blood. Not just an ideal. What would Sophie and Louis Black do if they were here? What would they do if they had to choose between a daughter and a son?

Never, ever let the Ward catch up with you. Never let them find you.

That was what his mother had written. And his father's words had been much the same:

You must never, NEVER let them catch you.

But all that was three years ago. So much had changed since then. He had scoured this land for the Crowman in every waking hour; even in his sleep he had pursued him. As he'd walked the fields and forests, as he'd passed through the ruined cities, he had given what help he could and he had waged an uncompromising war on wickedness.

He could see Jude weeping now and struggling weakly in Skelton's pudgy grip. Here was his sister and protector for so many years. The war was almost won and the future the Crowman promised was perhaps only a few days away. Jude needed that future more than he did. Gordon's lips moved silently:

Mum, Dad, I've done enough. I've got to give her a chance now.

Gordon approached the carriage, stopping fifty yards away.

"Send her out to me," he said.

"You come to us," said Skelton. "And then we'll let her walk away."

"No. She comes to me first."

Skelton removed a cutthroat razor from his trench coat pocket. He unfolded it.

"Come to us, Gordon. Or watch your *very* long-suffering sister bleed."

Gordon's feet began to move before his mind caught up. He walked slowly towards them, watching the hedges for movement. Pike, huge and stone-faced, stood motionless, as though switched off, but Gordon watched him anyway, alert for any movement.

"You can't win, Gordon," said Skelton. "Your problem is you care. That means you have no real power. I control this situation precisely because I *don't* care about your sister's welfare. Paradoxical, isn't it?"

Gordon's footsteps slowed further as he neared the group. The driver of the carriage tried to look unconcerned but Gordon knew the man had been picked for a reason. It was only when Gordon was five yards from them that Pike's dormant engine seemed to fire up, he seemed to expand and come to life. Skelton grinned and manhandled Jude to create a shield between himself and Gordon. The driver's hand slid inside his jacket.

Gordon's left hand moved towards his breast. He placed his palm over the Crowspar and allowed his eyes to close.

Once more. That's all I ask. Of the land. Of the sky. Of the crows. Once more and then I'm done.

There was nothing. Only the weight of a dead crystal beneath the fabric of his shirt. He heard the voices of his mother and father, speaking the warnings of their letters:

Never let them find you.

Never let them catch you.

Sometimes children disappoint their parents.

"I have to," he whispered, his eyes still shut.

"What did you say?" asked Skelton.

As if his decision had unlocked the Crowspar, it transformed him. He was the confluence of the earth and the sky. He was the animal in every human. He was the beginning and the end of everything, the Black Light manifest in flesh and blood.

A wind gathered around them, agitated at first then swiftly furious. Skelton looked up and around to discover the source of it. Gordon moved in that moment, rage and love surging through him, his black feathers giving him lift. He leapt at Skelton whose fat hand now moved towards Jude's neck. Pike began to lunge forwards with more strength than grace and the driver withdrew a long knife from the sheath inside his jacket.

The distance between Gordon and Skelton's razor hand was impossible but he covered every pace of it in the air, his arms outstretched ahead of him, his black coat flying around him. He saw true fear in Skelton's remaining eye. Pike's slow, clumsy dive missed him and Gordon brought his knife down on Skelton's wrist as the razor touched his sister's neck. Skelton screamed, the sound of a castrato, as Gordon's blade opened his forearm to the bones. Skelton dropped the razor and let go of Jude. Gordon's momentum sent the blubbery Wardsman careening back into the side of the carriage. The base of Skelton's head collided with the running board, knocking him senseless.

"Run, Jude!" shouted Gordon.

He saw the look of bewilderment on her face. This should have been the moment when they could finally embrace, reunited after so long. Instead, without even a touch, Gordon was commanding separation.

"Don't look back. I'll find you."

Pike lunged for Jude, but she slipped out of his grip. From where he now stood on the running board, Gordon slammed the sole of his boot into the side of Pike's face, knocking him to the ground. From the corner of his eye, Gordon saw the driver's knife flashing towards his neck. He ducked to his left and the knife slammed deep into the wood of the carriage, sticking. Gordon slashed backhanded at the driver; that single swipe opening the man's neck wide. The driver fell from the carriage, blood forced from his wound under such pressure it covered Gordon and Skelton as a mist.

Pike struggled to his feet and Gordon leapt at him from the running board. The lumbering man sidestepped with surprising alacrity and Gordon's knife slit nothing but air. Pike's massive fist came around in a wide arc, pounding into Gordon's wounded shoulder and sending him to the ground. He rolled and was up before Pike could grab him.

Now they faced each other.

From Pike's sleeve slipped a steel cosh, small but heavy. He held his arms wide and advanced. Gordon was sure he could hear the man's tendons creaking, his joints grinding like corroded gearwheels. Behind him, Skelton had rolled over, the back of his head sopping with blood. He staggered to his feet. To Gordon's disgust, the froglike man was grinning, his one eye wide and bulging with delight.

"My, my, Gordon. Haven't you grown? And what a fine specimen of a young man you've become."

Gordon risked a glance back to the fields. Jude was well out of range and still running, albeit weakly. He knew she'd make it to the Green Men now. The fleeting moment spent looking back had been a mistake and Pike, seeing him unguarded, struck. His cosh came diagonally downwards. Gordon didn't have time to counter or even to block it. All he could do was shrink from the blow and pray it missed. By some miracle the only thing that touched Gordon was the sudden, cold wind left by Pike's massive hand.

The attack left Pike wide open but when Gordon slashed at Pike's exposed shoulder, he missed his target. It was the simplest of disabling moves, one he'd executed successfully a hundred times. Both he and Pike stared at each other, neither understanding. Gordon raised his knife to cut again and stopped, staring at his hand. The cosh had snapped the worn blade of his father's lock knife; all he held now was its handle.

It was then that the rustling came from the hedgerows nearby, the sound of thirty Wardsmen with crossbows stepping clear and levelling their weapons at him. Gordon's hands dropped to his sides. The broken knife fell from his bloodied fingers.

The Black Light had gone out.

62

Denise watched Jerome dress.

Gone were the drab greens and browns of his filthy First Guard uniform. Now he stepped into stiff grey flannel trousers, a keen crease along the front and a thin charcoal stripe extending from hip to ankle. He pulled on a grey cotton shirt and tucked it in, snapping a pair of leather braces over his shoulders. The Ward trench coat was broad at the shoulders and reached almost to his knees. A single star on the epaulettes marked him as a low-ranking officer but he wore the uniform as though he were already a general. Tactically, perhaps he was.

If Jerome suspected her of being complicit in Gordon's escape, he never mentioned it. Perhaps she was too valuable a prize to risk losing over the ensuing argument. Besides, Jerome had delivered Gordon, as agreed, and got everything he wanted in return. Like Gordon, he wasn't much more than a boy and Denise knew many ways to keep a boy happy.

"Come back to bed," Denise said.

He turned to her, clearly tempted.

"There's not enough time. I have to assist in the transport of prisoners."

"You're losing interest in me."

"This is my first duty as a Wardsman. I need to get it right."

"Last night you said you loved me."

This much was true.

As the mortar fire had popped and thudded in the distance, raining destruction and chaos on Green Men in Yelvertoft, Jerome had flung himself on Denise, his passion at once sincere and inexperienced. She'd had no trouble pretending her feelings matched his and when he'd said, "I love you", she'd mirrored him effortlessly in reply. Now, his cheeks flushing deep red, he approached the bed and knelt, careful not to rumple his uniform.

"You're a beautiful woman, Denise. You're everything to me. But I have orders to follow and they will always come first."

She was shocked by his candour, by his unspoken denial of words spoken in darkness and lust. Power was more important to him than anything else. It only stung for a moment. Inwardly, she shrugged. She didn't care whether Jerome loved her or not as long as he took care of her. If what she suspected was correct, *her* might soon become an *us*. What was not possible was that Jerome was the progenitor. But she would always encourage him to think he was. Another month or two and she would give him the happy news.

"Do you understand what I'm telling you?" he asked.

"Of course," she said.

And to herself: you're just another man who thinks he controls everything around him.

"Can you live with that?" he asked.

The implication of commitment in the question was better than any declaration of love from Jerome, even if it had been true. She took his face in her hands, leaned forward and kissed him on the lips, a soft and lingering contact. When they parted, she looked him in the eye and smiled.

"Go to work," she said. "Make me proud."

Face still flaming and unable to hide his grin, Jerome left the vicarage.

Skelton and Pike addressed their officers in the windowless and burned-out village hall. At least, Skelton addressed them. Pike merely scowled, the muscles at the angle of his jaw bunching and rippling as he ground his teeth together. Skelton had not seen him do this before. It took him a while to realise that Pike was trying to contain his impatience. He was eager to be at the boy, keen to finish the job.

Skelton permitted himself a thin smile as he imagined what Pike would do. They had talked about it a lot over the years. Especially late at night when one or other of them had woken and could not return to sleep. Discussion of Gordon Black's punishment had been a way of both relaxing and staying positive. Indeed, in the darkest hours of the night, when Pike's mind was on the boy's destruction, these were the moments when he was most… Skelton reached for the word… accessible. When he thought about it, despite the hardships and seemingly unending disappointments along the way, the pursuit had brought Skelton a good deal of joy. Whether the same had been true for Pike, he couldn't say. He wasn't sure the man was capable of such an emotion. Seeing Pike now, his jaws twitching, his giant hands knotting in his lap, Skelton felt a rush of lascivious impropriety.

Governing himself, he turned his eyes to the crowd of grey-coated officers, their most recent and most useful recruit, Jerome Proctor, among them.

"Gentlemen, congratulations are in order. The mortar attack on Yelvertoft has all but decided this conflict. Close to half of the enemy have fled into the surrounding countryside but, as we have captured most of their officers, they won't be able to organise any meaningful response. A significant number of their remaining troops are also our prisoners now. The rest, we can assume, have regrouped but it will make no difference. Today, we are going to cut the head off these Green Men!"

A cheer went up from the assembled officers. Skelton waited for silence before he continued.

"You'll all be more than familiar with the local geography by now. Less than half a mile northeast of us is a good sized bump on the land. It's known as Cracks Hill. Appropriate really, as that is the place where we will crack the resolve of the Green Men once and for all. What I want you to do is range the prisoners in view of this hill and place our troops around them. Leave only a token force in the village. I want as many of us as possible to witness the end of this war. It's been a long hunt but it's finally over. Gordon Black has given us the Crowman. Everything you've fought for and every sacrifice you've made has been justified, my friends. The prophecies of doom will never be fulfilled. In capturing the boy, we have secured the future. We, the Ward, will be the architects of that future."

While the officers cheered, hugged and clapped each other on the shoulders, Skelton watched the twitching in Pike's jaw spread to the rest of his body. He laid a soft, white hand on Pike's shoulder and the man's face snapped towards him in shock.

"Soon, Mordaunt, my man. Very, very soon."

Skelton's fat fingers kneaded the tissue below his partner's uniform. Pike's bones resisted like an iron chassis, his muscles and tendons taut like rope and steel cable.

Skelton ached with joy at the impatience of the machine beneath his fingertips. Soon that machine would go to work, but first... well.

Skelton had his own reason for impatience.

63

Whether wounded, bloodied or merely carrying a weighty sack of defeat around their shoulders, the tens of thousands of Green Men taken prisoner were marched at gunpoint and spear tip into the fields around Cracks Hill. Their boots and weapons had been taken. Those who could walk carried the maimed or dying between them. The fields in this part of the village, once verdant and fertile, were barren now; the hedgerows skeletal and black. The grey, dusty earth had been churned and stirred by the feet of warring troops, by the tracks of tanks and trucks and by the impact of explosive shells. It was a sea of cold, dead dirt where nothing grew, nourished only by the blood of the fallen.

Through these fields at the base of the hill ran a broad but decaying country road. The fences and dead hedges to either side had crumbled to sticks and dust. The road hugged the southern base of the hill like a cuff, extending northwest and southeast away from the obstacle it delineated. Captured Green Men stood all along this road, to its north on the lower slopes of Cracks Hill and to its south in the fields. Their numbers extended almost half a mile to the east and west of the hill's southern face, and around this mass of defeated humanity stood even deeper ranks of Wardsmen. Many of the Ward troops could approach no closer than the northern borders of the village, so crowded and choked were the fields that gave onto the hill.

The hill itself would have been inconsequential if not for the flatness of the land all around. Its southern face was barren and grey. Evidence of a colony of rabbits remained in the form of dozens of eroded warren entrances but the tiny tunnels had long been abandoned. When the wind blew, as it blew today, it tore the lifeless dust away in sheets flung high and far. When it rained, the loose earth washed down into the fields and onto the road, creating dune-like pseudopodia which extended in every direction. The hill was slowly being devoured by the elements.

Once home to a small forest of mature oaks, now only one remained. It was as lifeless and black as the hedgerows all around, more like a gnarled charcoal monolith than a tree. The leaves and outermost branches had been gone for years; dried out, fallen and blown to dust along with the earth of the hill. What remained were the strongest, thickest limbs and the powerful, squat trunk. But the tree was dead, like everything else around it. Long dead. It looked as though it had been tortured and beaten into its present shape. The trunk leaned out far to one side and then bent back on itself, crippled and twisted like a tubercular spine. Mutated, like arms with too many elbows, the last few branches reached tentatively skyward, as though anticipating more punishment. The tree cowered, in spite of its ugly bulk. Wind had bent and snapped it. Hail and rain had lashed it. Lightning had scorched it. Yet, still it stood, solitary and stubborn even in death, its roots clawing into the south face of Cracks Hill like crooked black fingers buried deep in decaying flesh.

It was to this hill that the Ward led a tall young man. It was to this tree that they brought him.

He was dressed in black finery, elegant as a funeral groom. Black feathers decorated his flowing black coat. They danced in his long black hair at the touch of the wind and quivered in his hat band. Though his wrists were tied and the attending Wardsmen both dragged and goaded him, he walked with grace and dignity, his long legs striding with great confidence, his black-booted feet utterly certain of the ground.

Jerome warned Denise not to leave the cottage for any reason. If he hadn't bothered to return with that caution, if he hadn't said a word about it, she probably would have spent the whole day in bed.

As it was, her curiosity was irreversibly piqued.

"Why not?" she asked.

"Because it's going to be... dangerous out there today. I wouldn't want you to be hurt."

"What's going on, then?"

"Nothing you need to worry about. Just stay here until I get back tonight."

"Jerome, you'd better tell me what's happening. I'm not staying cooped up in here all day without any idea of what's happening out there."

Jerome, short of time anyway, sighed.

"Look, Denise, they're going to execute the Crowman this afternoon. They're making an example of him. All the POWs are being forced to attend and it could get ugly. I don't want you anywhere near. Understand?"

Denise frowned and shook her head.

"I don't believe it. How did they find him?"

"They did what they've been doing all along. Following Gordon Black. He led them right to him."

She tried to hide her shock but judging by Jerome's quizzical expression didn't completely succeeded

"You alright, Denise?"

"Yeah. Yes, I'm fine. Felt a bit dizzy for a moment, I guess."

"All the more reason why you should stay here. I'll see you tonight."

Jerome was so rushed and tense he hadn't even kissed her before walking out the door again. As soon as he'd gone, she was out of bed and dressing as fast as she could. In the bedroom wardrobe there were still clothes – left by the previous vicar and his wife, she assumed. She found a crocheted grey shawl of the softest wool and pulled it around herself, cowling her head, before setting off.

Now, having sweet-talked a couple of Wardsmen, she stood in the ranks of spectators, north of the road and at the base of the hill, directly below the twisted black oak. Beside her stood a filthy blind cripple, dressed entirely in ropes of rag. The smell from him was worse than the odour of the unwashed. He stank of decay, as though he were rotting alive. He swayed from foot to foot and nodded to himself like a madman, pointing up the hill with crooked, nail-less fingers.

Unlike the captive Green Men, he was undaunted and uncowed by the situation. The Wardsman appeared not to be bothered with him; he seemed too crazy and too physically broken to be of any use to either side. She would have given him a wider berth had it not been for the press of the throng all around them. There was nowhere else to stand.

64

Dempsey had managed to evade capture with his small band of sub-commanders and fighters. Other collections of battle-ready survivors had made good their escape too, having met and agreed on a plan in a field near the canal bridge outside Yelvertoft.

The simple reality was that they had neither the numbers, the equipment, nor the supplies necessary to face the Ward in open combat a second time. They might never be able to muster such a force again. There just weren't enough people left with the strength to fight.

No. Their war would become a guerrilla affair once again and, as before, they would take to the still-living parts of the land and hide there, in the hills and the forests, living wild. All the towns where they'd had influence would now be taken over by the Ward. Even Coventry would fall.

They're welcome to it, thought Dempsey.

What good was a city now to anyone? Nothing would grow there. No clean water flowed there. There was no game to hunt and nowhere to keep animals. That the Green Men had held the city had been good for morale. Such a triumph had been a source of pride. But now, for the sake of survival, they needed to go deep into the land and stay there. It was the one place the Ward had no understanding of and no interest in, a place where their agents couldn't survive for long.

Dempsey had brought his fighters on a circuitous route to a group of abandoned farm outbuildings to the east of the Ward's position. He would have kept his men moving if he hadn't had his binoculars. He used them regularly to make sure they weren't being followed and they'd shown him the massing of humanity around the base of a single, bald hill west of their temporary hideout.

He spent much of the morning glancing at the activity, shocked by the numbers of Green Men that had been captured. It had been a brutal and utterly demoralising defeat from which they could only run and hide. It shamed him and he saw the same disgrace in the eyes of every one of his cobbled-together troop. He feared the Ward were rounding up the captives for a mass execution.

That was until he saw a small group of Wardsmen leading one man up the hill and into the shadow of an old, dead tree.

He managed not to say *"Oh, dear God"* out loud.

His fighters did not need to know about this. But Dempsey needed to know so that he would have something to tell them, some outcome that they could take away from this, even if it was merely a story about how evil the Ward had become. It was better that they hear it as a story and not see it for themselves.

When he began to weep that afternoon, his binoculars held to his streaming eyes, they asked him what was wrong. He didn't reply. He watched and cried until nightfall when, under the generous cloak of its darkness, he led them on into the countryside, away from the cities forever and into the waiting arms of the land.

••••

Skelton struggled to walk up the hill, even though they traversed it to make it easier for him. He held his bandaged forearm close to his body. When their party reached the top, he was perspiring in spite of the heartless wind and cold, and his chest was hammering dangerously. A sharp pain under his breastbone caused his sweat to chill.

Don't let me die here! Not now!

The pains became an ache and ebbed away. Skelton heaved several sighs. Once his pulse had settled he cast his eye over the assembled throng.

There were faces, of Green Men and Ward, watching from every southerly direction, ranged as far back as the outskirts of the village. He was impressed – he'd never seen such a vast mass of people and he knew, as he looked at them, that news of what they were about to do would extend from every mouth assembled here to the ears of every person they ever met and so on, possibly forever.

Only now did the Ward's achievement really begin to hit home. They were saving history and making history all in the space of an afternoon. All the work, all the logistics of the chase, the nights spent awake, the treks back and forth across the country, the loss of life, the loss of his eye and of the mobility of Pike's leg, all of this now had meaning, all of this would now be paid back to them in the public destruction of one man.

65

Skelton turned back to regard their captive.

The boy stood between two hefty Wardsmen, but with his top hat he still appeared to tower over them. He was secure enough, though, with his wrists restrained behind his back by an old pair of police handcuffs. Four more Wardsmen stood ready. Pike, vibrating with singular intent, held in his right hand a crude brown leather bag which had exuded heavy clinks and rattles as they'd walked to the hill from their carriage. Pike, his hands like slabs and his face like granite, dwarfed them all. In Skelton's mind he was greater than any other man, a giant walking among mortals.

"Take him to the tree," said Skelton.

A blowtorch gleam lit Pike's eyes and Skelton faced the throng. There was no need to hold up his hands; the crowd was almost totally silent already. In the tones of a wheezing headmistress, he addressed everyone assembled.

"They said he was evil made flesh. They said he would bring Armageddon. But we, the Ward, who swore to protect this world, have hunted him down since the days of the first prophecies. And now our future is assured. Forget what you've heard. He is not a demon. He is not Satan. He is *not* almighty. He is just a man. A powerful man, true, but mortal like any other. Neither he nor anyone is powerful enough to stand against the Ward. Let his death unite us, for in his death we will all find salvation. People of the future, I give you the Crowman!"

Skelton stepped back and presented the scene unfolding behind him with a flourish. Pike stood apart from the tree while the six Wardsmen bound their prisoner to it. They used rope to stretch his hands up and back around the trunk, forcing his chest forwards. Ropes also held his torso, hips, knees and ankles keeping his legs apart. This made an X of his body without permitting his feet to touch the ground. Pike checked the ropes and nodded to the Wardsmen who retreated from the hill and joined the silent crowd.

Skelton approached the tree. He assessed the prisoner with satisfaction.

"Everything you've taken, you'll give back today."

He looked at Pike.

"Whenever you're ready."

Pike dropped his bag to the ground. It landed with a muffled clank and its slack brown lips parted to reveal dull glints; shafts of metal, shafts of wood. Skelton retreated a few yards and then, quickly realising he would be the useless third wheel, descended the hill to stand at the head of the crowd.

Pike forced Gordon's fingers open with the edge of his left fist and held the point of a tarnished four inch nail to the centre of the boy's palm. He looked into the boy's eyes. A single strike from the lump hammer, with Pike's strength behind it, sent the nail cleanly through the centre of Gordon's hand and an inch into the tree. The second strike forced the nail head deep between his carpal bones, pulling the skin of his palm into a deep pucker.

A scream accompanied each metallic thump.

Pike stood back. Not satisfied, he drove a second nail into the hand just above the wrist, this time breaking through the bones within to pound the nail home. He spiked Gordon's other hand in the same manner. For the elbows and knees he used six and eight inch nails respectively, six inch nails again for the boy's feet and ankles. Pike cut the ropes which had prevented Gordon from struggling, leaving his body supported by twelve slim junctions of steel and dead oak.

With his victim thus transfixed, Pike was ready to begin his work.

At the sound of the first hammer strike, the entire crowd drew breath, Green Men and Wardsmen alike. If it was the sound of wind whispering over water, the Crowman's scream was the coming of the storm.

Denise's hands flew to her mouth to stifle her response. As the hammering progressed, her fingers stole down past her breast to cover her womb. She was certain Gordon's child, not much more than a soul circling a few cells at the moment, would be able to hear the death of its father; a death that had afforded her a little more life.

This was wrong. So, terribly wrong.

Gordon was not the Crowman.

She knew that because she had spent a little time sharing the journey Gordon had taken *in search* of the Crowman. No. This was nothing more than the Ward using Gordon as a decoy and a symbol of their supremacy and power. If they could catch and kill the Crowman, they were almighty and indomitable. It was a trick to destroy all resistance. When she looked at the haggard, beaten faces all around her she could see the trick was working; better than any magic or miracle the Crowman himself had ever performed, whether real or imagined.

Truly now, the Ward held the future in their grey-gloved fist.

Beside her the stinking ragman danced on the spot, his body tugged and jerked by excitement or madness; it was impossible to say which. He seemed to find the unfolding horrors at the top of Cracks Hill delightful and amusing. She kicked out at him, striking the calf of one crooked, diseased looking leg. He stopped his manic jigging for a moment and turned his blind, pockmarked face toward her.

"There's no call for violence," he said, his voice like gravel under hobnailed boots.

"You can't see what's happening," she said, weeping. "They're torturing him. They're going to kill him."

The blind man shrugged.

"Unlikely."

Without eyes in his head, it was hard for Denise to decipher his expression.

"You don't understand. He's only a boy."

"He's not a boy." The ragman seemed to glance up the hill, which she knew was impossible. "He's a man. And soon he'll be so very much more."

Disgusted with his insanity, she spat on the man's rags.

"He'll be nothing if he's dead, you cretin."

The madman ignored the spittle dribbling down the front of his pauper's gowns. He turned back to her and his face seemed to look down towards her belly.

"He'll be survived," he whispered.

"What did you say?"

That was the moment when Pike, satisfied with his joinery, slit the bonds holding most of Gordon's bodyweight. The ropes fell away and the boy's cries took on a more anguished edge. Again the assembled masses reacted, this time in a low murmured wail.

Pike parted Gordon's coat and tore open his shirt in a single movement. He took a hunting knife from his workbag and held it up for Gordon and his audience to see. He used it to slit Gordon's belt and the waistband of his trousers and underwear. His coat gaping wide, and his body exposed both to eyes and implements, Gordon's breathing came fast and deep. His lithe chest expanded and contracted with great heaves and his pale stomach ballooned and flattened in time. Those standing near enough could see the high-speed rhythm of his heartbeat pulsing many times during each snatched round of respiration. The muscles in his legs tightened and quivered. He strained against his rivets, unable either to free himself or ease the effect of gravity.

At the centre of Gordon's chest hung a dark amulet and Pike snatched this from him, seeing it only as an obstruction to his work. He flung it high and far down the hill. Instinct driving her, Denise held up her hands and caught the falling object. It seemed to come right to her, to *home*. She pressed it close to her chest and then hid it in a pocket before pulling her grey shawl even tighter around her. It was cold enough that day, but the wind brought the temperature down still further. She didn't know if it was cold or shock making her shiver but she was unable to stop herself from shaking. Nor did she want to watch what Pike did to Gordon but her eyes would not close.

They observed; and they recorded everything.

As Pike positioned himself to one side of his captive and raised his knife, giving the greatest number of people a view, a noise rose up from every direction. Denise prayed it was a rallying of Green Men, ready to attack the unprepared Ward and set Gordon free. Even Pike, deaf to his victim's screaming, seemed able to hear this new sound. He paused. Looked around and then up.

It seemed like distant laughter at first. Laughter coming down from the sky. Faces in the crowd turned this way and that, much as Pike had done. They saw what he saw: dark clouds progressing from every point of the compass. It could have been a storm, some kind of tornado. The clouds converged from four directions in a spiralling pattern, gradually closing a circle of darkness overhead, shutting out the light like a tightening black whirlpool. At first the eye of the twister was almost as broad as the horizon but when the clouds approached, darkening and thickening as they streamed into one another, the eye contracted. The light began to be choked from the sky.

The laughter was not laughter at all but the solemn cries of every corvid in the land. The magpies; the jackdaws; the crows; the rooks; the ravens. Their mingled calls grew louder as they approached, becoming a single harmonised voice, a single tone; the sound that came before the world was made; the sound that echoed still throughout creation. Like a vast choir of black feathered monks, they sang this note into the ears of every assembled witness, sending the vibration into their very bones, causing every chest to hum, every head to throb with their beautiful terrifying chant.

The aperture of brightness above Cracks Hill was strangled to a tiny pupil through which a column of grey light illuminated the black oak, its black-coated hostage and his black-hearted tormentor. Pike looked up into the light, into the impossible vortex of birds that wheeled above him, his face more grim and determined than ever, his sunken eyes resolute.

The sky was black but for that one pinpoint of light. Denise looked at the people around her. The captive Green Men held expressions of hopeful astonishment. Was this their reprieve? Nature putting a stop to the madness of the Ward? The Wardsmen's faces showed fear and doubt. Had they been fighting for the wrong side all this time? The wind created by the beating cyclone pushed straight down. The black feathers decorating many of the captives fluttered. Rags and uniforms flattened against their wearers.

The cawing ceased but the vibration remained, buzzing in the bones of every man, woman and child. Denise felt it deep in her belly. Above them now the only sound was the sweep and whine of wings. The neat hole at the centre of the birds became ragged edged. It cracked open as the birds broke formation. They began to descend, looking for perches wherever there was space. In seconds every tree for miles around was black with their gleaming bodies. Every rooftop in the surrounding villages was blanketed: rooks and magpies, wing to wing with jackdaws, crows and ravens. Those who could not find a perch landed on the ground and took up their places facing the black oak. Cracks Hill itself was smothered save for a ring around the tree.

The grey day they'd woken to was gone. Sunshine lit the landscape bringing colour to everything it touched. The sky was so blue and cloudless Denise wished she could fly up into it. It was a cold day but the air was still now and the touch of the sun on every head and every pair of shoulders was like a blessing from a kindly and forgiving creator.

The world was utterly silent and Cracks Hill had become its focal point.

66

Megan took her place at the front of the crowd.

No one appeared to see her. Perhaps they were too focussed on the tree at the top of the hill to notice. She pulled the fur-lined hood tightly over her head and held it closed below her chin. Though it was a clear bright day, nothing could warm away her dread.

The one called Pike, a man who reminded her of the things she'd seen in the cave below the windmill, stepped forward and raised his knife. Perhaps the assembled masses thought his opening actions were symbolic in some way but she knew better. The first two cuts were simple revenge.

Gordon, his muscles strained and quivering watched with wide eyes as Pike stepped forwards and placed the blade against the top of his right thigh, in the dip below his pelvic bone. With a single draw, Pike opened his flesh, cutting ligament from bone. Gordon's twitching thigh muscle collapsed towards his knee and was still.

His screams began anew.

Pike moved his blade to the left side of Gordon's face. Holding the boy's hair to keep his head still, he dug its tip into the left orbit, scooped his knife in a rough circle and liberated Gordon's eye. He threw the ruined, sagging organ down the hill to Skelton who crushed it under his boot.

To Megan, Gordon's very screams were knives, cutting into her body, cutting away at the ties that bound them together, slicing through the weave and taking this precious boy away from her. Nauseated and weak, she fell to her knees.

Pike removed Gordon's genitals next and threw them to the crows. The birds hopped back, flapping and startled. Then they closed rank to squabble over the tender off cuts. All around Megan, people began to weep and moan, Wardsmen and Green Men together, to hold out their hands to Gordon even though they could neither touch nor comfort him.

Pike used his blade to open Gordon's belly from sternum to groin. He held the dripping red blade in his mouth as he forced his massive grey fingers into the wound to tear it wide open. He looked into Gordon's face as he snagged a loop of intestine around one thick, callused finger and backed away down the hill. Gordon's guts followed, tumbling out of him onto the dirt. Mist rose from them and from the great cut in his abdomen. The slippery mass of coils disentangled and lengthened as Pike receded from the tree until, several yards away, they reached their limit, pulling Gordon's grey-blue bowels through the lower lips of the knife wound and momentarily exposing his stomach at the top. When Pike dropped his piece of intestine, Gordon's tugged-upon stomach disappeared again.

Pike walked back up the hill, with difficulty because of his damaged leg. At the top he wiped his knife on a cloth and returned it to his battered leather workbag. He regarded the boy for a few moments before picking up his tools up and limping stiffly away. Crows and magpies scattered as he stomped between them but they soon closed rank behind him and, when he reached a safe distance, they leapt onto Gordon's entrails and began to feast.

Megan looked back into the crowd. Every face was pale, barring a few Wardsmen who seemed to find the cruelty amusing or even boring; nothing they hadn't either seen or performed themselves in the basements of some dark Ward substation.

A girl had fainted near the front of the throng. Megan took a step towards her and saw the hand which still gripped the Crowspar. She knew this girl. At some point in the future, in a city somewhere much nearer Megan's home, Denise would either drop or throw this crystal, leaving it for Megan to one day seek out by journeying through the weave. She found herself wishing that Denise, racked with guilt, had killed herself in the dry fountain where she'd retrieved the Crowspar.

Gordon's voice made her look away.

"Help me," he whispered. "Please. In the name of the Great Spirit, I beg you. Somebody help me."

Some of the Green Men in the front ranks moved tentatively forwards but the armed Wardsmen stepped into their paths. Gordon wept and screamed at the sight of his unmade body, pecked at now by hundreds of hungry corvids. He begged for an end to his pain but he could not die.

"Why?" he cried out eventually.

Megan stepped away from the crowd. No one tried to stop her. It was clear that none of these people could see into the weave but the starving corvids scattered at her approach. She walked straight up the hill, careful to step over Gordon's extruded offal. When she stood before him, his good eye was closed as he shook his head in denial of everything.

"Why is this happening to me?" he cried.

"You sacrificed yourself," she said.

Gordon stopped shaking his head and stared at her with his single eye.

"You." He almost smiled. "I thought I'd never see you again."

"I've been with you all along."

"Can you help me? Please? Help me to die quickly at least. Not like this."

"I'm so sorry, Gordon. I can't change any of this."

Bloody tears of frustration and anguish coursed down his cheeks. Megan caught glimpses of his lungs pumping within his deflated torso. It was almost more than she could bear to see him like this but if he had to suffer it, she knew she must at least be a comfort to him for as long as she was able to stay. Forcing himself to concentrate, his entire body quivering with the effort of focusing on Megan, he said:

"Tell me one thing, then. I know you know the answer. Where is the Crowman? Where is he? He promised he'd be here. He gave me his *word*."

"He is, Gordon."

Gordon scanned the crowd with his blood misted eye.

"I... I can't see him."

"You don't need to. You *are* him. You are the Crowman, Gordon. He is what you were born to become."

Gordon twisted his head from side to side in, almost laughing at the stupidity of what she was saying.

"No, no, no. That can't be. I've been searching for him..." He seemed to weaken then, to become confused. "I thought I'd found him... but I lost him again. He left me alone."

"No, Gordon. He is with you. Your spirit and his are united now. He has become part of you and you a part of him. You made the ultimate sacrifice. You have given us the future."

"I'm so tired," he said. "I've come all this way and..."

"It's alright, Gordon, I promise you. This will soon pass."

Gordon stiffened against the nails holding him to the tree and screamed.

"I don't want to die!"

Blood shook from his face, spattering her coat. She heard the whisper of wings and glanced up. Three crows landed in the highest branches of the black oak. They sat there above him, cawing in mirthful disdain.

His voice dropped to a hushed breath, the whisper of a small, frightened boy.

"Please... Please don't let me die."

She saw his breathing slacken and his heartbeat wane. His head dropped forward. She reached up and held his face in her hands.

"You mustn't be afraid, Gordon," she whispered. "You cannot die. And we will meet again someday. I swear it."

She kissed his forehead, his blood-sticky lips.

Something pulled at her, drew her back. She thought she was slipping away down the hill at first. The draw became stronger and she knew than that *he* was bringing her back, back through the weave to her time. Gordon must have felt it.

"Don't leave me," he said, his face still falling towards his chest. "I've been so alone."

"I'll never leave you, Gordon Black. I love you."

The pull was irresistible. It lifted her from the ground, up and away from the hill. To her left, the sun had dipped low towards the horizon, it was red now; stained by his blood.

In the tree, the crows called out their throaty rattle, proclaiming the death of Gordon Black and the coming of the Crowman. Megan rose higher, saw more. She was able to see behind the black oak where Gordon's body now hung, mercifully limp and relaxed. Walking away from the tree was a tall man in a coat of black feathers and wearing a black top hat. Many more feathers poked from its brim and twirled in his long black hair.

He turned back to her, removed his hat and bowed with a flourish.

67

Megan has to hold a kerchief to her face and sit back from the book to make sure she doesn't dampen the pages or smudge the ink with her freely flowing tears. When she has written the final word, the only space left is the last verso inside the back cover of the book's leather binding. She blots the still glistening ink, closes the book quietly and gently and sits back in her chair.

For some time, she has no notion of how long, she is able to do nothing but stare from the wind-eye, her eyes moving across the landscape in random sweeps and vainly trying to see back into the weave. Sitting at her desk though, her only power is that of the journaler and archivist. At this moment, the ability to pass into other realms might never even have been hers.

In gradual increments the will and ability to move returns to her and she packs away the writing implements and book into their box. Outside it appears to be midmorning, though it is cloudy again and she hasn't kept track of the movement of the light.

Megan has run out of road. The purpose that has animated her in waking and sleeping for the last several months has been fulfilled. She has never felt emptier. There are no more tears left to cry and she is no longer confident of the purpose of her world or her place in it. To be without a compass is frightening. It is this simple fear that motivates her to rise. She packs the black box into a knapsack, pulls on her furs and leaves the bedroom. At the front door she pulls on her winter boots. Her mother is busy in the kitchen, preparing cakes and pies for the Festival of Light.

"Going far, Meg?"

"Not sure. I have to see Mr Keeper."

Her mother turns then and sees Megan's face. Megan can only assume that what Amu sees there is beyond deciphering.

"You'll be back in time for the celebrations, though, surely."

"I'd like to be. But I… don't know for certain."

"Megan Maurice, no one misses the Festival of Light. You make sure you're back in time."

The instant the words are out Megan can see Amu regrets them. She is talking to a little girl and there is no little girl in the Maurice homestead any longer.

"I'll do what I can, Amu. You know I wouldn't miss it unless there was something…" There isn't any point in trying to explain. Megan goes to her mother and embraces her. At first Amu is rigid, then she returns the contact just as fiercely. When Megan draws away, her mother is unwilling to release her. She kisses Amu on the cheek. "I really have to go."

Walking along the snowy track through the village, Megan wishes Tom and Sally would appear. It would make leaving the village again more bearable – especially if she isn't able to return in time for the festival. There's no one on the road with her, though, and she departs the borders of Beckby alone.

Returning along the track through the pines is far easier for Megan than when she left almost two weeks before.

When she arrives at the clearing she is surprised to see Mr Keeper outside the roundhouse; even more surprised to see two horses tethered and saddled nearby. Their saddlebags look heavy and are collecting flecks of snow. Mr Keeper holds up a hand to her even though he's facing the opposite direction.

As she reaches the roundhouse he turns to her, looking irritated, and says, "Where have you been all morning?"

"I was... working."

"No you weren't. You were sitting staring out of the window."

There was nothing she could say to that. It was easy to forget how far Mr Keeper could see when he chose to look.

"I'm sorry. I was... gathering myself."

"Really? Well, at least you're here now. Pick a horse – this one's mine."

"What? Where are we going?"

"Not far."

"But... The Festival..."

"We'll be back in time for that."

"Are you sure? Only–"

"Megan," he says, his eyes a-twinkle, "Have I ever let you down? Come on, girl. Mount up." He holds out his hand. Finally Megan reacts and hands him the box from her knapsack. He removes the book, tucking it under his arm while he stows the box inside the roundhouse. "I'll read as we go along," he says. Once again she is amazed at how he swings from grumpy to cheerful in the space between moments.

"I don't much like horses," she says.

"Nonsense. Get your behind in that saddle before I throw you up there myself."

Warily, Megan complies. If her horse even notices she's sat on top of his back, he doesn't show it. Mr Keeper unties both mounts and climbs onto his. Megan watches his movements. Some of his energy has returned, she's relieved to see, but he still moves with difficulty and his back remains subtly bent. His hair seems to have lost bulk and his face is thinner. Getting into the saddle causes him obvious discomfort and Megan suspects that his wounds mustn't yet have fully healed. Still, he seems happy enough and happier still to be moving.

He nudges his horse and it walks off towards the path. Her horse follows without her having to do anything. She notices Mr Keeper's reins are loose and he already has the book open in his lap.

They travel east and their journey takes the rest of the day. Mr Keeper is the least talkative she has ever known him and at no point does he stop, not even to smoke his pipe. Megan contents herself with watching the landscape slowly alter as they move through it, keeping her eye open for signs of the Crowman. There is nothing. Not even the crows themselves. Some of the route they take she recognises from their journey to Shep Afon but they turn onto a lesser-used track quickly and the land here is new to her once more. This alone breaks the monotony of journey.

The horses maintain the same unconcerned, unhurried pace throughout the day. They appear to know exactly where they are going, which is fortunate because Mr Keeper never once looks up from the book. Sometime before dusk she notices a lump in the landscape. This seems to be where they are heading. It is too small to be a hill and too large to be roundhouse or dwelling. The lump is situated at the centre of a generous but slow rise in the land, higher up than the rolling hills that surround it in every direction. As they begin the gradual climb that will bring them to the grassy bubble at the top of the rise, Mr Keeper thumps the book closed.

He makes no other movement or sound.

Even when they reach the mound and he tethers the horses to a wooden stake driven deep into the turf, he says nothing. He dismounts, walks around to the opposite side of the mound and disappears beneath its rim. Megan climbs down and follows him.

He really has disappeared. For a few moments she is utterly disorientated. Walking a little farther around the mound she finds grass-covered steps leading down to a dark opening. A stone door, thick as her thigh, stands open. Light flickers inside.

She descends towards it.

68

A few steps below the surface of the land, the earthen mound becomes a small stone cavern, its walls cold and slatey to the touch. Megan traces her hands along them to steady herself and dips her head to keep from hitting it on the low ceiling.

The cramped passage gives into a small oval space with embrasures at intervals around it. It is in between these hollows that Mr Keeper now moves, lighting tallow candles. At each end of the oval an aperture leads into a new space. Megan steps partially through to find another room of exactly the same dimensions with one difference; the room they occupy is three-quarters lined with black books exactly like the one she has been writing in these past many months. The rooms beyond are empty.

"What is this place?"

"It's the Keepers' Library for this land."

"This land?"

"There are many lands, Megan, each with their own Keepers and their own libraries. Like all those others, this is where past and future, near and far, the day world and the night country meet. It's where we can see the weave in all its magnificence. This is where the world continues. We tell its stories and thereby keep it alive."

Mr Keeper's eyes shine in the warm yellow glimmering. Are those tears she sees, ready to spill at their corners? She looks around trying to guess the numbers of books here; perhaps four hundred in this room, with room for a couple hundred more.

"How long has it been since the Black Dawn ended?"

Mr Keeper shakes his head.

"I don't know. No one does."

"And how many Keepers are there?"

"Not many. Not enough, that's for certain. Well, until now, of course."

Megan frowns, moves to the stone shelves and runs her fingers over the spines of the identical black books. She stops and looks back at Mr Keeper.

"Why must we keep telling the same story over and over again? Once we tell it, won't it stay told?"

Mr Keeper grins and holds up his finger.

"Ah. Now. *There's* a question. Perhaps you ought to find out for yourself." Mr Keeper plops down on the stone floor and finally reaches for his pipe and tobacco. He fills the bowl with gentle fingers and lights up from a candle nearby. "But first, there's one more thing you need to do." He opens up Megan's book to the last page, the blank verso. From a slot in the wall he draws out a raven quill and a pot of ink. He hands them to her. "Your name," he says, nodding towards the parchment. "Right there, please. Large as you like."

She hesitates only for a moment before dipping and writing:

Megan Maurice

near the top of the page. She hands the quill and ink back. Mr Keeper places the ink beside him but keeps the pen.

"Pass me the book," he says.

She returns it and he adds, underneath her name, a single line of handwriting:

Keeper of the Crowman, Guardian of the World

Her own eyes fill with tears now. When the ink is dry, Mr Keeper adds her book to the shelves, filling a row. He comes back to her and holds her in his arms.

"Well done, Megan. You've been an inspiration to me."

They sit quietly then and he attends to his pipe, drifting away from her on wafts and twirls of smoke.

After some time he says, "We'll stay here tonight and return in the morning. You'll be back in time for the Festival of Light."

Megan doesn't miss the implication.

"What about you?"

"I've some travelling to do."

"But why? Where to? Why can't you come to the celebrations?"

He waves her questions away like bothersome flies.

"We can talk about that later. I'm going to fetch our bedrolls. Meanwhile, I want you to read…"

He stands up with some difficulty and searches the shelves until he finds what he's looking for.

"…this. I'll be right back."

The first thing Megan does is turn to the back of the book where she finds, the name:

Aaron Alwin

The handwriting is the same as Mr Keeper's, if a little steadier.

She opens it and begins to read. After a couple of pages, she frowns and reads back over a section. She reads a page more and then flicks ahead. Not satisfied, she removes her book from where it has barely had the chance to settle and reads sections from each. There's a swish and a solid thud from the direction of the door. When Mr Keeper returns, she has both books open on the stone floor and is lying on her front with the index finger of each hand resting on the parchment of each book. She doesn't look up as Mr Keeper rolls out their bedding and prepares them a meal of cured pigeon and chunks of oatbread.

69

Megan reads in silence for a long time – it must be hours because when her concentration breaks and she looks up, Mr Keeper is asleep. She reads on into the night, comparing the books until she's quite certain of her conclusions. She does, eventually, sleep but all too soon she hears Mr Keeper preparing his first smoke of the morning. She wants nothing more than to go back to sleep. For a month or more.

"Pleasant night?" he asks.

She sits up.

"Far from it."

He passes her a skin.

"Drink some water. You'll feel better."

"No, I won't. I want to know what's going on."

"Questions, Megan? There's a surprise."

Megan sits up from her bedroll. Furious with Mr Keeper's nonchalance.

"This may be amusing to you but it means everything to me. Everything. Can't you understand? Don't you remember what that feels like?"

He lays his pipe down half smoked and lets his eyes meet hers. Immediately she is full of remorse. She has gone too far now. Broken the respect that has gone tacitly between them all this time. Mr Keeper ages in those silent seconds and she can't bear to hold his gaze. She looks away.

"You're quite right, Megan. I'm sorry to be so... curmudgeonly. Laughing at things has become my way of dealing with what can sometimes be a confusing and painful experience."

"Being a Keeper, you mean?"

"I mean life."

Megan doesn't know what to say.

"Look, Megan, I know what you want to ask me and it's OK. I asked my Keeper exactly the same thing and everyone who writes this book and completes this journey is bound, literally bound, to ask the same question. You want to know why the stories aren't the same. Right?"

Megan nods.

"The truth is, we receive the story of the Crowman through spirit, by being in touch with something that is not entirely of this world. None of us hear it in identical terms, no matter how hard the Crowman tries to speak it the same to all of us. The language of spirit is different from ours. It's a miracle that we hear it at all."

"But, Mr Keeper, some of the *names* are different. Even some of the places. The way it begins. The way it ends..."

Mr Keeper picks up his pipe again and continues to smoke now that they are over what he seems to think is the worst of it.

"Would you agree that the stories are broadly the same?"

Megan sighs. She can't help but feel a sense of bone-deep defeat.

"Yes, but so what? Aren't the differences between them big enough to invalidate the whole story?"

"That's a question for a Keeper's own heart, Megan. I can't answer it."

"I don't understand. Is any of it even real? Did any of it even *happen*?"

Mr Keeper finished his smoke and put the pipe down again.

"Megan, come here."

"No."

"Come here and sit with me for a moment. Please. I ask as a friend. We are friends aren't we, you and I? After all that's happened, surely you can allow me that one assumption."

Megan is weeping even before she reaches him.

"Of course we're friends," she stutters. "Of course we are. I just… it feels like you've taken everything away from me. I *love* him. You can't go telling me Gordon Black is just something I conjured from my imagination."

Mr Keeper folds her into his arms and rocks her for long moments. For now, she is too upset to listen but she knows he's waiting for her to be calm enough to take in something more. She works hard to regain control. Gently he takes her shoulders and pushes her away from him. He looks into her eyes.

"Remember this, Megan: if the story wasn't real, none of us would be here now. There would be no world. It would have ended generations ago. It's true, we created the Crowman by telling his story, but his story existed long before we did. It can't be a myth any more because we've made it real. Do you understand?"

"Are you saying that the myth created us before we could recount it?"

"Yes, Megan. That is exactly what I'm telling you."

"But how much of it is the past and how much is just…" Megan breaks down. She can barely get the words out of her mouth. "…a story?"

"I don't think anyone will ever know. Not for certain. There was certainly a boy who grew into a powerful man. There was certainly a force of evil on earth so powerful it almost ended the world. The boy certainly opposed it and through his self-sacrifice, defeated it. There were prophecies. There were earthquakes. There were storms. There was famine and sickness. There was a war. And this boy, this boy who became a man – as he does in every book in this library – led an army against the forces of evil. And though they lost the battle, his death, his passing back into myth, won the war. That is the story we Keepers tell and by telling it we keep this world alive. Yours is the most beautiful and powerful ever placed in this library.

"What you must ask yourself today, Megan Maurice, Keeper of the Crowman, is not how much of the story is true but how much of it is *alive*. My answer would be that every page of it is alive with the presence of the Crowman. I have seen him with you from the start, Megan, and the two of you share a special connection. I could see that in the way he first presented himself to you.

"The spirit of the Crowman was born long before humans but his *story* could only be told after we had come to that point in history, that place in the weave, at which we would either end ourselves or be reborn. We were always going to come to that moment of crisis; it was built into us and it still is. That was the trigger that caused his energy to enter. That was when we called on his spirit, not merely as individuals, not as a nation, but as a world. His seed was alive in all of us and we called from a deep place in ourselves that most people don't even know exists. That is the place where Keepers work from, Megan. Once we'd summoned him, the Crowman prophecies began. By keeping his story alive, we keep the dark side of ourselves in balance by *allowing* his darkness in.

"You have kept the world alive, Megan. But not, as the Keepers who came before you have, for one more generation. You have reunited us with the land forever. You should be proud, Megan."

"I don't feel like I've done anything more than tell some silly fireside tale."

Megan weeps harder into Mr Keeper's shoulder. He holds her tight for a few moments more.

"Megan."

When she doesn't respond, Mr Keeper gently breaks their contact.

"You have to stop crying now, Megan. There's work to do. It's time for you to share his story with the folk in Beckby and hereabouts. After that, you must take it to the other Keepers. You are the last of us. The one who carries the Crowman's tale. It is as perfect and fragile as a snowflake and you must find a way to keep it safe for everyone."

Megan sniffs and wipes the tears from her face. She heaves a sigh and nods to her mentor.

"I'll do everything I can."

He grins.

"I know you will. And it will always be enough, Megan. I've never known anyone worthier of such a responsibility."

Megan glances around the library and shivers as she thinks of all the Keepers who have travelled the weave in pursuit of the same words. Even then, after so many generations, only one book is correct. And now her dark angel, her guide in the realms of spirit has stepped back once more into shadow.

"He told me he had to leave me for a while," says Megan. "And that I was to look for him in inconsequential things."

Mr Keeper nods, smiling as though he remembers a similar admonishment from a distant moment in his own life.

"He said there's a part of him that knows me from a time before. From a time in my story. He says I'll be reunited with that part of him some day."

"That's between you and the Crowman, Megan. Not for my ears."

"I think I know who I was. He watched me die a long time ago. I think I loved him even then."

Mr Keeper places a hand on her arm.

"Are you going to be alright, Megan? Do you understand now?"

"I think so. I…"

"What is it?"

"The men from the mill. Do you think–"

"They won't bother you again, Megan."

"No. It isn't that."

Mr Keeper looks impatient.

"What then?"

"Not just them, but all men who still seek the power of technology. They'll never stop, will they?"

Mr Keeper struggles to his feet, his joints clicking loudly, the sound echoing off the stone.

"Come on, Megan. We can talk about this on the way home. If we don't leave soon, you'll miss the celebrations."

For a few moments, Megan doesn't move. He's evading the question. Putting her off in the hope she won't pursue it. Why? Before it becomes an issue she stands up too, feigning a breezy mood and a keenness to be on her way.

She mimics Mr Keeper's packing up of his bedroll and follows him as he makes sure they have everything before blowing out the candles. The only light now comes from the passage leading up to the door of the library. He guides her out and up, pulling the door shut with a solemn thud. The horses look as though they haven't moved and seem very content considering how they've spent the night.

Mr Keeper puts his horse into a trot and Megan's mount follows its lead. She does have questions but they are fewer than she imagined. Much of their trip is silent but for the sound of hooves on hard ground. Everywhere Megan looks and in all the creatures and plants and shapes of the land, she sees the touch of the Crowman. He may no longer be with her but it is as though he has been there before them and left his sign. She can no longer put it into words but it she understands better now than ever she did before. She smiles and is glad in her heart because she *knows* the Crowman is close and real. He is more real than she.

70

It is midmorning when they reach the village and Megan can see the black Crow Pole the villagers have erected in the centre of the circular hub.

At the top of this tall wooden mast sits a carving of a huge white crow. Below it hang streamers of black and white. Tonight the children of the village will dance in and out of each other, weaving the black and the white together, and Megan now knows where this ritual originates, even though most of the villagers no longer remember. The white crow is the light that is always above us. The black pole is the blackness of the human heart. The black and white streamers are our potential for evil and for good. By dancing, by binding them together, we can keep the blackness of our hearts in check forever. The Crow Pole also represents the tree where the Crowman died, the darkness and the light that streamed down upon him from above.

Seeing all this and making such simple sense of it gives Megan a deep aspect of peace. She rides behind Mr Keeper through the outskirts of the village and back into New Wood, happier and more content than she has been since her journey along the Black Feathered Path began.

At the roundhouse, Mr Keeper busies himself with unpacking the saddlebags. For a long time he disappears inside and she thinks that, as is often the way, this is his version of goodbye. But before she walks away from the clearing he emerges again, this time with a heavy pack and wearing his thickest winter furs.

"Haven't you gone yet?" he asks and then grins before she has time to be upset.

"I was waiting for you."

"Ah. Well, I'm not coming."

"You can't miss the Festival of Light!"

"I haven't attended for years. It's not really the thing for Keepers to be part of the community in that way."

When she thinks about it, Megan realises he must be telling the truth. She doesn't remember seeing his face at any of the festivals.

"Now, I want you to return these fine animals to Mr Lilley at Hay Cottage and tell him how well-trained they are."

"Where are you going?"

"I've got some travelling ahead of me."

Megan's glad heart is falling into shadow.

"When will you be back?" she asks, not sure she wants to hear the answer.

"Well, I'm not sure *exactly* when. It could be a while."

There is silence between them. The silence fills with portent. Mr Keeper clears his throat.

"So, I've been meaning to ask you if you'd look after the place for a while." He nods towards the roundhouse and looks quickly away. "Just until I get back."

"Of course. I can come over every couple of days and–"

"No, Megan." His look is a glare for a moment. It softens immediately. "You have to stay here. You're a Keeper now. You can't go home. People will need you and this is where they will come to find you. Do you... understand?"

She is very afraid that she does.

"Where will you go?"

"Oh, north, I suppose. To begin with. And then east." He nods to himself. "Yes, definitely east after that."

"Mr Keeper?"

"Let's not make this more complicated than it already is, Megan." He sets off for the forest path. "Come, I'll walk with you to the edge of the wood. Bring those horses. After you drop them off you can join the celebrations." He looks back. "But this will be the last time you attend, alright?"

She is unable to speak. It is not alright. Not at all.

But she has made her vows and she will honour them. She has taken an oath and she is marked with the sign of the Crowman. She can alter none of this and, in her heart, she knows doesn't want to. The Black Feathered Path is a long, long road. Megan realises now that, for her, it is only just beginning.

At last she uproots her feet and follows Mr Keeper, leading the first horse by the reins, the second following dutifully. She doesn't so much walk with Mr Keeper as stare at his bulky back pack as he hobbles along. Time and his injury have worn him down. He is not the powerful man she remembers, the man who came to their door and enchanted her, what now seems like years ago. And yet he is still adept and strong in ways less obvious. Power walks with him, if not within him.

They reach the edge of New Wood far too quickly and Mr Keeper pauses before turning. She waits for the moment, afraid of what she will see on his face: dismissal; the putting of her behind him. A faraway look already in place so that she is able to say goodbye only to the ghost of him. Perhaps just the simple sadness of a man who has already lived most of his life and has little to look forward to in what remains of it.

When he turns to face her, he is grinning. As full of mischief and trickery as he ever was. And he is kindly too, just like he was one the day they first talked in Amu's kitchen.

"Stay on the Path, Megan Maurice. Watch for the Crowman in everything you do and wherever you go. Look for him in the folk you meet, whether hereabouts or distant. And never doubt for an instant that he's as real as you or I. That's your duty, Megan. Do you hear me?"

"I do, Aaron Alwin."

"Ha! Well, you've earned the right to call me whatever you like, I suppose."

In the village hub, fire-crackers explode in rapid-fire. They both jump a little.

"You'd better go and join the party." His eyes meet hers. "I'll see you soon, Megan."

"See you soon, Mr Keeper."

He turns and walks to the outskirts of the village. From there he heads north. His journey will take him past the meadow, the fallow field and Covey Wood. Megan gives him a head start before following with the horses.

71

Mr Lilley is not at home so Megan lets the docile horses into the stable beside Hay Cottage and shuts them in.

She walks slowly to the village hub, uncertain what she will do when she arrives. She pulls her hood up, not for the sake of the cold but because she feels safer not being noticed. The villagers not already at the hub are making their way there now, noisily and merrily. The wine and ale will have been flowing for most of the day. When she reaches the edge of the hub, she sees her parents standing nearby and she goes to them. They move apart and she squeezes between, letting their arms hold her tight.

In the centre of the hub the children are already dancing, wrapping black into white and white into black. They laugh and sing as they skip between each other to the music from a fiddle and drum. Someone lets off more firecrackers and everyone cheers. She can see Amu and Apa are ruddy cheeked with wine and for a few moments she loses herself in the celebration, remembering how only the previous year, she had danced around the Crow Pole with her friends. Tom and Sally stand on the far side of the hub, laughing and clapping with the music. They haven't noticed her and for that she's glad.

She spends a little longer between her parents and even manages to dance with them a few times, though much of her joy is reserved. When dusk comes, the celebrations begin in earnest.

Barrels of ale and wine are ceremoniously broken open and more musicians join the band. Many people are dancing now and she is sure that somewhere in the crowd, not far from the pole at the centre of the hub, a tall man in a long black coat and a black top hat dances with them.

She kisses her mother and father. Over the noise of fireworks and shouted merriment, she says:

"I'll see you soon."

And then she slips away.

ACKNOWLEDGMENTS

Black Feathers and *The Book of the Crowman* were originally written as a single, epic tale. Owing to the length of the work, however, the story was eventually split and published in two parts. For this reason, these acknowledgments remain largely unchanged from book one. However, there were omissions and, since then, more individuals have joined the force who've worked so hard to bring the Crowman to life.

The perception that writers birth their creations in lone, agonised acts of heroism is mostly false. Ideas are often triggered by those we meet, later to be fed and watered by others, long before the writing even begins. Once work commences, though we may sit alone to do it, there are many people who make that sitting possible, who encourage it and give it their blessing. When the writing is done and the idea has entered the world, raw and crudely formed, there are many more – the midwives, obstetricians and nannies of the publishing world – whose input is crucial to the process. This tide of energy adds something immeasurable to a work of fiction. Without it, books would be incomplete in ways that would make them hardly worth reading. Many wouldn't reach a first draft.

Black Feathers and *The Book of the Crowman* contain a great deal of shared effort and history. Without such positive influence from so many sources, this tale would never have made it from brain-spark to manifestation. If I haven't thanked you – yes, you, the one I always forget – it's because I'm an airhead; it's not because I don't care.

When I was thirteen, I made a batik in art class. The subject was three crows, perching in a dead tree at sunset. It was the first time I'd really *studied* the corvid form and I've loved crows ever since. So, dear art teacher whose name I don't remember, thanks for being there at the beginning.

Tracy Walters, you first spoke the Crowman's name. In that instant, you personified a mythical creature who gestated in my subconscious for more than fifteen years before finally being born into these pages. For that and other inspirations, I'm very grateful.

My heartfelt thanks to vision quest guide, David Wendl-Berry, a man more connected to the land than anyone else I know and whose wisdom and kindness has brought many individuals much closer to it. I hope this tale will reawaken a desire for that same intimacy in many more.

Sun Bear, all I can do is hurl my gratitude into the spirit world as I never met you. Your book *Black Dawn, Bright Day* did much to shape my apocalypse and its aftermath.

Michael Meade, of the Mosaic Multicultural Foundation, your work on myth, the hero's journey and the initiation of the soul has been a great inspiration. Thanks for enriching me and so many others.

To Vanessa Blackburn of Corvid Aid, whose charity cares for injured corvids, thanks for patiently answering all my questions about crows while I wrote the first draft. The limping crow who foraged outside my office window throughout that year still visits me now.

I'm especially grateful to John Jarrold for helping me

knock the first draft into something readable – no small task considering the size of the original manuscript, also to Fraser Lee for very specific and useful notes, which I used throughout the editing process.

On the subject of re-working written material, 2012 became the year of a very steep learning curve for me. Without the input of Steve Haynes, my editor on *Blood Fugue*, I doubt I'd have been prepared for the magnitude of re-write that was essential for *Black Feathers*. My attitude, a direct result of working so closely with Steve, meant that I was ready – and willing – to step up and swallow some big cuts and changes. I owe you about a zillion pints and my soul on a plate, Steve!

This "critical maturity" has been a long time coming and was a turning point. Without it, I would also not have been ready for Brie Burkeman, an old-school literary representative who wanted my serious commitment to change before she would take me on. There's a very special place in all this for her, hyper-agent and no-bullshit driving force that she is. Thank you, Brie. You're a guiding light.

In these days of social media and instant online communication, it's possible to forge connections and alliances with people you may never actually meet. For me, one such is Helen Maus – a friend of a friend and someone I've yet to speak to in the real world. Helen, you gave me help and advice at a time when things were looking grim. Without that input, I doubt things would not have turned out this well. Whenever the moment arises, lunch is still on me.

Several authors have given me a great deal of their time and support while this book developed. Their combined contribution is monumental. To Will Hill, Alison Littlewood,

Graham Joyce, Tom Fletcher, Tim Lebbon, Mark Charan Newton, Carole Johnstone, Conrad Williams, Paul Meloy, Matt Cardin, Cliff McNish, Jasper Bark, Don Roff, Sam Enthoven, Adam Nevill and John Costello my sincere and humble thanks.

Big hugs to the bloggers and reporters who read and react to my work most frequently. This is just a few of you: Jim Mcleod, Geoff Nelder, Paul & Nadine Holmes, Colin Leslie, Nat Robinson, Lisa Campbell of *The Bookseller*, Mark Goddard, Adele Wearing, Dave de Burgh, Ben Bussey and Clare Allington.

Two gentlemen warrant particular mention for their backing: Michael Wilson of *This Is Horror* and Adam Bradley of *Morpheus Tales*, both of whose support has been constant and unflinching. Thanks, guys. I appreciate everything you've done.

Others who've had a hand in the evolution of this novel include Kim Harris, Mary Ann von Radowitz, Rob Goforth, Kim Hoyland, Philip Harker and Anna Kennett. A black feather for each of you.

Of course, the manuscript would never have become a book without the fine team at Angry Robot taking it on, guiding it to readiness, clothing it, displaying it and inviting the reading world to witness its birth. Thank you, Lee Harris, Marc Gascoigne, Darren Turpin, Caroline Lambe and Roland Briscoe.

Most important of all, my family. Each of you have always done everything you can to help me write, never giving up on my efforts, even when the way forward seemed impossibly blocked. I know I'm hell to live with when things don't go to plan, so my love and thanks to all of you for keeping the faith.

And to the limping crow who visited daily through the many months spent quietly in the office, you know best of all that I did not write this book alone.

When duty and honor
collide...

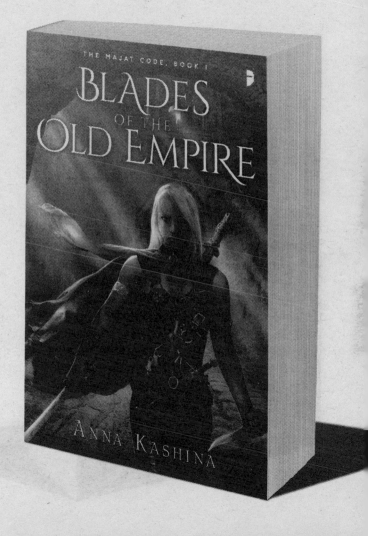

**Gods and monsters roam the streets
in this superior urban fantasy from
the author of _Empire State_.**

David Gemmel meets *The Dirty Dozen* in this epic tale of sorcerous war and bloody survival.